Bart Davis

Bart Davis was born and raised in New York. After graduating he became an English teacher, specialising in disruptive students, and taught for eleven years. He also acquired a Master's degree in social work and a brown belt in karate, and became a licensed hypnotist and a therapist. He has lectured frequently on education, social work and writing. His first thriller, *Blind Prophet*, was published in 1984, and was followed by *Takeover* and *Black Widow*. His last novel, also featuring Peter MacKenzie, was *Raise the Red Dawn*. He and his wife live in New York State.

From the reviews of *Raise the Red Dawn*:

'Underwater excitement . . . all the tensions of *The Hunt for Red October*.'
Oxford Times

'Splendidly tense stuff, not least the final, nail-biting battle deep below the ice, as *Seawolf* and *Akula* stalk each other in a deadly game of Russian roulette, a scenario to which author Bart Davis brings the graphic realism of film.'
Eastern Daily Press

'A Soviet submarine is in deep, deep trouble under the Arctic icepack . . . a ramrod of a thriller.'
Peterborough Evening Telegraph

'Taut, tense thriller writing of the highest order.'
Manchester Evening News

'Suspense as chilling as the Arctic seas.'
ED RUGGERO, author of *38 North Yankee*

BY BART DAVIS

Takeover
Blind Prophet
Black Widow
Raise the Red Dawn
Destroy the Kentucky

BART DAVIS

DESTROY
THE KENTUCKY

HarperCollins*Publishers*

This book is a work of fiction.
Names, characters, places and incidents
either are products of the author's imagination
or are used fictitiously. Any resemblance
to actual events or locales or persons, living or dead,
is entirely coincidental.

HarperCollins*Publishers*
77–85 Fulham Palace Road,
Hammersmith, London W6 8JB

This paperback edition 1994
1 3 5 7 9 8 6 4 2

Published simultaneously in hardback by
HarperCollins*Publishers*

First published in the USA by
Pocket Books 1992

Copyright © Bart Davis 1992

The Author asserts the moral right to
be identified as the author of this work

ISBN 0 00 647639 2

Set in Meridien

Printed in Great Britain by
HarperCollinsManufacturing Glasgow

For Sharon –
for everything.

ACKNOWLEDGMENTS

My sincere thanks to RADM J. Weldon Koenig (ret) for his invaluable technical assistance; to Mr William Miola for his crew's eye view; to Mr Robert Gottlieb of the William Morris Agency for his continued support; and to Mr Paul McCarthy, my editor, for the wisdom he continues to inspire and, especially, for that most wondrous lunch from which all things sprang.

I am also indebted to the writings of many others on the Soviet Union and its peoples.

ONE

NATO Air Force Base, Scotland

This night security was doubled.

Armed soldiers covered the airfield and the surrounding woods from guard towers twenty feet over the tarmac. Automatic weapons twitched like deadly divining rods covering the dead zone between perimeter fences topped with barbed wire and razor sharp concertina coil. In the shadows, restless guard dogs pulled at their sharp-eyed handlers' leashes, scurrying back and forth, panting hotly.

The reason for all the extra security had just landed on the runway and sat bathed in the light of the control tower floods. At first glance it was just another Boeing 747, but upon closer look the familiar silhouette was distorted by an odd 'hump,' actually a second craft mated to the fuselage between the cockpit and wings. This particular 747 belonged to NASA and was used to ferry space shuttles back to the Kennedy Space Center in Florida after desert landings on the west coast. The black 'hump' on the 747's fuselage, now the center of intense activity by coveralled technicians, was not a shuttle, however. It was the navy's newest minisub, the USS *Kentucky*. The *Kentucky* had just completed the first leg of its journey from the construction yards at Newport News to its eventual destination – the sub pens at Holy Loch, the American fleet's main submarine base in this hemisphere.

The black, teardrop shaped *Kentucky*, perched piggyback on the big plane's spine, sat outlined in the glare of truck lights and runway beacons. Crewmen crawled over the hull to release the transport moorings, their breaths misting in the cold Highland air.

The navy had experimented with minisubs before, but none had come near the *Kentucky*'s striking success. Ultrafast computers and superlight alloys had made it possible to cut the size of the ship radically, and thus the size of the crew. Only three men were needed to operate the relatively simple controls. The propulsion system was based on new high-temperature superconductors that eliminated the need for noisy nuclear reactors with their attendant large cooling pumps and heavy turbines. Unique in the world, she was very fast for such a small ship.

Miniaturization made armament smaller, too, enabling the *Kentucky* to carry two modified MK-48 torpedoes that could be fired quickly and efficiently from *Kentucky*'s single torpedo tube in a kind of automatic weapon 'clip' arrangement. Her combat system was an advancement on the latest BSY-2 carried by the new SS-21 USS *Seawolf*, but much smaller, with navigational satellite relays. By far the *Kentucky*'s biggest offensive threat was her four tube-launched cruise missiles, modified Tomahawks designed to wield a limited nuclear capability against poison gas-capable enemies. All this was contained in a forty-foot hull with a twelve-foot beam, shaped by the new stealth technology into a flattened teardrop coated with black sound-absorbing tiles.

A honey of a ship, the *Kentucky* could dive to five thousand feet, more than twice the depth of our deepest diving sub, or if need be, operate in shallow water less than thirty feet to back up a land invasion. Her deep-diving ability gave her 'bottoming-out' capabilities in most oceans of the world. She had a bathyscaphic sphere amidships with a viewport and, like the Deep Sea Rescue Vehicles from which she was partially descended, a remote controlled manipulator arm which stored within the outer hull.

Potentially, the *Kentucky*'s greatest strength, one that made the Anti Submarine Warfare boys in the navy think tank at Crystal City in Washington jump for joy, was that the *Kentucky* had proved virtually impossible to detect at speeds up to twenty knots by any sonar the navy possessed, including those of the *Seawolf*.

Crewmen with hooded flashlights jockeyed the big unloading crane into position, a three-story boxlike affair built like an inverted U, open in the center. There was a coveralled air force driver in the cab and a computer operator. They rolled the crane slowly over the nose of the 747 and sat poised like a huge spider. When the last bolts holding the *Kentucky* to the 747 were removed, grapple arms reached down and lifted the minisub off the plane.

The crane rolled back from the 747 and a sixteen wheeler transport slid into the space underneath it. The minisub was lowered onto the flatbed and crewmen threw special tarps over the black hull, securing them with heavy line. The truck started up and drove along the tarmac, moving through its gears with a higher and higher whine. At the main gate a jeep with four armed marines and a .50 caliber machine gun mounted on the back gunned out of the darkness and moved in front of the truck. A second similarly armed jeep slid in behind it. The three vehicles passed under the raised barrier and out onto the dark and winding road that cut through the heathered moors and low hills of the Scottish countryside.

A short distance away, a fisherman watched the convoy's steady approach from a concealed position. As it left the main gate he spoke into a radio in his native language, Turkmeni, a derivative of Turkish spoken by the Moslem inhabitants of Turkmenistan, one of the Soviet Central Asian Republics.

'They're coming, Raza. Two jeeps, one in front, one in back, each with four marines and a fifty caliber gun.'

'Acknowledged. Pull back,' came Raza's voice.

Raza, the leader of the operation, was crouched three miles away in the darkness on the crest of a hill overlooking the road. Dressed in the combat fatigues of a colonel in the Soviet Special Forces – Spetsnatz – Raza shook his head at what he had just heard. 'Stupid,' he muttered, pulling the bolt back on his assault rifle. Raza also spoke in Turkmeni, forsaking the despised Russian whenever he could. All the men he brought with him spoke Turkmeni, most born in Ashkhabad, the capital city of Turkmenistan.

'Criminally stupid,' he amended to himself. 'Guard the plane with a hundred men, guard the truck with only eight.'

He waited until the convoy drew close. Three of Raza's men were in a trench on the side of the road below his position, three on the other side of the road where the grade was lowest. All were armed with grenades and assault rifles and wore starlight-gathering night glasses. Raza motioned to his second-in-command across the highway, a big man with a dark, scraggly beard and no mustache, named Azrak. Azrak nodded in the darkness, made a sign with his hand and then dropped out of sight.

The first of the jeeps was no more than a hundred yards away. Raza fingered the detonator in his hand. The American soldiers were lazy. One was smoking. The soldiers manning the .50-cal guns hung casually over their weapons. Raza doubted the guns were even cocked. After all, who was expecting anything? This was Scotland and the cold war was over. Wasn't it?

The truck and the jeeps were almost upon them when Raza pressed the detonator. As he had instructed his men to do, he kept his eyes closed to avoid any night blindness the plastique flash would create, depending only on the sounds his ears picked up to know that the explosion had not caught the first jeep underneath as he had wanted, but a little ahead, so that it spun into the trench at the side of the road rather than going up in flames.

The sound of gunfire told Raza his men were already up and onto the road before the jeep stopped spinning. Two of the marines tumbled out of it only to be mowed down, jerking like crazed marionettes under the withering fire. With a sudden *crack wumpf*, the jeep's gas tank exploded.

Behind the truck, Azrak and his men had made short

work of the second jeep. But the truck driver was nobody's fool. He gave no thought to the slaughter going on around him and gunned the engine, sliding off the road onto the treacherous shoulder. The truck inclined so acutely that it almost tipped over. He managed to hold it steady and steer around the burning jeep. He shot past Raza's men who brandished their weapons to get him to stop, but feared harming his cargo too much to shoot directly.

Raza dropped his rifle and raced down the hill toward the truck. They had to end this quickly. The truck certainly had a radio and help would soon be on its way. Ahead, he saw a boulder jutting out from the roadside. With a little luck . . .

The truck was closing the distance and for a moment he feared he might not make it. But too much was at stake. Too much planning and too many lives. Clamping down on his doubt with a will that years of Spetsnatz training had forged into steel, he shot forward with a burst of speed, jumped onto the boulder and leapt into the air as the truck, still held back from full speed by the narrow road and the weight of its cargo, passed.

Raza hit the truck bed and felt the thick tarpaulin under his hands. It stopped his fall. Righting himself, he crawled toward the truck cab. The wind blew his hair back and made his eyes tear. He drew a pistol from his tunic.

In one motion he swung down onto the running board outside the driver's door and plunged the gun through the window glass. It shattered, spraying the wide-eyed driver who for the first time had believed himself safe. Raza pressed the barrel into the driver's neck and pulled the trigger. The explosion was barely audible above the wind noise but the force of the blast almost wrenched the driver from behind the wheel. Yanking the body out of the way, Raza slid in and applied the brakes carefully. The truck came to a stop on the suddenly quiet road.

Raza forced his pounding pulse under control. The light from the burning jeep cast strange gyrating shadows on the hills around him. He saw his men coming in the truck's big rearview mirrors.

Azrak was the first to reach him. His smile was fierce. 'And here I thought so many years with the Russians made you slow and fat,' he said proudly.

Raza laughed. 'Teach you to think ill of your betters.'

'It was a good run. Maybe you haven't lost your nerve yet.'

Raza motioned back. 'Do we have any casualties?'

'None. There are three of them left alive. We did what we could for them. I think they will live.'

'Good. Get the men on the truck. We must go.'

Azrak disappeared for a moment, then came back and slid into the cab. 'All loaded, including the lookout. How much time do you think we have?'

'This will amaze you. Look.'

Azrak did, his craggy face suddenly breaking into a grin. The radio was in shambles from a direct hit.

'We've done it, Raza. Praise Allah!'

'Allah be praised,' avowed Raza with appropriate gravity. His reputation for piety needed shoring up anyway. He slid the truck into gear and moved it down the road, picking up speed for the short run to the coast.

Two wooden fishing trawlers were harbored in the rocky basin. The ancient pier that led out to them looked barely able to support the weight of a few men, much less the *Kentucky*, but Raza's men had reinforced the old timbers with steel beams months ago, publicly, the prelude to a never-to-come cannery.

Here we are then, he thought, walking down the path to the pier. *What was ordained has come to pass*. On the road above the rocky crags his troops had been met by fishermen from the trawlers and together they were working the off-loading ramps from the truck. He felt a sense of awe that it had all worked. *Who knows?* he wondered. *Maybe I am getting religion in my old age.*

12

Slowly, the soldiers and the fishermen slid the *Kentucky*'s great black mass onto a trolley which rested on a set of steel rails leading all the way down the cliffs and along the pier to the ship. Raza saw Azrak and another man raise a black hatch and disappear inside the *Kentucky*. Using only pulleys and sweat, the rest of the men hauled the *Kentucky* toward the boat that was to be its home for the next few critical weeks while they uncovered its secrets.

The *Kentucky* reached the side of the first trawler. It was far too big to be put down any of the hatches and Raza wondered idly how they would get it on board. He shouldn't have. Ancient tools. That was all they had, anyway. Ancient tools and ancient ways. And his training. The entire side of the trawler was lifted away, revealing a hold large enough to contain the minisub. Once it was inside, the side was replaced and a horde of fishermen swarmed over it, nailing and caulking and resealing.

Azrak emerged on deck and signaled to someone. A boom with a cargo net was lowered into the hold. When it appeared again, it carried two eight-foot cylinders with tapered nose cones, ten feet shorter than the original Tomahawks – half the *Kentucky*'s complement of cruise missiles. They were transferred to the second trawler and disappeared down into its hold.

Azrak came down from the trawler and walked up the pier. 'Allah has two hands,' Raza quoted when he was in earshot.

Azrak made a fist, his face serious. 'Open for the righteous, closed for the infidel,' he finished the quote.

Azrak didn't know it, but Raza had spent considerable time collecting a list of these little pieties to be parceled out at moments like these, half-remembered from their shared boyhood and the underground schools that had been the foundation of their Islamic education years ago. The Russians had taught him that a good officer understood what motivated his men. God, how little they had under-stood what motivated *him*. Turkmenis were driven first and

13

foremost by a fierce and unorthodox piety. A simple pat on the back or a 'good job' wouldn't be enough for men who were risking their lives for God's will and their country's future. He had spent too many years away. For them to follow him with his suspiciously secular reputation, piety was doubly important.

'We must go, Azrak. The tide is ours only for a little while longer. Tell the men they fought well.'

'The killing was justified, blessed by Allah.' Azrak's eyes had a heretic twinkle. 'The Russians taught you *that* well enough.'

'Be careful in the desert,' Raza said seriously. 'The way will be long and dangerous and they'll come after their prize. Be sure of it. And remember what I taught you.'

'The day I need an old has-been to teach me anything is the day I teach my children Russian.' Azrak laughed. '*You* be careful, Raza. This sea is not the kind one of our youth.'

'You set the timer?'

Azrak nodded. 'You worry too much.'

They embraced, clapping each other on the back. Then Azrak boarded the trawler with the missiles and Raza got onto the trawler that held the *Kentucky*. A half mile out to sea, Raza looked back.

The first explosions ripped through the steel railings and sent them tumbling down the cliffs into the sea. The pier was dragged under by rocks the size of small houses. The road crumbled, sending the truck tumbling in slow motion down the cliffs into the sea. More explosions followed. A cloud of black dust rolled out over the water.

When the smoke cleared, the cove was empty.

TWO

Norfolk, Virginia – Two Weeks Later

The color of the day was the same dull gray as the oily water that slid past the submarine USS *Farley*'s hull as it entered the channel into Norfolk Naval Station. Fat gulls stitched the drab sky to the cold sea. A fog bank was rolling in. Capt Peter MacKenzie stood on the bridge watching the crew secure lines to the tugs that would bring the *Farley* into port. The featureless grayness suited him, precisely matching his mood.

'Good to be home, sir,' said the navigator, Lt Ron Thompson, beside him.

MacKenzie decided it was just an innocent remark. Thompson had worked well with him on the milk run from the Med. If he'd harbored doubts about MacKenzie's fitness to command, they wouldn't be surfacing now. *You have to stop*, MacKenzie reminded himself for the hundredth time, having wondered about most everything said about him within earshot during the entire voyage. Thompson's simple statement was just that. He eased his grip on the damp bulkhead steel.

'It's always nice to come home. Do you have any plans, Ron?'

Thompson nodded. 'I'm gonna get some rest. Then take some advanced training near the longest, whitest beach Detailing can find me.'

MacKenzie smiled. 'I forgot, you're single.'

Thompson shrugged philosophically. 'Tough to keep up a steady relationship when you're always leaving on seventy-day cruises. I suppose your wife will be waiting, sir. Must be a nice feeling.'

MacKenzie felt a familiar sinking sensation in the pit of his stomach. Like swallowing a table, his wife, Justine, used to say. No, he wanted to tell the younger man standing beside him, my wife will not be waiting. She is somewhere I can't reach her. Mostly, he could admit to himself now, because she could not reach me. Instead he said, 'Her job takes her away sometimes,' and left it at that.

'Coming up on the markers, Skipper.'

MacKenzie spotted them and spoke into the headset mike connecting him to the control room below. 'Right ten degrees rudder. Make minimum turns.'

'Right ten degrees rudder. Minimum turns, aye,' repeated the diving officer below, relaying the instructions to the helm.

MacKenzie ran a hand over the sharp planes of his rugged Scottish features and felt the deep lines wind, weather and responsibility had put there. There was more gray in his thick black hair than there had been a year ago. The tiny lines around his blue gray eyes were more pronounced, too, the result of the stress of command – and other things.

MacKenzie looked ahead. Bridges crisscrossed the network of Norfolk's internal waterways. Navy ships of all sizes were docked at concrete piers. Sleek subs, razor-prowed destroyers, huge, vacuous subtenders that looked like floating junkyards. Squat, round fuel tanks were everywhere, along with repair yards and graveled parking lots filled with cars. But over everything, the bridges. MacKenzie wondered to himself, *Have I burnt mine*?

'Bridge, Communications. Skipper, naval air station just called to say there'll be a plane waiting for you when we dock. You're routed straight through to Washington to met with the CNO.'

'Acknowledged,' MacKenzie responded. 'Have a car meet me.'

The chief of naval operations, Adm Ben Garver, was an old friend and there was a pleasant glow attached to the

16

name. Careful, MacKenzie caught himself. Old friends are the most dangerous. They expect things to stay the same. But even disregarding Ben Garver's superior rank, he owed him too much to stall the meeting.

'Good to be home, sir,' Thompson said again.

Once, it had been.

MacKenzie turned his attention to docking the *Farley*.

Take it one thing at a time.

THREE

Washington, DC

It was wet and cold the way Washington springs can be, so the big fireplace in Adm Ben Garver's comfortable den in Tingey House in the Washington Naval Yard had several logs burning in it. A uniformed orderly escorted MacKenzie in from the front door. The fire gave the nautical furnishings a warm glow, banishing at least part of the rainy gloom that had followed him from Norfolk.

Garver was seated in front of the fireplace talking to a man wearing lieutenant commander stripes. Somewhere in his fifties, MacKenzie judged. Both had snifters filled with an inch or so of brandy. Garver got up as MacKenzie entered, his smile warm and his hand extended.

'Mac, good to see you. Just got in?'

'Hello, sir. Right from the boat to here.'

'How was the trip from the Med?' Garver asked it lightly, but MacKenzie heard a more serious tone underneath. His face tightened. A year ago, Garver wouldn't even have asked about a routine ferry job. But then he had to admit to himself that a year ago, he wouldn't have been given a routine ferry job. A lot had changed since he had captained the *Seawolf* against the Russians under the arctic ice.

'It went well, sir. The *Farley* could use the refit. We had some problems with her steam fittings on the way over.'

'Nothing you couldn't handle, I assume.'

Again MacKenzie felt the probe of hidden meanings but let it pass. 'No, sir. Nothing I couldn't handle.'

MacKenzie was acutely aware of the presence of the other man in the room. Garver had not yet introduced him and he couldn't tell what that meant. Garver never did anything without a reason. The man had said nothing so far. He just remained standing casually by his chair, calmly observing their interchange. He had very clear brown eyes in a round face with small, neat features and an academician's professorial fringe of thinning hair. MacKenzie clamped down on his curiosity and his insecurity and ignored the other man the way Garver was doing. If this was a test of his self-control, he wasn't going to fail it by asking questions out of turn.

'Like a drink, Mac?' Garver asked.

'Whatever you're having will be fine, sir,' MacKenzie responded.

'Good.' Garver smiled. 'Brandy. Just the thing to ward off the chills on a day like this.' He walked over to a tray of crystal decanters on a mahogany lowboy and poured some of the brandy into another snifter.

'Cheers.'

'Good health,' MacKenzie toasted, taking a sip and liking the fiery trail the thick liquid left as it rolled down his throat. ''That's very good, sir. Thank you.'

His excessive politeness aggravated Garver. 'Yes, sir. Thank you, sir. What gives, Mac? We go back too far for you to sir me to death in my own home.'

Was this a test, too? The other man still hadn't said a word. 'I'm not sure why you wanted to see me, Ben.'

'Something has come up.' He turned to the other man. 'Doug, maybe you'd better wait outside for a bit.'

'Yes, sir.'

'Before you go, let me introduce Captain Peter Mac-Kenzie. Mac, Commander Doug Wallace.'

'How do you do, Captain.'

'Pleasure, Commander.'

Wallace had a pleasant voice, animated and educated. His eyes never left MacKenzie's face. MacKenzie had seen eyes like that before. In a sudden flash of intuition he knew who, or rather what, Wallace was and why Garver had brought Wallace here. He said nothing. The knowledge, or at least his firm suspicion, was a possible advantage in whatever was to come with Garver. Instinctive reaction. Take the high ground. Old habits did die hard.

Wallace left and Garver dropped into one of the leather chairs in front of the fireplace, motioning for MacKenzie to take the other. It was a comfortable chair, one to doze in with a book on your chest and a big red dog lying on the floor beside you.

'How are you doing?' Garver asked quietly.

MacKenzie sat back and studied the amber liquid swirling in his glass. 'Hard to say, Ben.'

'Any pain?'

'A little. Comes and goes. Still some stiffness.'

Garver laughed. 'Sounds no worse than just being my age.'

MacKenzie's smile was fleeting. 'I'd like to tell you I feel fine. That I'm the same guy I used to be. But it isn't true.'

'Better or worse?'

'Maybe a little of both. Funny. You start monkeying around with some things, taking them apart, you're not always sure how to put all the pieces back. Like a model ship with parts left over at the end. It looks okay on the outside, but you know something's missing.'

'What is missing?'

'Well, for one thing,' MacKenzie began, 'I don't trust myself.'

'C'mon,' Garver said with a little irritation. 'You were and are the best there is. A natural.'

MacKenzie smiled ruefully. 'So I carry the natural's curse.'

'Which is?'

'Which is what happens to you the day you discover you have to work at it like everybody else. That it isn't natural anymore. That your mind or your body just might not deliver whatever you need like it always did. That deep inside you is a time bomb, maybe just like the one everyone else has, but that doesn't matter. *You* never had it. And if that bomb inside went off once it might go off again, but this time you might take a hundred and eleven men along with you, instead . . .' He paused. Garver was studying him intently. He had been waiting for this. '. . . instead of just yourself.'

'It wasn't attempted suicide,' Garver protested. 'The investigative board never ruled that and I don't think you should call it that or think it was. It distorts the truth.'

'The truth is I don't know whether or not it was me. With all the pain and the pills I don't know what I was thinking. All I know is that suddenly, for the first time in my life, the unthinkable wasn't unthinkable anymore. That's scary, Ben. It scared me right down to my roots.'

'So get unscared.' Garver frowned. 'I'm too primitive for all this stuff, Mac. I don't go for shrinks messing with a person's insides. Like you say, I don't know if they can put back together what they take apart. Willpower, Mac. Tell yourself it was nothing and it was. Move on. Command.'

'I don't know if I can anymore,' MacKenzie said honestly. 'There I was on the *Farley* on a mission a Sea Scout could handle. No stress. Nothing even remotely approaching a combat situation. I was as nervous as a whore in church. Everyone I met I wondered – has he heard? Does he know? Was that just an innocent remark or is he needling me? I second-guessed myself continuously. I wasn't sure of the simplest order. I was never so happy to see Norfolk in my life. Frankly, Ben, I don't know how I got through it.'

'Will it help to know what your XO said?'

MacKenzie had to laugh. 'You work quick.'

'I had his report faxed to me while you were in the air.' Garver reached beside his chair and picked up a folder, thumbing through the papers till he found the ones he wanted. 'Here. Your XO said, and I quote, ''Captain MacKenzie is a thorough professional who inspired all his officers and men to their finest standards of performance. When a steam leak scramed the reactor, it was Captain

MacKenzie's personal courage and leadership that returned the ship to an operating posture and prevented serious injury to two of the engineering room crew. Details follow." ' He looked up. 'Now that doesn't sound like some green uncertain kid to me, Mac. It just doesn't. It sounds like the old MacKenzie.'

'All they see is the outside. I'm in here looking out. And I know what I feel.'

'Fuck what you feel. I'm only concerned with what you do. Most of us used to shit our pants before every cruise in 'Nam. And if not before, during. Everybody's scared, Mac.'

'Not of themselves.'

Garver considered that for a while.

'Why did you bring me here?' MacKenzie asked. 'You've got shrinks who could do a better debriefing.'

Garver remained silent for a while longer. Then, he asked, 'What do you know about the *Kentucky*?'

'The new minisub? I hear it's a pistol. I haven't actually seen the trial reports yet.'

'I've got them here. She lives up to her rep and more. Runs too quiet for anything we have to pick her up. Capable up to a thousand feet with torpedoes and cruise missiles. She could sneak down a sewer pipe if we asked her to, with a crew of three and enough punch to make the difference in a small war.'

'I'd like to drive it sometime,' MacKenzie said.

'That's another thing,' Garver interjected enthusiastically. 'Trim, ballast, pitch, planes, course, everything is automatically adjusted by computer. Given the operating manuals and enough time, you wouldn't really need to be a trained sub driver. Who knows? Maybe we just invented the world's most expensive carnival ride.'

'Or a toy for rich kids. Hey, Dad, can I borrow the keys to the sub?' Talking about the *Kentucky*, Mac felt some of his old exuberance return for a moment, but it was fleeting. It faded, and the familiar lethargy of spirit he had come to know settled over him again. He asked, 'Where's it stationed?'

'Two weeks ago we shipped the first operational unit to Scotland on board a seven-forty-seven. Unfortunately, it was stolen.'

'What?'

Garver drained his glass and got up to pour himself another. 'You?'

'No, thanks. Did I hear you right? It was stolen? By whom?'

Garver sighed. 'Turkmenistani guerrillas. God help us. We get through fighting the Soviet Union as a whole, now we've got to take on every goddamned separate republic.'

'I'm just a sub driver, take it slow will you.'

Garver folded himself back into his chair and his voice took on a lecturing tone. 'Turkmenistan is a mostly desert republic in Soviet Central Asia. It was occupied or conquered by so many invaders up through the last century it doesn't pay to name them, except for some folks called the Oghuz from Mongolia who gave the region its Turkic character about a thousand years ago. They still speak a Turkish dialect there. Britain was concerned enough about Russian expansion toward India in the late 1800s to fight for the area for a while, but by 1924 the Brits withdrew and the Red Army wiped out enough Turkmeni citizens to gain control. Turkmenistan became a Soviet republic.'

'You know a lot for an ex-jock.'

'I'm a quick study. Anyway, over the years the central beef these folks had with the ethnic Russians is that they are Moslem, a religion the Russians actively suppressed. They also wanted to speak Turkmen and the Russians want them to speak, well, Russian. KGB political assassinations took out every serious Turkmeni leader for decades. Moscow controlled their schools, their trade, even their architectural styles. Making matters worse, the Russians did as piss poor a job of housing and agriculture there as they did everywhere else.'

23

'Look, I know this may be heresy,' said MacKenzie, 'but why do we or anyone else care about some crummy desert?'

Garver smiled. 'Because the world's third largest gold and oil deposits reside in this crummy desert. Along with untold cubic feet of natural gas and other assorted chemicals like bromine and iodine. The Russians spent billions creating an infrastructure in Turkmenistan. Wipe it out and you eliminate one of their few remaining sources of hard currency. They're broke. They can't afford to write off that investment. No money, no food. No food, well, we don't like to think about what could happen to democratic reform if half the Russian population is starving to death.'

MacKenzie said, 'The hardliners could try it again.'

'Precisely. Russia and Turkmenistan, all the republics, need a political solution to the problem worked out over time, not a military coup.'

'Where does the *Kentucky* fit in?'

'I'm coming to that.' Garver took a sip of brandy and continued. 'Before the cold war ended, cultivating the Turkmenis' strong nationalist tendencies was the subject of intense CIA efforts. They built a relationship with an emerging radical group called *Skobelev.*'

'*Skobelev* sounds Russian.'

'It is. Or rather, *he* was. A Russian general brought in after the Turkmenis defeated his predecessor at a place called Geok Tepe. Skobelev took Geok Tepe and gave no quarter to the defenders. Over eight thousand men, women and children were massacred. As Skobelev himself put it, "The duration of the peace is in direct proportion to the slaughter you inflict upon your enemy." Nice fucking guy, huh?'

'The name, I take it, now indicates that the radical group shares that philosophy?'

'It's certainly possible,' Garver agreed. 'American funds strengthened Skobelev to the point where it was a first-class organization with international connections. Then all

24

the changes occurred and our government decided to slow things down in Turkmenistan. The radicals, however, as is so often the case, weren't as easy to control as the CIA would have liked.

'The head of Skobelev is a guy named Raza, a native Turkmeni who was culled from the population early and sent to Moscow for special training. He ended up a colonel in the Spetsnatz, their version of the special forces. He is tough and smart. He is also the mastermind behind the theft of the *Kentucky*. Unknown to his superiors, he set up a special SIGINT unit within his command to monitor US intelligence traffic. Ironically, he probably used our money to finance the entire operation. He learned about the *Kentucky*, and understanding the strategic use such a weapon could be to him, he plotted to steal it. Two weeks ago he succeeded, leaving five marines dead. We've been looking for the *Kentucky* ever since.'

'How do we know all this?' MacKenzie asked.

'Because the Russians told us,' Garver said baldly. 'You've got to remember, we're not the enemy in this scenario. Raza has nothing to gain from pointing cruise missiles at the US. But you can be damn sure one day soon, whenever he's set up what he thinks is a pat hand, and that includes having bypassed the safeguards on those cruise missiles – and they're pretty formidable – he's going to call whoever's in charge in Moscow and announce that the Russians don't own squat in Turkmenistan anymore and if anybody has a problem with that, he will be more than happy to wipe out whatever target is within *Kentucky*'s range and happens to please him that day. Believe me, Mac, the clock is ticking. Raza's kind of nationalism could consume the whole region. Everybody who's cleared to know about this is worried sick about it, including the President. We are on the verge of having a world where political solutions rule the day. We can't permit nuclear terrorism to succeed.'

A log split in the crackling fire, sending sparks up the

chimney. MacKenzie said thoughtfully, 'You know, Ben, events being what they are, Raza holds some pretty strong cards.'

'That is also the opinion of the higher-ups who have lost a lot of sleep studying the situation,' Garver said with growing intensity. He looked at MacKenzie squarely. 'The real danger is that this could explode into war between the republics. It is not in the best interests of the United States to let that happen. There are several thousand nuclear weapons which could fall into unstable hands. Additionally, we are not at all pleased with having a billion-dollar submarine stolen from us. To put it mildly. We all think it is an excellent idea that word go out that no one, including Raza, can profit from this activity.'

'It's hard not to sympathize with him in part,' MacKenzie said. 'Depending on how you look at it, the man's a patriot.'

'He's a thief and a murderer,' Garver said angrily.

'The British once said that about the man this city is named after.'

'This is policy, Mac.'

MacKenzie shrugged. 'I'm not going against it.'

'Good.'

'I'm just making a point.' MacKenzie got up and put his glass on the table. His gaze traveled over the books on the shelves. Naval history, classics, the State Department series on the countries of the world. Garver was still nursing his brandy, looking pensive.

Why had Garver gone to so much trouble to give him the background on the missing *Kentucky*? And Doug Wallace's presence still hung in the air. MacKenzie decided it was time to play that card.

'How come you asked the shrink to leave, Ben?'

Garver looked startled for a moment, then shook his head admiringly. 'See? I told you there wasn't a thing wrong with you. Or your instincts. How'd you know?'

'The eyes. The manner. I talked to enough of them before I was recertified for duty. I'm not wrong?'

'No. I brought in Dr Wallace to consult on your case if I felt I needed him. Or if you did.'

'Why? What's so special now? I told you I'd hold off retiring for a while longer and see how things worked out. I made the run with the *Farley*, didn't I?'

Garver held up a hand. 'It isn't any of those things. It's something else. Something more important.'

'Guessing game's over, Ben.'

Garver sighed. 'Here's the deal. If we were able to locate the *Kentucky* where she is in the North Atlantic, we'd destroy her for all the reasons I just gave you. But so far the sub has proved too quiet to be picked up by any sonar we have. We've shifted a massive naval presence into the area and so have the Russians. We have LAMPS helicopters in the air as thick as mosquitoes and Orions flying nonstop. We are monitoring every radio transmission and there isn't a fishing boat or a merchant ship or even a pleasure craft in the North Sea that hasn't been stopped and searched. The CIA's gone the other route, putting manpower into Turkmenistan itself to pick up something from the Skobelevs. Moscow has combined KGB and special forces teams out looking for Raza all over the world. All that and there hasn't been one damn trace of him or the *Kentucky*. We were tearing our hair out. Until five days ago.'

'What happened then?'

'The Russians told us they have an experimental sonar capable of hearing the *Kentucky*.'

'But that would mean . . .' MacKenzie began.

'Right. It would mean a much greater capability than any we suspected. It means *Seawolf* might not have the edge we hoped for or the new refits on the LA class might not be sufficient to conceal her and who the hell knows what else. In the growing spirit of international cooperation, the Russians have asked for our help in destroying the *Kentucky*. For strategic reasons they are willing to let us use the new sonar if we are willing to sink the ship. And believe me, we'd very much like to. It has not helped our new relationship that we've been covertly supporting these folks all these years.'

'Why not just sink it themselves?'

'First, because they're not sure they can. Remember, they know nothing about the *Kentucky*'s capabilities and we're certainly not going to educate them. They don't want to risk Raza's launching those cruise missiles. Second, it's bad precedent letting a foreign navy sink one of our ships, even a rogue. So we asked them to give us the sonar and we'd do the job.'

'And?'

'And they refused.' Garver grinned. 'They're not stupid, Mac. They knew that ten minutes after we had the sonar it would be in pieces in the Defense Advance Research Projects Agency's labs. They're still smarting about *Red Dawn*, or have you forgotten?'

'I haven't forgotten.'

'A compromise was reached. An American officer will be allowed to captain the Soviet sub equipped with the new sonar in full command of a Soviet crew. His mission is to destroy the *Kentucky*. I needn't tell you that it is also the intelligence community's fervent hope that this particular captain will be clever enough to bring us back the data on the sonar. If not, completing the primary mission will be sufficient.'

MacKenzie felt the world growing smaller.

'The Russians want you, Mac.'

'No. Absolutely not.'

Garver shrugged. 'We gave them a list. They rejected every name.'

'I resign my commission, effective immediately.'

'You can't. You're needed.'

MacKenzie's eyes were pleading. 'Look, you just said they were still smarting about the *Red Dawn*. If that's true, why me? I was the one who beat them to it.'

Garver's expression was mild. 'You have to understand

the Russians' way of thinking. In their books that simply makes you the best. But that wasn't the clincher. It was what happened between you and the *Akula*'s captain at the end that made the difference. We've learned his name was Vassily Kalik, by the way. How many lives were saved because of your decision, Mac? Evidently, Kalik included that in his report and the Russians haven't forgotten it. They believe you are a moral man. We cannot shake their faith. They want you.'

MacKenzie felt the familiar tightening in his chest. It was hard to breathe. He controlled his rising panic and said more steadily, 'I can't, Ben. There's too great a likelihood that I'll fail. I'm not running from this. I'm just trying to give you an accurate picture. If you asked me how well a weapon system worked, I'd give you the facts as I saw them. I'm doing that now. I'm not the same man I was. I don't know if I can function in my old environment, much less a radically new one.'

'You're the same man, damn it. The same man!'

'I wish I was,' said MacKenzie sadly. 'But I'm not. I don't have it anymore and I don't know how to get it back. On the *Farley*, I was just going through the motions. It was an old routine I knew well enough to fake. But command a Russian sub? Who the hell is going to translate?'

'The Russian captain who will function as your XO can speak English as well as you do. So can the crew. They start it in grade school. Anyone who couldn't was replaced. Next problem.'

'Getting used to a totally different design.'

'Subs go up, subs go down. What the hell difference does it make if it was built in Norfolk or Novodny? Sure you'll have to train quicker than anyone has a right to expect of you, Mac. We all know that. But time is the one thing we do not have and the stakes are too damn high to go slow. Raza could act any time he gets those missiles armed. He could kill millions. We don't know if you'll be the one that has to face him, Mac, but you'd better get that ship ready damn fast because so far it's shaping up that you may well be the only defense we have.'

MacKenzie shook his head. 'Alone in Russia with a crew that's indoctrinated from birth to hate Americans. Christ, Ben, I wondered what they were saying about me on my own ship.'

'The Russians say it's you or no one. Your country needs you. Don't make me remind you of your patriotic duty. Your personal considerations have no place here.'

MacKenzie shook his head. 'You're not listening. I don't believe I can do it. Admiral Garver,' he said formally, 'I respectfully submit my –'

'Just a minute. I didn't want to do this, Mac. I hoped we could work this thing through just between us. Old friends. But if you insist on going formal there's not a damn thing I can do to stop you. So before you do, listen to one more thing. When's the last time you saw Justine?'

'What's she got to do with this?'

'Answer me.'

'Three months,' MacKenzie said bleakly. He held up a hand to stifle Garver's protest. 'She wasn't wrong to leave me, Ben. I know that. I was . . . unreachable. I hope to tell her that. Maybe we can start over.'

'I hope so, Mac. For both your sakes. In light of that maybe you'll want to reconsider your decision.'

'Why?'

Garver's words cut like a knife blade into MacKenzie's heart. 'Because three months ago your wife volunteered to be one of the agents the CIA sent into Turkmenistan,' he said, 'and at this moment she is in a Skobelev prison.'

For one moment, Garver saw it. The undefinable quality that had always made MacKenzie a man to be reckoned with. Garver savored it, relieved it had not been lost – and if it hadn't been lost it could be restored. One instructor had called it total concentration. An instant 'on' switch, another had said. Garver felt it the way you feel a storm build around you until finally lightning strikes. Nothing had changed physically. MacKenzie still sat holding his glass and his facial expression could not have changed more than a millimeter, but somehow there was a cold light in his eyes that had not been there before, and the room was charged with a crackling energy for which he was the locus.

'Has she been hurt?' he asked quietly. A world of questions in one.

'No. Not to our knowledge.'

The energy subsided.

Garver said, 'I'll tell you the rest.'

Twenty minutes later, Garver left MacKenzie mulling over what he had been told and walked through a raised panel mahogany door into the adjacent room. Dr Doug Wallace was wearing headphones that let him listen to what transpired in the den. He slid them off when Garver entered.

'You heard?' Garver demanded.

'Everything. Decidedly against regulations to eavesdrop this way,' Wallace said mildly.

'Stuff the regs. Can he do it?'

Wallace considered. 'MacKenzie is an interesting case. Everyone, including you, seems convinced he is still a fully functioning command officer. Everyone except MacKenzie himself. Does he have higher standards than the rest of us? Is he just being insecure after trauma, something not so extraordinary. Or does he know something that we don't, to wit – that he really can't function under serious pressure.'

'Yes or no, Doc.'

'Given his time on the *Farley* and the rest of the reports, including the XO's, I'd like to give you a hesitant yes. But it's not that simple. I've read his record. It strikes me as consistent that he would be harder on himself than anyone else. I take it he has yet to resolve his marital problems?'

'You have to know Justine to really appreciate how she went to bat for him. She's as tough as he is. An experienced combat vet, too. She understood what he was feeling. It was just like he said, he was unreachable. It was part of the reason she went back into the field. Maybe he's willing to open up now. I dunno.'

'Yes, you do. And I wonder if you didn't use his guilt over her now being in danger because of him as a lever to get him to accept this assignment.'

Garver shrugged. 'Maybe. Like I said, personal considerations have no place here. Yes or no, Doc?'

'I'd like the chance to speak to him before he goes. Then I'll tell you.'

Garver nodded. 'I gotta get back.'

'Well?'

'I shouldn't take this assignment given what I think of my combat readiness. But there's Justine. Take Raza out and we weaken all of his units. That will help her directly.'

'Then you'll go?'

'I'll go. And off the record?'

'Sure.'

'You are a stinking manipulative sonofabitch.'

Garver was expansive. 'Now that's the Mac I know and love. I tell you, it'll be all right, son.'

'A Russian ship. Jesus Christ,' MacKenzie swore.

Garver was smiling the smile he saved for huge successes. He pulled out a cigar. 'Let's talk.'

FOUR

Ashkhabad, Turkmenistan

The tiny desert mouse poked its head out of a crack in the mud and brick wall of the cell and looked around, its whiskers twitching cautiously. It searched for the slightest motion, found none, and slowly ventured out to eat a crumb on the dirt floor. It moved on to another, then another . . .

Justine Segurra MacKenzie held a string that hung down from the rafters and held her boot suspended over the last crumb. She had made it by unraveling the wool blanket on her cot. The mouse came closer. She let go of the string. The boot fell on top of the creature, trapping him.

'Gotcha,' she said proudly. The mouse had been eluding her for a day, and with little else to do in the barren cell, its capture had become a real focus for her.

She reached into the boot, palmed its furry smallness and brought it out. 'You're a cute little thing, aren't you?' There was panic in its eyes. 'Don't worry,' she said soothingly, 'there's nothing to worry about. I don't eat friends.'

This was obviously a comfort to the mouse and it snuggled into her hand. Justine had a cage already prepared, a tight basket weave of desert grasses she had pulled out of the mattress. She was taught how to weave by the campesinos of her native country when she was a child. She put the mouse in and dropped some food through the strands.

'Home sweet home.'

The mouse's capture was a real achievement, but as with all such successes she now had to figure out what to do next. Choices weren't many. The dirt-floored cell had a door, a naked light bulb, a barred window, a chamber pot, a bed with a grass-stuffed mattress and a blanket made of Karakul wool, the native sheep of this region. No books, no writing materials, no instruments. Just time.

Normally, all her energies would have been devoted to getting out. After three days in the cell she'd have had half a dozen escape plans formulated. But the same apathy that had characterized her work since the breakup with Mac had affected her here, too. She had to admit that if she was up to her usual standards, she wouldn't even be in this mess in the first place.

Unbelievable, really. Raza was a trained professional, like she was. It would have been one thing if she had fallen to him. But the pair of local yokels who had taken her because she was stupid enough to get up on a horse with a rigged saddle – it was too much. She was thrown to the sand and while stunned they had trussed her up like a Christmas turkey and thrown her in here. She tried to work up a sense of indignation but couldn't even manage that. Instead, she wondered what to name the mouse. She sighed. It was obvious.

'Hey, Little Mac.' The mouse raised no objection to the name, settling in to gnaw on his food.

Raza was long gone with the rest of his group. He had come back to Turkmenistan only briefly, anyway, from the North Atlantic. That she had been able to find out, but for what purpose she couldn't ascertain. Then he was gone again. Great work, Justine.

The clever bastard had fooled them all. The CIA thought he was controllable in exchange for supporting his group. The Red Army and even the KGB with whom he frequently worked, as many Spetsnatz had, thought he was a loyal officer. Only the people here, members of his Skobelev organization, knew that all the while he was working for them, setting up the *Kentucky* gambit that had the super-powers jumping. From Moscow's point of view it was all or nothing. For better or worse, both countries agreed he had to be stopped.

Raza had still outflanked them. The incredible number of operatives in the region had managed to learn that Raza had taken two of the cruise missiles off the *Kentucky* and transported them into Turkmenistan as additional insurance. Justine was one of the people whose brief it was to find those other missiles and eliminate them.

She'd made a mess of it. Choosing to work alone, she ran an agent onto one of the higher up Skobelevs with whom she'd had contact before the whole organization went rogue. Just when she thought she was getting some decent product, his men pulled the horse trick that landed her in here. She hadn't learned enough to pinpoint the weapons, only that they were somewhere in the vast Kara-Kum Desert.

Her own people might not even know she was in here. It was time to get out on her own. Sooner or later some very unpleasant questioning would begin. Probably only Raza's presence elsewhere had forestalled it till now. She forced herself to stretch. Throw some kicks. Get the blood moving. She began a slow *kata*, holding each movement a long time, flowing into the next, letting the isometric interplay of muscles provide resistance. After a few minutes she felt better.

The guards would be arriving in a few hours with her afternoon meal. There would be two, as usual. One held a rifle on her while the other put down the new tray and picked up the old. The chamber pot came and left the same way. Evidently, they knew something about her talents. The man with the gun never took his eyes off her. But now she had something to work with.

'About goddamned time,' she needled herself, and set about her task.

The jailers came as they usually did, a little while after afternoon prayers. She needed no clock, the prompt voice of the *imam* singing out prayers in the city gave her sufficient time to get ready. She placed the old tray and the chamber pot on the floor by the door as she did every day and sat down on the bed, hands folded in her lap, also according to her captor's instructions.

The bolt on the other side of the door snicked back and the door swung open. Her jailers wore traditional Turkmeni clothing, dark, knee-length robes over blousey shirts, loose fitting trousers, and boots. They looked like brothers and could well have been. Large families were the norm throughout Central Asia. The one with the rifle watched her closely but he couldn't see the end of the string she was holding behind her. It trailed under the cot all the way to the mouse's cage hidden by the door.

'*Salam*.' The one with the tray put it on the floor and placed a clean pot beside it. The used pot went on the dirty tray. He swept both up together. Just like always.

'*Sag bol*,' Justine said. Thank you. Every nerve was lit up now. Her energy boiled, waiting for the moment when it could all burst out in a sudden rush. Like the sun and the moon approaching eclipse there was one configuration that had to present itself before she could act. One alignment that had to be there. It happened. The man with the tray stepped in front of the man in the doorway holding the gun. She pulled the string and the tiny cage came undone. A long, black, ropelike creature slithered out.

'Snake!' She leapt up onto the bed. 'Help! Cobra?'

The animal's motion caught the gunman's eye lending credence to Justine's cry as she leapt to her feet, wide-eyed.

Both men reacted instinctively. The tray bearer jumped back in panic ramming into the gunman who took his eyes off Justine and his finger off the trigger as he backpedaled in fear of the deadly creature it was illegal to kill. Justine shot off the bed and hit the tray bearer like a football lineman adding to his momentum and smashing him even harder into the gunman. All three shot out into the corridor and crashed into the wall. Justine took one quick glance around. The corridor was deserted.

Both Turkmenis were almost to their feet. She took the

gunman first, the known danger. Her right foot shot out and kicked him solidly in the groin, doubling him over. The gun slid out of his hands and he clutched at his privates. She stepped in and chopped down hard on the nerve bundle at the side of his neck. There was a dull internal crunch and the man dropped to the floor like a stone.

The tray bearer was up and circling now. In spite of what she had done to his friend, his contempt for fighting a woman was evident in his casual stance. He must not have taken lessons from his elders, Justine thought as he circled her not even bothering to call out a warning or for help. Turkmeni women had often fought alongside their men during the wars. She let him come in with a long loping right and blocked it feebly. Grinning, he grabbed her shirt high up on the shoulder and pulled her to him.

It was a mistake. Justine brought her arm sharply around and underneath the man's elbow pushing up with all her might. The tray bearer's face broke into a grimace of pain as his arm straightened from underneath, a direction elbows do not bend, and the joint broke with a snap. A cry of anguish tore from him. Justine, clamping down on the damaged arm and using his shoulder for leverage, ran him headfirst into the wall. He dropped beside his fallen brother.

She dragged both men into her cell and shut the door. The entire fight had taken less than a minute. No alarm had been raised. She took enough of their clothing to cover her jeans, work shirt and boots and trussed them both with Karakul twine, gagging them with pieces of ripped blanket.

The men were no longer a concern but she was worried about the mouse. She owed it something. Without its timely diversion, she might never have had the chance to make a break.

'Ah, there you are, Little Mac,' she said happily, spying it in a corner. It was struggling tangled up in the braid of dark twine she had fixed to its tail – the cobra's 'body.' The illegality of killing cobras, a Russian law, sprang from the need for their venom for medicinal purposes. Catchers had to be called in whenever they were found in populated areas. She freed the mouse and put it back in the crack in the cell wall. As a parting gift she took one of the meat pies called *fitchi* from the tray and pushed it into the hole.

'Have a feast,' she said, munching the other pie.

A few moments later, dressed like a Turkmeni male with the rifle slung casually over her shoulder, she left the cell.

Above the building, on a roof across the street, Spetsnatz Brigadier General Goren Ivanovich Karansky watched the jail through a pair of binoculars with ever mounting concern. Three days of staking out the jail had strained his self-control. What if he had figured things incorrectly? Given Justine Segurra's reputation, she should have been out of there long before now. He ran a hand under his cap over his bald skull, pensive. At least the harsh sun had eased. He could afford to wait, he decided. She'll be coming. He would give it one more day and then leave, in spite of the problems that would cause him.

Karansky was on top of a relatively new building with a fine view of the jail. Most of the buildings in Ashkhabad were new. A nine-point earthquake had leveled the city back in 1948. The jail was one of the few mud and brick buildings left, with a walled courtyard in front of it. Skobelevs stood guard checking the papers of all who entered and left.

He was just about to put down his glasses and come back at the next mealtime when he saw her framed in the front doorway. Was he certain? Yes, it was the American all right. The boots gave her away. She was dressed like a Turkmeni male, her hair hidden under a woolly astrakhan hat. the clothing must have belonged to her jailers. He smiled appreciatively in the gathering dusk. Well, she was supposed to be good. He began to relax. He had figured things correctly after all.

To leave the compound she would have to get on the line of people in the courtyard who were slowly filing past the guard post having their papers checked. The barrier across the courtyard gate was only opened when the guards gave the signal. The open street lay beyond. The American got on line. Fine. He had a clear field.

He took out his sniper's rifle, set the stock carefully on the pillow his jacket made folded neatly on the low roof wall, and lined up the crosshairs in the scope on his target.

Justine saw the guards outside the door and knew she had a problem. But the damn building didn't seem to have any other way out and there was a limit to the amount of time she could spend wandering around muttering 'Salam' with downcast eyes. She fished out the jailer's identity papers and got on line in the courtyard. If she could get close enough to the barrier a few well placed shots might create enough confusion to let her get away.

The line moved across the courtyard and several people at the head were passed through the barrier into the tree-lined street. Turkmenistan was ninety percent desert but Ashkhabad was built in the middle of an oasis. Trees were plentiful. She edged forward. The rifle was an old 9mm bolt-action. There was already a cartridge in the chamber. She held a second between her fingers. Abruptly she came to the guard post.

'Papers?' the guard demanded.

Justine shoved the identity papers in front of his face and moved forward as if nothing could be so stupid a waste of time. It almost worked. For a second she heard no protest. She was almost at the barrier. Then she felt a hand on her shoulder. It's a universal, that hand. It means you have been found out.

She didn't pause to consider any implications. She thrust the offending hand aside and unlimbered her rifle, aware that cries of alarm were already spreading. Soldiers were running. Whistles were blowing. She ducked into the panicked people pushing against each other. The guards would start shooting the moment she was in the clear.

39

'Stop! You . . . stop!'

The robe constricted her. She threw it off and raised the rifle but there were too many innocent bodies in the way. Children were screaming. Guards from other stations were leaping barriers, running toward her. One got to her and threw his arms around her in a bear hug, pinning her arms to her side. The rifle dropped from her hands. She stomped down against the man's instep and he let go of her with a cry of pain. She turned and rammed the heel of her palm into his nose. He reeled away, blinded by the pain. She ran for the barrier, ducking in and out of the stampeding crowd in the courtyard, trying to stay low, using the people for cover. She didn't see the soldier who tackled her till his arms encircled her legs. She went down hard. Another one jumped on her and before she could get out from under them a third pushed her over and twisted her arms behind her back. An officer ran over and put a gun to her head. They levered her to her feet.

'You!' the officer cried, panting. 'You are a demon, but we have you now!'

He was wrong. A red hole blossomed in the center of his forehead and he crumpled to the dusty ground. The gun slid from his lifeless hand. The other two soldiers went open-mouthed in shock, looked at each other and then grabbed for their guns. They never made it. The lower half of one's jaw disappeared in a red mist and the force of it spun him away into a group of cowering people. The other soldier's tunic suddenly had a dark wet stain on the chest as he fell, too.

Justine grabbed his gun, a bulky ancient pistol, and ran. She couldn't guess the sniper's identity, but whoever it was, she owed him. More soldiers were coming and shots rang out. Bullets plucked chips from the masonry. But she was too close to the barrier to be stopped now. She hit the striped wooden pole with both hands and vaulted it, hitting the street beyond in a dead run.

*　　*　　*

40

She didn't slow till the sounds from the jail were distant enough to blend in with the ordinary street noise. She pulled up to a walk, breathing tightly, struggling to control her heaving chest. She had to get off the streets. A Western woman was just too easy to spot. Even though European clothing was rapidly replacing national dress, her jeans, work shirt and boots were too modern not to be noticed.

She cut across Lenin Prospect onto Karl Marx Street, thinking for the hundredth time that Main Street had it all over Karl Marx as an eternal appellation. She crossed into Karl Marx – again the thought – Square. As always, the central fountain gushed happily and there were people sitting by the beautiful flower beds laid out in the designs of the local Bukhara carpets, the region's most famous product. She passed the Town Hall, and Aeroflot office and the bank, hurrying on. The streets fanned out from here into the suburbs. Most of the people lived in the hilly southwestern sections, in brick houses with terraces on the shady side. *Yurtas*, the traditional dwelling tents of the once nomadic Turkmen tribes, were reduced to being set up in the backyard as a kind of summerhouse.

She made it into the department store on Pervomayskaya Street and carefully extracted the currency hidden in her boot. A few minutes, and about half of her rubles later, she was wrapped in native clothing. Most Turkmeni men still wore red or crimson robes over a white shirt with high, shaggy sheepskin hats. The women wore long sack dresses and narrow trousers decorated with bands of embroidery at the ankle. With such a dress and pants over her jeans and shirt, and her hair thrust into a native headdress decorated with coins, Justine could walk the streets unnoticed.

There was an open-air *shashlik* bar on a low hill behind the not very up-to-date Turkmenistan Hotel. She took a table off to the side that had a view of the street. A woman alone caused some stares but she was careful not to meet male eyes and since most Turkmeni women did not wear the veil, she was not bothered. The guard's heavy old revolver was a reassuring weight in her lap.

She ordered a rich, lamb filled *fitchi*, and *chok-chai*, the native green tea, and pondered her situation as she ate. Raza had taken everything out of her apartment, her communications equipment, weapons and papers – and Raza was long gone. She couldn't venture into the Kara-Kum Desert without a guide and provisions. Although the agreement between Moscow and Washington sanctioned her work here, the locals knew nothing about her.

That left her alone and isolated, with a desert to search. She had little choice but to contact her own people and start over again. Maybe somebody else'd had better luck. A thought struck her. After the deaths at the jail she was probably pretty high up on the Skobelev most wanted list. If she was caught again they might not just throw her into jail for questioning. She took another bite, pondering options. Damned if she could see many others. Just dandy.

'Pardon me.'

Her eyes didn't look up, but her ears directed the gun in her hand under the table toward the source of the voice.

'Pardon me,' the voice said again. 'May I sit?'

She raised her eyes slightly. The man was dressed in desert khakis, with well-fitting leather boots. His bald head glistened, as richly tanned as the rest of his skin. It seemed natural, the baldness, oddly masculine, and it accentuated his clear blue eyes. He had high cheekbones and the planes of his face were flat and strong above a full mouth, white teeth and a firm chin. Ethnic Russian, she guessed. Military, she decided. He was trim and moved with athletic sureness. He put something on the table. Carefully, so as not to provoke her.

'I am aware you are pointing a weapon of some kind at me from under the table,' he said quietly in nearly accent-less English. 'Please, examine these first.'

She flicked her eyes from the man to the table and back again, but she saw what he put there. Shell casings. Three of them. Big ones, maybe three hundred grain. For a long shot. A sniper's shot.

'You would not have gotten away without my help,' he said.

'Maybe,' she replied. 'Maybe not. I got out of that cell without your help.'

The man's tone was derisive. 'It only took you three days.'

'How do you know that?'

'I've been watching.'

Justine gestured to an empty chair and he sat. Easily, just sort of folded into it. She poured him some tea. 'Lot of help, watching,' she said.

He grinned. 'With your reputation, I figured it was only a matter of time before you got out by yourself. I wanted to see if you were as good as they say. Why break in, kill a lot of people, and betray my presence here? In the end you left me no choice. By the way, what took you so long?'

'I couldn't find the right mouse.'

'Excuse me?'

'Never mind.' She put the gun on the table and extended her hand. 'Justine MacKenzie.'

'General Goren Ivanovich Karansky, at your service.' He held her fingers lightly and gave a slight bow, lips pursed.

'For God's sake don't kiss it. I hate when anybody kisses my hand. Feels like I've been licked.' She gave her best shudder.

'As you wish.'

'You can click your heels if you want to.'

He smiled pointedly. 'Out of style. As is the dress you're wearing.'

'Fair enough. Army?'

He nodded. 'Spetsnatz.'

'Ah. One of the tough guys. Like Raza.'

His face was cold. 'No. Not like Raza.'

'Sorry, no offense.' She motioned to the waiter for a

43

check. 'Am I right in thinking you've got something arranged?'

'Yes.'

'God, that's good news.' She sighed. 'Let's get the hell out of here.'

'I *hate* Russians.'

Justine looked up. 'Are you a ventriloquist?'

Karansky shook his head. 'It wasn't me.' He shrugged over toward the bar.

'All Russians are scum,' said a fat man poised there. One of the waiters. 'I don't think we should serve them here,' he said loudly to his companions. Most of them nodded, muttering.

'Tell him you don't eat them,' prompted Justine.

'That's pretty good,' Karansky said admiringly.

'Very old. Ignore that asshole and let's get out of here.' He stood. 'As you wish.'

But the fat man took Karansky's lack of response as a sign of weakness. It made him bolder. His friends continued to egg him on and he strutted forward, a *kesser*, the sharp, little curved knife used for cutting wool, appearing in his hand. 'You get out of here,' he said harshly, brandishing the knife.

'We were just leaving,' said Karansky easily. 'There's no need for that.'

But the man was not so easily mollified. 'Don't tell me what to do. You're just another Russian throwing his weight around.' Moving pretty fast for a big man, he swung the curved blade at Karansky's chest.

Justine knew it was coming but did nothing. It was far more instructive to observe. Karansky didn't duck or dodge or even move his feet that she could see. His fist simply shot out in one short, perfect motion like a rocket, turning over karate-style. It caught the fat man square in the solar plexus. One punch. That was all. The *kesser* never even reached the plane of Karansky's body. He was pretty quick, she decided. The fat man simply stopped all in one motion,

44

as if he had run into a wall, and the knife dropped from his hand. He made one impossible gasp for the breath that his paralyzed nerves could not take into his lungs and then his body fell to the floor and took his head with it.

Justine tossed some coins on the table. 'Twenty percent's probably too much when you consider,' she said.

Karansky looked at her curiously and followed her out the door.

It was a warm night and the sweet smell of roasting lamb carried in the air. They walked the few blocks to the racecourse on Swoboda Prospect carefully avoiding the troops on the streets. Karansky seemed familiar with the city. He took them down back streets and soon they arrived. Racing was a very popular sport with Turkmenis.

'You ride, of course,' he said.

'It's been a while.'

'Time to get reacquainted.'

He turned down a long row of attached barns and stopped at one and knocked. Someone peeked out and Karansky said something in Russian. A moment later, two men slid the tall barn door aside.

'They're mine,' Karansky said, going in. Justine followed. The men shut the door behind them.

Racing bridles and harnesses hung on the walls from wooden pegs. There were two horses in the stalls, already saddled and waiting. Turkmenis were justifiably proud of their horses which were world famous as far back as Marco Polo. These two were Argamaks, a stunning breed with great endurance. One was a dark red chestnut, the other was black with a white blaze on its forehead. Their heads were long and aristocratic with dished faces and thick muscles that rippled under dark, lustrous coats. Karansky's men led them out of the stalls. They waited expectantly.

Justine patted the red's neck. 'Where are we going, General?'

'All in due time,' he said. One of his men handed him a

45

heavy quilted jacket and he shrugged into it. 'We have to leave now.'

'Not yet,' she said.

Something in her voice made Karansky turn. She was pointing her pistol at him. He was too far away for any offensive response, but of course she knew that. He heard his men moving behind him and stopped them with a hand motion.

'Tell me something,' Justine said. She cocked the pistol. It made a loud noise in the small room.

Karansky said, 'Leningrad.'

Justine eased up. 'The proper response to that is "St Petersburg." ' She lowered the hammer. 'Sorry. I'm all for personal charm, General, but I had to be sure Moscow sent you.'

'Now you're sure?'

She shrugged.

'Fair enough,' he said. 'Here. Take these and mount up.' He reached into a locker against the wall and handed her a shoulder holster with a Beretta 9mm automatic, and a quilted jacket identical to his. She checked the clip on the Beretta, made sure a cartridge was in the chamber, and then slipped into both. The firepower of the Beretta was reassuring. She handed the guard's heavy pistol over to one of Karansky's men.

'Sorry to be a bother, General, but before we go anywhere I need to call home. Is there a phone handy?'

He took a black cellular phone out of the same locker. 'Here, use this.'

'Direct satellite?'

He nodded.

'Thanks.'

A few minutes later she had reported as well as she could over an unsecured link. Karansky put the phone into the black horse's saddlebag.

One of the men put his hands out and vaulted her onto the chestnut. It was a heady feeling up on top of the big, restless horse. Next to her, Karansky put a foot into the stirrup and mounted the black in one fluid motion.

'They will be looking for you on the roads tonight. We can't risk using a car,' he explained, tightening the reins.

'Where are we going?'

'South. To Firyuza,' he said.

'In the mountains? The desert is north.'

'Right. Open the doors,' he directed his men.

Karansky spurred his horse out of the stable. Justine followed. The hot pulse of the animal beneath her was a heady feeling. There were horses on her father's estate before the revolution. Her brothers had taught her to ride. She began to take the strain in her legs, leaning forward. Balance. Seat. The horse was exquisitely bred and ran effortlessly. Crisp air streamed past her face.

She left the racecourse. Karansky was heading across a field in the distance. She followed, settling into the cadence of the ride. Somehow the horse fit this ancient city. The houses began to thin into open pastures. The foothills of the Kopet Dagh Mountains beckoned ahead. She caught up to Karansky after a mile or so and rode beside him quietly for a while. This was a pleasure not to be missed, or diluted with words. Firyuza was maybe twenty miles south, a resort town in the mountains favored by the city dwellers. The long last rays of the sun made the fields glow. It would be dark soon. Whatever was to come, she would remember this ride and the total freedom of it. Karansky was a good companion. He understood and said nothing.

She reined in her horse on a lower slope and turned back to Ashkhabad. The sun was a red ball in the sky over the city. Most of the houses in the long, sprawling city were hidden by trees. Only a few buildings rose out of the greenery, the ornamental tower of the textile mill, the dome of a mosque, a thin gilt tower in the center.

She turned back, spurred her horse forward and began to climb into the mountains.

FIVE

Odessa

The long translantic flight to the NATO base in Turkey, and then the shorter hop across the Black Sea to Odessa on the southern coast of the Soviet Union had made MacKenzie physically tired, but his mind was in high gear overflowing with thoughts, feelings and impressions.

He put down the last of the guidebooks he'd studied on the way over. The 'western gate of the Soviet Riviera' they called Odessa. Sight-seeing was never much his heart's desire and apart from the beaches they raved about, he had as much interest in visiting medieval churches and art museums as watching paint dry. Another character flaw, he decided ruefully, this lack of interest in churches and museums. On vacation in Paris once, Justine tried to imbue him with some culture. It didn't take. He much more enjoyed sitting in a cafe watching people passing, or seeing a good movie. A visit to the Louvre confirmed his long held suspicion that if a genuine masterpiece was put next to something from Woolworth's he would be unable to spot the one considered 'art.' A cultural black hole, Justine called him.

The place came in low over the choppy sea and he got his first look at Odessa's harbor. Cruise ships and freighters were tied up at the piers. Wide beaches lined the shore. The fishing fleet made its home a short ways down the coast. Wide stone steps led from the modern looking dock to a seaside promenade high above the water. From the guidebook's description these were the Potemkin Steps. Behind them the city spread out in rising rings till the view was lost in the hills on the horizon. Narrow, winding streets, two- and three-story brick buildings. It was an old city, you could tell that, with an old city's charm.

Justine was just a few hundred miles to the east. To reach Turkmenistan all he had to do was go east to the end of the Black Sea, then cross the Caucasus Mountains and the Caspian Sea. He mulled over what Garver told him just before he left. Justine had managed to let her superiors know that she'd escaped from jail and linked up with a Russian general whom Moscow had sent to find the second set of *Kentucky*'s missiles. MacKenzie breathed easier knowing she was no longer a prisoner. Given some room to move, Justine was pretty good at taking care of herself. He spent much of his last night in the States thinking about her and a lot of the things he should have said months before.

Months before. Time passed so damn fast. Was it only eighteen months ago all the trouble had begun? That triggered memories. He tried to put them out of his mind, but these kinds of memories were no respecter of will. He stared out the window, remembering . . .

It was a late snow, later than anyone could remember falling in the Washington area. People had already changed their snow tires. Cans of windshield deicer in the trunk had been replaced by picnic blankets weeks before. MacKenzie, like everybody else, including those responsible for clearing the roads, was caught by the sudden drop to subzero temperatures. No one blamed him. It was all understandable. The car ahead of him didn't see the solid sheet of ice covering the roadway. Neither did MacKenzie, swerving out of the way, until he hit his brakes and felt the sickening loss of traction when his tires failed to hold. He fishtailed across the intersection frantically trying to straighten out his car, out of control. That's when he saw them . . .

Stop it! MacKenzie buried his head in his hands and pressed his temples as hard as he could to stop the memories. *Enough!* What would it take to keep them away? He had to compose himself. The plane would be landing soon and the Russian captain was supposed to meet him at the airfield. It was too late to back out. Like it or not he was in charge of this mission and more than just his own future rested on it. Without the *Kentucky* and her weapons, Raza's power was reduced to a fraction. That could only help Justine complete her end of the mission. Then perhaps they could both come home and maybe start over. He picked up the guidebook. An item caught his eye.

The mud of Odessa's estuaries is rich in sulphur and other chemicals which are efficacious in the cure of rheumatic, nervous and skin diseases. Because of these natural assets there are over fifteen rest homes and thirty sanatoria on this part of the coast.

MacKenzie snorted ruefully. Worse came to worst he could check into one.

'Capteen MacKenzie! *Zdrav'st-vuytye* . . . Hello!'

MacKenzie walked down the airplane gangway to the tarmac carrying his duffel bag over his shoulder. He located the source of the booming voice that hailed him. It was remarkable. If that was his Russian counterpart, he didn't at first see how the man could *fit* into a submarine, much less captain one. He had a huge head and deep, dark eyes. The lower half of his face was covered by a thick black beard and mustache. Black ringlets leaked out from his cap. His shoulders were thick and wide to support the massive head, and his arms were the heavy limbs of a weight lifter or a shot-putter.

The man rumbled forward. 'So, you are MacKenzie,' he boomed. 'I am Captain Nikolai Vladimirovich Raskin, of the Soviet navy. I welcome you.'

MacKenzie wondered if his crew had to wear ear protection. 'Pleased to meet you, Captain Raskin. Thanks for meeting me.' They shook hands.

Raskin smiled expansively. 'It was no problem.' He picked up Mac's duffel bag and slung it over his shoulder. It looked half the size. But suddenly he looked concerned.

'Oh, I am sorry,' he said innocently. 'Perhaps you have some secret things in there. Spy stuff or the like. I don't want you to think I am meddling, yes?'

MacKenzie sighed. Less than ten seconds and the needling had begun. In a way, he was surprised it had taken so long.

'That's okay, just don't jar the nuclear stuff. Radiation.'

Raskin was all smiles. 'Come, I take you to your hotel.'

The Intourist hotel he was booked into was called the Odessa and it was located at Primorsky Boulevard 11, Primorsky Boulevard being the promenade overlooking the harbor MacKenzie had seen from the air. The room was clean and neat and there were pleasant white curtains on the windows, a patterned comforter on the bed, and a wooden wardrobe painted light blue. It had its own toilet and shower, a luxury never to be sneered at. The view from the balcony was superb. The Black Sea stretched out to meet an azure sky dotted with wispy clouds. The briny smell blowing in was a tonic after the plane rides. He took out the 35mm point-and-shoot camera he had brought and took some pictures for posterity.

He'd left Raskin waiting downstairs while he washed and changed. During the short ride over, the Russian had kept up a steady stream of tourist information that gave MacKenzie no clue at all as to what he thought about the situation. MacKenzie wasn't going to ask. Ultimately, they both had a job to do and it was best served by old-fashioned discipline and straightforward adherence to orders.

He pulled on a clean uniform. Whatever Russian-American team had dreamed up this craziness had decreed that MacKenzie could wear his own uniform on board ship. The use of 'Comrade' would be dropped and the crew would use the American naval custom of addressing the officers, including their former captain, Raskin, as 'Mister.' MacKenzie alone would be called Captain. All communications were to be in English. Touchy areas like weapons and sonar would be dealt with by the security officer who was most assuredly going to have an ulcer by the time the operation was finished.

MacKenzie finished dressing and walked down to the lobby. Raskin was folded into a wooden chair with a carved high back reading *Pravda*.

'I'm ready, Mr Raskin,' MacKenzie announced, crossing the lobby. 'I'd like to see the ship now.'

'Of course . . . Capteen. We can take the car if you like. But it isn't very far.'

'Fine. I could use the air.'

The breeze was warm and salty, and gulls circled the ships in the harbor. Raskin set off at a brisk pace, almost trotting down the wide Steps. MacKenzie was surprised at first that Raskin, who was so much bigger than he was, wasn't much taller. Closer, he could see why. He had almost no neck and he was bandy-legged, like the sailors of old who spent years on the rolling decks of sailing ships. Even though Raskin was very broad, those things probably cost him several inches. He was only slightly taller than MacKenzie's six-foot-one. Powerful – MacKenzie decided that was a good word. He was a powerful looking man, with his thick curly beard and dark eyes.

MacKenzie was anxious to see his new ship. Navy pride was navy pride. Foreign or not she would be his home for the foreseeable future. He wondered what the Soviets had chosen for them. Years before, in the Caribbean Sea, he had fought a rogue Victor III sub stolen from the Soviet navy. Later, he did battle with the state-of-the-art Akula-class submarine under the North Polar ice cap, commanded by the cleverest strategist he had ever come up against. Both episodes ended satisfactorily. At least from his own point of view.

Several of the end piers were empty, a buffer zone between the commercial ships and the jet black submarine moored at the last one. The Soviets had balked at having an American captain at a functioning naval base for any

52

length of time. Later they would fly to Kola Bay, the main submarine base for the Soviet northern fleet and their eventual point of departure to hunt the *Kentucky*. All the preliminary training would be done here in the Black Sea.

The concrete pier was surrounded by fencing that looked newly installed. An armed soldier stood guard at the gate. It took MacKenzie a moment to identify the type of submarine and he had to hide his surprise. This was no state-of-the-art nuclear boat. No Akula or Sierra. The sub was an aging Victor II.

The Victor II had its first operational capability in the seventies and had mostly been replaced by newer Victor IIIs, Akulas and Sierras. It was 100 meters long with a 10-meter beam and a submerged displacement of 5600 metric tons. Its main weapons were ASW and antiship torpedoes, possibly the longer range versions. It could also fire ASW missiles. MacKenzie had no way of knowing whether or not this sub carried them.

'So here we are, Capteen. A fine ship, eh? Good and reliable. You recognize it?' Raskin asked.

'A Victor II. Er . . . a good ship.'

'You sound disappointed.'

MacKenzie's voice was neutral. 'A bit surprised, maybe. I expected a more heavily armed boat. Something like an Akula.'

'This is a good ship. The crew are all experienced men. The intelligence reports say you have engaged a Victor and an Akula. Is that true?'

'Yes, but under widely different conditions.'

Raskin seemed genuinely interested. 'Perhaps we can discuss the tactics some time. This is a rare opportunity for both of us.'

'I would enjoy that,' said MacKenzie honestly.

Raskin showed the guard his identification and they were passed through.

The sub's name was stenciled on the prow in white letters

but MacKenzie couldn't read Cyrillic. Before he could ask Raskin to translate, other things caught his eye. This close he could see signs of disrepair. These were paint patches on the hull, and rust spots on the planes. There were fresh welds on masts that had been repaired too many times for his comfort. She was possibly almost twenty years old. Time and the sea had not been kind to her.

As he walked along the pier, MacKenzie felt the hostile measure of the crewman standing watch on deck. What could he say to him? To any of them? How could he transmit confidence? What were the words that would reassure them – a feeling he could use himself right now. He was a stranger in a strange land and all the naval traditions and lore, all the unspoken understandings he was used to, didn't apply here. For the first time in his career he was truly and completely alone.

'*Zdrav* – ' the crewman began, but Raskin cut him off.

'English, Vladimir. From now on, English.'

'I am sorry, Cap . . . *Meester* Raskin. I forgot.'

'Vladimir, this is our Capteen MacKenzie. Capteen, Helmsman First Class Vladimir Radovich.'

The crewman's slicker was dirty and needed mending. He looked at MacKenzie with ill hidden hostility and made no move at all to salute. 'Capteen,' he acknowledged through tight lips.

'Helmsman,' MacKenzie responded, at a loss. Maybe the man had a right to be hostile. What *was* he doing here? But something in the young man's defiant stare stirred his command reflex. He met the hostile gaze. 'Where are you from, son?' he asked.

'Tbilisi, Comr . . . Capteen.' The hostility was unabated.

'In Georgia. I heard that's a pretty town. You call it that, don't you? Just "The Town" . . . *Kalaki*.'

'Yes . . . we do. But how did you know?'

Because I read guidebooks, MacKenzie thought. Instead he shrugged in that omniscient way common both to very good commanders, and parents desperately maintaining an edge over their six-year-olds. 'Are the hot springs as good as they say?' he asked.

Some things are universal. Pride in a birthplace, the local sports teams, my dad can lick your dad. MacKenzie saw it in his eyes.

'Better,' the helmsman proclaimed, heavily rolling the r's. A grudging smile broke over his unlined face. 'People say they can cure anything.'

MacKenzie said, 'Maybe I'll get to see them when we're done with our business here.' He turned to Raskin without waiting for a response. 'I'm ready to see the ship.'

Raskin had been studying the interchange closely. 'Of course, Capteen.' He grabbed the railing over the hatch and hunkered down. MacKenzie followed, noticing rust spots where there should have been none.

There is a feeling about submarines. It starts with the clang of your shoes on the ladder and ends with the compression in your ears when you secure the hatches. It is a feeling of power and technology, of force harnessed and a group joined by a single idea. The captain is the head of this corporation created to do battle. A sub is a supremely well oiled, state-of-the-art machine, every man polished and ready, endlessly studying and striving to perfect his duty.

There was none of that here. What MacKenzie felt he could only describe as a kind of deadness, like a pillow around your head. Men stood idly at their stations as Raskin led him through the ship, somewhat curious but almost insolently indifferent. The air was damp and close as if no one had bothered to exhaust it in hours. The cramped berths in the crew's quarters were unmade. Dirty clothing hung over stanchions. Cassette players were precariously taped to the bulkheads. In the mess, several off duty crewmen stared at him with surly faces. The smell of unwashed bodies was strong.

It got worse. The trash room had a strong odor emanating from it. The corridor floors needed washing. The galley – well, it smelled of things MacKenzie didn't want to identify.

Jury-rigged electrical connections had been stuffed back into the ceiling wiring. Pipe fittings looked ready to explode.

If Raskin saw anything out of order he didn't mention it. The appalling thought that this was normal occurred to MacKenzie.

'Gentlemen,' Raskin announced, entering the control room, 'meet our new commanding officer. Capteen Peter MacKenzie of the United States Navy.'

The announcement was greeted with about the same enthusiasm as if he had said, Lunch – borscht again. No one came to attention. The navigator looked up from his chart table but said nothing. The radioman slid his headphones off and turned to stare. A *Michman*, a rank MacKenzie knew was equivalent to a petty officer's, made no sign of moving away from his board. The rest barely paused in their tasks.

'Good day, gentlemen,' said MacKenzie into the thick silence. 'Mr Raskin, is the full crew on board?'

'Most are still on shore leave in the city.'

'How soon can they be gotten back here?'

Raskin frowned. 'Many just left. They are not supposed to report till tomorrow.'

'Get them back. Use the military police if you have to but I want every member of the crew back on this ship within two hours.' Men grumbled. MacKenzie ignored it. 'Begin preparations for getting underway at that time. Is that clear?'

'Yes, but – '

'Then carry out my order.'

With a you're-making-a-big-mistake look on his face, Raskin shrugged acquiescently. 'Whatever you say, Capteen.'

'When that's done, assemble the division officers in the wardroom. I want to speak to them. Now please show me to your . . . er, my cabin.'

*   *   *

56

Raskin's cabin, now MacKenzie's, had its own head and MacKenzie shut himself inside relieved to be alone. He splashed water in his face and stared at his reflection in the mirror. You can't do this, he told himself. This ship and everybody on it is a disaster. Did the Soviets want the mission to fail?

His head felt tight. It was hard to breathe. He held out his hands and saw they were shaking. He felt out of control again. The tiny room constricted around him and memories came flooding back. He was suddenly back in the snow . . .

. . . *fishtailing out of control across the intersection he desperately tried to straighten his car out. Another car hit the ice and was hurtling at him head-on. He turned the wheel into the skid and gave his car gas. He straightened for a second. The oncoming car flashed by and he thought he was out of the woods but traction disappeared again and the car spun out wildly. That's when he saw them. They were standing on the corner in front of a grocery store. The woman was holding her little girl's hand in hers and clutching her coat together. The little girl looked up and saw the car coming at them. Her face creased into a smile. Look, Mommy, she must have said, look at the nice car . . .*

He grabbed his head and pressed his face against the cold glass till the spinning stopped. He grabbed a towel and rubbed his face vigorously. For the hundredth time he pushed his ghosts back into private places.

He sat down on his bunk weakly. The Soviets had provided the Victor II's engineering manuals. Get to know his ship. That was his first order of business. He put his feet up and began to study.

An hour or so later there was a knock at his door. It was Raskin. MacKenzie ushered him in. The two of them barely fit into the cabin together, but Raskin squeezed by and perched on the bed.

'The officers are waiting, Capteen. But could I talk with you for a second?'

'Of course. What's on your mind?'

'Capteen MacKenzie, perhaps I am talking out of turn, but I feel I must explain some things to you.'

'All right. I appreciate your speaking freely.'

'Very well,' said Raskin. 'I could not help but notice your reaction to this ship. I can only tell you that there was substantial opposition to this mission among many members of the Admiralty and this ship was the compromise. Possibly the secrets you would have been exposed to on one of the latest classes seemed too perilous. I can not say. I can only tell you that those who support this mission, as I do, believe this ship and this crew are capable of performing the required tasks.'

'I am glad to hear that, Mister Raskin.'

'May I continue?'

MacKenzie reclined against the desk. 'Of course.'

'The ship aside. I do not think we do things here the same way you do them in your navy. The men are mostly conscripts with very little education and only a few of the officers are career men. In a way, most are just, how would you say it . . .'

'Just putting in their time?'

'Yes. That's the truth. So we overlook some things, and bear others, and in the end we manage to get the job done. Maybe a little slower than on board the fancy new subs, but then again, we do not get so many gray hairs. You see?'

'Yes. I do.'

Raskin beamed. 'Good. I hoped you would. Now come. The men are waiting.'

An orderly brought in mugs of tea and a tray of sweet rolls and set them down on the wooden table separating MacKenzie from the officers who watched him warily. There was none of the banter he was familiar with, none of the usual questions about home or family or sports. They showed him no more respect than they had earlier, and he felt the undertone of their hostility keenly.

'All of you know that our ship has been chosen for a special mission,' Raskin began, 'one that is vital to our country. Most of you have met our new commander, Capteen Peter MacKenzie. Capteen, for your ease, and to conform to Western customs, I will leave out our patronymic middle names. This is our navigator, Lieutenant Alexi Chernin. Lieutenant Mikhail Kortzov, our weapons officer. Chief Engineer Ari Prudenkov. Senior Sonar Officer Pytor Kotnikov. Lieutenant Yuri Golovskoy, our communications officer. Diving Officer Viktor Petrov. Lieutenant Igor Dainis is the ship's security officer. Comrades, before the capteen says anything, I want to tell you I have spoken with him and I believe we can all get along on this mission. The capteen is an understanding man.'

MacKenzie shook hands with each man and tried to fix him in his mind, like a flash picture. The navigator, Chernin, was a small neat man with glasses. Kortzov, the weapons officer, was a handsome man with shiny black hair. Kotnikov, the sonar man, had a round face with a hawk nose and chin-strap beard. Golovskoy, the communications officer, had wiry hair, bushy eyebrows and deep black eyes. Petrov, the diving officer, had a narrow face and big ears with a shock of blond hair that grew almost straight up off his head. Like a carrot, MacKenzie thought. Dainis, the security officer, was gaunt with a bad complexion and folds of skin between neck and chin that resembled a chicken's. His whole manner was protective and haughty, as if he alone were worthy of holding the keys to the kingdom.

They relaxed a bit at Raskin's comforting words. It was going to be business as usual, boys. Sloppy business. A pity their relief wasn't going to last very long, thought MacKenzie.

'Mr Raskin is right when he said I am an understanding man,' he began. 'I understand that this is a difficult situation for all of us and I understand that we must all go beyond our normal limits to do our jobs. What I do not understand, however, and what I will never tolerate, is sloppiness, disrespect, tardiness, and the altogether lax attitude that governs this ship. I am appalled at its condition and I am even more disturbed by your lack of concern for it. Is this a normal state of affairs?'

'Capteen, I tried to explain – ' Raskin began.

'Those kinds of explanations are not acceptable,' MacKenzie said with a hard edge to his voice. 'Is the crew on board yet?'

Chernin answered. 'Yes, Capteen.'

'Good. Make preparations to get underway. Mr Chernin, I want to see the area charts. Now.'

Word spread fast. Grumbling men were returned to the ship escorted by military authorities or harbor police. Tales of the new captain's tongue-lashing of the officers spread and soon amplified. The officers' misgivings trickled down to the men. In the crew's quarters, one group huddled close together.

'Can you believe it?' demanded a seaman named Ivan Kutsky, a big-boned man with tattooed arms and a knife scar over his left ear. 'I had another day of leave and suddenly those big goons grab me and tell me I have to come back. I thought it must be a big emergency. Then I get here and find it's just the impatient American captain who's done it.' His expression became a leer. 'I tell you I had a girl waiting for me today with tits like torpedoes. I did.'

'I think this American's a real bastard,' said Yuri Tartakov, a thin man with a peaked, batty face and thin black hair. 'He thinks he can throw his weight around, does he? We could show him a thing or two.'

'Make his life miserable,' agreed Kutsky.

'I heard Raskin asked for reassignment but they said no to him,' said Tartakov.

'I can understand he would feel that way. How would you feel if they gave your ship to a foreigner?' said a young blond seaman named Purzov. 'But me, I'm withholding judgment.'

'Well, I'm not. And I'm not taking this lying down. I didn't ask for this special mission crap,' objected Tartakov. 'It is a dangerous thing. Soon we'll start thinking we're better than other ships. That's an American way to think. Well, I'm not better. I want things the way they were.'

'Then we're agreed,' said Kutsky. 'We'll teach him a lesson.'

'I think we should wait,' argued Purzov.

Tartakov ignored him. 'I'm for having a little fun with the American.'

Other heads nodded. War had been declared.

MacKenzie entered the control room and felt the indignation like a heat wave. Word had already spread that the new CO was a bastard. He closed his mind to the turmoil and got to the task at hand.

'Mr Chernin, you have those charts?'

'They are here, Comr . . . Capteen.'

MacKenzie looked them over. 'This is the hundred fathom curve?'

'It is. You can begin the dive there. What course?'

'Don't ask. Wait for my order. Understood?'

Chernin bristled. 'Yes, Capteen.'

'Mr Raskin, station the maneuvering watch.'

'All right.'

MacKenzie turned on him. 'Not "all right." Yes, sir. Crisp. Move it now.'

MacKenzie located the intercom. As with the gauges, there were markings in English over the Cyrillic. He found the all-ship and opened a channel. 'Engineering, this is the captain.'

'We are here.'

'No. Not "we are here." Engine Room, aye. Got it? I want a crisp response to my orders, is that understood?'

'Yes, Capteen, but – '

'Stand by. Captain out.'

MacKenzie blew out a deep breath. It was like trying to move an elephant by kicking him all the way. Everybody performed their jobs with such a surly slowness. It was maddening. 'Mr Raskin, report.'

'The maneuvering watch is stationed, Capteen, and the ship is ready to get underway. We are prepared for dive except for the deck.'

Hallelujah. MacKenzie hit the intercom. 'Engine Room, this is the captain speaking. Stand by to answer maneuvering bells.'

Silence.

'Engine Room!'

'We are ready to answer all bells, Capteen.'

MacKenzie checked his watch. 'Take in all lines,' he ordered, timing them. On the *Farley*, this would have taken about twenty seconds. Here it took a full minute and a half till Raskin finally announced, 'Lines coiled below decks.'

MacKenzie bit back a rebuke. That would come later. For now he just wanted to get out of here in under a week. 'Michman, status of all hatches.'

'All hatches secured, Capteen.'

In navy parlance, the chief would have reported 'straight board.' MacKenzie let it pass. At least the damn doors were shut. A sudden thought crossed his mind.

'Mr Raskin.'

'Capteen?'

'It just occurred to me that I don't know the name of our ship.'

'It is the *Riga*, Capteen. That is the – '

'. . . capital city of Latvia,' MacKenzie said, feeling like a school kid taking a quiz. 'All right, Mr Raskin. Into the fray.' He hit the intercom. 'Engine Room, answer all bells. All engines slow astern.'

Slowly, the *Riga* backed out of her slot. 'Navigation, depth.'

'Fifty meters and increasing.'

62

'Helm, right ten degrees rudder. Repeat that and all other orders before executing them, Mr Petrov and Mr Radovich.'

'Right ten degrees rudder, Capteen.'

MacKenzie slowly swung them around. 'Navigation, why aren't you giving me the depth?'

Chernin looked hurt. 'You said to wait until you asked, Capteen, no?'

'No.'

'One hundred meters then.'

MacKenzie sighed. He saw Raskin hide a smile.

'We are out of the channel,' Chernin reported.

'Very well. Prepare to submerge the ship,' MacKenzie ordered, keeping a lid on his own pressure.

'The deck is clear and the ship is rigged for dive,' Raskin said.

'Submerge the ship,' MacKenzie ordered. 'Take her down to six zero meters. Steer course zero nine zero.' He waited. 'Mr Petrov?'

'Oh, *da*. Six zero meters. Zero nine zero.'

'Engine Room, all ahead two thirds.'

'Two thirds, *da* . . . yes.'

Hesitantly, the *Riga* slid beneath the Black Sea.

An hour out of port things had settled down to a more or less comfortable level. MacKenzie pushed and cajoled and managed to get the crew to respond. It became a maddening game. They never took long enough to provoke a verbal reprimand, just long enough to be a constant drag on his patience and control. A tenth of a second pause, a quarter second delay. Not such big things – until you added up all the lost tenths and quarters. Then they turned into seconds, and the seconds turned into minutes, and the drag on effective performance grew.

A good cruise was one where nothing unexpected happened. That was the oldest rule of command. If you covered all the bases and returned to port with your ship and everyone in it in good shape you had a successful cruise.

But there was *always* the unexpected. That was the reason for the endless training. Later, MacKenzie realized if he'd been his normal self, under normal conditions, things might never have gone so far. But in his present state of mind . . .

All of a sudden the *Riga's* bow developed a pronounced up angle tilting the bow up almost twenty degrees. The loss of trim – the sub remaining on a horizontal plane – got worse. MacKenzie had to grab a railing to keep from falling back.

'Michman, watch your trim. Add ballast to the forward tanks.'

'Yes, Capteen.' The michman hit a pump switch on his board and water flowed into the forward tanks, making the bow heavier. This reestablished trim and the ship returned to the horizontal.

MacKenzie saw the security officer, Dainis, watching him. He would not be at ease until MacKenzie was off the ship for good. Dainis hovered by the sonar room and MacKenzie wondered what he would say if he tried to go in there. Well, the man had to sleep sometime and – the bow dropped so suddenly that again MacKenzie had to grab for a railing to keep from being thrown into a bulkhead. Raskin and Chernin hung on for dear life. The rest of the men clung to their instrument consoles.

'Michman,' MacKenzie roared. 'I told you to watch your trim. Blow ballast in the forward tanks. Get that bow up. Now.'

'I am trying to stabilize us, Capteen. But every time I do the weight shifts. I swear it, Capteen,' the michman complained, hitting switches. The ballast pumps whined and the ship righted itself. As if on cue, the bow shot back up.

'A very impressive display of seamanship,' Dainis said, his voice dripping with sarcasm and loud enough for everyone to hear.

MacKenzie's face got hot. He looked like a fool. What

the hell was going on? He used the railing to climb up to the michman's station and peered over his shoulder at the board.

'Here. Like this,' he said, closing the switches himself. 'Blow the ballast in the forward tanks. Keep the pressure intact in the aft. Transfer the center . . . here.' The deck came back down to the horizontal.

If the seesaw action kept up he was going to have one hell of a seasick crew, MacKenzie thought. Sure enough he heard someone running, followed by the first sounds of vomiting somewhere aft.

'We are in trim,' the michman reported.

He spoke too soon. MacKenzie again heard the sound of running and for the fourth time they lost trim, the bow dropping like an express elevator. MacKenzie tasted bile as his stomach heaved.

'Capteen, do something,' the helmsman complained.

What the hell was it? Equipment failure? Pump overload? A problem in the engine room or in the computers? Something gnawed at his subconscious. He went over the engineering manuals again in his mind.

'Blow ballast in the forward tanks,' he ordered.

This could not go on. Men were running through the corridor. Someone was violently retching. What equipment could be . . . wait a minute. Running? It came to him in a flash and he hit his forehead with his hand. They had done it to him very neatly. He had fallen for a trick pulled on new execs by veterans in his own navy. It wasn't the ship. It was the crew.

The tilt of the deck returned to normal and MacKenzie bolted out of the control room with a hasty, 'You have the conn, Mr Raskin.' If he was right, they were probably near the trash room about now. He almost skidded on an oil slick on the deck and made a mental note to have the floor scrubbed. He liked that thought. He probably had some good candidates.

Ten men racing down the corridor almost ran right into

him. 'Stop,' MacKenzie commanded. 'All of you. Right here.'

They skidded to a halt. Apprehension replaced the glee on their faces. They looked guilty as hell. MacKenzie decided they were very strong men. They would have to be to run at top speed with the seventy-five pounds of metal slugs they were carrying, slugs normally used to weigh down trash containers jettisoned from the ship. Multiply seventy-five pounds times ten and add the weight of the men and you had over twenty-seven hundred pounds suddenly shifting from the stern to the bow and back again. No wonder the michman couldn't keep the ship straight. The crew was having a Trim Party.

The men looked sheepish. 'Hello, Capteen,' said one. 'We were just – '

'Yes. I know. You, the leaders. What are your names?'

'Seaman Ivan Kutsky,' said the thick-bodied man with a scar over his ear defiantly, 'and this is Seaman Tartakov.'

MacKenzie noticed that Kutsky was carrying not one, but two sets of weights, almost a hundred and fifty pounds. And he was barely breathing hard. He motioned to the trash room with a quick thrust of his chin. There was no protest. The weights went back inside with a clang.

'How did you know?' asked Tartakov.

'In the American navy veteran crews sometimes do it to welcome a new executive officer. There's the man trying to impress the captain and the ship won't stay still. Drives him crazy till he figures it out.'

'We wanted to welcome you on board, Capteen,' said Kutsky disarmingly.

'And so you have. In fact, it is the first thing anyone's done around here I can really appreciate.'

Kutsky grinned a greasy smile. 'Then not so many hard feelings, eh?'

'No. Not so many.' MacKenzie smiled, but something flared in his gray eyes that made the men wary. They drew back, suspicious.

MacKenzie put a hand on Kutsky's shoulder. 'I would like to return the welcome. Running through a ship is such a poor way to see it. You've got to get closer to appreciate the fine points. Much closer. At the Academy we used to call it toothbrush close . . .'

All eyes were on MacKenzie when he returned to the control room. Raskin's face was so blank MacKenzie was certain he'd figured out it was a trim party, even if he hadn't necessarily played an active part in it. But he actually felt better than at any time since he had boarded the ship. Discipline was a function of his authority to command. Word would spread. It was a start. He would deal with other situations as they came up.

'Mr Chernin. Lay in a course for home. All ahead two thirds.'

'A course for home. *Da*, sir.'

MacKenzie figured it would take them about three hours to get back – roughly the same amount of time Kutsky, Tartakov, and the trim team would need to clean the entire length of the *Riga*'s main corridor with their toothbrushes.

SIX

Turkmenistan

Justine and Karansky rode south to Firyuza across tilled fields and grassy plains, then moved higher along a deep ravine to the lower summits of the Kopet Dagh Mountains. Her equestrian skills came back quickly and Justine found herself in far better control of the fine chestnut animal than she'd anticipated. They stopped during the night in the village of Bagir to rest the horses and she caught a quick few hours of sleep. At dawn, a woman brought her a breakfast of fruit and tea and with it a little washing kit that included a small hand mirror. She did what she could to erase the tired circles under her eyes, scrubbed her face clean, and tied her straight black hair back. Then she and Karansky rode off again.

The mountain air was crisp and cold. She was glad of the heavy jacket he had given her. The region was spectacular. The mountain summits ahead rose majestically into a clear blue sky. Groves of chestnut trees dotted the hillsides. Clear flowing streams cut through the rocky terrain.

By lunchtime they reached a place called the Golden Spring. A beautiful rush of water cascaded down the mountain, and Karansky called a halt. 'We can follow this into Firyuza. But let's rest a bit first.' He dismounted and took some meat pies and a jug of wine from his saddlebag.

Justine tethered her horse beside Karansky's under a chestnut tree and they sat down to eat. The red and black horses munched grass happily. The mountain air was sweet and clear and the sun warmed her back. She stretched tired muscles. 'I can see why they come up here,' she said. 'It's beautiful.'

'It's hard to believe the desert is so close,' Karansky said. 'The contrasts here are quite startling.'

'I know. At first I didn't see the beauty of this region. Too damn hot and dry. But then you realize how lush a single stream can be against a dry plain. Or how one twisted tree trunk against the desert sky can be as magnificent as crashing waves. There's an ecology of sparsity here. It forces you to readjust your thinking.'

'You're quite a poet, Mrs Segurra.'

'Mrs MacKenzie. Segurra is my maiden name.'

'You're married to a navy captain, yes?'

Justine nodded agreement but had no reason to talk about her marriage with Karansky. It was private, and besides, she was still very much in turmoil about what had happened between them. She wondered how Mac's cruise from the Med had gone. It was his first since returning to active duty. He'd probably be home by now. God, they had fought so much. What was it about marriage that made it so easy to be angry at the other person? By the end they were treating cab drivers and waiters better than each other. It surprised her. For most of her life she thought she would never marry. Then, with Mac, she thought she would never be unmarried. But as things got worse, leaving seemed the only way. Every day he sank deeper and deeper into depression. It seemed kinder somehow to let him find his own way. Maybe by now he had.

'You do that frequently,' Karansky observed.

'Do what?'

'Become still. Inward. Any particular reason?'

She bristled at the question, then relaxed. 'Old habit. Rest when you can. Get your balance back. Never know what's coming next.'

'Savor the quiet times, prepare for the difficult ones.'

'That. And sometimes you remember just how far away you are from the things that really matter.' She picked up a stone and skipped it across the stream. It made five neat rings. 'Don't let my mood worry you, General. I haven't lost the knack.'

'My name is Goren. People I've killed for are allowed to call me that. May I have the same privilege?'

It was there for a brief moment in those clear blue eyes. Interest. His gaze traveled down her lean body and lingered for a moment on her high breasts and trim hips. A silent question. But it found no resonance in her. She saw him record that and accept it as he might any other feature of their working relationship.

'Sure,' she said. 'Justine. And I wanted to thank you for that straight shooting back at the jail.'

'Not at all,' he said in the same manner as if he'd been thanked for lunch.

'But you didn't help me out because it's be kind to jailed Americans week,' she said. The knot in her long black hair had come undone. She began to retie it.

'No,' he admitted. 'But first, tell me what "Leningrad" meant to you?'

'That you're part of the operation looking for the second set of weapons stolen from the *Kentucky*. That you aren't one of Raza's men. Just that.'

'The rest is more complicated.' He sat back against a rock and took a sip from the jug. 'We know the weapons are somewhere in the desert. But that's like saying they are somewhere in the ocean. You were working on one of Raza's men. Did you learn anything?'

'I can confirm they are in the Kara-Kum somewhere. Nothing more.'

'That's too bad. It was one of the reasons I wanted to talk to you.'

'Sorry to disappoint you.'

'No matter. It isn't the only reason. After much effort, those with responsibility for this matter concluded that all our vaunted technology was not going to locate the weapons. Buried six feet under the sands of the Kara-Kum our planes and satellites could look forever and not

70

find them. We realized we needed human resources, not electronic ones.'

'It's a common problem. We have it, too.'

Karansky took another sip and corked the jug. 'Another route was opened. A tribe called the Karadeen live in the Kara-Kum. They are nomadic like the Bedouin, with whom they share similarities, but Turkic in descent. They are brilliant horsemen, good fighters, and have deep family traditions which do not include subservience to Raza. If anyone can locate the weapons in the Kara-Kum, we believe they can.'

'So why do you need me?' Justine asked.

For the first time, Karansky looked uncomfortable. 'Because they hate Moscow almost as much as Raza does.'

Justine laughed. 'You really haven't done a very good job in the PR department, you know.'

Karansky shrugged. 'Things are changing. The Wall fell. Almost everywhere the Party withers and dies. Just a few years ago it would have been inconceivable for us to talk as friends, much less work together. There is an inevitability about things, Justine. We have stopped lying to ourselves in the Soviet Union.'

'It won't be much of a Union if the breakaway republics have anything to say about it.'

'That too can change. What would your southern states have said about Washington just a century ago?'

'Probably not much worse than they say now, but your point is well-taken. Look, this isn't my beef. It's your country. I'm just after the missiles. What do we offer the Karadeen to get them to work for us?'

'Up to five million in gold bullion.' Karansky grimaced. 'Please try and remember we're pressed for hard currency. The lower the figure the happier my superiors will be.'

Justine shook her head. 'Look, I may have been born at night, but I wasn't born *last* night. I don't buy it. If the Karadeen hate you guys enough that you need an

American to barter with them, a little gold isn't going to do it. You're not telling me everything.'

Karansky chewed on a blade of grass thoughtfully. 'Sadly, that is true. There is something else that the Karadeen want. Something that means far more to them than the gold. Do you know what the term *Mahdi* means?'

'Some kind of religious leader.'

'Not some kind of leader. *The* leader. It means "He who is guided right." According to Moslem traditionalists, Mohammed declared that one of his descendants, the imam of God, would fill the earth with equity and justice. This imam would bear the name of al-Mahdi. He is the hidden deliverer who will one day appear and fill the oppressed world with righteousness. The Karadeen and other Moslems believe in the Mahdi as a kind of religious warrior who will lead the faithful to victory in a holy war.'

'What has this got to do with us?'

'Everything. There have been lots of Mahdis over the years. Every petty tyrant who got near the top proclaimed himself Mahdi as justification for a lot more killing. As you can imagine, very little equity and justice ever followed.'

There was an odd light in Karansky's eyes. Justine could see he was caught up in his own narrative as he went on.

'Despite all that, there was one man who by all accounts seems to have at least come close to fitting the bill. His name was Ali-Kahdri and he was born in this desert somewhere around the turn of the century. Some of the reports about him are a little hard to believe. He fought ten men and subdued them. He killed a tiger with his bare hands. He crossed the desert on foot after being betrayed by a rival and left to die. That kind of stuff. But if even half of what was said about the man is true, he was as wise as Solomon and had the heart of a lion, the fighting prowess of a samurai and the soul of a poet. He was also a brilliant leader, a devoted father and a faithful husband. On top of all that, he was also supposed to be quite handsome, too.

'Ali-Kahdri never spent a day in a traditional school as

72

you and I know it, but by the time he was twenty-one, most of the tribes in this region were allied under his rule.'

'What happened to him?' asked Justine, fascinated.

'You know that this region was coveted by Russia and Britain and even Turkey in those years. Ali-Kahdri fought them all. But in the end he realized he had to throw in with someone. He chose Russia because the Kremlin offered him free rule over his people once the others were defeated. With his help, the Red Army took the whole region and this became the autonomous oblast of Turkistan.

'For a while things went as agreed. Turkistan was prosperous and peaceful under Ali-Kahdri's rule. But things changed in Moscow. Stalin came to power. He didn't want a single Turkic nation within the USSR and decided to break it up into five separate republics according to his principle of nationalities. He tried to impose stern Party rule. Naturally, Ali-Kahdri refused to accept any of this. He told Stalin where to stick his plan and led the tribes in revolt. Stalin's generals were ruthless. Thousands died. But Ali-Kahdri knew the desert better than anybody and no matter who Stalin sent, Ali-Kahdri managed to hit-and-run and survive. Finally Stalin had no choice but to sue for peace. Ali-Kahdri accepted the offer, under the same terms as before.

'The meeting was set for Ashkhabad. The chiefs of the various tribes under Ali-Kahdri's rule were all there for what was supposed to be a big celebration. Stalin himself was supposed to come and present the new treaty to Ali-Kahdri. What came instead was an elite unit of Stalin's political police who had been smuggled into the city days before and were waiting for Ali-Kahdri and his chiefs to gather. They were supported by aerial attacks that drove the horses and camels mad even as the chiefs tried to escape. Half the city was bombed out in the process. Hundreds were killed, including most of Ali-Kahdri's sons. What was left of the tribe escaped into the desert. Ali-Kahdri himself was captured and imprisoned.'

'This was so long ago, Goren. What could it matter now?'

'Justine, Ali-Kahdri is still alive. He is nearly ninety years old and has spent the last sixty years in a cell in a monastery in a part of the Soviet Union that's about as remote as the moon. But he has been treated well. Stalin and the other rulers after him could never quite be sure they wouldn't need him sometime. For my money, I wonder if they weren't just a little afraid of him, too. So he has been given the freedom to read and write. He even has a television, a wonder I am told he never tires of. So he is well versed in the global politics of this past half century and has lost none of his mental acuity.'

The light grew stronger in Karansky's eyes. 'I've met him, Justine. It was an experience I shall never forget. Even at ninety he is an imposing man with a presence that seemed to fill the room. I am almost prepared to believe he is the Mahdi of whom they speak. But whether he is or he isn't is not the issue. We are willing to trade Ali-Kahdri for the weapons. If the Karadeen will locate *Kentucky*'s remaining missiles for us, they can have their Mahdi back.'

'Aren't you afraid he'll lead his people against you as soon as he's out?' Justine asked. 'You're just trading war with Raza for war with the Karadeen.'

'The Karadeen don't have nuclear bombs. We'll deal with one revolt at a time. Look, conditions have changed. There's oil wealth here now, an agricultural economy, too. The canal irrigates the entire region. This sort of infra-structure requires a modern nation. Or at least a modern nation's help. Ali-Kahdri will taste melons grown on land that was once only sand.'

'Who rules the Karadeen now?'

'His grandson, Kemal, rules the tribe. He is a direct descendant of Ali-Kahdri and from all reports may be as much of a man as his grandfather. It is Kemal we are here to meet.'

'What's the catch?'

'Pardon?'

Justine had been feeling a funny itch between her shoulder blades for some time now. It had alerted her to the small, almost imperceptible movements in the rocks all around them. Men were moving into position. She forced herself to concentrate on Karansky.

'Goren, there's no such thing as a free lunch. You still don't need me for this. Here's your grandfather, Kemal. Go find my missiles. Why complicate it with me?'

Goren smiled. 'You're very perceptive.'

'And I play a neat piano. Give.'

'When they were first approached, the Karadeen saw this as just another possibility for Russian treachery. They demanded a hostage. A highly placed American who would be valued enough by his or her government to guarantee the Mahdi's delivery.'

'Why American? Why not Russian?'

Goren came closer to looking shamefaced than she would have believed possible. 'They think we would willingly sacrifice one of our own.'

'I see.'

'Kemal is no backward desert rat. He went to school in London. He has contacts in the intelligence community. Your dossier is long and your reputation established. The name Doña Justiñana of the Nicaraguan revolution, and later, of the CIA, is known to many. We knew you were in Turkmenistan so we contacted your government and they gave us the brief to make the offer. Kemal accepted. I would have broken you out of that jail if you hadn't done so yourself. Of course, I'm supposed to tell you that you have the right to refuse this hostage deal. It could put you in a difficult position.'

'Sure. And I have the right to remain silent. A deal's a deal.' Justine appraised the situation honestly.

'Just one more thing. Remember Kemal has sworn a blood oath. If the Karadeen complete their part of the bargain and we don't turn Ali-Kahdri over to him, he swears you will never leave the desert alive.'

'So I'm dependent on Russian integrity.' Justine shook her head ruefully. 'Tell me that's not a contradiction in terms.'

'I give you my word. That's the best I can do.'

'What happens when we find the missiles?'

'I call in an air strike. We vaporize the area.'

'Leaving a small radioactive crater. Ecologically speaking.'

He shrugged. 'It's a big desert. No one will miss a little piece.'

'One last thing,' she said. 'What stops you from calling in your Spetsnatz paratroops and taking two of my country's most advanced weapons? You can't tell me you wouldn't like to get your hands on them.'

'Just as you would if our positions were reversed. But the danger here is too big to take chances. The deal is as I've just presented it. No tricks.'

Justine's senses were extended outward. There was growing movement in the rocks about fifty feet from the stream. More in the chestnut grove below them. She shifted slightly and put her hand on her gun. Karansky caught the movement.

'You're aware we're not alone,' she said quietly.

'For a while now.'

'Do you know who it is?'

'It could be Raza's men,' he said. 'Or Kemal's. I can't tell.'

Justine motioned with her eyes. 'Some behind the rocks and in the grove below us. Anywhere else?'

'The trees to your right. I think the only way out is up.'

Justine moved her legs and found her balance. 'No time like the present, eh?'

There were sudden shouts from the rocks and men dressed in desert garb leapt out and began running at them, maybe ten in all. Another ten came rushing up from the grove. 'Go,' Goren yelled, grabbing his horse's reins. He vaulted into the saddle, reined the big black horse around and shot forward up the mountain.

Justine hit the saddle from a run and tore the reins out of the branches of the chestnut tree. The horse sensed the tension in her hands and needed little incentive to race after Karansky's mount. Behind them, the men were still yelling. They were already at the spot where Justine and Karansky had eaten lunch. But something was odd. The distances were not that great and they were heavily armed, yet they weren't shooting.

Karansky was crouched low on his horse ahead of her, racing up the mountainside. She saw where he was heading. A path was cut into the hillside where some ancient stream had worn down the rocky cliffs. The boulders on either side were too big to ride over. A sudden suspicion formed in her mind. It was too neat. The shouting, the lack of gunfire – it all began to feel like they were being herded to that spot. She called out to Karansky but her voice was lost in the wind. Karansky got to the pass and darted in. Acting solely on intuition, Justine pulled back hard on the reins and brought her horse to a sliding stop.

Karansky was almost through. He was leaning far forward, giving the horse his head to run along the rocky path. The wind whipped the horse's mane as it surged on. Its ears were flattened against its head and it was blowing hard from its nostrils. An open field was ahead of him and Justine began to wonder if she had made a mistake. Karansky would be through in a matter of seconds. She held the chestnut back, ready to follow him if she had made a mistake.

The net that dropped from the boulders on either side of the pass caught Karansky's horse in full stride. It lost its footing and tumbled forward squealing in fear going down like it had been shot. Karansky's momentum threw him from the saddle into the netting, helpless. He twisted head over heels and landed flat on his back, immediately surrounded by desert men who yanked the dazed general to a standing position and took his weapons.

Justine looked back. Men were closing on her but there was still no gunfire. That and the net proved they wanted them alive. The men in the pass began moving down the mountainside toward her. Those below were coming up. She was caught in between.

She spurred the chestnut back down the mountainside toward the rushing men. They stopped, confused for a moment. Then they spread out in staggered pairs, waving their hands, ready to rip her from the saddle as she passed. She put her head down and rode straight at them. They held their ground. At the last minute she yanked back hard on the reins and dug her feet down into the stirrups throwing her weight back. The chestnut was magnificent. It reared up on hind legs scattering men before it, but that wasn't all she had in mind. There were more men coming up from the grove below and she saw no chance of getting through the trees at high speed. Instead she yanked hard on the reins again and dug her heels into the horse's side. The chestnut spun around throwing up stones and sand like a fishtailing sports car. She spurred it back up the hill hard, taking the men who had just run out of the pass totally by surprise. She raced for the cut between the hills. Maybe they had one net ready, but two was unlikely. If she could make it past the men who held Karansky she might be free.

The chestnut stallion never faltered as she ran straight into the pack of men coming down the hill. They tore at her legs but the great horse was too big and fast and the offending hands were torn loose from the force of their passage. She wanted to turn and yell her defiance to them but the wind was a raging storm in her face. The pass lay ahead. She bent low, spurring her horse on with a sharp slap to its flanks.

She felt the compression of the air as she sped between the rocky sides of the pass. The men who held Karansky tightened their grip and pressed him back. Still there was no gunfire. Justine grinned. Well, who the hell said they wrote the rules? She yanked the Beretta from her jacket and her first shots blasted stone shrapnel from the rocky walls. She emptied the clip. Karansky's captors loosened their hold on him to duck. It was all the general needed. His left foot shot out and blasted into the man next to him. His elbow struck the second in the side. The third was bent over and Karansky's kick straightened him up fast. Justine leaned out and extended her arm. Karansky timed his leap just right. She barely had to slow. Suddenly he was in the saddle behind her.

Justine spurred the horse on again leaving Karansky's still recovering captors behind. Open ground lay ahead. They shot out of the pass onto a broad grassy plain leading up to the next plateau. Justine urged the horse on. There was froth on its muzzle and its great chest heaved with the exertion, but he never wavered. The wind screamed in her ears. The rhythm of the stallion's hooves pounding on the turf matched her heartbeat. She wanted to shout her victory. Then she felt something flick at her back and she heard Karansky cry out and felt his hands leave her sides. When his weight suddenly disappeared she knew it was not over yet.

She reined in the stallion and looked back. A man in flowing black robes mounted on a brilliant dapple gray stallion with a long silver mane and tail had stopped chasing her long enough to drag Karansky's unconscious form back to him using the rope he'd obviously just lassoed the hapless general with. It took him only a moment to tie Karansky and leave him on the ground for his men to recover. Then he slid back up on his horse like a stream of water. No introduction was necessary for Justine to know she was watching a different class of man than the ones she had just ridden through. He moved with the economy of motion usually only truly gifted athletes possess and he rode with such assurance that he appeared to be nothing less than a powerful wind rolling across the grassy plain.

Well, first he had to catch her. She turned and raced for

the summit. The stallion felt her need and gave it all he could. Its legs pumped. It surged ahead. Still Justine felt the presence of the man in black behind her. When she looked back he was closer. It occurred to her that his mount might well be fresh and she had been riding hers since dawn. All right. If she couldn't outride him, maybe she could outsmart him.

It was all in the timing. He'd use the lasso again. She felt him gaining on her. She urged her horse on again. Again it responded. The plain sped by beneath her. Every one of her muscles was strained from the pounding she was taking, but adrenaline spared her the pain. The plateau lay ahead. One last hurdle before she reached it, the man in black.

Timing. A rearview mirror would have been handy. She had the next best thing. The little mirror given to her in Bagir that morning was already in her hand. She could see the man in black coming up hard behind her. His horse seemed to float over the plain. With one eye on the ground ahead and the other on him, she saw him take another rope from his pommel and commence a long looping movement that sent it spinning out into the air toward her.

She ducked at the last minute and the rope hit her body instead of settling around her. She was able to grab it. When she felt the man in black take in the slack sharply, two things happened at once. She threw her weight forward and yanked her horse's reins harder than she would have wished on such a courageous animal, and just as suddenly she let go of the rope. She felt a sudden weight on the end of it that just as suddenly fell off. She looked back. It worked! The man in black had overbalanced and fallen embarrassingly backward off his horse. He hit the ground rolling. She spurred her horse on again, but slower this time. It would take him too long to remount and catch up to her again.

She took a look back. It was her first and last mistake. The whirring sound penetrated her consciousness a split second before her brain identified what it was and the mental picture of the man in black standing on the plain whirring the odd looking balls over his head clarified.

The bolas hit and wrapped themselves around her horse's legs, tripping the fine animal as he ran. Its knees hit the plain and it heaved forward squealing, throwing Justine right over its head. The ground came up fast and she had time only to hear the man in black give one final infuriatingly gratified laugh before the mountain came up at her, and all the lights went out.

SEVEN

Odessa

With a few final fits and starts, MacKenzie brought the *Riga* limping back into port. He was utterly exhausted from the strain of constantly pushing lethargic officers and crews. He watched them from the sail bridge as they departed along the pier, grumbling among themselves. They were just as annoyed and surly as before. It was going to be a tough road earning any respect or admiration from this bunch. As far as they were concerned, he was a royal pain in the ass. And as far as *he* was concerned, the success of their mission at this point was a total impossibility. Time pressure and Garver's warning to be ready with all haste weighed heavily on him. He had to get this crew into shape. But how? For the conceivable future, if Raza had a school kid for a pilot and a guy with an engineering degree from Uzbek U. to run the engines, the *Kentucky* could take the *Riga* no contest.

'So, Capteen,' boomed Raskin's voice from below. 'Not a bad first trip, eh?'

Raskin's enormous head filled the hatch. MacKenzie almost laughed. 'Were we on the same ship?'

'Oh, not to worry. We just have different ways of doing things. We will reconcile them in time. Will you have dinner with me?'

'I'm pretty tired. And I want to go over the duty rosters.'

'See? That is another mistake. Never turn down a friendly invitation. You have yet to see the Odessa nightlife. Consider it a part of your Russian education.'

'All right. Let me get cleaned up.'

Raskin squeezed through the hatch onto the bridge. 'We

are going to eat, not get married. You look fine. Forget your problems and come with me.'

A few hundred yards away, Igor Dainis, the *Riga*'s security officer, entered a dark sedan parked along the promenade above the harbor.

'He is an average seeming man for one with so many military accomplishments,' said Viktor Volchek, the Operations Director of Soviet Naval Intelligence who had been watching the *Riga* through binoculars since it docked. Volchek was a sturdy, flat-featured man with thin hair slicked back on the sides of his head. A career intelligence officer, he had three children from two different marriages and the kind of personal sensibilities usually found at book burnings. He wore a Suvarov Naval Academy ring.

Dainis was happy to be speaking Russian again. 'He is a competent enough commander. Of course the crew hates him because he is driving them too hard.'

'And Raskin?'

'Raskin accepts the situation because he has to. For the moment he is neither helping nor hindering MacKenzie.' He told Volchek about the trim party.

'I'm not sure I like that,' Volchek said. 'The *Kentucky* is a priority. We don't want anything getting in the way.'

'My advice would be to leave MacKenzie to his own devices. I think there is more to him than meets the eye. If anyone threatens to be truly obstructive, I can step in.'

'What about the new sonar?'

Dainis shook his head. 'So far he has made no effort to see it. Frankly, Comrade Director, I don't see how it can be prevented given the confines of the situation. The same with the weaponry.'

'I am forced to agree. Which is why I am here. Those who supported the mission rammed through a compromise to use a competent enough crew on an older sub. That is supposed to sufficiently minimize security loss. I don't hold to that. Neither do our more conservative elements.

83

Regardless of the operating unit there is simply no way to prevent MacKenzie from learning much too much about us. The sonar may be the biggest prize, but it is not the only one. Our operational movements, our codes, our running routes and frequencies, these and other incidentals can be just as important in the long run.'

'What can be done about it?'

'Comrade Dainis, you know that your selection for this assignment puts you in a very special category.'

'And I am grateful, Comrade Volchek.'

'Good. Because your responsibilities are now increased. We have to live with this mission, but we have constructed a scenario whereby we can prevent security loss and even encourage the *Riga* to succeed. You will do your best to support Captain MacKenzie in his mission to destroy the *Kentucky*. Make sure nothing stands in his way. But when that mission is completed, we want him to have a fatal accident. If it can be done in the aftermath of battle, so much the better. But this is important – it must appear to be an accident. That way we can deliver his body to the Americans with full military honors and the secrecy of our operations intact.'

Dainis nodded. 'That would be a very successful ending to all this.'

Volchek rubbed the jewel in his ring around the palm of his other hand. 'I can also tell you that some of us feel that this will pay Captain MacKenzie back for his interference with *Red Dawn* and his attack on the *Akula*. We have a long memory. It will be good for the Americans to wonder about that. So plan his demise, but in the short term do not stand in his way. He will need the sonar and the torpedoes. Let him have them.'

'What about Captain Raskin?'

'Raskin is a well-disciplined captain but he can also be an idealist. Watch for that trait. Be careful of it. Remember they share certain bonds. I had papers prepared in case you need them. Yours is the ultimate authority. If Raskin gets in your way, supersede him. If he resists, well, his failure to return won't be a major blow to the Soviet navy.'

Dainis slid the papers into his pocket.

'Do you have any idea how long the training will take?' Volchek asked.

'If today was any example,' Dainis said, rolling his eyes, 'a lot longer than anyone expected.'

According to Raskin, some of the best food in town was found right in the Hotel Odessa. They ate under the trees in an open air courtyard overlooking the harbor. MacKenzie let Raskin do the ordering. He wasn't a very adventurous eater, but the food in the hotel proved to be excellent. There were *blinis*, thin little pancakes stuffed with caviar and topped with sour cream, then cold soup called *akroshka*, which Raskin explained had a beer base. Then a better Chicken Kiev than any MacKenzie had eaten outside the Russian Tea Room, and finally dessert of rich ripe local fruits. All of the above, however, was accompanied by glass after glass of ice-cold vodka which Raskin consumed like water.

'*Na zdoróvie*,' Raskin toasted for the fourth or fifth time. MacKenzie had lost count.

'Health,' Mac returned the toast, sipping the same glass of clear fire he had been consuming all dinner.

'I tell you, Capteen MacKenzie . . .'

'Mac, okay?'

'Mac . . .' Raskin's mouth twisted around the unfamiliar syllable.

'Not muck. Mac. *A* like it "at." '

Raskin tried it again without much improvement.

MacKenzie frowned. 'I can't see myself spending the next few weeks being called Muck.'

'Do you have another name? A middle name, perhaps. As you know, we Russians have patronymic middle names derived from the names of our fathers. My father's name was Vladimir. So my full name is Nikolai Vladimirovich Raskin.'

MacKenzie said, 'Peter,' much the same way a child says 'liver.'

But Raskin smiled expansively. 'Peter ... Pytor. It's almost the same here. A good Russian name. Can I call you that?'

'You're the only one. I swear. Not even my wife does.'

'Well, Peter, if you don't mind my saying so, I think you must learn to relax a little.'

'We have a job to do, Nikolai.'

'Yes, but it's not good to work so hard all the time. The cruise is past. Move on.'

'I keep anticipating some new version of the trim party.'

Raskin grinned. 'That was pretty good your figuring it out so quick. I've seen some officers go half crazy trying to keep a sub in trim while the crew runs back and forth with the trash weights. And making them clean the deck with their toothbrushes – wonderful! I thought Kutsky was going to burst his spleen. He's not so bad by the way once you come to know him.'

'I could tell we made a great impression on each other.'

'Forget Kutsky. Forget all of them. It's a beautiful evening. Let us ponder the meaning of life.'

MacKenzie sighed, trying to figure out what he had done to deserve all this. 'So much depends on this mission, Nikolai. It's hard to forget why I'm here.'

'Even for a few hours?'

MacKenzie shook his head. 'How can I? The situation is a disaster and you know it. The crew needs a completely different level of discipline and a whole lot more training if we're going to get through this in one piece. This won't be just cruising around the Black Sea. We could get killed fighting the *Kentucky*. I warn you, she packs a lot of punch. We have to begin combat exercises as soon as possible. Help me, Nikolai. What makes the men so difficult to motivate? Aren't we all after the same thing?'

'Yes,' Raskin said, 'and no. It is not easy to understand the Russian soul. Have another drink, Peter. It will put you in a better frame of mind.'

'I'm fine.'

'You don't want me to have a bad opinion of you, do you?'

'Well, one more.'

'Good.' Raskin beckoned the waiter to pour another round. When his glass had been drained again he grew pensive, sifting through his thoughts for the right words. 'This is going to be difficult,' he said, finally. 'It's hard to explain such things. You are going to have to leave some of your basic ideas about life behind. Or at least be open to new ideas. Some people can't. You are a man who believes in definite things. It is easy to see that. Hard work, dedication, individual initiative – things that are, by the way, typically American. I spent time in America a few years ago, as part of the naval mission attached to the embassy in Washington by the way. It was easy to see why Americans value those things. But here . . .' He gave a shrug that MacKenzie was beginning to see as universal here, part wistful, part resigned. 'Here things are different. We have had a single Party controlling everything from the schools to the economy for seventy years. You can not imagine the impact that has had. Over the years people here have had to learn different ways to survive, much less prosper. If you are unwilling to pay bribes, or trade favors, or use the black market, your family will probably end up doing without. Your American way of doing things would not produce the kind of results here you might think. Work harder than your neighbor and you will not earn his respect, you will earn his envy and rancor. This is part of what you feel from the crew. It surprises you, I can tell. Well, it is real, I assure you. All our lives we have been taught to hate and fear the man who puts himself over others, over the collective. Of course, this has a price. You are not the first to notice we have become a nation of

87

indifferent workers, dependent on the State for all things, unable to produce a decent television set or create adequate housing or make furniture that isn't squat and ugly.'

'You're an industrial country. A superpower. How can this be acceptable?'

'To some degree it isn't acceptable any longer,' Raskin said seriously. 'Our very survival is at stake. We produce a bumper crop of potatoes and half of them rot in the storage sheds or fall off broken-down trucks bouncing over potholed roads on the way to the market. People wait in line for hours a day to buy the most basic necessities. Everyone knows the old story about the man who walks into the empty fish store to buy meat. "Go across the street," the clerk tells him. "That is the store where they have no meat." '

MacKenzie laughed, seeing in the humor of the story the deeper despair it carried. By now the vodka had given him a pleasant glow and he felt some of the tension of the voyage dissipating.

'But if you are going to understand us you must look deeper,' Raskin continued. 'Underneath what seems to be just laziness and sloth you must see that there are very basic values operating. It is not just a system of madmen. Ask a Russian if he's afraid of losing his job or his apartment and he'll look at you like you're from the moon – or from America. He'll laugh because he knows he could spend every other day drinking at the *banyas*, those are our public bathhouses, and never be discharged. Arrange men by order of competence? Never. That would be unseemly, placing the work over the man, something most Russians feel deep down in our bones is in some way, well, spiritually wrong. Work is a *thing*. It should not be made more important than the people who perform it. We are a people country, Peter. Few outsiders really understand that.'

'Nikolai, I just won't buy the "competition is evil" stuff,' MacKenzie objected. 'A healthy amount of it makes people stronger, produces better products and brings out the best in the lot of us. It's another form of pride. We're not robots, Nikolai. Compassion and charity run just as strong in us. But when you get into an airplane don't you want to know that the pilot is there because he's competent, and not because he was given a job by some political hack? And even if you're willing to risk that, what about when your wife and kids get on that plane?'

'No, of course not. In such an area we would have very little disagreement.' Raskin signaled the waiter for more vodka. 'But not every place is so vital, is it? Not all work is so crucial.'

Mackenzie allowed his glass to be refilled. 'I don't know. If it's right for airplane pilots, maybe it's right for doctors or film directors or electricians or breakfast cereals. The marketplace is an ancient device for bringing out the best.'

'The best . . .' Raskin's smile was rueful. 'I have heard much about this quest for the best in your country. Look at the price you pay for it. How many men and women in your country can't sleep at night with worry about their jobs and their future, or the future of their children? "One paycheck away from the edge" – that was a phrase I heard a great deal when I spoke to your countrymen. The edge is a place that is very real for Americans. It is a place where there is no one to help you and nowhere to go because someone faster or smarter or better connected than you got the job you depend on. Competence – ' His tone was derisive. 'How humane. How noble. Did you ever ask yourself, Peter, why a man's basic needs should be hostage to competence? Why doesn't every man, woman and child get them just because they exist in this world and are entitled? Economic slavery can be just as evil as the other kind. It is true we don't live as well as you, but food and housing and education and medical care are all subsidized by the government. Prices haven't changed much in twenty years. We Russians are amazed you can function every day without that safety net, why anyone would *want* to. You make better cars, and your living standard is the envy of the world, but what is the cost in ulcers and fear and isolation and loneliness? You are so *alone*, Peter. It is true we stand in line for bread, but at least we stand in line together.'

MacKenzie drank some more. For some reason the vodka had lost its bite. 'So your economy isn't falling apart and there aren't any class distinctions and I'm not getting drunk on this vodka which you all drink too damn much of?'

'Alas, all three are true.' Raskin drained his glass again, and again it was refilled. 'By the way, don't drink it like that, one sip at a time – not even ladies drink it that way. Tilt your head back and knock it down in one shot. Better for the afterglow. You won't get such a hangover.'

MacKenzie shot down the rest of the vodka and felt like someone hit him in the back of the head. His eyes must have shown it.

'Eat something,' Raskin suggested. 'A little of the *blinis*, maybe. A Russian never drinks vodka without eating something. Even a piece of buttered bread.'

'Right.' MacKenzie shoved some pancake in his mouth. 'But to continue, I still can't imagine keeping a man on who couldn't do his job. What would you rather know, that a man who didn't know how to do his job kept it or the man who did did?'

Did did? Christ, he was getting shitfaced. He hadn't drunk like this in a long time. MacKenzie shook his head. He'd better stop. It was unseemly to get drunk with Raskin. He had to maintain professional distance. Control.

A man carrying a guitar came out of the hotel and perched on a stool in the center of the courtyard. The sun was setting and the lights in the trees glowed with color. Below, the harbor was a sprawling net of sparkling jewels. The singer gently strummed chords and began humming, softly calling attention to himself.

'You like music?' Raskin asked.

'Some. My wife was a musician once.'

Raskin leaned back. 'I have heard this one. From the Odessa Conservatory. But here he sings folk music. He is very good.' Raskin winked. 'Very Russian. See what you think.'

The singer was dressed in a simple white shirt and dark slacks. He was a thin man with a narrow face and dark eyes. His voice was deep and throaty. The people in the courtyard turned to listen. Maybe it was the vodka – of course it was the vodka – but MacKenzie felt himself drawn in to the songs, compelled by the smoky raspiness in the man's voice that seemed all at once to speak of things that were old, and lost, or buried deep in private places.

Raskin said happily, 'You are lucky tonight. He is singing the music of Vladimir Vysotsky, a very famous actor and folksinger. Very important to the Russian people although he was never officially recognized. But people recorded his music on tapes and passed them along hand to hand, from one to the next till there were millions of copies. Underground, I think is your word for it.'

'What is he saying?'

'Listen even without knowing the words. Do you feel it? Truth is a force which pierces your heart, Vysotsky said. Let the music in, Peter.'

The singer's hoarse baritone filled the courtyard and an awareness without words nibbled at the edge of Mac-Kenzie's mind. There was pain. And sadness. MacKenzie listened. The people had tears in their eyes, nodding slowly, feeling the emotions with a freedom that surprised him. He heard the melody repeating and realized the song was being sung over again. This time, eyes moist, Raskin leaned over and translated.

> We're on time,
> for a visit to God.
> No one is ever late.
> So why are the angels singing

with such evil voices?
Or is that a bell
that's sobbed itself out of tune?
Or is it me,
screaming to the horses to slow down?
Slower, horses,
just a little slower.
I beg you just gallop, don't fly!
But somehow the horses seem cruel.
I didn't finish living.
I pray to finish my song.
To my steeds I'll sing
and I'll finish this verse,
for a moment is all I have left.

The singer strummed the final chords and grew silent. Tears leaked from Raskin's eyes.

It affected MacKenzie deeply. The vodka, the stress, the lyrics. All of them seemed to combine and suddenly MacKenzie felt a place hidden within him, one he had refused to look into for so long, well up and threaten to consume him. He fought for control. Raskin was watching him now, sensing a struggle he had no way of understanding. He reached out a hand to help but MacKenzie swept it away. He pushed his chair from the table and walked away stiff legged. 'I've got to go. Good night, Nikolai.'

'Peter, wait. What is wrong?' Raskin called after him.

'Early morning. Plan for battle drills. I'll see you on the ship.'

'Peter, please wait.'

But MacKenzie kept on walking, till the music finally faded and he could hear it no more.

Mac slammed his door and went out to the balcony to clear his head. His hands were unsteady on the railing. His mind was reeling. The wind streamed past his face and the waves slammed unmindfully into the harbor walls below. What was this place with its vodka and poetry doing to him? Tearing him apart, it seemed. And the strain of the mission was a constant debilitant, undermining his confidence. He was sinking lower under the weight of uncontrollable emotions.

I don't have the strength.

Raskin came out of the hotel and got into his car on the promenade and drove away. Mac watched the lights dwindle. The wind cooled his hot cheeks. The waves curled into white froth as they raced in and out, beckoning. What would it take to fly off this height and sink below them forever?

The singer's lyrics were like fire in his brain.

> *. . . is it me,*
> *screaming to the horses to slow down?*
> *Slower, horses,*
> *just a little slower.*
> *I beg you just gallop, don't fly!*

How could the song so correctly identify his torment? He felt his pain beating within him. He fought it back. He couldn't allow himself to feel it in total. If he let it come crashing in all at once it would consume him. He fought it back. Control. He had to stay in control.

Sweating despite the cool sea breeze, he threw himself down on his bed and tried to block out the noise.

Only when the gulls cried out that the morning was near did sleep come for him.

EIGHT

Kara-Kum Desert, Turkmenistan

Justine woke up on the floor of a tent. A quick inspection from behind compressed lids told her so, and that a sleepy-eyed man in desert garb was sitting cross-legged a short distance away holding a rifle across his lap. Her arms and legs weren't bound and she felt instinctively that the man was not so much guarding her as watching over her. She made no move to go for the gun. She rose to a sitting position and swept her hair from her face. He shifted slightly and looked at her.

'*Salam*,' she said.

'*Salam*,' the man responded, and spoke a few sentences. It was too fast for her. But she thought she could make out the word *Karadeen*, which was reassuring.

She shook her head. '*Men dushemok.*' I don't understand.

He shrugged and got up, gesturing for her to remain there. He ducked under the tent flap.

Evidently, she was not a prisoner. She could run if she wanted to but it seemed wise to wait. She checked her body. The fall off her horse had been hard enough to knock her out, but the terrain was forgiving and apart from a few scrapes and bruises there was nothing seriously wrong. She wondered where Karansky was. The last time she saw him he was being hog-tied by the man in black. Damn. If not for those damned bolas, or whatever they called them locally, she would have gotten away. She hoped her horse wasn't hurt. The big chestnut was a valiant animal who had given her all he had.

The tent was a traditional *yurta* similar to the ones she had become familiar with during her stay in Ashkhabad,

94

but this one was no mere backyard remnant of a nomadic past. It was a real home with a lived-in feel. Gaily colored Turkmeni rugs were on the floor and the walls were hung with bright tapestries and woven bags which held clothing and household utensils. It was held up by an intricate inner wooden framework and covered with a combination of rush and felt.

She wondered why the Karadeen had set an ambush for her and the general. Treachery? Or did their leader, Kemal, just consider a trap prudent given the Karadeen's quite valid reasons to mistrust the Russians. She was pondering that when the tent opened and the man came back in. He held the flap open and gestured for her to come out. Justine smoothed out her clothing and ducked outside under his arm.

The sun was so bright she had to shield her eyes. They were no longer in the mountains. The Kopet Dagh peaks that had towered into the sky were gone, replaced by a ring of low hills around a sparse, grassy plain. The canopy of deep blue sky overhead was so vast she could almost feel the weight of its arc stretching from the sandy dunes a few hundred yards away to the horizon. Around them, scores of other *yurtas* were arranged in neat rows all the way back to the rocky hillside. Horses and camels were tethered in front. But the camp had a deserted feel.

'Where is everybody?' Justine asked. The taciturn rifleman gestured over the dunes and started walking in that direction. Justine fell in behind him.

The unmistakable clamor of a festive occasion hit her when they crested the high dune. Cheers and barks of laughter, the heavy rumble of men competing, the high-pitched cries of women spectators. She stopped for a moment to view the scene spread out beyond.

The Karadeen were gathered in a tree filled oasis eating, drinking and taking part in varying sports contests. Trays of food and drink were laid out on carpets. Families sat in small knots, eating or relaxing. The rest watched the various athletic contests.

Men stripped to the waist wrestled in the hot sun. Their bodies glistened with sweat. Others threw knives at targets. Something like a dice game was in progress. Out on the plain, groups of thundering horsemen charged back and forth over a roughly staked out course, battling over a small object Justine couldn't make out. They beat on each other freely and pushed each other off their horses. It looked like a cross between polo, keep-away and a gang fight.

She walked into the shade. They were a good-looking people, the Karadeen, swarthy and dark haired with lean bodies and the kind of carriage that comes from high self-esteem. It spoke well of the rule of Ali-Kahdri's grandson, Kemal. No beaten down group this. Their faces were relaxed and happy. Most of the men had facial hair of some kind and were dressed in loose fitting pants, white shirts and crimson robes. The women weren't wearing veils but most had on traditional headdresses adorned with coins and other trinkets. They looked at her as she passed by, engrossed in caring for the small children. She felt no menace, no sense that she was an alien to be feared. When she reached the carpets laden with food and drink an old woman smiled and offered her a cup of tea. Justine realized how thirsty she was. '*Sag bol*,' she said gratefully. The woman smiled again and pointed to the food with the universal 'help yourself' gesture. Justine took a meat pie. Then she moved over to the edge of the oasis to watch the horsemen out on the sand.

They rode with exquisite skill and even the hardest tumbles didn't faze them. They banged on each other wildly as they rode and the blows would have done credit to a prizefighter.

'A bit of madness that, eh?' said a voice behind her. It was Karansky, still dressed in his khakis, looking none the worse for wear. He had no sidearm.

'The last time I saw you,' she said, 'you were doing a pretty good imitation of a roped steer.'

'I suppose this was from your tactical vantage point facedown in the sand.'

She chuckled. 'Who could have expected those bolas, anyway?' Then, more seriously, 'It was Kemal, wasn't it, the man in black?'

'That it was,' Karansky agreed. 'They start about the age of four throwing those damn things. Do it for sport, too. There's a group of them over there, see?'

She looked to where Karansky pointed. Boys and girls were throwing bolas at stakes planted in the sand. Most of the bolas hit true, wrapping themselves around the stakes with a sharp, clacking noise.

'What's going on here exactly?' she asked.

'It's called a *toi*,' Karansky explained. 'A festival to mark a wedding or the birth of a child or some other big deal. In this case, the birth of that squealing thing in that cradle over there, apparently Kemal's newest nephew. Everybody here is a guest of the parents. They're treated to refreshments and entertained with sports contests like the ones you see going on.'

'Did you get an angle on why the ambush? We would have met them anyway in a few miles.'

Karansky shrugged. 'Kemal wasn't going to trust any damn Russian and get played for a fool like his grandfather. This way he was in control from the start. As simple as that. But he told me not to worry, we were his guests.'

'Translation, hostages.'

Karansky nodded. 'Exactly. They took my guns and my phone.'

It seemed unlikely that an old pro like Karansky wouldn't have made procuring another weapon his first priority but she let it pass. 'Where's the headman now?'

'Where else? Right in the middle of the pack.' Karansky pointed out to the battle on the plain. 'See? Over there.'

Justine picked him out. She had the same feeling as in

the mountain pass. He was a classic horseman, a powerful figure. Kemal drove his horse dizzyingly in and out of the pack and was often in front of the careening herd for long periods of time, usually carrying the 'ball.' At closer range it looked to be a stuffed animal skin of some kind.

'What are the rules here?' Justine asked.

The general ran a hand over his shaved head. 'So far I've not been able to determine any.'

Kemal was wearing the same kind of loose fitting black pants Justine had last seen him in, but the black tunic had been discarded and the wind and exertion had pulled his flowing white shirt open to his waist. She watched as the pack of horsemen careened around and someone smashed the 'ball' out of Kemal's hands. There was a mad scramble for it. It changed hands a few times as riders bashed it from each other's grip, then Kemal grabbed it again. He sprinted around the others passing close enough to the edge of the oasis to give Justine a chance to see him clearly for the first time.

Karansky had said that Ali-Kahdri was a good-looking man. Evidently, it ran in the family. Kemal was strikingly handsome, with fine features and a lean physique. Sinewy muscles lay flat on his bones. His chest and stomach looked carved out of marble. He had a dark visage as bold as some satanic knight's, but his sparkling gray eyes held warmth and laughter. Those eyes glinted as he rode, as much boy as man in his competitiveness. His skin was as smooth as polished hardwood and his high cheekbones and thick eyebrows made those gray eyes all the more penetrating. Wavy black hair fell in tangles over his ears. A thin beard outlined his jaw and curved around his upper lip to join the mustache that framed his full-lipped mouth.

Kemal's fierce eyes were fixed intently on an opening in the pack. He kicked his horse forward to outdistance the other riders. The muscles of his chest and arms were even more clearly defined by the effort. Someone rode up on him and gave him a clout across the shoulders that would have unseated a lesser horseman or a weaker man. Kemal's mouth just curved into a grin and his eyes sparkled as he absorbed the blow with only a deep hunching of his back. Guiding his horse with his knees, he backfisted the other rider in the head and the other man had to grab his horse's pumping neck with both arms to hang on. Kemal laughed and shot ahead, reveling in the game.

The pack caught up with Kemal again and he spurred his horse into a full gallop turning everyone toward the outside of the course, the lead animal of the herd. It brought them back toward Justine and she could study Kemal again. As he passed, his head turned and for a moment their eyes met. She saw something register in those wide gray eyes. It could have been simple interest in her presence. It could have been male appraisal. Justine knew she was attractive. He would not have been the first man to stare. But in that split second there was something more. In that second his gray eyes seemed to reach out and fixed her so intently that not even the speeding horse under him mattered. The totality of his concentration pulled her into his gaze. Then his attention swung back to the course, breaking the connection. Thundering past, he was gone.

Divots of earth fell back to the turf and the smell of hot animals dissipated on the wind. She felt the impact of Kemal's physical presence even after he was gone. The horsemen fought over the animal skin a while longer, then the game broke up and the riders drifted back to the oasis. Waiting families were gathered around carpets covered with food and drink. Out on the sand, Kemal spoke to one of the horsemen, who nodded, wheeled around, and rode over to Justine and Karansky.

'*Salam*,' he said dismounting. 'My lord Kemal asks for the honor of your sitting with him and his family on this happy day.'

'We're honored,' agreed Karansky, courtly as hell.

Kemal's place was at the head of the gathering. His relatives and their families sat on deep red Bukhara rugs.

The baby slept peacefully in a cradle of wood and woven rush next to his parents, undisturbed by the noise of the gathering in his honor. Mother and father's proud smiles needed no translation.

'Which is Kemal's wife?' Justine asked.

'My lord Kemal is as yet unmarried,' their guide said.

'Isn't that a bit unusual?' asked Karansky.

A voice nearby said, 'Not if you haven't found the right woman. We gave up political betrothal years ago.'

They turned. Kemal stood before them, regally clad in a black robe with a single red band down the center. He said with a wink, 'Not everyone agreed with the change. Some of the tribal elders will not forgive my British education. General. Mrs MacKenzie. Welcome to my camp.'

Karansky extended his hand, almost bowing. 'A pleasure, Lord. I look forward to sitting down with you and discussing our mutual goals at the earliest opportunity.'

Kemal's personal magnetism was as strong as the desert sun, but Justine could read distrust for the Russian general beneath the surface. 'Tomorrow morning,' Kemal said regally. 'We'll talk after the *toi*.'

He turned his gaze on Justine. His appraisal was instantaneous and intense, like a flash picture that he would fully develop later in his mind for closer study. She bridled under it, uncomfortably aware that his inspection made her conscious of being a woman. Damn hormones.

'Mrs MacKenzie, I am aware of your outstanding achievements. They are remarkable. Will you join me for some refreshments?'

It was a kind and generous offer under the circumstances. So what was bothering her? Maybe it was too nice and neat. The desert lord, the fawning Russian courtier, the acquiescent woman hostage. Some instinct told her it was time to cut herself out of the herd. Her guts were telling her that she would be well advised to give Kemal's kingly manner a jolt and at the same time to distance herself from Karansky's fawning lest Kemal think she was part of it, too.

The feeling grew stronger the more she thought about it. She had her own interests to protect. She wasn't Karansky's flunky and she wouldn't be Kemal's, sitting on her behind while the men figured out what to do with her.

Sometimes the best plays came straight from the guts, without a lot of planning. She said loudly enough to be heard several yards away, 'For the record, Prince Kemal, I was ambushed on my way to a meeting with you to discuss the cooperation of our countries and brought here against my will. Most of what I know of this wasteland was literally stuffed down my throat after you crippled my horse. For the record, you have personally attacked me and I reserve the right to respond at a later date. If I am a prisoner here, I expect you to contact my embassy at once so terms for my release can be negotiated. If I am a guest, I want a horse saddled within ten minutes because I'm leaving. I've been treated better in waterfront bars.'

She thought Karansky was going to choke. Kemal looked like he'd been shot. It was a little wordy and melodramatic, but it seemed to have the desired effect. There were angry rumbles from some of the men nearby and Justine heard the low snick of arms being cocked. She stood her ground. It was a dangerous moment. Karansky shifted his weight and his right hand fluttered near his hip. So the old bastard *was* armed after all, she thought. Behind him, the parents of the newborn looked sick with anxiety and fear.

Kemal swallowed slowly. 'I was under the impression you . . .' He stopped, all eyes on him. He stood even straighter if that was possible, and settled back into himself with a confidence and power that permitted him to do nothing more than wave a hand to defuse the situation. Justine was impressed. It was a neat trick, controlling things with only your personality. Maybe this guy was the genuine article.

Kemal said for all to hear, 'I fear I have been mis-informed. My apologies to you and your government for this misunderstanding. It is not necessary to saddle your

101

horse, Mrs MacKenzie. You may have my own if you wish.'

Justine knew she'd won. Actually, the element of shock had almost assured she would. The tough part was going to be backing down gracefully. Costing Kemal more face wasn't going to improve her position. She'd gotten his attention and put him off balance. That was enough for now. She could see the strain in the desert chief as he waited for her to say something. Even though the threat of violence was over, the parents for whose child the *toi* was thrown still looked as if the world were coming to an end. A thought occurred to her. She decided to take a stab at it.

'Under ordinary circumstances I would be inclined to leave. But we are new to each other's customs. Misunderstandings can occur. I don't want to cast a cloud over this gathering.'

She saw it in the parents' faces. Relief. She'd guessed right. Both of them looked back to Kemal with pleading eyes.

He nodded slowly. 'An incident at the *toi* would ill omen the boy for life. How could you know it?'

'I respect the accomplishments of the Karadeen,' she lied. 'I would welcome your invitation if it's still offered.'

Someone let out a long breath. Karansky's hand dropped away from his side. The parents sighed with relief and life seemed to return to the immediate area. Kemal held out his hand to her. 'I would be honored if you would sit with me and my family.'

She let him lead her back to his carpet. She was acutely aware of his masculinity. God, he was a compelling man. He wore authority as easily as a cloak. His hand was rough from riding, but well formed, with long, graceful fingers. This close she could smell his scent. It was the clean crisp odor of sand and the desert wind.

She was old enough to know that she was reacting to him on a sexual level. She worked with men all the time and most were just another species of plant as far as she

102

was concerned. But this one. She'd rather not be dealing with the feelings Kemal stirred in her. Did he feel it, too? She ignored the question. She felt unfaithful to Mac just thinking such thoughts. Besides, she was a professional. It bothered her that she could respond in such a schoolgirlish fashion. But it simmered just below the surface. She'd have to watch herself.

They reached the carpets and Kemal bade her sit. 'Here we are, Mrs MacKenzie.'

'Justine,' she said sweetly.

He looked at her curiously, caught off balance. He shrugged and sat down beside her. 'Justine,' he repeated, baffled as all men are when they learn that women were created by a fierce, vengeful and capricious God.

Justine, being a wise woman, knew this already.

NINE

The Black Sea

MacKenzie was wondering whether shooting the crew was within his authority.

The animosity had transformed itself into a war of nerves. The atmosphere became one of grudging silence, reticence in obeying orders, and there had even been one attempt at sabotage.

It wasn't sabotage exactly. It was more a practical joke, at his expense. But it made him mad enough to entertain murderous thoughts. The personal sanitation arrangements in a submarine are fairly complicated, involving a pressurized system within a pressurized system. With over a hundred men on board, sooner or later the sanitary tanks are filled to capacity and must be blown out to sea. In order to pressurize a tank, it is first sealed off. A red warning bulb is lit, alerting anyone in that delicate position not to flush or they will experience a backflow of most unpleasant proportions. When the tank is blown and the pressures corrected, a white bulb lights up.

Someone switched the bulbs.

Like the trim party, it was hardly the Caine Mutiny, but it was an annoying breach of discipline and an indication of the men's basic resentments. More importantly, if one looked at it as another step in the escalating war between captain and crew, it carried the message that he had better watch his back. MacKenzie took the incident stoically, changed, and strode back into the control room. His attitude was hardening. He could take the slights and the difficulties. He was going to get this crew into shape no matter what it took. He found he was feeling better than he had in a long time. Maybe the anger was good for him and had a kind of cleansing effect. Although he was still prone to wonder if he was to blame for the animosity, the struggle was having the opposite effect from the one the crew intended. The harder things got, the more he felt like digging in.

Raskin looked up. 'Yes, Capteen?'

'What?'

'You said something.'

'No. I was just thinking.' They were two hundred miles out of Odessa, at sea for over twenty hours. He had made his presence felt all over the sub, virtually standing behind men and urging them to give faster and better performances. He discovered that on Soviet ships junior officers did the work normally done by chief petty officers in the American navy. The junior officers were the hands-on professionals who took care of maintenance in their departments. The enlisted specialists were little more than low-level technicians.

Sloppiness, at least by his standards, was everywhere, but one department could tolerate it least. A trip to the engineering compartment had resulted in a new maintenance schedule and cleaning details for all present, along with a brief, private, no-nonsense conversation with Chief Engineer Prudenkov. All over the ship, men were set to scrubbing, cleaning, checking and rechecking their equipment. The reorder list for equipment when they returned to dock grew larger by the minute. Maybe it was just wishful thinking, but soon the *Riga* began to have a lighter, brighter feel.

'I haven't seen the ship look so well in years,' complimented Raskin. 'But we are depleting the stores at a rapid rate.'

'Call whoever is in charge of this mission and get more,' MacKenzie said flatly. 'I want this to be a ship we can depend on. No blown circuit is going to cost us an attack run, or worse, lives.'

'As you wish, Capteen.'

'Where is Security Officer Dainis?' MacKenzie asked.

'Probably in his compartment. Do you want him?'

'Tell him I'm going into the sonar room.'

Raskin made an I-can't-wait-to-see-this face and summoned the security officer over the intercom. A few moments later Dainis came into the conn. 'Yes, Capteen?'

'As you know, Mr Dainis,' MacKenzie said, 'I'll be depending on your new sonar when we go into battle so I'm going to have to become acquainted with it sooner or later. Do you agree?'

Dainis took it in stride. 'I have decided that security must take a backseat to your tactical needs in this case. My superiors have decreed the *Riga* is your ship, Capteen. Run it as you will.'

Raskin, who had been waiting for the explosion, looked shocked. It was as if the Pope had said, 'Sure. Convert.' He searched Dainis's face for signs of ulterior motives but didn't detect any. Which didn't mean, he thought, there weren't any.

MacKenzie walked into the sonar room. The same heaviness of design that characterized most things Soviet was present here – heavy consoles, bulky trim – but the layout was similar enough to American subs that MacKenzie could find his way around. There was one newer stainless-steel console that he assumed housed the special sonar.

The sonar officer was Pytor Kotnikov, a round-faced man with a hawk nose and chin-strap beard. Two other sonar technicians were present. One was fleshy faced and hairy. Tartokov, MacKenzie remembered. From the Trim Party. The other was a boyish looking young man with blond hair. They both stiffened when MacKenzie and Dainis entered.

'Mr Kotnikov,' MacKenzie acknowledged the sonar officer.

'Capteen. Mr Dainis.'

'Be at ease,' said Dainis.

'I remember Seaman Tartakov from my welcoming trim party. What is your name?' MacKenzie asked the second technician.

'Seaman Purzov, Capteen.'

'Very well. Seaman Purzov and Seaman Tartakov, we are going to engage in a little old-fashioned competition. I want to see which one of you is the faster operator. Using passive sonars you will scan the area. As soon as a contact is made, I want a solution on its course, speed and range. If we are fortunate enough to pick up a submarine, I also want its depth. The faster man will be considered our sonarman first class and be the one I want on station when we go into battle. Understood?'

The men looked even more uncomfortable. Kotnikov stepped back and didn't say anything either way.

'Begin your sweep,' MacKenzie ordered.

Both men leaned closer to their instrument consoles, studying their readings. Tartakov was openly antagonistic. MacKenzie saw that Purzov was trying to ignore the other man and work.

'Capteen,' said Kotnikov, 'we usually don't – '

'When we go into battle,' MacKenzie snapped, 'I will be depending upon our sonar to give us the advantage. Physical size means nothing underwater. A torpedo half as big as the ones the *Kentucky* carries would be enough to sink us. Plus she's smaller and more maneuverable and better able to hide in ambush. We must have the element of surprise on our side. At thirty knots a torpedo travels three thousand yards in three minutes, almost fifty feet per second. A two-second advantage gives us a hundred-foot edge – easily the difference between a hit or a miss. Now you tell me how important it is to have the best man in this chair.'

'It could be the difference between living and dying,' said Kotnikov.

'Capteen?' It was Purzov. There was something on his screen.

MacKenzie was glad he was first. 'Yes, Mr Purzov?'

But Purzov hesitated in reporting the contact he obviously had. He glanced sideways. Tartakov was still scanning.

'Capteen,' said Purzov, obviously stalling. 'There may be – '

'I have a contact,' said Tartakov, interrupting the other man. MacKenzie checked his watch. A full four seconds had elapsed since Purzov established contact. 'The course is – ' Tartakov began.

'Two seven zero,' said Purzov. 'Speed . . .' He hesitated again. MacKenzie could tell he had the complete solution. But instead of giving it he was waiting for the other man to catch up. It was maddening. From Raskin's explanations the night before it was sadly understandable. Wanting to be first was not an honorable ambition, it was a moral defect.

'Ten knots,' finished Tartakov. 'Range, one thousand yards.'

'Thank you, gentlemen. Based on this preliminary test, Seaman Purzov will be sonarman first class.'

'But why?' demanded Tartakov hotly. 'I had the solution at the same time.'

'Seaman Purzov had the solution first. He waited for you to compute it so he would not be accused of putting himself over you. I do not agree with such thinking, even though I am learning to understand it. Also, Mr Tartakov, the next time you question one of my orders for any reason, I will have you removed from this ship. Is that clear?'

Tartakov responded tightly. 'Yes, Capteen. Clear.'

I'll have to watch this one, MacKenzie thought. Tartakov and Kutsky both. He wondered if he should have them removed from the ship. But if he started that kind of cutting, when would it stop? He might lose half the crew before he was done. No, he had to play the hand he'd been dealt. It would be a mark of failure to dismiss even one of them. Somehow or other he was going to have to win them over. Even the Tartakovs and Kutskys.

Purzov looked up. 'I have no wish to be disrespectful, Capteen, but I am sure we both had the solution.'

Tartakov looked smug.

'My order stands,' MacKenzie said. 'But I plan to have Mr Kotnikov order such drills periodically. In fact, we are going to be instituting them in almost every department. Should Mr Tartakov's time improve over yours, I will consider replacing you.'

'*Da*, Capteen.'

'We're going to have a new way of doing things on the *Riga*,' MacKenzie said. 'It may take some getting used to, but damn anyone who doesn't get with the program. The best man does the job. Nothing more, nothing less. I don't care what your politics are. The best man does the job. That's the way it's going to be. Now, Mr Kotnikov, I want to see the new sonar. Mr Dainis will stay for the show.'

Kotnikov hesitated. Dainis gave him the go-ahead. 'Capteen MacKenzie can not use what he does not understand. We all want to come home, yes?'

'Yes . . . of course,' said Kotnikov in a way that gave MacKenzie the clear indication that Kotnikov was as surprised as Raskin at Dainis's cooperation.

The way most Russians could say things and yet not say them was another thing MacKenzie had begun to notice. They always wore two faces, one carefully observant of authority, the other private and warm, rarely lacking in emotion or humor. Take Raskin. He was an ebullient, emotional man, much given to honesty. But when Dainis was around he was as closed as a clam. It was more than just a normal reticence around an officer with more power or a different brief. It was fear. Speaking your mind here was dangerous. The concept of free speech suddenly took on more meaning. He saw the effects of growing up without it.

'The basis of the new sonar is an innovation on the

fiber-optic sensors. We understand you also are using these on your new submarines,' Kotnikov began. 'Is that correct?'

'As a working assumption,' MacKenzie said carefully.

'You understand the basic principle then,' Kotnikov went on. 'A beam of laser light is split into two parallel coils of optical fibers. Acoustic pressure waves, sounds, hit the sensing fibers and induce a tiny shift in the phase of the light which can be detected by measuring and comparing the wavelengths. It is converted in a signal processor at the bottom end of the system into recognizable data. When the computers build up a recognition system, well, the rest is easy.'

'How sensitive is the system?'

Caught up in what was obviously a real love for his work, Kotnikov plowed on with the specifics of increased sensitivities, new ranges and contact times. MacKenzie busily converted them into attack distances. The new sonar was at least a five-to-ten percent improvement over their best. To view the extent of the problem from another angle, it meant that the American fleet was in real danger of being heard long before they could hear the Soviets.

Quietness had always been the hallmark of American submarine technological superiority. Quieter reactors which could rely on natural flow cooling for longer periods of time and at higher speeds had produced classes of ships that were like trying to hear a flashlight in the ocean, as one sonar tech put it. Smart torpedoes and sub launched rockets had taken any real tactical advantage out of speed and even deep diving ability. The capability to lie in wait in ambush, or to sneak up on an enemy unsuspected, those were the modern combat advantages. Quietness became even more important when the submarine was arrayed against the formidable defenses of a surface group's anti-submarine helicopters and ASW missiles.

The advantage in the Soviet system lay in two areas, the computer program and the type of laser. From the way Kotnikov eyed the stainless steel cabinet, MacKenzie figured the system computers were probably housed inside. He tried to keep his eyes from it with Dainis watching him, but even peripherally he could see no seams or openings in its gleaming surface.

'I hope those specs run true,' MacKenzie said finally. 'The *Kentucky* is quieter than any ship we've ever built.'

'If you get us close enough, Capteen,' said Kotnikov, 'we will hear her.'

'That's the spirit, Mr Kotnikov,' MacKenzie said approvingly. 'See if you can spread it around. Now stand by for battle drill. Keep both Mr Purzov and Mr Tartakov on the scopes. I want a record of their times in each engagement. Later we will establish new PQS's for this and other stations.'

'PQS, Capteen?'

'Personnel Qualification Standards. Back to the conn, Mr Dainis.'

Raskin was huddled over the chart table with the navigator, Lt Alexi Chernin, a small, neat man with a habit of holding his glasses out from his face like magnifying glasses. 'I have the conn, Mr Raskin,' said MacKenzie.

'Aye, Capteen,' Raskin responded.

MacKenzie's hand flashed out and hit the battle alarm and the strident sound rang around the ship. He picked up the intercom and selected all-ship. 'This is the captain speaking. We are going into battle. As is the custom on American ships, there will be no notice, unless I choose to announce it, of when the alarm signals a real battle or just a drill. Therefore you will always act as if the alarm signals the real thing. Seconds count. Pride in your work makes a difference. Remember, you are warriors in the service of your country. All hands prepare to go hunting. Captain out.'

MacKenzie looked around the conn. 'Make your depth one zero zero meters, Mr Petrov. Steer course one eight zero.'

Petrov turned back. 'All right, Capteen.'

111

MacKenzie sighed. 'Not "all right." Acknowledge the order verbatim, followed with "Aye, sir." Crisp. Helm, mind your heading. Five degrees down bubble.'

'Five degrees down bubble . . . aye,' Petrov repeated.

MacKenzie hit the intercom. 'Engineering, this is the captain.'

'We are here, Capteen . . . er, Engine Room, aye. Yes?'

'Yes.' He took a deep breath. 'Very well. All ahead one third. Maintain natural flow in the reactor. No noise.'

'One third, Capteen, aye. No noise.'

Better. MacKenzie moved on. 'Mr Raskin, rig for ultra-quiet. If it so much as sighs shut it down.'

'Aye, Capteen.'

'We are at the depth you ordered, Capteen. One hundrd meters.'

'Very well. Helm, rudder amidships. Remember to repeat that and all other orders before executing them.'

'Rudder amidships, Capteen.'

MacKenzie nodded. It was still slow, but it was better. 'Sonar, begin your sweep.'

'Sonar, aye, Capteen.'

That was Purzov's voice. The young man had possibilities. MacKenzie settled in to wait. For the moment, the sub was running well. The officers in the control room seemed to have at least tacitly accepted his presence, and the animosity from the crew had abated somewhat. But it was one thing to sail a sub in a straight line without incident, quite another for captain and crew to function well together under the stress of combat.

Sonar called in with several contacts over the next few hours, but MacKenzie rejected them. He wanted a demonstration of what he could do, what the *Riga* could do if properly handled. Like going to meet a date's parents for the first time, first impressions were everything. He was going to get one chance to score with this crew. It had to be an impressive victory. A successful run would give the crew confidence in itself and his leadership.

'Capteen, Sonar Room.'

'Saying Conn – Sonar will be sufficient, Mr Purzov. What have you got?'

'Contact, Capteen. We're tracking another ship. It's a submarine. In the shallow zone.'

'Course, speed and range,' MacKenzie ordered.

'Course two seven zero, speed twenty knots. The contact is six thousand meters south-southeast of us. It looks like it is running a search pattern.'

'I wonder what they're after,' mused MacKenzie. 'Can you identify the contact?'

'We are working on it.'

MacKenzie threw up a mental map. It was a textbook setup for an attack run. The 'enemy' sub was moving due west, six thousand meters, or three miles, off his bow. He could take *Riga* in slowly, move into position and rake the other sub with a blast of active sonar, the peacetime equivalent of a torpedo shot. Nothing really fancy about it. Basic tactics. This was the one.

'Mr Chernin, assume our contact maintains her present speed and course and we hold to a speed of five knots. Plot a course that will bring us to a point about two thousand meters due north of the contact's track. We will then go to all stop and let him drift across our bow into firing range.'

Chernin went to work on his chart table. MacKenzie waited, gratified when Purzov's voice came over the intercom. 'Capteen, we have identified the contact as a Sierra-class attack submarine. It is the *Lenin*.'

'A big prize,' said Raskin. 'I know the ship. They finished sea trials only last year. State of the art. Her captain is Rear Admiral Boris Karolov. Strong as an ox with a personality to match. He is the Commander of Submarines. The *Lenin* is his flagship. By the way, you might want to know he was deeply opposed to this mission.'

'Thanks, Nikolai. Good work, Mr Purzov,' said MacKenzie. At her present speed, the *Lenin* would have a hard time hearing much of anything. Her sonars would be fouled by the noise from her props and bow wave. Once in position, the *Riga* would be almost impossible to detect.

'Capteen.' It was Chernin. 'Steer course one nine five. At five knots we will be in position in six minutes.'

'Thank you, Mr Chernin. Helm, right ten degrees rudder. Come to new course one nine five.'

'Ten degrees right rudder, new course one nine five,' returned the helm crisply.

'Mr Raskin, maintain ultraquiet.'

'Aye, Capteen. Good hunting.'

MacKenzie could feel it. The excitement of the hunt was overtaking them all. This was what a submarine was created for, what all the preparation and training was about. His problems with the officers and men were forgotten for the moment. Men stood straighter and peered at their instruments more intently. Everyone urged the ship on, caught up in the rising hot blood of the pursuit.

'Steady on new course one nine five,' reported the helm.

'Acknowledged,' MacKenzie responded. 'Maintain present depth.'

'Conn, Sonar. Contact maintaining course and speed. Turn count steady.'

'Conn, aye. Mr Purzov, set your active sonar for maximum power. Continuous ping.'

'Aye, Capteen. Set active sonar to maximum power.'

'Fire Control.' MacKenzie looked over to the handsome weapons officer with his shiny black hair.

'*Da*. Fire Control, aye, Capteen.'

'Mr Kortzov, match sonar bearings. I want a constant solution on the Sierra. We'll simulate shooting two torpedoes, one from tube one and another from tube two. Make a complete engagement tape. We'll all be studying it later.'

'Tapes running . . . now. We are computing a constant firing solution.'

'Capteen.' It was Chernin. 'Five minutes to mark.'

'Acknowledged. Mr Raskin, please come here.'

Raskin looked up from behind the diving officer. 'Capteen.' He strode over.

'Nikolai, what we're going to do next is an old page out of American combat tactics. It's been used before to good advantage, against the *Akula* in fact. I've spent a lot of time worrying about the *Kentucky*'s turn-and-shoot agility and this maneuver is one I want firmly ingrained in everybody's mind.'

'I understand, Peter.'

'Right after we shoot, the Sierra's going to be looking for a target to fire back on. We could go all stop and drift and let her try and pick us up, but she might do just that and then we're sitting ducks.'

'What is the alternative?' Raskin asked.

'As soon as we shoot I'm going to execute a high-speed turn and cavitate enough bubbles to fool their sonar, give them a false target to lock onto. We call it a "knuckle." '

'Two minutes to mark, Capteen.'

'Acknowledged, Mr Chernin.'

'Conn, Sonar. Contact maintaining course and speed.'

MacKenzie turned back to Raskin. 'Pay attention.' He hit the intercom. 'Maneuvering, this is the captain. Stand by to answer all ahead flank in ninety seconds.'

'You will have it, Capteen,' came Chief Engineer Prudenkov's voice staunchly. 'As much as you need.'

'Was that pride I heard?' MacKenzie said to Raskin happily.

'Don't be smug, Peter. Pride is not confined to one navy.'

MacKenzie started. For the first time since he met the man, Raskin's voice was hard. And for the first time MacKenzie saw that underneath the controlled exterior was a very proud individual, one who, even though he had been pushed aside, was mature enough to respond with support rather than bitterness.

'I apologize, Nikolai. I mean it.'

'Please, I should not have spoken here.'

MacKenzie put up a hand. 'We'll talk later. For now . . . ?'

Raskin nodded. 'The *Lenin*.'

'Okay. Helm, on my order give me hard right rudder. We'll pivot at flank speed, turn her as fast as you can.'

'*Da*, Capteen.'

'Thirty seconds to mark, Capteen,' said Chernin.

'Acknowledged. Fire Control, simulate open outer doors tubes one and two. Set torpedoes to enable in the shallow zone.'

'Outer doors simulated open. Torpedoes set for shallow zone. Constant solution plotted.'

'Three . . . two . . . one . . . Mark!' said Chernin.

'Maneuvering, Conn. All stop. Get ready to kick her in the tail, Mr Prudenkov.'

'No problem, Capteen,' scoffed Prudenkov from the engine room. 'This is Russian steel.'

'Conn, Sonar. Target in position. Two thousand two hundred meters off our bow . . . one hundred . . . two thousand . . .'

'Conn, Fire Control. Ship ready, solution ready, torpedoes ready.'

'Fire Control. This is the captain. Final bearing and . . . Shoot unit one.'

'Unit one simulated . . . away.'

'Shoot unit two.'

'Unit two simulated . . . away.'

'Mark,' said MacKenzie.

Nothing happened. No torpedo actually left the *Riga*'s tubes. The course tracks and the contact's bearings were all stored in the fire control computer for later analysis. But it felt good, MacKenzie thought to himself. It felt damn good. Now for a little icing on the cake.

'Sonar, go active. Max power. Continuous ping. Maneuvering, ten seconds to flank speed.'

* * *

In the *Lenin*'s control room, commander of submarines for the Black Sea Fleet Adm Boris Karolov grabbed his ears and cursed loudly. 'What the hell is that? Sonar?'

'We are picking up a contact, Comrade Admiral. It's coming from a submarine close off the starboard beam.'

'An American submarine?' demanded Karolov, shocked.

'Comrade Admiral ... the computers tell us it is a Russian sub. The *Riga*,' came back the astonished voice.

Karolov was a tough, veteran commander who made a religion of personal fitness and his warship and seemed to worship an almost mystical connection between the two. Nearing fifty, he still had the body of the trained Olympic decathlete he had been almost twenty-five years before. He also had a hair-trigger temper that was legendary in the fleet. Many claimed that he looked back on his family's aristocratic roots with pride rather than shame. He ran a tight ship, and could often be found in his off-hours engaged in arm wrestling contests with the crew, contests he never lost.

Karolov's eyes narrowed. 'So the *Riga*'s captain finds us even before we find him. Our meeting was destined from the start and this is proof of it.' Adding to 'destiny' was the fact that Karolov had been searching for *Riga* since leaving his home port at Nikolayev. When Naval Command ignored his objections to having an American command one of his subs – especially *this* American with his confirmed Soviet kills – he had decided to challenge the man himself. He told no one except his exec of his intentions as he took *Lenin* into the Riga's stated test waters. Who could say their meeting was not an accident? Things had fallen into place nicely. Lesser captains might have fallen to MacKenzie, Karolov would show everyone which navy produced the better man. This engagement would be MacKenzie's turn to fall.

His communications officer looked up from the coded printer. 'There is no mention of any authorized combat exercises in this area, Comrade Captain.'

'Of course not,' he snapped. 'Do you think we could have been caught so unprepared if there were?' Karolov clutched his ears as the pinging raked them screechingly again. 'Enough! Sonar, where is the *Riga* now?'

'They are all at stop. Holding position.'

'Then he will get a taste of his own medicine. Sonar, maximum power, continuous ping. Helm, pivot to course . . .'

'Three six zero,' supplied the navigator.

'. . . three six zero. Sonar on max power . . . now.'

'Contact, Capteen,' came Purzov's excited voice from the speaker. 'Full contact. They will be very hard-of-hearing for a while. Wait, they are scanning . . . turning . . . they have us, Capteen.'

It would have been impossible to avoid. Although active sonar was far more accurate than passive, the captain who used it to range a target pinpointed his own location as well. As soon as he went active on the *Riga's* active sonar, the *Lenin* would have an accurate fix. MacKenzie wasted no time. 'Maneuvering, all ahead flank cavitate. Helm, hard left rudder. Steady to course zero nine zero.'

MacKenzie and everyone else in the conn had to hold on to something as the *Riga* spun through her turn. Her propellors churned up a huge wake of bubbles to reflect the *Lenin*'s sonar, creating a false target.

'Capteen, they are thinking the bubbles are us,' came Purzov's excited voice again. 'They are sweeping them with active sonar. Maximum power.'

'All they'll get is a lot of bubbles with headaches,' retorted MacKenzie. 'All stop,' he ordered. It was time to hide from the big boy's wrath.

He saw a smile of approval on Raskin's face. He looked around. All around the conn the men were wearing similar looks, the kind that came from completing a successful engagement.

'Very nice work, Peter,' Raskin said without any begrudging. 'Very nice.'

Sonar Officer Kotnikov had gone into the conn on MacKenzie's order, leaving Purzov studying his screen admiringly. 'They are looking for us but can not find us. You've got to admit that was a good run,' he said to Tartakov.

'He fools a ship that is half asleep and managed to escape by throwing up a few bubbles that any veteran captain wouldn't bother with in combat. He is no genius.'

'Maybe not. But he is not so bad either.'

'You like being the first sonarman so much, is that it?' Tartakov sneered.

'You know me better.'

'I know those stains on your nose look brown to me.'

Purzov turned, his face hot. 'That's not it at all. I just say credit where credit is due. Maybe he's better than we first thought.'

'And I say you think you're better than me. *Sukhovaty*.'

The word meant 'dryish,' as in cold, or lacking human warmth. It connoted the kind of person that would put his work, or himself, over others. As an insult, it struck to the core of Russian sensibilities.

'You have no right to say that,' said Purzov, hurt. 'I am just trying to serve the ship. What would you have me do?'

'Be one of us,' said Tartakov slyly.

'Who's us? You and Kutsky? Against the American? You are against everything. Always complaining about things. Why are you so angry? First the trim weights and . . . why do you look like that?'

'Because you have not checked your screen for the last twenty seconds. Maybe you are not so much smarter than me after all, eh?'

Galvanized by the smirk on Tartakov's face, Purzov twisted back to his screen in alarm. It took no longer than a few seconds to see the source of the other man's satisfaction. The *Lenin* had changed course and was coming on fast in a stop-and-start search pattern, heading right for the silent *Riga* which it could not possibly hear.

He hit the collision alarm. 'Conn. Sonar . . . emergency!'

On board the *Lenin*, Karolov heard the *Riga*'s powerful sonar ping and knew at once they were close, too close. Sonar's anxious voice echoed the thought. 'Comrade Captain, the *Riga* is two hundred meters off our bow signaling with active sonar. We are on a collision heading.'

Karolov almost gave the order to turn. It was pure luck he had stumbled on the *Riga* because his own sonars had not been any help. The *Riga* was equipped with the advanced laser sensors – another abomination. His own ship had not yet been updated. The American captain obviously heard them coming and let out the sonar burst to inform him they were there. At this point it would be an easy matter to turn the *Lenin* aside. But Karolov was still smarting from being caught off guard by an American – he had read the man's file – especially an American who had defeated Russian captains before.

'All ahead, two thirds,' he ordered.

He didn't know the game was called chicken, but he was very good at it nonetheless.

'He's not turning, Capteen,' Purzov's anxious voice came over the speaker.

Raskin snorted. 'He's letting you know he's not going to be pushed around twice.'

The men were watching him wondering what he would do next. MacKenzie decided to use the situation to make another statement. By Soviet logic he had won the engagement and a right thinking man would now let the other captain save face by turning away himself. Zero sum. Everybody walks away. Well, although there were certainly times when that might be best, he needed this crew to have more pride than that. He needed winners. His gut feeling was that it was going to take innovation and audacity to defeat the *Kentucky*. These were men who'd had those qualities trained out of them since birth.

'Hold our position,' he ordered. 'Sonar, range to contact.'

'Two hundred meters, Capteen. They are making ten knots.'

'What do you have in mind, Peter?' Raskin asked.

'You said this captain's a stiff-necked bastard. Let's show him he's not the only one.'

Raskin frowned. 'Peter, Karolov has a lot of friends in high places. Technically, the *Riga* is under his command. Why push him? He could use this to go after you personally.'

MacKenzie's voice was as hard as stone, his tone deadly serious. 'Nobody beats us. Not at anything. I want that clear at the outset. Listen to me, Nikolai, listen, all of you. If there's a single man on this ship who thinks otherwise let him get off now.'

Raskin looked at him narrowly. 'So you are a hard man, too, eh?'

'Not hard, Nikolai. Navy. It's time you all found out what that means. Michman, flood our forward and aft tanks. Be prepared for emergency dive on my order. Diving Officer Petrov, twenty degree down bubble. Got that? We're going to take her deep fast.'

'Aye, Capteen. Emergency dive, twenty degree down . . . bubble.'

'Maneuvering, be prepared to answer all bells. All ahead flank on my order.'

'Maneuvering ready, Capteen.'

'Listen, everyone.' MacKenzie turned to the men in the conn. 'The captain of the *Lenin* expects us to turn aside. He's saying he's the big boy on the block and we'd better get out of his way. Well, I for one have too much pride in this crew and this ship to be pushed around. And I expect all of you to feel the same way.' He fixed each man with his eyes. 'But that's not something I can order. It's got to be your choice. Pride has got to be your choice. Each and every man, freely given. So if so much as one man wants to turn aside, I swear I'll do it.' He stopped and let that sink in. 'We've got to be in this together. You may think you know about collectives. Well, this is the American collective. We're a team. This ship is our ship. We don't run from man or beast. Now you tell me, who wants to turn aside?'

'Capteen, Sonar. Thirty seconds to collision.'

MacKenzie waited. He saw their fear, their confusion. He was a madman, they were thinking, who called to their courage and told them to stand up as individuals and become a team. Who was this crazy captain who said one dissenting voice would be enough to fold on? But MacKenzie saw the beginning of understanding, too. No one had ever asked much of them before. Choice was not a natural part of their belief system. There was a correct ideology and you adhered to it. Voluntary submission to a higher ideal – MacKenzie watched their faces and saw them struggling with that one.

He was experiencing emotions he had thought all but lost to him. Here he was on a Russian ship in the middle of the Black Sea playing chicken with a Soviet admiral. Yet something in the absurdity of that position seemed to anchor him more strongly to reality, like seeing yourself from the outside; disassociating, only to return. He felt real power rise inside him coming from an almost Zen totality of being all here, truly here, now. And he felt something else arise in him that he hadn't felt for too damn long. Facing death, the intense desire to triumph, to win . . . to live.

No one said 'turn aside'.

'Very well,' MacKenzie said. 'Maneuvering, all ahead flank.'

'Admiral,' came sonar's panicked voice. 'They are not turning. They are coming straight at us. Flank speed.'

'What?'

'Collision in fifteen seconds ... fourteen ... thirteen
... twelve.'

'Hold your course,' Karolov ordered. Sweat broke out
on his brow and body and slid down his sides. He had
guessed wrong. The American was not a fully known
factor. His dossier was, of necessity, incomplete. Who could
know what he was thinking?

'... ten ... nine ... eight ... collision course.'

Karolov broke first. 'Emergency! Hard left rudder! All
stop on port engine, Helm.'

The *Lenin* broke to the left. Karolov held his breath.

'Right full rudder,' ordered MacKenzie at the last second.

'No, Capteen, that's the way they are turning!' yelled
Raskin. 'We are too close.'

The momentary mistake paralyzed him. MacKenzie felt
sweat break out on his body. The compartment got smaller.
Memories flooded back. Not an attack now, he almost
yelled. Not now! He couldn't afford to think of anything
but the submarine coming at him, but it was hard to breathe
and his chest was tight.

*The hospital room. The pain. Every nerve was on fire. Later
they told him the people were all right. He wanted to see them
but he couldn't fight the drugs ...*

'Capteen!' yelled Raskin.

MacKenzie stared at him. *The pain. There was more pain
in him than he ever imagined there could be. He was lost down
a long black tunnel and no one could find him. He wanted to
shout but he was too far away.*

His command authority suddenly deserted him. The
pressure was too much. He tried to pull himself back. He
couldn't handle it. Which way to go, up or down, right or
left? One moment he was all right and the next he felt all
the horrors that pursued him. He had left too little time to
avoid the *Lenin*. He'd made a killing mistake.

'Peter!' shouted Raskin. 'Your orders!'

'Emergency deep,' MacKenzie gasped, grabbing a railing to hold on to.

The michman flooded the tanks and the *Riga* plummeted like a stone. A Sierra was almost one hundred and ten meters long and the *Riga* was only six meters shorter. In such close quarters they could easily ram each other. There was the shriek of tortured metal.

'Capteen, we are hit,' yelled Kortzov. 'The sail.'

MacKenzie had to tear himself out of his paralysis. Icy water was spraying into the control room. The electrics were in danger of shorting. Raskin leapt to the overhead under the sail and was shutting pipes by hand. Still MacKenzie couldn't move. Gratefully, he watched the flow of water diminish and stop.

'Depth five hundred feet,' reported Petrov, relieved.

'Zero bubble, Mr Petrov,' he managed. '. . . Nikolai?'

Raskin pushed wet hair off his face. 'Just a few fittings. They're secure now.'

'Conn. Sonar. Contact is moving off.'

MacKenzie heard grateful sighs. No one realized how far gone he was. Raskin's attention was on the sail area. Fire Control Officer Kortzov mopped his brow and clapped the little Chernin on the back so hard he almost dislodged the navigator's glasses, remembering only that *Lenin* had turned aside first. Each man relived what they had just been through. In spite of the near collision, there was a good feeling in the air. They savored the victory.

MacKenzie hid his bitter self-recriminations. *They think we won. They don't know how close we came*. In spite of how he felt he had to address the men. He opened the all-ship channel. 'This is the captain speaking. If the engagement tapes bear me out, the *Riga* has just had her first successful combat run. You have my personal "well done." Captain out.'

As if in response, the hot printer chattered across the compartment. The radioman took the coded copy and ran it through the decoder. Raskin read it. His face grew worried.

'What is it, Nikolai?' asked MacKenzie.

'Peter, I told you that Admiral Karolov was not a man to trifle with. He is bringing you and the crew of this ship up on charges with Fleet Command. Reckless endangerment. We are ordered to return to port at once. This is very serious, Peter. We could end up losing our ranks.'

Fear brought a chill to the conn's atmosphere like a cold north wind. MacKenzie felt the sudden change. The men's eyes were on him again, but this time they weren't friendly. He had asked them to risk, and they had, and now instead of reward they were going to suffer for it. The elation of victory was replaced so quickly by the dread fear of consequences that MacKenzie wondered if they would remember it at all.

'I'm responsible for the actions of this sub,' he said firmly. 'If this Admiral Karolov wants somebody's head, let him come after mine. But mine alone. I want everybody to understand that.'

'We appreciate the brave speech, Peter,' said Raskin. 'But there is more to this than you understand. It could be a very bad business for us. You don't understand how things work here.'

MacKenzie understood this much. Here individual rights meant as little as, well, brave speeches. He cursed Karolov bitterly. All the good work undone.

'Lay in a course for home, Mr Chernin,' he said, not letting anyone see his disappointment. 'Nikolai, you have the conn.'

'Aye, Capteen.'

MacKenzie went to his cabin feeling deathly tired. He had failed under pressure. Maybe he was the only one who knew it, but he had almost taken two ships and several hundred men to the bottom. He felt the icy hand of fear squeeze his chest till it hurt. How could he go on? Everything had come to bear in that instant. His personal life was a shambles, and now his fear had been borne out that he couldn't count on his professional skills either. He agonized over his decision to go after Karolov. He could find no peace.

He ran his mistakes over and over again in his mind like a film loop with no beginning or end, just the constant torment of repetition. If his instincts had deserted him what could he trust?

In the end he was left unsure, weakened and vulnerable. And very much alone.

TEN

Kara-Kum Desert

The Karadeen's athletic contests went on well into the night. Everyone was caught up in the spirit of the *toi*. The proud parents beamed. The guests ate and drank. The sportsmen burnt their bodies in the hot sun and then basked in the cool evening breezes.

Justine was relaxed but watchful. Kemal was absorbed in the contests and seemed to have forgotten her for the moment. Karansky was resolutely betting on every horse race with the Karadeen equivalent of local bookies.

Kemal was the key to her success here, possibly her survival as well. Understanding what made him tick and finding ways to manipulate him could mean the difference between life and death. This wasn't just some desert bar mitzvah she was attending. She was being held hostage to guarantee payment after they located deadly nuclear weapons. If the Russians didn't release Ali-Kahdri, Kemal made it clear that she wouldn't make it out of the desert alive. Analyzing the opposition was a priority. What did Kemal think? How would he react?

Kemal was an unusual combination, a Moslem tribal chieftain with a modern British education. Part old, part new. She was an odd combination, too. A Western woman of Spanish ancestry, now an American intelligence official. Where was their common ground? Probably in the universals. He was a man, driven by many of the same things that drove all men, all people.

From the looks of things around the *toi*, male and female labor among the Karadeen was divided along fairly traditional roles. The horsemen, knife throwers and wrestlers were all men. The cooks, child-watchers and cleanup brigade were all women. The elders on the dais were somewhat uncomfortable with her, she could feel it. Denying Kemal any respect surely added to that. On the other hand, Karadeen women didn't seem unhappy or particularly subservient even if they weren't on the cutting edge of tribal decision making. They seemed happy. But it was clear that the men in this culture were the authority figures, carrying an implicit assumption of superiority.

Well, for a variety of reasons, the most important of which was the desire to be taken seriously – she wanted an opportunity to challenge that assumption.

'Come, you'll want to see this,' Kemal said.

She followed him over to a clearing in the oasis where men and women were arranging a big circle of carpets on the ground. Others began to drift over. There was an air of expectancy. People encircled the area.

'What's going on?' she asked at his side.

'The last competition of the *toi*.' He was a little startled at how easily she stood close to him. Given his age, which she put roughly at thirty-five, it had been a long time since he went to school in the West. He was having trouble remembering how to deal with free women. 'The strongest men in the tribe will fight,' he said. 'The winner has his pick of our best breeding stock. We consider it a great honor, especially if the winner is from the child's family.'

As he spoke, two large men both stripped to the waist entered the circle. They faced each other, standing straight and still. At Kemal's nod they crouched low and began circling, arms extended. The crowd was five and six deep now, jostling for a better view. Shouts of encouragement filled the night air. Bets were placed.

'What are the rules?' Justine asked. The space around Kemal was clear. Standing with him she had a perfect view.

'Only one. The man who leaves the carpets loses.'

The men were careful at first. A few feints and starts, then one got hold of the other's arm and pulled him in, gripping his shoulder in a way that gave him leverage. The other man held his position for a moment, but the first man had too good a hold. He levered the other's arm up behind his back and brought him literally up on his tiptoes. A quick shove sent the man out of the circle.

The crowd shouted approval. Money changed hands. New bets were placed.

'What do you think?' asked Kemal.

'Oh, he's . . . very good,' she tried.

'Damned with faint praise,' said Kemal. 'Just watch.'

A new man entered the circle and bent into a crouch, circling the winner. They locked arms, but this new man was faster than his predecessor. He spun inside and used his hip and flipped the former winner out of the circle onto the sand. It was a good move, well executed. The crowd loved it. Several pulled the dazed man to his feet and brushed the sand off his back. He smiled ruefully and gave a quick wave of acknowledgment to the winner.

The new man in the circle waited for another challenger. One came onto the carpets almost at once. They circled. The winner tried the same hold but the challenger was too fast. He slid under the winner's arms and punched him solidly in the midsection. The breath burst out of him like a popped paper bag. The man had such a hard time catching his breath the challenger was able to lead him off the carpets like a bridled horse. There was good-natured laughter and catcalls. More money changed hands. The new winner stood proudly in the circle.

'What isn't allowed?' Justine asked.

'Can't rip off body parts,' said Kemal casually. 'Other than that . . .' He shrugged.

Another challenger came onto the carpets. He was a good-looking young man, well built, with dark hair and a thick mustache. There were shouts of encouragement. Justine looked to Kemal.

'The child's father,' he explained. 'My brother, Radi. He's showing everybody how brave he is, coming into the circle so early. It is for his boy.' He frowned. 'He will have to hold it a long time. He will be very tired.'

'Can he do it?' Justine wondered.

Kemal looked at her. 'Who can say what is written?'

Justine felt his impact again. It was a visceral thing. A jolt on the hormonal level, like the fear that came from facing a wild animal, or the involuntary smile a baby brought to your face. Did he know he was doing it? Was he doing it deliberately? She pulled her gaze back to the circle.

The winner tried the same move, blocking and punching to the body, but Radi took the punch and delivered his own blow to the winner's jaw. It snapped his head back. Radi stepped in and swept his legs out from under him. The man went down on his back and Radi rolled him onto the sand.

More cheers. More laughter. More money. Radi defeated three more comers. He was strong and fast in an un-schooled way, with a really wicked right hand.

Radi looked around for another challenger. He was breathing through his mouth, his chest heaving. For a moment, Justine thought no one would challenge him. Maybe a nice kind of 'fix' was in, a general agreement to let the child's father win. She should have known better. In this environment strength would always be a prime virtue. The next challenger came into the circle, and she understood what had concerned Kemal. This guy was big and well muscled and moved with more assurance than any of the others. A flicker of concern crossed Radi's face.

'Ezek,' said Kemal under his breath. 'He is the strongest. If Radi can hold him, others may not try.'

'Will you fight Ezek if he doesn't win?' she asked.

'It is not permitted,' he said, and she saw how frustrated he was.

Radi and Ezek faced each other warily. One punch wasn't going to stop either of these men. She decided Radi had to stay out of Ezek's powerful grip. Ezek would have to guard against exposing his head and body to Radi's powerful punches. Ezek made the first move, diving low to grab Radi's legs. Radi stood his ground and slammed both of his cupped hands down on the back of Ezek's neck. Ezek went to his knees, but did not let go. His big arms stayed wrapped around Radi's thighs. He drove his feet into the sand moving Radi back like a tackle dummy. Radi dug in. Unable to free himself, he pounded on Ezek's back. The big man absorbed the punishment like a sponge.

It was soon apparent that Radi would not hold Ezek. They came closer and closer to the edge of the carpets. The crowd was going wild. They shouted for Radi to hold. Radi tried a last desperate move, driving his knee up under Ezek's chest. The blow would have caved in the ribs of a lesser man, but Ezek took it, getting an arm under Radi's leg and trapping Radi's leg against his chest. Off balance, Radi fell back. Ezek gave a mighty push and shoved him off the carpets.

There was a sigh from the crowd amidst the cheers. Radi was the favorite on the day of his son's *toi*. Panting, Radi picked himself up from the sand and gave a short wave to Ezek, who accepted it graciously. You could see the disappointment on Radi's face. He went back to his family, and his wife dutifully swept the sand off him, cooing soft words of support. He took defeat well, managing a small rueful smile.

Ezek bounded around the carpets looking pleased with himself. His sweaty muscles glistened in the firelight. He was an imposing figure, big as a house and a good fighter. There seemed to be no one else to fight him.

Kemal was stoic, but she could feel his frustration and disappointment. He wanted to enter the circle himself for his nephew. Universals. What we all want for our children. It gave her an idea, but before she had time to put it into effect, a bemused look came over Kemal's face.

'It seems there's one more challenger,' he said to her. 'This is an interesting night in many ways.'

Justine turned and did a double take. Karansky had

131

taken off his shirt and entered the circle with Ezek.

It was going to be a contest. Karansky was almost as big as Ezek. He was better trained of course, but she judged him not much faster. And Ezek was no fat waiter in a *shashlik* bar. He was tough as nails from a lifetime in the desert. Interestingly, it changed a lot of the dynamics of the contest. You could tell Ezek was happy the Russian was in the circle. Radi was a fellow tribesman. Beating him cost Radi's son the prize so his victory was tinged with some regret. But he could pound on the Russian till doomsday and feel just fine about it. The crowd knew it, too. Defeating what amounted to a hereditary enemy would be just plain fun. They roared for Ezek. No split loyalty here. They wanted Karansky to go down and stay down.

The two men came together in a classic arm over arm standing wrestler's hold. They felt each other out. Karansky looked confident and strong, as if he thought this desert yokel would be no match for a trained commando. Muscles bulged as they tested their strength against each other. It was an odd sight, the hirsute Ezek and the hairless Karansky jostling together in the firelight. They seemed pretty equally matched. For a moment, neither had the advantage. Then a slight frown of puzzlement crossed Karansky's face. He was forced back a pace and the frown increased. He strained harder. Karansky moved back another pace. They were still locked together, vying for definitive leverage, but now there was sweat on Karansky's body. Justine thought she understood what was happening.

Karansky had entered the circle after seeing Ezek fight Radi. He'd judged Ezek's performance and abilities by that. She had wondered if a fix was possible, and clearly it wasn't, but what if Ezek had been easier on Radi than he could have been? It would have embarrassed Radi to throw him out of the circle too easily. The long, tough fight made Kemal's brother look good on the day of his son's *toi*. She began to suspect that Ezek had reserves of strength he hadn't even begun to use.

She was right. Karansky, realizing he had under-estimated the other man, tried to get it over fast. With a huge upward thrust of his arms he broke Ezek's hold and punched him in the jaw. It sounded like he hit a rock and she saw him pull his hand back in pain. Ezek shook it off. Karansky tried a chop to the neck but Ezek blocked it, dodging the vicious front kick that Karansky tried to hide. The crowd shouted and hooted, cheering Ezek on. So far, Karansky had been unable to do any damage.

With the basics not working, Karansky tried an ill-advised fancy move. It was his first and last mistake. He lunged to the side and Ezek moved to intercept him, but Karansky jumped up and launched a flying side kick at Ezek's chest. For a moment it looked like it had caught the big man off guard and the force of Karansky's weight would drive Ezek out of the circle. But Ezek was far quicker than he had shown in his fight with Radi. He ducked under Karansky's leap and Karansky landed in Ezek's arms like a baby into his mother's embrace. Ezek spun Karansky around with the motion a jai alai player uses to catch and throw a ball, released him, and the Russian flew out of the circle landing unceremoniously on his rump in the sand.

The applause and shouting were tumultuous. Ezek clasped his hands over his head in the universal victory sign. Coins and other trinkets landed at his feet. He looked around perfunctorily for other challengers. No one stepped forward. Justine took a deep breath.

'May I?' she inquired of Kemal.

Kemal didn't realize at first she was talking about entering the circle. 'May I? Oh, you mean . . . ?' He shook his head firmly. 'You are a woman,' he said flatly.

'I'm lots of things. Right now that's the least of them.'

'Not to my men.'

'I outrank General Karansky. If he can play, why can't I?'

'Play? Is that what you think this is?' Kemal was growing exasperated. 'Justine . . . I can not explain it to you any better. Please, accept my word.'

Justine shucked off her boots and socks. Her jeans were a little tight, but if she took them off here it would cause a riot. She rolled up her sleeves and tied her shirttails across her stomach, leaving her midriff bare and giving her more freedom to move.

'What are you doing?' Kemal demanded.

'Getting ready.'

'But I told you, you could not.'

Justine leaned close enough so that no one else could hear. 'You look pretty good, Kemal. But I'm better. So don't try me. If you lose you'll only be embarrassed in front of your tribe. Can you afford that?'

She thought he would explode, but he surprised her. 'With an attitude like that I have half a mind to let you,' he whispered back, grinning.

She winked. 'Live dangerously.' And she stepped into the circle.

The crowd noise changed at once. It wasn't hostile exactly, more curious and doubtful. There was an undercurrent of anger, sure, probably from the older men. But she was a guest and a Westerner and not of their rules. The general reaction seemed to be if she wanted to get thrown into the sand by Ezek, let her be. Besides, in her strange country, many had heard, the women and the men did the same things anyway. Who could understand such reasoning? Ezek himself looked at her from at least eight inches higher and shook his head, a little bit confounded. He glanced over to Kemal. Justine waited. Kemal's grin had receded, but not vanished. He nodded.

Justine moved. Figuring Ezek would be slow to start she grabbed the advantage. She knew now how fast he was and how strong. Fall into those big meaty arms and she was done for. She had one chance against him. She had to break him down muscle by muscle. He thought she was playing right into his hands. He wanted her to come to him, standing there, hands extended, waiting. Sorry, it was time to execute her own program. Just outside his grasp she leapt up and executed a perfect spinning kick, her right foot lashing out with incredible centrifugal force into Ezek's outstretched hand. Something cracked. He yanked it back in pain and surprise.

First blood. The crowd knew it and murmured with interest. So be it. But Justine was already moving in again. Again her foot lashed out, this time into Ezek's other hand. A cry of pain came from his lips. Rubbing his hands together he advanced on her. She backed up warily like a cornered cat. Every time he reached out she went for his hands. Once she faked the hands and went for his side, only to go back to the hands as soon as he reached for her again. Again and again she hit those big hands, using his size against him. Every time he lunged for her she either ducked or kicked, till he was completely unsure of what she was going to do.

There was pain in his eyes and his hands were clutched like talons. But he was fast and the circle was small. When she had to stand and fight it was always a quick in and out, never directly challenging his size or his strength. She threw a fake front kick and he made the grab for the leg he thought was coming. She wrenched it out of line and brought it smartly up and around his hands into a round-house kick to the head. The ball of her foot caught him squarely on his cheek. His hands came up to his face automatically. It was a mistake. She put all of her weight into a kick to the solar plexus and he doubled over and went down.

She moved in, but Ezek was trickier than she imagined. His hand shot out and grabbed her leg, yanking her down to the carpet. She hit the ground with a thud and got the wind knocked out of her. A fist the size of a ham hock blasted into the side of her head and a wave of blackness passed over her eyes. She could hear the crowd shouting wildly but it was too far away to matter. She tried to clear her head. The fog was too thick. Ezek got his hands around her wrists and rose to his feet, bringing her up with him, dangling like a hooked fish.

Justine wasn't sure she could get out of the hold but she put all of her strength into it – and broke free of his hands. It was the payoff for all the damage she had done with the kicks. In the early stages of the fight she never could have broken his grip. Ezek looked surprised, almost boyishly curious that his hands could not hold her. But it was too late to counter the damage. Only inches from his body, she was already moving, throwing her last close quarter move.

A full crescent kick is particularly difficult to throw because it uses the whole leg, launching it in an arc directly from the hip like a propellor blade, only inches from your own face. But precisely because the entire leg is involved, it has unparalleled striking force. Justine's foot came up and around and blasted into Ezek's head with all the power she could muster. It turned his lights out. His eyes glazed and he stumbled backward, landing in a heap in the sand outside the circle of carpets.

Back in focus she could hear the noise now. The Karadeen were cheering. Universals. A great contest was a great contest. She had given them a show to remember. There were looks of appreciation on the men's faces, looks of wonder – and of pride, maybe? – on the women's. Men helped Ezek up. He gave her the same small wave Radi had given him. She returned it. As for Radi, there was no dishonor in losing, no rancor in another's victory. It told her much about the Karadeen. These were people with character.

Kemal walked over to her. 'Are you all right?'

'A little dizzy. He's got a fist like a tree stump.'

'You were quite remarkable,' he said. 'I'm glad I didn't try to stop you.'

'Are you? Why?'

He gave her her boots and socks and squatted on his haunches beside her when she sat to put them on. 'Ezek has only been defeated once in my memory. You moved like a tiger . . . no, like a dancer with the power of a tiger. Where did you learn that?'

'I had an . . . atypical childhood.'

'Will you tell me about it later?'

His request was so sincere that she nodded. 'If you like.'

'I would. But please – ' he stood up. 'You must come with me now.'

She had no time to ask where they were going as he propelled her along in the direction she suddenly realized all the other Karadeen were going. They walked out of the oasis and onto the open sand. The night sky was filled with stars and the air was crisp and cool. Faces around her were kind and happy as they made a path for her between them. She caught a quick glance of Karansky who looked pleased in a professional way. Then he was lost in the crowd.

A string of horses were tethered together on the sand. She had never seen their like. Beautiful Arabians with trim neat ears, widely spaced eyes and tapering muzzles. Aristocratic horses. Their coats all shone in the moonlight, but one outshone them all. A golden colored mare with a white mane flowing behind a refined head and neck, and a short, level back. The eyes looked as intelligent as a human's, but kinder.

She pointed to the gold. 'Kemal, what is that one?'

He smiled. 'You have a good eye. She is an Akhal-Teké. The finest saddle horse God ever created. You may have one other as well.'

'What do you mean, have?'

'You won them by defeating Ezek. They are yours. Pick.'

Justine walked over to the golden mare. The animal snorted softly and bent its head to nuzzle her. For a moment she was sorely tempted to keep it, it was such a beautiful creature. But she hadn't gone to all this effort to gain a horse, even such a remarkable one as this. It was a tribe she was after. She raised her voice to make herself heard above the murmuring crowd. 'Prince Kemal, I was honored by your invitation to join the *toi*. The golden mare will go

137

to Radi's son as my gift and good omen, and this splendid Black will go to Ezek who was a worthy opponent.'

It was, as they say, the right move.

The Karadeen swept her up exuberantly and carried her off.

It wasn't until some hours later that she finally found herself alone. Radi had insisted on toasting her, then big Ezek insisted, then all the people who liked the fight insisted, then all the people whose first names began with the letter *A* insisted, and so on. It was a damn good thing there was no alcohol, or she would be lying on the floor, well, the sand, by now. As it was she got a quick lesson in desert personal sanitation.

Most of the Karadeen had retired to their tents. She walked out onto the sand to the tethered horses., The golden mare was still there. The splendid animal shivered, sniffing some faraway scent carried on the wind, eyes narrowing with pleasure and the desire to run. She had given her own present away. It wasn't the first time. She could hardly remember a time when she hadn't put something or someone over her own needs. Some part of her felt like that was a shame.

'Are you very sad?' said his voice.

'A part of me would love to keep that horse,' she answered honestly, another part of her automatically registering that she hadn't actually heard him come up behind her.

'But with it you bought my tribe's favor and loyalty,' Kemal observed correctly. 'Radi's son has a golden horse for his *toi*. Ezek sings your praises and he is a man of some importance. And I am personally indebted to you for the gifts to my family. It was for all of those things that you fought, wasn't it?'

'In part.'

'What was the other part?'

'I wanted to impress you.'

138

He shook his head. 'You are either the most devious or the most honest woman I have ever met.'

'In a woman it's the same thing.'

He laughed. 'There is great wisdom in that.' His face grew serious. 'Why would you want to impress me?'

'So you'd be forced to come to the conclusion I was your equal. A force to be reckoned with. Then I would be close to the center of power, both to be in a better position to see the mission completed, and to protect myself, if it should come to that.'

'Can you?' he asked. 'Protect yourself I mean.'

'You saw.'

There was the slightest note of deprecation in his voice. 'That was Ezek.'

She sighed. There was a soft rustle and then something hard pressed into the hollow under Kemal's chin. The sharp metallic snick of a handgun's hammer being cocked sounded loud in the stillness of the night.

'Where did you get that?' he asked, surprised. 'You were searched and disarmed when you were brought in.'

The gun disappeared back under her jacket. 'I took it from Karansky who hid it in his pile of clothing when he was fighting. Everybody was watching him, not me. Where he got it I can only speculate.'

Kemal picked up a handful of sand and let it stream through his fingers. 'Tell me about your childhood. Is this part of it, always being ready, always anticipating violence?'

It was so dark that she could barely see him sitting nearby in the sand. His rich and resonant voice seemed to hang in the air, almost disembodied. Maybe that helped her to talk about it. In the daylight she would have had more protection. Her defenses would have been strong and her self sealed up. Here in the desert the anonymity of being with a man who was almost a total stranger, and perhaps the melancholy feeling violence always carried in its aftermath, seemed to free her in a way that only Mac had done before.

'I was born into a very old and important family,' she said. 'Very aristocratic. Very wealthy. Deeply involved in the fabric of the nation. We traced our lineage all the way back to Spain. My grandfather was once elected president of Nicaragua. All my relatives were ambassadors, statesmen, publishers, artists and the like. My father . . .' She heard the subtle betraying catch in her voice, 'My father was a remarkable man. In some ways more remarkable than any of them. He was a gifted musician, a famous concert artist. He played all over the world. I had two brothers, Sebastion and Miguel. My father taught us all to play and later we accompanied him when he toured, giving concerts ourselves. People called us prodigies. It was easy. I had the music in my head. It helped to sustain me.

'What no one knew was that my father was also a leader of the revolution against the dictator Somoza. No one but the leaders ever knew. His tours were a way to open the borders so they could smuggle arms into the country. We would stop at a border crossing and my brothers and I would entertain the National Guardsmen while my father went inside the guard post with our papers. He was a national figure. No one ever suspected he was anything else. We carried our instruments in the back of an old pickup driven by a family retainer named Lucho.'

Her voice took on a ghostly quality in the darkness. 'I played the piano. I was pretty. The guardsmen always stopped to watch me. My brothers had weapons hidden in their instruments. Sebastion's machete. Miguel's terrible needle. My father could hear us, he *had* to hear us because at a certain point in the piece my brothers would attack the guards outside and he would kill the guards inside. I always heard his gunshots. I waited for them. When I heard him shoot I knew he was alive, and the guardsmen were dead. Playing for the dead, that's what I was doing. Playing men into their graves. I tried to let the music drown out their cries. It never did. I couldn't stop playing till he came out and lifted my hands off the keys.

'Later on we had to flee and join the rest of the rebels in the mountains. Then there were other things. We children had to stand on both sides of the road where guardsmen were going to be ambushed and scream at the tops of our lungs to panic them. It was an unholy sound, guaranteed to frighten the bravest of men. They called us *el coro de los ángeles*, the Angels' Choir. The line of guardsmen would break and run and they would be slaughtered.'

'All this,' Kemal said wonderingly, 'and still a child? Your father was a committed man. I respect him. And you.'

His reaction surprised her. 'You don't think he was wrong? My husband did. Does.'

Kemal let more sand pour through his fingers. 'Your husband is an American?'

'Yes.'

'That's a big part of it. It will always be hard for Americans to understand necessity. They have too much. The British are basically the same. Narrower, perhaps, but all they really have is a drab little island.'

'You really think that? You're unusual.'

'Can you imagine Gandhi's peaceful revolution succeeding if anyone but the British had been in charge? He would have been dead by poison or gun shot in a week if it had been the Russians or the South Africans or the likes of your Somoza. Take the Persian Gulf war. Is there any other country but America that would use half a million troops and enough air power to bomb the region into the Stone Age to take the biggest oil reserves in the world and then choose to give it all back?'

She had to laugh. 'Not when you put it that way, no.'

'Didn't you feel it when you got to know them? I did my postgraduate work at Stanford. Americans are unique. Believers in fairy tales and man's good nature. I once advanced the theory that a nation that produced Frank Capra and Walt Disney could never understand evil in the world. I am a student of history – an undeniable record of man's inhumanity to man. How could your husband, or anyone from that culture, understand what you were raised to do?'

'But you understand it.'

'I was raised to understand it,' he said simply. 'As my father was before me.'

She heard sadness in his voice but said nothing. There was unguarded emotion here and she didn't want to break the spell cast by the night and the desert and the powerful intimacy strangers sometimes find. His words spilled out, followed by reflective pauses as if talking about himself was hard for him to do, something he wasn't used to, but wanted to do nonetheless.

'Americans have a hard time understanding that there really are people in this world who deprive others of their freedom,' he said, 'and that most of the people in the world live under governments that will not hesitate to use force against them. Guns and knives and fists and prisons. That naiveté staggers those of us who lived under Communism. Justine, you and I know it is a living breathing thing, this desire to subjugate others. Sometimes I think it is as strong as the desire for freedom.' He shook his head. 'An amazing place, America. Four children shot by state militiamen at one of your universities thirty years ago, not even regular soldiers, and it almost brought down the government. There are still repercussions. In China, they roll over them with tanks by the hundreds.'

His voice grew heavy. 'I've always known my responsibilities. When Stalin betrayed my grandfather and the tribes fled back to the desert it was decreed that we would never accept foreign rule. My father resisted it his whole life and when he died I took the same vow. Now it is Raza and his ambitions. I live with it as you lived with your promise to your father. Springtime flowers and happy memories of childhood were for others. We are the responsible ones.'

'Don't you resent it sometimes?' she asked.

'The fish was once asked what it was like to swim in the water all the time. "What water?" he replied.'

142

'You're saying it's become our way of life. We know no other.'

'There *is* no other. Fate selects things for us. For a believer in Islam I am remarkably Greek in my conception of Fate. I believe we may make it better or worse, but we can never escape it. If Oedipus hadn't been so stubborn he would still have slept with his mother, but he wouldn't have been *blind* and sleeping with his mother.'

She laughed. 'I've never heard it put quite that way. You have an intriguing philosophy.'

'I think we have a lot in common.'

'Does it help you to know that Raza is going to have to work on the missiles if he intends to use them?' she asked, well aware she was changing the subject.

'Considerably,' he said. 'If his only purpose here is to store the weapons,' his hand swept out toward the horizon, 'the black sands of the Kara-Kum are deep and wide. But there are not so many places to do technical work. Water, shelter, power. Not so many places have those. We will have to go into the desert and see.'

'Karansky says his people will airlift whatever we need. Do you trust them?'

She could feel him shrug. 'Of course not,' he said. 'But it doesn't matter. They will deliver my grandfather whether they want to or not.'

'But you can't believe my presence here will guarantee that. What do they care if Karansky or I make it out once we locate the missiles? All the government protests in the world won't – ' She stopped suddenly. 'Wait a minute. You know that. It's the weapons themselves! That's it, isn't it? You won't call in the Russians once you find them. You want to play the same game as Raza. Use the missiles to force the release of your grandfather.'

Kemal's silence went on for some time. 'We did not steal them,' he said finally. 'I am a man of my word. Once the Mahdi is returned, the weapons will be destroyed.'

Justine tossed away the sand in her hand, startling

143

the horses. 'So instead of just being able to find the damn bombs and call in an air strike to vaporize that particular area of desert, you want to take the weapons yourselves. Well, that's nuts. It's fine to take potshots at the occasional Red Army patrol that comes into the desert every few months, but you haven't come close to a serious engagement in who knows how long. We trained Raza's people ourselves. I know you and your men are tough and committed, and you've been fighting with the Russians for a long time, but you're still using hunting rifles and revolvers. What the hell do you know about automatic weapons and laser sights and night vision?'

His voice had just the slightest hesitation. '*You* know about them.'

She had to shake her head as the implications set in, amazed at his duplicity. 'You conniving bastard! Is that why I'm here? You knew a hostage wouldn't mean a thing so you never really wanted one. You were after a guerrilla leader to help get those missiles.'

He held up a hand. 'Actually that's only part of it. I also had to figure out a way to prevent the Russians from just sending in their troops to take the weapons once we located them. I needed a player in whose interest it would be to prevent it. An agent of your government was the obvious choice.'

She saw it. The full scope of what he had done. 'Remarkable,' she said admiringly.

'I thought I was being rather clever in a Byzantine sort of way,' Kemal admitted. 'Ethnic Russians are a prejudiced lot. They were happy to believe I was just an unsophisticated camel driver. Your being in Ashkhabad was fortunate. I knew you were perfect as soon as they showed me your dossier.'

'What do you think Karansky is going to say when he finds out you won't let him destroy the missiles?' Justine asked.

'He will only learn of my ultimate intentions if you tell him. Till then, we are united by a common goal.'

She couldn't help but admire his thinking from a professional point of view. 'I've got to hand it to you, Kemal. You set this up beautifully. Everybody rushed to give you what you wanted thinking it gave them the upper hand and all along it was just the opposite. You caught me, too. I went to all that trouble to impress you when I was supposed to be in charge all along.'

'Actually, it worked out well,' he said easily. 'The men will follow you now.'

'Wait a minute. Why should I help you? Especially now that I know what you're really after. It's a lot less dangerous just to call in the Russian fighters. It's what my government wants.'

Kemal leaned closer. His eyes held her. He said, 'Because above all you fight for justice. And because your father would.'

It stopped her. 'Do you ever make a wrong move?' she said softly, off balance.

'Justine, our fight is a hundred years old. Help me win it.'

She couldn't believe he had tied her up so deftly in so many ways. She'd always had a mission, now she had a moral imperative. It was an almost irresistible combination.

He bowed his head slightly, a significant gesture for a prince. 'Help us. We are yours to lead, Doña Justiñana.'

She said harshly, 'Don't call me that. That was another time. Another fight. It's long over.'

'Is it?' His voice was fierce. 'I said we had much in common and we do. Both our lives have been dominated by a single idea – the fight to free our people. I understand your father because I understood mine. They were total fighters. That is our bond, Justine. The shared pain of being less important to them than their ideals were. Isn't that really it? Do we ever really forgive them that? Do we ever really recover? But I think I am luckier than you.'

145

'Why?' she asked softly.

'Because once Ali-Kahdri is free I will have done much to accomplish my goal. I will have peace. What can your peace be?'

She said tremulously, 'There were too many sides after the revolution. My brothers chose theirs, I chose mine. One died. Even then nothing was clear. But I have a home now, a husband. I'm tired of fighting. And you're wrong about one thing. I learned a lot about peace over the years. Almost as much as about war.'

'And what did you learn?'

'That you make it on a daily basis. I had it once with Mac, I'll have it again.'

'Mac . . . yes, your husband. A navy captain.' When she nodded he said, 'Is that your sadness? There is trouble between you?'

'You are too perceptive by half, Kemal. And I don't know why I can talk about it with you. I couldn't with anyone else. It's a funny thing. Until this minute I thought Mac was the one who caused our problems. He had an accident. There were . . . complications. But there came a time when I thought he should be over it. I waited, but he still wasn't better. So I gave him some more time and even then he wasn't over it. Look at me, I used to say, you know what my life's been like and I learned to live with it. What's wrong with you? Enough already. And in my arrogance I left him. Because I needed him to have *my* peace. And he was failing me.'

She felt him framing a response, but her words came rushing out. 'Kemal, I've been miserable for a lifetime, how could I have given him a time limit? You're right about Americans – and Mac's as American and optimistic as they come. Don't get me wrong, he's nobody's fool, smart and tough, with more nerve than I'll ever have. But this is a guy who had tears in his eyes when they took down the Berlin Wall. Pictures from the Mars satellite made him stand up and cheer. He sees possibility and hope when everybody else is pulling the sheet over the patient's head. When he had to confront his own hell, he wasn't prepared for it. How could he have been? So how could I have left him, Kemal? I know about pain. How could I have failed him so totally?'

'Perhaps the bonds were not as strong as you thought.'

She was defiant. 'They're strong. I was selfish. Mac gave me a reason to get up in the morning. He gave me a way to be lighthearted and happy. Listen to this. Before the accident he heard on the news that there was a breakthrough in the treatment of some horrible children's disease. He said we should go out to dinner to celebrate.' She felt her eyes well up, making the stars scintillate. 'The world stinks. I always tried to make him see that. It was like a test. As long as I couldn't convince him, then maybe I was wrong. Maybe the world wasn't so bad. And when he stopped giving me that I acted like a spoiled brat whose allowance got cut off. Instead of being there for him, I got mad and walked out and looked for someone else to make the payments.'

'You're crying . . .'

'You're damn right I'm crying.' She sniffled. 'Why should that surprise you? Just don't try and do anything, okay? Permit me the dignity of being left alone.'

'That is female and very contradictory,' he said.

'So what's it to ya?'

'Yes . . . er, well put.' Kemal didn't like feeling helpless, and no man is more helpless than when he's confronted by a crying woman who doesn't want to be held. But he waited, and after a while her breathing returned to normal.

'Do you feel better?' he asked.

'As a matter of fact, I do.'

He kept his distance. 'We are a strange pair, Justine. I believe that God will deliver my grandfather to his people. I believe he sent this mission as his vehicle for it. He also chose to send you. I ask myself why.'

'He's economical?'

147

'Don't blaspheme. This isn't Washington.'

She felt his touch, as light as a feather. She remained very still. 'Pain's a lousy thing to base a relationship on, Kemal.'

'All your travels have brought you here. How can you know what is to come? We are a new page, yet to be written. An unanswered question.'

There was an undeniable ache in her body. How good it would feel to have his hands on her right then and there, to thrust up against him in the warm night and blot out everything else. She dug her fingers into the sand to clear her mind, then felt it take her even further. She didn't want it to be, but desire hung between them like a third person. Moist heat rose from her. Her nipples stiffened involuntarily. She forced herself to breathe evenly, but he could feel it. He knew.

His hand brushed over her taut breast, gentle, but more insistent now. His hunger was suddenly evident. She fought to clear her head. Desire was the ultimate arousal. It passed between them, rose on the wind. The horses sensed it and grew restless, snorting and stomping their hooves on the sand. The mare tossed her graceful golden head from side to side and her mane flew white and wild.

'I can't,' Justine said finally, as softly as his touch.

Kemal said nothing, waiting. His silence asked again and she had no answer.

'Please,' she whispered.

His hand dropped away.

For a time, they remained still. Poised. Then a cool breeze swept over them. It dispelled the heat, evaporated her sweat, cooled her skin. The moment had come and gone. They were just two people again, sitting together on the sand. The horses seemed to sense the change and grew calmer. Kemal rose to check their tethers. She was grateful for his self-possession. She need offer him nothing more.

'It will be an early morning,' he said from near the horses.

'Who do I see to put in a wake-up call?'

His grin was unmistakable, even in the dark. It made them both feel better. 'I assigned a woman to tend to your needs. She will come to your *yurta* and wake you and do the cooking.'

'Great. I'm a disaster in the kitchen. You don't know it, but you've been saved from a life of horrible indigestion.'

Again the grin. 'I am grateful.'

She felt her poise returning. She got up and brushed herself off. The camp fires burning by the *yurtas* would provide enough of a beacon to steer her back. She turned back to him.

'I will help you, Kemal,' she said, watching him stroke the Gold's graceful neck. 'We'll talk in the morning.'

'As you wish.' The golden mare stilled under his gentle touch. Kemal was a prince again. He looked over to her, 'You will not regret this, Justine. Ali-Kahdri is a man worth fighting for.'

So's my husband, she thought to herself. Maybe I just had to remember that. 'Good night, Kemal,' she said.

'Sleep well, Justine.'

She walked toward the *yurtas* but suddenly remembered something and turned back.

'By the way, you never told me. Who was the only other person to beat Ezek?'

Kemal smiled briefly but didn't answer – which was answer enough.

ELEVEN

London

The suite at the Dorchester was opulent. Crystal chandeliers, sweeping velvet draperies and a grand piano dominated the living room. Eighteenth century antiques set off every piece of intricately carved furniture, all antiques themselves. Yet the opulence was of no interest to either of the room's two occupants.

'I'm concerned about when I can leave,' said Dr Winston Lavenhal, his face etched with deeper stress lines than his fifty-three years should have put there.

Raza didn't like his chair's soft cushions. Everything was too overdone here, from the silk wallpapers to the plush robes hanging in the closet. Desert-minded, he was ill at ease without sparsity.

'How close are you?'

'Another few days, a week at the most,' replied Lavenhal, fidgeting out a cigarette. 'But how do I know you'll let me go then?'

It was odd to see an American smoking these days, Raza thought, what with the barrage of health news these people got. Actually, he knew from Lavenhal's KGB file he had given up the habit years before. What Raza had put him through in the past two weeks had brought it back.

'I keep my word,' Raza said, wrinkling his nose. 'But there are other considerations. I need your best work. I don't want to find some booby trap you built to guarantee your security in case I am lying to you. Also, the skills you provide to me are invaluable and I may need you again. Perhaps most to the point, you are already compromised. Your work for the KGB would be enough to convict you

150

of treason. Remember this?' He threw a document on the table. 'So I'm not worried you will tell anyone about me. You were a Soviet asset before I borrowed you, you will be an asset when you return. No one the wiser.' He gestured around the suite. 'I tried to give you pleasant memories of your vacation.'

'Sure,' muttered Lavenhal. 'It's been great.'

Raza ignored the sarcasm. 'Get ready. We're going to the warehouse.'

Lavenhal went to get his instruments.

There were three main centers in the United States for nuclear arms, the Los Almos National Laboratory, the Lawrence Livermore National Laboratory and the Sandia National Laboratory, the last having special expertise in nuclear security. The document Raza had thrown on the table was a copy of a top secret study done at Sandia, a highly classified analysis called the 'Comprehensive Report on the Recapture/Recovery and Standoff Vulnerabilities of US Nuclear Weapons Deployed in NATO.' Standoff referred to stopping a terrorist attack on one of the nuclear weapons storage facilities in Belgium, Italy, Greece, the Netherlands, Turkey, Germany and Britain. Recapture meant tracking down and recovering a stolen weapon. The Spetsnatz, who would most likely be the ones to breach such facilities in time of war, had been after the report for a long time. Lavenhal, a spy for the KGB, had provided it.

Lavenhal was a senior researcher at the 8,500 employee Sandia Lab that produced internal and external protections ranging from door locks and weapon tie-downs to comprehensive security force training. Raza knew he would someday need Lavenhal if his plans were to work. When it came time, he triggered the come-in-immediately code Lavenhal's handlers used, an urgent cable from Britain that a sick relative needed him at once. Lavenhal booked passage to London and registered at the Dorchester as he knew to do, and had in fact done twice before, expecting his familiar handlers to meet him. Instead, he found Raza.

Lavenhal had no deep ideological devotion to world Communism as the spies of the fifties and sixties often had, or any grudge against the system to be used and exploited, as the malcontents of all eras had. He was one of a newer breed who had simply been seduced by money, and not even by vast sums at that. Some analysts saw it as a product of the 'me-first' eighties. Others saw it as a logical outgrowth of the fundamental spirit of get-ahead-at-any-cost capitalism. Raza had spent time in the United States and he agreed with one perceptive researcher who called it a result of the 'few thousand more' syndrome – the constant ache most Americans felt for just a few thousand dollars more to make that payment on a nicer house in a better neighborhood, or that better car, or a private school for the kids – things just out of reach. It was much less grandiose than dreams of a secret fortune. It was just getting by better.

The KGB had a long-standing policy of planting 'recruiters' in communities surrounding places like Sandia or Livermore. More than likely Lavenhal's recruitment started with a friendship with a man or a woman, a neighbor or a fellow worker it might have been, who lived just a little better than the rest of the people around and offered a sympathetic ear, over a tennis game maybe, about how those government salaries never really did pay you what you were worth, wasn't that the truth? Maybe sometime there was an offer of some money to help with alimony payments or the kids' college costs. He only wanted some simple stuff at first, unclassified material. Just to help a friendly competitor. But it began a pattern. A few thousand more here and there. A few more documents. Another few thousand to entertain friends and go to finer restaurants. When the pattern was undeniable and Lavenhal was in too deep to get out, he was sent on a trip to Europe for advanced training where he met his future handler, learned letter drops, safe communications and preset signals. In the end, he was a source.

Raza explained who he was to Lavenhal and what he

expected him to do. He had to breach the safety devices in the missiles and activate the nuclear warheads. Lavenhal was hardly in a position to refuse. Raza could set either side on him. He'd been a basket case the first day, totally unable to work. Raza understood. Lavenhal's handlers had an intimate relationship with him. They were the only people he could really trust, the only ones who knew the truth. It was profoundly shocking to be 'used' by someone else, like a wife finding out she'd been loaned to another man for the weekend.

That was almost two weeks ago. Now time was a pressure. There was a limit to how long he could keep Lavenhal without compromising him. If Lavenhal thought he was blown, he might think he had nothing left to lose – a dangerous attitude for a man handling nuclear bombs. But he couldn't press him too hard. Without Lavenhal, the *Kentucky* was nothing more than a deep diving sub. Securing the nuclear weapons that were on board her had been one thing. *Activating* those weapons was another matter entirely.

Nuclear arms couldn't be fired like an artillery shell. You couldn't just shove one in the breechblock and pull the trigger. Safety devices were built into every weapon's basic design, protection against theft or accident. Unless the correct numerical codes were sent to the remote controlled electromagnetic locks in the arming circuits, called Permissive Action Links, or PALS, the weapon could not be activated. The codes were numerical sequences with as many as twelve digits – over a trillion combinations. You had to get around the PAL to breach the internal security system even before you got to the other internal locks and traps. They were all put in to build up what was referred to as 'bypass time' – the time a terrorist would need to deactivate the safeguards and trigger the weapon should he get it into his possession.

The most formidable safeguard, used on advanced arms like the *Kentucky*'s cruise missiles, was a superthin membrane just inside the weapon's casing laced with electronic sensors and powered by long-life batteries. If the membrane was penetrated for any reason, the sensors sent out signals deactivating the weapon.

Lavenhal had been working for almost two weeks now to arm the warheads. They were essential to Raza's plans. Raza lived with the daily frustration of feeling dead in the water. He could not go forward, he could not go back.

He had to keep pressure up.

He needed a demonstration. He needed those bombs.

They drove across London to a warehouse Raza's men had rented months before. This close to the Thames the air was moist with an undercurrent of decay from the river. The warehouse was a run-down brick building with corrugated metal sliding doors. Paint had long since peeled off the window trim. With space at a premium, expensive high-rise buildings were encroaching from the east. Many of the buildings here were due to be torn down. Raza was not much given to humor but he had to smile at the thought of how quickly urban renewal would occur if Lavenhal made a mistake.

The modern workshop inside the warehouse belied its external appearance. Portable walls blocked out the paint-peeling bricks. Surgical lamps supplanted naked ceiling fixtures. Lasers and oscilloscopes, microscopic scanners and racks of electronic test equipment sat on dust-free gray steel shelving. Both missiles that had been left on the *Kentucky* were now secured on long slate-topped workbenches, their open panels revealing multicolored spaghetti bundles of wiring. Lavenhal had been studying the units, much the same way as a diamond cutter studies an uncut stone planning to make one perfect cut. He had to be quick and precise and bypass the locking systems in one series of flaw-free movements. Time itself was a safety device. If he took too long once inside, the firing mechanism would automatically deactivate.

The process had taken its toll on Lavenhal. He was chain-smoking and increasingly short-tempered with his assistants, men Raza had culled from special army units trained to handle nuclear arms. Time and time again Lavenhal lectured them about the risk of crippling the weapons, and the danger of accidently triggering the powerful explosives in the warhead used to create the nuclear blast. There was actually less worry about a nuclear accident. In a planned detonation, an electrical impulse fired the high explosives and the resulting shock wave compressed the nuclear core, starting a chain reaction. If the triggering mechanism was deactivated, or not activated correctly, or even activated at the wrong angle, setting off the high explosive wouldn't compress the core for fission – it would just blast the radioactive core into dust and send radioactive plutonium and poisonous fumes spewing out. This once happened to a Bomarc missile which caught fire in New Jersey. From what Raza had seen of New Jersey, it was likely the toxic crater went unnoticed.

Lavenhal put on a white lab coat and moved to the lighted magnifier bent over the first missile. After a while he looked up and found Raza, blinking from the change in focal length.

'After getting to know you, I'm sure you will take what I'm about to tell you as a sign from God. But I prefer to look at it as an incredible breach of security. Maybe neither of those is true and you're just plain lucky.'

'Will you explain that, please?'

Lavenhal pointed into the missile. 'I couldn't be sure at first. It's taken me all this time to verify it, but you remember when I explained the PALS to you?'

'The number sequence, yes.'

'There is no such link in this missile,' Lavenhal said flatly.

'What?'

'I had heard that the navy resisted fitting its weapons with Permissive Action Links. And that even when it did, it had a policy of leaving them unlocked on deployed weapons. It makes a certain kind of sense. Ballistic missile subs are the last leg of the strategic triad, deployed under the ice pack to wait for the nuclear war to be over and then, wham, deliver the final punch. Who's going to be around to send the sequence to unlock the PAL if Washington is a nuclear cinder? The commander's got to be able to launch weeks or months later. On other ships the theory obviously is that no one could steal a big cruiser or a carrier the size of a small town. Until you came along and grabbed the minisub, that is.'

'Are you telling me that there is no need to bypass the links?'

Lavenhal nodded. 'The electromechanical lock in this weapon's arming circuits is open. I suspect the others are, too.'

Raza felt a great lift to his spirits. 'What about the sensors on the inner membranes?'

'Intact and fully functioning. But I've got a way around them.' Raza heard it in Lavenhal's voice. He was warming to the task. It had ceased to be a matter of whose weapon it was, or the purpose to which Raza would put it. It was a scientific puzzle, one which involved his life's work. He was bent on solving it for the sheer mental conquest.

'Did you ever see that demonstration when the first lasers came out? They took a colored balloon and blew it up inside a clear balloon and then broke the colored one without bursting the clear?'

'Yes.'

'It works because the clear balloon has no color and therefore absorbs no light energy. The dark one absorbs it and bursts. Using the same principle I'm going to burn away the battery connections inside with a special laser and never penetrate the membrane. When the sensors die, the membrane is functionless. I can remove it and get to the rest of the locks. It's going to be a very precise operation, but it should work.'

'How long?'

'Seventy-two hours.'

'The weapons in the desert, can you arm them the same way?'

'Now that we know we don't have to deal with the PAL, and assuming you can airlift the equipment there, they can be bypassed in the same time frame. Maybe less as I get better at this.'

'That's excellent, Doctor. You've done all that I asked of you and it will be rewarded. Ten thousand dollars a missile. Forty thousand dollars in your hands and a ticket back to the States. No one to be the wiser. I trust it will compensate you for this inconvenience.'

'It will do quite nicely, thank you,' Lavenhal said, lighting another cigarette from the tip of his last. He turned back to the bombs.

Raza hid his disgust. A man could be loyal to many things and still have his respect. But to money? That was a whore's mentality, regardless of the sums involved.

The tactical part of Raza's mind turned to the next phase of his plan. The Russians understood terror. That was why they could train men so well in its uses.

He had worked hard on selecting the target. It would be a powerful message.

Worthy of the ancient General Skobelev himself.

TWELVE

Odessa

MacKenzie let Raskin drag him to dinner only because the alternative was eating alone in his room. Memories of the crew's brief elation were tantalizing remnants of the day, a day suddenly bitter because of his own mistakes and Admiral Karolov. He wondered if the Soviet authorities would scrap the mission. Did Karolov have that kind of clout? Given his own performance, maybe he should just resign and save everybody a lot of trouble.

When he got back to port they had been advised of a hearing the following day at 1700 hours at the naval base. The order included Raskin, Chernin, Chief Engineer Prudenkov and senior officers. It made MacKenzie angry. He'd worked hard to give the crew some spirit and he resented anyone's trying to break it.

'What's on your mind, Peter?' asked Raskin, downing vodkas at a rate that would paralyze a lesser man. They were in a waterfront bar like those found in every seaport in the world. Raskin said its name translated roughly as the Storm-at-Sea. Hard-drinking men sat around pock-marked tables lit by candles, and at the long wooden bar. The mirror behind the bar was dirty, barely reflecting the bottles set up in front of it. Ratty fishnets and nautical touches adorned the walls, once decorations, now dust traps.

There was a mix of merchant sailors and naval men in the place. They were tough, hard men, and they gave the atmosphere in the place a charged feel like a storm was building. The dowdy, thick-armed waitresses looked like they could bench press their considerable weight. But the seafood chowder was better than any MacKenzie had ever eaten, thick and spicy with tender lumps of fish and potatoes and vegetables, and the bread was thick and sweet and freshly hot out of the oven.

'Besides getting on my own case for a lousy performance today, I was just thinking I'd like to have five minutes alone with that Karolov character,' MacKenzie said, munching on the bread. 'It burns my ass, Nikolai. I had them. I really had them for a minute. They won. They stood up and they won. And they liked winning.'

'First,' said Raskin, 'your performance was not lousy. You had a momentary lapse. It happens to us all. I knew a captain once who ordered his periscope raised.'

'What's wrong with that?'

'He was under a bridge at the time.'

Both men laughed.

'Anyway, I liked it,' Raskin said expansively. 'It's a heady feeling to lead with your balls.'

'But not such a good feeling to get them chopped off. How far do you think Karolov will go with this?'

Raskin shrugged. 'He is as thick necked and stubborn as they come. Very old school. You made him look bad. He lost face in front of his crew. And since there was an actual collision he has solid grounds for the reckless endangerment charge. Listen, do you know what he likes best? To go into the crew's mess and challenge them to arm wrestling contests. Especially new men who haven't heard about him. He takes off his uniform blouse, I swear he's got arms as thick as your leg. His wrists are like iron. He can go at it for hours. Nobody ever beats him. Now in some captains it might be a way of forming a bond or relieving some of the pressure, yes? Well, with him it's not a social thing. He never stays after with the men, never talks to them. He just beats them. So you tell me. You think he wants this hearing to kiss you for making him turn and run and then hitting his ship?'

'I suppose not.' MacKenzie stirred his soup idly. 'Why is it you're not afraid like the others, Nikolai?'

Raskin pursed his mouth thoughtfully. 'I suppose because I have accepted my position in life. I am not on the top, but I am not on the bottom. I do my job well enough, and as things go I will retire in a few years with a pension. Maybe if Anna were alive it would be different. I would have something to lose.'

'Anna?'

'My wife,' Raskin said. 'She died three years ago. A good woman. Strong. Like the defenders of Leningrad in the Great War. I never really thought of myself as Soviet, you see, I thought of myself as hers. She was the one I kissed good-bye when I went on a cruise. She was the one I came home to. Those two points were my north and south, my compass. In between I did my job. You know, Peter, I really think I was promoted because nobody could find a reason not to. Not because they said, that Raskin – he's the stuff captains are made of. You know what I mean? Other more ambitious men made mistakes, or got someone angry, or had the wrong politics, or became the targets of jealous superiors. I just came to whatever boat I was assigned to and did my job and went home, a threat to no one. After a while, the others fell by the way and they made me captain. It's hard to scare a man who doesn't care, Peter. That's why Karolov's hearing doesn't really frighten me. It's my secret weapon.'

'I'm sorry, Nikolai. How did your wife die?'

'Cancer. In her bones. Maybe in your country she might have had better care and lived a few years longer. But I am convinced in the end it would have been the same. So I drink to her when I drink, and when I cry it is about her. A good woman.' He nodded for a few moments, lost in reverie. 'A good woman.' He lifted his glass. '*Na zdoróvie*,' Raskin toasted.

'*Na zdoróvie*,' MacKenzie echoed, shooting the ice-cold vodka down his throat and munching on a piece of bread.

'You look almost Russian doing that,' complimented Raskin.

'*Spaseeba*. I'm getting the hang of it.'

'Look,' said Raskin. 'Some of our crew.'

MacKenzie turned. There was Purzov and Ivan Kutsky, and round-faced Tartakov and a torpedoman named Vysov along with about a dozen men in all. They took a table off by themselves. If they saw Raskin or MacKenzie they didn't say anything.

'Popular place,' MacKenzie observed.

'Very. The drinks are not watered down and the waitresses are not so ugly here.'

MacKenzie looked at him cautiously. 'They're not?'

Raskin grinned. 'I was just testing to see if you were still sober. If they actually looked good to you it was time to take you home.'

MacKenzie watched the crew. They put their drinks away as fast as Raskin did, no small feat. He still felt alienated from them. Who were these men? What did they believe in? How could he undo a lifetime of training and instill the kind of pride his standards demanded? MacKenzie found his glass empty, for all of two seconds. Raskin poured him another. Maybe he should start to wonder not so much if he would survive the battle with the *Kentucky*, but the alcoholic binge leading up to it.

'More coming,' said Raskin.

This time it was *Riga*'s officers, Chernin, Kotnikov, Weapons Officer Kortzov, Chief Engineer Prudenkov, Communications Officer Golovskoy, Diving Officer Petrov, and Igor Dainis. The place was filling up.

'I'm surprised to see Dainis with the others,' MacKenzie said. 'He's a tight sonofabitch.'

'Political officers are an odd breed,' said Raskin. 'You have nothing like them in your navy. It takes a very committed man with a strange sort of inner ugliness to want to invade the minds of others deeply enough to control them. A man who can tolerate no disorder. I believe

161

that at their roots they are fascists, zealots. But he seems to be on your side. Frankly, I am surprised.'

'Me, too. What do you figure?'

'I can't tell. You are everything he had been trained to hate. Daring, impudent, independent. You behave like a capitalist. Self-assured. Unmindful of others. But he hasn't rallied the crew against you and he didn't bat an eyelash when Kotnikov gave you the new sonar as easily as a copy of *Das Kapital*.'

'Is it inconceivable he might want to make the mission work?'

'The way you mean it, going against regulations, yes, frankly it is. Flexibility is not a trait associated with political officers. But I don't know. We will have to see.'

MacKenzie took another drink. It was new to him drinking this much on a steady basis. Alcohol had never been one of the ways he dealt with his despair. Maybe in the States it would have been a sign of his further collapse, but here it somehow seemed right. It helped to loosen him up more than all the months of therapy at the base hospital. He was beginning to understand that there was something about these Russians with their steady supply of vodka and the easy accessibility to their feelings that opened him in ways the doctors hadn't. He downed another shot. The pleasant glow expanded within him.

'That soup was good. Any more of it?'

'Here.' Raskin ladled some into his bowl. MacKenzie dipped his spoon in and lifted it to his mouth. Good and peppery. It went down like fire, warming him – until he saw the expression on Raskin's face.

'What?'

'I don't believe it,' said Raskin.

'It isn't soup. You translated wrong. It's shoe polish.'

Raskin frowned. 'Stop drinking. You're getting stupid. But you must be able to foretell the future. Didn't you say before you wished you had five minutes with Karolov?'

'I did.'

162

'Well, you may get them. He just walked in with half the *Lenin's* officers.'

'Point him out,' MacKenzie directed.

'There. That's him.'

Karolov and his men were shown to a large table by waiters who obviously knew them. MacKenzie took in the admiral's powerful physique, his confident manner. His officers sat around him like disciples at the Last Supper, worshipful, ready to do the master's bidding. Bottles were set down on the table and one poured the first round. Karolov shot it back to a chorus of *Na zdoróvies*, his men following suit. His glass wasn't empty a second before someone rushed to fill it. Actually, MacKenzie had to admit it was not a totally unfamiliar scene. Powerful American military men with a lot of charisma blended with needs arising from personal insecurities often demanded and got that kind of sycophantic loyalty. MacKenzie had always found it personally distasteful. It reminded him of high school, where there was always the toady whose claim to fame was being the quarterback's best friend and who lorded that relationship over others. Power through affiliation. It lowered his opinion of Karolov that he would cultivate those kinds of officers. But it was time to put his feelings aside. He had to think of his own men first.

Raskin said, 'I don't like the expression on your face. What are you thinking?'

'I'll go over, we'll have a drink. Settle this out of court, so to speak.' He stood up, swaying slightly.

'Peter, this is impossible.'

'Nothing is impossible. This is America, remember?'

'This is . . . what? Peter, what are you doing? You've had too much . . . you have no idea . . . Peter!'

'Not to worry,' MacKenzie called jauntily back over his shoulder.

A lot of people had arrived while he and Raskin ate. The place was shoulder to shoulder with people. They were two and three deep at the bar and every table was filled.

Karolov was laughing at something one of the officers said. He looked up as MacKenzie reached the table and pressed in between two of them. There was no sign of recognition.

'Admiral Karolov?'

'*Da?*'

'Excuse me. I am Captain Peter MacKenzie. Of the *Riga*. I am pleased to met the captain of the *Lenin*.' He held out his hand.

MacKenzie heard a familiar Russian voice speaking rapidly right next to him. He was surprised to see Raskin standing next to him, translating. But the expression on Karolov's face had changed with the speed of a storm at sea. 'That's enough, Captain Raskin,' he said angrily. 'I speak fluent English. But any talking I do with the American will not be during my dinner. It will be at the hearing tomorrow. You are both dismissed.'

'That's all, Peter,' Raskin said. 'Let's go.'

'Admiral,' said MacKenzie, pressing in. 'I hoped you might let me explain. The situation today was my fault entirely. As one captain to another . . . '

Karolov didn't rise from his seat but his voice was strong enough to carry over the noise in the room. People turned to listen. 'We are not officers together, as you suggest, Captain MacKenzie.' Karolov glared. 'You have no right on board a Soviet ship of the line. I have expressed that opinion before, wisely I think in light of your performance today' – which, he thought to himself, played right into his hands – 'You endangered us all with a reckless maneuver that damaged both ships. Lives could have been lost. You are dangerous. Possibly a saboteur. You should be sent back to your country. I will make that case at the hearing.'

MacKenzie felt his cheeks flush. 'I hoped you might understand the difficulty of my position. I am trying to retrain a crew with little or no understanding of my own traditions.'

'We don't need your traditions in this navy. They are all

the more reason to disperse the crew and send them for retraining before everyone is infected beyond repair.'

'Be reasonable,' MacKenzie said. 'The crew follows my orders. This is a mission both our governments support. In the spirit of cooperation . . .'

Karolov folded his arms over his chest. 'I have nothing more to say. I told you to go. If you are part of our navy I outrank you. Are you incapable of following even the simplest order?'

Several of the officers laughed. Karolov brought his glass to his lips and shot back his drink. It was a nasty gesture, a dismissal of a lesser being. 'See?' he said to the men around him. 'This is the best the American navy produces. Fit only for a garbage scow like the *Riga*.'

In retrospect, MacKenzie wondered if he would have said what he said if he hadn't been drinking. But Karolov's arrogance was just too much. Noting with pride that Raskin, although silent, had not moved from his side, MacKenzie said coldly, 'Admiral, the only thing I see is a tight ass bastard who's too much of a fraud to admit that he was outmaneuvered today. You just didn't have the balls to make me turn first and your crew saw it. So now you're after me and my men as if that's going to wipe it out. Well, it won't. The *Riga* is a better ship and we proved it. So why don't we let the children go home and settle this between you and me. Outside or underwater. Your choice. Nikolai, translate that for anyone who doesn't speak English.'

'Peter . . .'

'Translate it!'

Later, MacKenzie was angry at himself for not anticipating what the reaction would be. Of course the dogs would want to show the pack leader how fierce they were. As it was he was unprepared for the swiftness of the physical onslaught. One spun around and sucker punched him right from his seat, doubling him over. Two held Raskin. The rest came up from the table like a wave and jumped him.

He gave a fairly good account of himself, Raskin told him later, tending his wounds back at the hotel, but he was no match for Karolov's men. He managed to do some of the things Justine had taught him as they beat him, catching one man in the solar plexus and another in the throat and using a last ditch hip throw that only partially worked on one monster that jumped him. They both fell, but it brought the man down on his side and kept most of his weight off MacKenzie.

They swarmed over him, pummeling him with their fists. MacKenzie managed to get in a good shot to someone's face before his own head started to get mushy from the blows. He felt like his head was wrapped in cotton. They pinned his arms to his side. One held him while the others hit him. It got rough for a little while, then. Karolov himself stepped up and drove his fist deep into MacKenzie's abdomen. His insides churned and he threw up. He tried to kick the grinning admiral, but they clamped down on his legs. After a while he couldn't do anything else but take it.

When the beating let up he was close to unconscious. Karolov's men dragged him to the door and threw him into the street. He hit the cold wet cobblestones and rolled helplessly into a foul smelling puddle. Somebody said something in Russian that had to be a curse. Somebody else laughed.

He lay there for a while, facedown in the dirty water, unable to move. The men went away. He tried to gather his legs under him but they were disconnected and he remained facedown. City noises filtered down. The smell of the sea. After a while he felt Raskin's powerful arms under him, lifting him upright. He sagged against him and would have fallen if not for the big man's support.

'You are an interesting man, Peter MacKenzie. Is it the whole Russian navy you want to take on, or just part of it?'

MacKenzie couldn't speak. Nausea came in waves. He

blacked out. When he came to Raskin had draped MacKenzie's arm over his wide shoulder and was walking him down the cobblestoned street to the car. MacKenzie felt blood well up in his mouth and spat.

'Here, wait a minute.' Raskin propped MacKenzie up and fished coins out of his pocket. 'I'll get you a mineral.'

Several bright blue soda machines on the sidewalk were against the brick wall of a closed shop. Raskin fed the coins into the machine and pressed one of three round steel buttons. Soda sizzed out into a glass in the chrome lined receptacle below. He lifted it out of the machine and raised it to MacKenzie's lips. 'Rinse your mouth and spit out the blood.'

'Hurt . . .' MacKenzie managed once his mouth was clear.

'I know,' said Raskin putting the community glass back into the vending machine where running water and brushes cleaned the vessel after each use. 'Hold on. The car's here.'

MacKenzie felt himself lifted into the front seat. The motor started. The car jerked forward. Darkness was coming fast, sending him down a long tunnel. His last thought was that what really hurt wasn't so much lying facedown in the street in the brackish water, covered with his own blood and vomit. It wasn't even the pain that coursed hot and throbbing through every part of his body.

What hurt was that not one of his men had stepped in to help him.

THIRTEEN

MacKenzie woke in agony.

He figured he wasn't dead; he hurt too much to be dead. This did not mean he didn't want to be dead. A hangover the strength of a major hurricane added to his misery. He managed to hobble into the bathroom. He threw up. He splashed cold water into his face, swallowed a couple of aspirin and ran a hot bath.

A salty breeze fluttered the white curtains and the pale light of morning glowed in the windows. Raskin had gotten him back to the hotel in one piece and helped him up here. Most of his cuts were superficial and nothing was broken. It was a brutal beating but not without intelligence. They had left his face alone and avoided really serious injury to his body. No broken ribs. No crushed spine. The purpose was to humiliate him. Or rather, to pay him back for his humiliating the revered Saint Karolov. Black eyes and broken bones would have raised questions at the hearing.

Rage as hot as lava coursed through him and every ache and pain compounded it. He couldn't let Karolov get away with this. His men had seen the beating. No matter they had not helped him. They had to know that he could take it. Maybe then they'd believe that *they* could take it. He would go to his post today if he had to crawl into the conn. He said it – now he had to show them how to live it. Nobody beats us. Not at anything.

He lay in the hot water flexing his bruised muscles. He had never seen himself as a violent man but he wanted to do violence to Karolov. He had approached the man in a civilized, if slightly tipsy, manner, and sued for peace. Karolov had him whipped like a dog and thrown in the gutter. It was personal now.

He lay in the tub working things through. There had to be an angle here he could exploit, a way to come out on top. He needed a strategy. He could sure use Tom Lasovic now, his best friend and XO on both the *Aspen* and the *Seawolf*. Even more he wished Justine were here. He'd let her down, he knew that now. He had stopped fighting. Maybe this thing with Karolov was all the more important because of that. He wasn't about to stop fighting again. Tactics. He needed a plan. He had an opponent and the opponent had vulnerabilities. He could exploit them. He lay in the hot water thinking.

'Peter? Are you here? I let myself in. Where are you?'

It was Raskin outside. 'In here, Nikolai.'

Raskin appeared in the doorway. The man obviously had an iron constitution. He looked none the worse for all the drinking and the lateness of the hour when he had finally left. 'Tending your wounds, eh?' he said mildly.

MacKenzie managed a pained grin. 'You should have seen the other guy.'

'I did. You're lucky you're not in worse shape. Can you walk?'

'Like I was seventy,' MacKenzie admitted. 'I took some aspirin. I don't know. But I'm heading for the *Riga* as soon as I can.'

'I thought you'd say that,' said Raskin. 'Knowing what shape you would be in, I got an idea. It's a venerable Russian tradition. Just what you need.'

'I'll die if this involves more drinking . . .'

Raskin held up a hand. 'Trust me. A few hours you'll be a new man. We have a hearing to get through later. Let me help you out of there.'

'I got in here okay, I can get out, thank you.'

'Americans.' Raskin sighed. 'I'll bring the car around.'

They drove into the city and stopped at a nondescript building with a stone facade on a tree shaded cobblestone street. Odessa was lovely close up. Teenaged girls wearing fashionable long skirts strolled along the sidewalks, children played soccer in the park. Apartment dwellers had pulled chairs onto the sidewalk and now sat in clusters in front of neat sand-colored buildings talking and enjoying the morning.

'It's beautiful here,' MacKenzie said.

'I'm sorry you're not in better shape to appreciate it,' said Raskin.

'I'll have to remember it. Take some pictures for me?'

Raskin took MacKenzie's camera out of the car and shot the roll. The little motor rewound the film.

'Where are we going?' he asked Raskin who was helping support him as they walked.

'To a *banya*, a communal bath. It will make you a new man.'

'I thought miracles were for churches.'

'To many of us' – Raskin grinned – 'this is as close to church as we get.'

Inside, attendants helped MacKenzie undress and store his clothing. Wrapped in a white towel he hobbled after Raskin into a big, white-tiled room with a bath so large it qualified as an indoor swimming pool. Lots of men were bathing. Others were playing cards and drinking beer. Even at this hour of the morning it was crowded, hot and moist, filled with people.

'Most of the people you see here,' Raskin explained, 'are playing hookey from work. So many hide in the *banyas* that in Moscow Yuri Andropov used to have his KGB men go in and chase them out. Are you hungry? There is beer and salted fish if you want.'

'Pass, thank you,' said MacKenzie.

The *banya* had a congenial atmosphere, like a locker room at a private club. Men talked, bathed, sat around or played cards. Raskin translated some of what was being said and it was the same as what was being said in Washington or Paris. Politics, the health of the kids, the

170

best place to buy – or in this case, trade for – food, the wife, women, and sports.

A burly masseur helped MacKenzie onto a table and proceeded to work the kinks out of his muscles, first gently, then with a growing kneading intensity that bordered on torment.

'Blood,' Raskin translated what the masseur kept saying. 'Blood back into the muscles.'

Blood back into the muscles. MacKenzie felt like the man was forcing his blood out of his body, but he hung in and soon the heat and the pressure relieved a lot of the pain. He was moving more freely and his balance was back again. He took the steam with Raskin and about a dozen other men. They soon picked up his accent and there was a flood of questions about America. MacKenzie was more of an oddity here in Odessa than he would have been in Moscow. The men were interested in everything. Raskin translated, though many spoke English, and MacKenzie soon found himself enjoying the exchange. Dealing with the *Riga* and the dangerous business at hand, it was easy to forget there were other people in the real city with their own lives and priorities. Forget dour-faced Tartakov for a while, he decided, and the arrogant Karolov. There were more than enough Purzovs and Raskins in here.

MacKenzie was beginning to get a feel for the Russians. Although they lacked a real work ethic and tolerated an impossible system of things, they were a kindly people, mischievous and full of warmth. One man with an infectious laugh told stories about his family. He had a son he kept trying to get out of the house to go to work. Why should he? another demanded. At home you get him his food. He goes to work he has to wait in line. There were plenty of jokes and stories, their way of enduring the paradoxes of life.

More steam, another massage, and a brisk beating with some kind of tree branches that actually felt good. He even ate some of the salted fish and drank a beer. Somebody was always ready with a toast. There was emotion here. He felt something within him thawing, something tentative, that had been frozen for a long time. What was it with these people that they seemed so able to touch him?

'I think you'll live,' pronounced Raskin, when after two hours he was able to move without agony.

'I've been thinking, Nikolai,' MacKenzie said as they dressed. 'Where is the *Lenin* berthed?'

'The base at Nikolayev.'

'Can we make it there and back to the *Riga* in time to sail on schedule?'

Raskin's eyes widened in alarm. 'Go to Nikolayev? What do you have in mind, Peter? Maybe I'm less nervous than most, but I still don't want to end my career where it's very, very cold, if you understand.'

MacKenzie slipped his shirt on gingerly. At least he could get his arms over his head now. 'Think tactically, Nikolai. We can't let Karolov drag us into a hearing we're going to lose. What military tribunal is going to let an American captain make a Russian admiral look stupid in his own ocean? If we walk in there we're finished. Karolov knows it. So does our crew. We've got to show them something better.'

'Which is?'

'That we can beat him. Karolov is a godsend, a real live dyed-in-the-wool enemy. Nothing unifies like a common enemy, Nikolai. History proves that. During World War Two we were allies, for Christ's sake. If we can beat him' – MacKenzie was excited – 'we can beat anyone or anything and that includes the goddamned *Kentucky*. One crew, one captain. All winners. That's *Riga's* new tradition. I tell you beating Karolov is a better lesson than all the sub pinging we could do in a hundred years.'

Raskin finished dressing. 'Assuming I accept your logic, what do you propose?'

'I want to make him so mad that winning at the tribunal

won't be enough. I want him mad enough to take a shot at us.'

'I don't want him shooting at you, Peter. I'm usually standing close by.'

'No. Not at me. At the *Riga*.'

'I'm losing you.' Raskin sighed. 'Have you noticed that seems to be happening more often these days?'

MacKenzie pulled on his jacket. He felt like a new man. 'C'mon. I'll explain it to you as we drive.' As an afterthought he added, 'Bring more beer.'

The base at Nikolayev wasn't as big as the main headquarters of the Black Sea Fleet at Sevastopol but it was a bustling port nonetheless. Raskin's naval credentials gained them admittance and they drove down along the dock looking for the pen that housed the *Lenin*.

'By the way,' MacKenzie said, 'I've been meaning to ask you. How come you speak English so well?'

'I studied it in school,' Raskin replied. 'Most of us do from a very early age. And I have read many of your classics.'

'Wait a minute, no way you got all those colloquialisms from books or even that tour in the States.'

'Well,' said Raskin, smiling. 'I also did a three-year stint in Naval Intelligence deciphering your radio signals. We had to be up on your popular expressions. You have a very colorful language, Peter. Excellent descriptive terminology. I particularly liked "Jive Turkey Motherfucker." One of our absolute favorites.'

'Keep your eyes on the ships. I don't read Russian.'

'I don't have to. There it is.' He stopped the car. A crewman was standing guard.

MacKenzie said, 'Fast talk this guy. I need to get out on the pier.'

'I should have my head examined.'

'Right.'

Raskin stepped out of the car and strode up to the guard,

a young crewman. He flashed his military identification. He pointed to the sail. The guard trotted off, crossed over the gangplank and disappeared down the forward hatch.

MacKenzie trotted down the pier. When he reached the sail he set down the bag of garbage he was carrying and began happily, methodically dumping it on the *Lenin*'s hull. First there were eggs, a gift from one of the men in the bathhouse. They made a delightful splat. Each of the beer cans caused a lovely clatter sliding down the hull. He shot several like a basketball player and sank one right down the open hatchway.

MacKenzie said, 'Swish.'

He was feeling good now. Better than he had in a long time. Maybe therapy was just release. Maybe it was the half-dozen beers. He tossed another egg.

'Hey, you!' The voice came from the sail bridge. 'You. Stop that!'

MacKenzie looked over. It was one of the officers from the night before. One with a particularly vicious right hand, if he remembered correctly. MacKenzie waved and lobbed another beer can. It sailed down the hatch. The officer dropped out of sight.

This should be it, MacKenzie thought.

Seconds later, Karolov himself appeared on the bridge. 'What the hell do you think you're doing?' he demanded. 'Didn't you have enough last night? Do you want me to send my men out there again, you fool?'

MacKenzie smiled. It changed the expression on Karolov's face. With the beating he got last night Mac-Kenzie should have been lying in bed for a week, not here now, tossing garbage onto the *Lenin*. More officers came onto the bridge. Karolov turned to talk to them. Maybe he was chewing them out for not really beating him badly enough. Their faces grew angry. They wouldn't botch the opportunity if it occurred again, he knew that much.

It was a small sound that stopped Karolov's tirade, but one that was unmistakable. Karolov had turned back to

MacKenzie to continue yelling. 'I demand you stop . . .'
Then he heard and saw.

'What are you doing? Are you insane? You think you
can do that to my ship and get away with it? I will hunt
you down. You are a madman. Get me a rifle. Someone
get me a rifle!'

Finishing, and thanking God he could finally let go of
all that beer, MacKenzie waved jauntily to both Karolov
and his wide-eyed officers, zipped his fly and walked
back to the car. He felt Karolov's eyes boring into his
back all the way. He wondered if he had misjudged the
admiral and he was capable of putting a bullet in him. One
thing he hadn't misjudged. Karolov was certainly mad
enough.

At the car, in spite of his trepidation, Raskin was doubled
over with silent laughter. When he got behind the wheel
there were tears in his eyes.

'To the *Riga*?'

'Absolutely.'

You have to feel good on a day like this, MacKenzie
thought to himself, getting in.

Raskin was still shaking with mirth as they left the base.
MacKenzie leaned back.

You really have to feel pretty goddamn good.

The communication came when they were a hundred miles
out to sea. Word of MacKenzie's exploit had already spread
throughout the ship and the crew was looking at him in a
new, if rather surprised, light. Whether or not he would
even show up to make the cruise had been the subject of
intense debate among the men. Showing up looking relatively intact after the brutal beating so many of them had
witnessed, and pissing on the admiral's sub to boot – that
was the stuff of which legends were made.

Communications Officer Golovskoy brought the decoded
message. He had already read it and MacKenzie knew it
was probably already circulating the length of the ship.

It was a simple message. Two words and some co-ordinates. And two times.

'Mr Chernin,' MacKenzie ordered. 'Plot these.'

'Aye, Capteen.'

MacKenzie thought over the hidden meaning and passed the message to Raskin, who read it and nodded admiringly. The two words on the message were 'Hearing Postponed.'

'Capteen?' Chernin passed him a chart. The four co-ordinates produced a box roughly a hundred miles on each side. The first time was twelve hundred hours the following day. The second time was twelve hours later.

With the message from Karolov on board the *Lenin* he knew the morning's escapade had worked. He had made the admiral angry enough to want a more personal victory over MacKenzie and his bastard ship. Karolov had also named the stakes. A hearing postponed could also be rescheduled. That's what they were fighting for. Win, and Karolov and the hearing went away. Lose, and they not only lost face – they would be back up on charges as soon as they reached port.

MacKenzie's dream of a proud and unified crew depended on winning. In a sense, he had already gained an important victory. The hearing was postponed. Audacity paid off. MacKenzie's thoughts turned to the problem of a dogfight with the *Lenin*, a superior ship with a tightly disciplined crew.

MacKenzie was reminded of more proverbial wisdom. *Awaken the sleeping tiger only if you're prepared to ride it.*

MacKenzie opened the all-ship channel to inform the crew they were about to ride the tiger.

FOURTEEN

Washington, DC

Adm Ben Garver read the report filed by the liaison to the Soviet Naval Command and found some humor in it despite the seriousness. Leave it to MacKenzie to get the entire Soviet admiralty's noses out of joint in just a few days. Phrases like 'reckless endangerment' and 'flagrant disregard for military procedure' ran through the pages like veins of ore in a mine. It was horseshit, Garver decided. Most of the screaming was traceable to one Admiral Karolov. The report had probably been sent to Washington just to calm Karolov down. If the Soviets were really serious about yanking MacKenzie they could have done so without all the noise.

They probably just wanted to let Garver know that the situation was potentially serious, but not yet serious enough to jeopardize the mission . . . yet. It did raise serious questions, however. MacKenzie wasn't over there to declare war on the Russians. He was an ally on a joint mission. Had MacKenzie indeed gone over the edge? Or was there some method to his madness?

He had MacKenzie's report, an addendum to Soviet Naval Command's. There was little he could say through unsecured channels. Mac was obviously being terse and noncommittal. 'Mission proceeding as planned.' That was all.

Garver could not disregard the possibility that it was Karolov who instigated the conflict. Submarine captains were not usually high-profile officers. It took painstaking intelligence to build up even the slimmest files on them. MacKenzie was different. If there was a rogue's gallery somewhere in Soviet Naval Intelligence headquarters, MacKenzie had to be in it. He was known to most of the fleet commanders for his role in the episodes of the *Kirov*, the *Red Dawn* and the *Akula*, Soviet subs MacKenzie was credited with killing, stealing and crippling, respectively. It wasn't so unlikely that a Soviet admiral who knew his reputation and had something to prove would go gunning for him.

It was up to Garver whether or not to cancel the mission. His own top brass had been alerted to the questions concerning Mac's fitness to command. He was under considerable heat over that. There was growing support for just bombing the hell out of the North Atlantic in the hopes of sinking the *Kentucky*, if only by accident. But there was more to this mission than just the minisub, as important as she was. Continued cooperation with the Soviets could continue to change the world. The diplomatic importance of this joint mission hadn't been lost to men of good will on either side. Garver himself had to admit to an additional, darker motive, one more subtle perhaps, but no less important. In these changing times, balance of power was a tricky thing that could change overnight. If there was a chance they could get their hands on the new sonar they had to go all the way.

The second document on his desk finalized Garver's decision. Within the last forty-eight hours, Raza had sent a communiqué to the Soviet president formally declaring a new Turkmeni Republic with himself as prime minister. He then announced its secession from the Soviet Union. All Soviet military and government personnel were ordered out of Turkmenistan by the fifteenth of the month, just ten days away. He also demanded control of the nuclear weapons stored in Turkmenistan within that same time frame or 'the fullest extent of Turkmeni power will be brought to bear on your northern centers.' The veiled reference to the *Kentucky* and her nuclear arsenal could not be more clear.

Of course, the Soviet president had refused and sent out the rest of the Soviet navy to find the *Kentucky*. Garver shook his head sadly when he thought of how fruitless that mission was. He had his own P-3 Orions and ASW surface craft all over that area and not one had turned up so much as a trace of the *Kentucky*. She could be moored under an island, or below a surface craft or an oil rig and they wouldn't know about her until she fired. Only the *Riga* with the new sonar stood a chance.

Less than ten days to nuclear warfare. Every psych profile of Raza agreed he wasn't bluffing, he would indeed launch the weapons. He was prepared for any number of people dying to advance his cause. It was a frightening specter. The *Kentucky*'s modified Tomahawk cruise missiles could reach Moscow itself. MacKenzie's mission had seemed a long shot when it was conceived but it was leading the pack right now. Well, the cards had been dealt. He was going to let Mac play out his hand, in spite of the uncertainty about his performance.

Ten days.

The clock was ticking.

FIFTEEN

Kara-Kum

Justine hated her camel. It wasn't just that it was ugly and smelled bad, enough of an indictment, it was also an ill-tempered, mean-spirited beast who took every opportunity to spit at her or bite. She was introduced to her mount when they had taken off that morning, just after dawn. Kemal led a party that included the big wrestler Ezek, Kemal's brother, Radi, Justine, Karansky and about a dozen other men.

It was clear that Karansky had noticed a change in the relationship – if that's what it could be called – between Kemal and Justine almost at once. Whether or not he attributed it to her performance at the *toi* the previous day, or to something else, she didn't know, so she drew him aside at the earliest opportunity. They had stopped to rest in the shade of a small oasis and let the camels take in water for the journey into the central desert. She walked off alone, motioning for him to follow.

'We've got a problem,' she said as he drew up beside her under a tree.

'You seem well placed to handle it,' he said.

'Don't be snide,' she countered. 'I worked damn hard to make that place. I didn't see you do so well in the circle.'

'I wanted it to be over too quickly. It was a mistake. Actually, you were very good. As good as I'd heard,' Karansky said admiringly.

'Thank you.'

'By the way, where is my gun?'

180

'How would I know?' she said.

'Do I look stupid?' Karansky said. 'Who else would have taken it?'

'Kemal, maybe?'

He reached out to touch her shirt. She batted his hand away. 'Sure,' he said. 'Kemal took it.'

'Next time remember not to leave things lying around. But forget about that. We need a weapons drop anyway. Then you can have something a lot better than the antique stuff these guys carry.'

'What's your plan?'

'It's not my plan,' she said. 'It's Kemal's. He's looking to put one over on you. He doesn't intend to locate the weapons just to let them be destroyed. He wants to grab them himself and play one up on Raza's game. The Mahdi's safe return for the weapons.'

'And what do you say about that?'

'Unhappily, it is my government's policy that the weapons be destroyed.'

'Unhappily?'

'If I had to pick a side in this, it wouldn't be yours.'

Karansky digested that.

Justine watched him. If he harbored any intentions of trying to take the weapons she wanted him to be sure that she would stop him. Beyond that, she felt sad and guilty betraying Kemal but her mission did not include the return of aging Mahdis or support for the Karadeen independence movement. Her government wanted those weapons destroyed. That had to be her highest priority. Nothing that happened during or after the *toi* changed that.

'When did he tell you all this?' Karansky asked.

'Last night.'

'Oh. I see.'

The simple 'I see' hung in the air. Justine felt her face flush. Ridiculous, she thought. My age and I'm blushing. 'You see shit,' she retorted. 'He trusts me.'

'He's obviously an excellent judge of character.'

Justine frowned. 'Are you trying to make me mad, or is this just your winning personality?'

'I don't like to be cut out,' Karansky said angrily. 'You play things too close to the chest for me, Justine. How do I know this isn't another setup?'

'I'm telling you exactly what he told me. Do you think I want to get involved in a firefight with Raza's men somewhere in this lousy desert over weapons we're supposd to destroy?'

Karansky was slightly mollified. 'What do you want to do?'

'Play along with Kemal. Arm his men. Keep them going. But I'm not playing Lawrence of Arabia with him or anybody else. As soon as we locate the weapons we call in the air strike. Then your people had better play it straight.'

'I'll need my transmitter back,' he said.

'I'll speak to Kemal.'

She found him at the edge of the oasis, looking at something in the sand.

'Kemal, I – '

'Shhh,' he said. 'Watch this.'

She got down to see. It turned out to be a funny looking little lizard with bright red ears. As soon as he touched it the creature shivered with such intense vibration that it dug its way right into the sand, out of reach of predators.

'Most people see only lifeless sand here,' Kemal said. 'But there are a thousand kinds of insects and a hundred kinds of birds. Foxes and wildcats, too.'

He has a habit of doing that, Justine thought. *All of a sudden he's as simple and honest as a child. That innocence makes my manipulations seem cheap and immoral.* But she had to remember that so far this 'child' was keeping several governments hopping. In many ways he had outfoxed them all. He was a complex man. Was he conscious of that complexity? Did he use it? Or was it just that Kemal had gotten further under her skin that she wanted to admit?

182

'I was born out here,' he said. 'My mother had her labor in a tent on the sand with only the other women to help her. They buried my birth cord in this desert. So I am a part of it, as it is a part of me. There is magic if you know where to look. What did Karansky say?'

'He accepts the need to arm your men with modern weapons. He'll call up an air drop if you'll give him back his transmitter.'

'What reason did you give him?' Kemal asked.

'I told him that if we stumbled onto Raza's men the antique garbage you're carrying wouldn't even let us fall back to call in an air strike. I told him I wasn't going to traipse around the desert with anything less effective than a modern strike force. Good enough?'

'You act like I was questioning you.'

Damn it, I'm going to have to watch that, she thought. We're too close now. I let him cross boundaries I should never have let him cross. He notices the slightest variation in my tone. The truth is I'm feeling guilty about betraying him so I'm short with him. Shit. What the hell do I have to feel guilty about?

'Sorry. I'm hot and thirsty and I hate my camel. How come nobody stores missiles in Capri? Forget it, okay? Let's get going.'

They took off under the hot sun riding one-humped dromedary camels that were belligerent about being torn from grazing on the sparse shoots that sprouted from the sand in rough tangled patches like stubble. Kemal showed her how to better manage the saddle with its tented canopy that blocked out the sun. The camels took up a slow padding lope, more surefooted than she had expected. The dunes slid apart as easily as powder as they traversed them. She began to have a grudging respect for the animals.

Karansky had made the call on his satellite direct-link transmitter, the same one she had used in the stable in Ashkhabad. That seemed like a long time ago. Kemal duly took the transmitter back. He wasn't letting either of them use it for any other calls. She saw Karansky watching him. The transmitter was a key of sorts. With it, they were air minutes away from safety or had the ability to bring a blazing holocaust down on the stolen weapons. Without it, they were ants crawling across a torrid desert as vast as the ocean, the only difference being the opposing design of its inherent cruelty.

She had to betray Kemal to complete her mission.

She kept telling herself that as she rode deeper into the desert that he loved.

SIXTEEN

The Black Sea

The crew of the *Riga* had talked about nothing else since MacKenzie told them about the upcoming duel with the *Lenin*. There were more opinions about the new captain and his recent actions than in a *banya* at World Cup time. However, the sides basically broke down into those who had begun to admire MacKenzie, feeling that he had demonstrated good seamanship in besting Karolov during their initial encounter and had showed deeper-than-had-been-suspected character by personally risking himself to get Karolov off their backs – and those who refused to forgive him for putting Karolov there in the first place, not to mention the collision that could have sunk them.

'I tell you that you are misjudging him,' said Purzov, with the rest of the off-duty crew in their quarters. The men were gathering there more often now that it smelled better. 'Yes, he can be *sukhoi*' – 'dry,' the word meant, without emotion – 'but not because he is without feelings. He just puts them aside to *do* things. It's different than the way we are.'

'He doesn't care a damn about any of us. It is the mission, only the mission,' Kutsky declared. 'We are things to be used and then discarded. He wouldn't risk a finger for one of us.'

'See? He divides us,' said Tartakov. 'First you think you're better than me. Then I think I'm better than you. Soon, what are we? Dogs fighting over scraps of meat and old bones. Just like Americans. Not comrades. Competitors.'

A radio tech named Vasilov shook his head. 'I don't

know. All the time the big shots tell us what to do, the *nomenklatura* get all the good posts, the stores, the upper ranks. It was just like Admiral Karolov to order us out of the way. Like we were just peasants and he was royalty. So what did MacKenzie really do? Told him to go to hell. Get out of *my* way for once. I tell you, fellows, it made me feel good to do it.'

'But look at the trouble we are in. The navy is a good career these days. Everyone else is starving. Does he care what trouble he has made for us?' demanded Tartakov.

'Already he has gotten the hearing postponed,' argued Purzov. 'If we beat the admiral, he will cancel it. The capteen is fighting for us. And he wants us to fight for ourselves. I tell you I think that's the truth of it.'

'I think we're going to hell,' said Kutsky flatly.

'I'll tell you what I feel bad about,' said Vasilov. 'We sat there last night and let those bastards from the *Lenin* beat him up without so much as a shout from us.'

'Raskin couldn't help him either,' said Tartakov. 'There were too many.'

'Raskin tried,' Kutsky said, guilt on his features, too. 'They held him. If it had been Raskin they attacked, I'd have done something. Maybe we should have anyway. I have to think more.'

'He is our captain. We should have had more pride,' said Vasilov. 'They spit on him, they spit on us.'

'The rules don't apply,' said Tartakov. 'He's not one of us.'

'Then why does he fight for us?' demanded Purzov. 'And if he saves our asses? What then? Will he be one of us then?'

'We will see,' pronounced Michman Rislov, having caught the gist of the conversation as he entered the room with the newest training schedule. He posted it on the bulkhead to a chorus of grumblings and groans. 'But I tell you this, comrades. If you do end up in hell, you will be the best trained corpses there. Drills in ten minutes. Go to your posts.'

MacKenzie received Garver's communiqué from Washington in his cabin. It only increased the pressure to get the men in fighting shape. He'd had less than the two weeks Garver had promised him to train *Riga*'s crew, and now there were less than ten days to Raza's doomsday. It was going to be damn tight. Too tight, maybe. Garver communicated quite clearly the general feeling that Raza would not hesitate to use the weapons. There were enough bodies lying around to support that theory. MacKenzie had to make the *Riga* battleworthy fast. Well, he was about to take the first step.

He had to have the officers first. They were the key. He couldn't go after the 'enlisted' men directly. No captain could. Any sense of a popularity contest was bad leadership and downright dangerous. One led by example. Pride, dignity, never settling for anything less than excellence – these things led to similar attitudes in the crew. But the officers were another matter. They understood more, saw beneath the surface of things. They might someday be in command themselves. The crew had to be shown, the officers had to be convinced.

Belief was the central issue. Everyone had to believe that the captain was the smartest sonofabitch above or below the sea, that he could protect them in battle or in an emergency and bring them back home safely. Under normal circumstances, your reputation preceded you. MacKenzie's combat exploits were well-known in the tightly knit, all-volunteer submarine service. You signed on with MacKenzie you were coming home. That counted when the pressure was on. It made the difference between hesitation and commitment – and that spread to the men like no other message. We are the smart ones and we believe; you can believe, too.

He had no reputation here. He was only someone who

disrupted their lives, got them into trouble, and hit another ship. His first victory, if pinging the *Lenin* aside could be called that, could well have been a fluke. He had to prove to them it wasn't. He had to prove to himself it wasn't, and that he wouldn't freeze in combat again. This time, Karolov knew he was coming. Karolov had the better ship and maybe the better crew. The difference was MacKenzie, and every officer on board the *Riga* knew it.

Which was why they all looked at him strangely when he ordered, 'All back emergency.'

'Capteen, with the *Lenin* tracking us?'

'Orders, Mr Raskin. Follow them.'

You couldn't do much in a submarine that made more noise than suddenly reversing spin on the main engine at high speed. It was a collision avoidance drill and it cavitated the water like a depth charge. A kid with a hearing aid could hear a sub half a mile away under a back emergency bell. To make matters worse, MacKenzie had been making as much noise as a tugboat captain all day. Ordinarily, even those officers and crew who weren't fans of his admired his deft touch at controlling the sub. Suddenly he had turned madly aggressive. He ran the cooling pumps at high speed and abruptly went from back emergency order to emergency surface and bounced *Riga* right up to the waves with the emergency blow. All of it created enough noise so Karolov would be able to pinpoint the exact location of the *Riga* any moment he cared to. By midmorning, even Raskin was wondering what the hell the captain was up to.

He finally asked. 'Peter, knowing you as I do by now, I am willing to believe you are up to something extremely tricky, but for the life of me I can not see what it is. Karolov must have a perfect firing solution on us.'

MacKenzie nodded. 'I think so, too. Judging from his track he's not being nearly as devious as if he didn't. Don't worry, we've got a fix on him, too. That new sonar is a wonder, Nikolai. I wish we had it.'

Raskin looked hapless. 'So you have Karolov and he has you. Given our relative strengths, isn't that a little like grabbing a bear and announcing you've got him?'

Chernin chuckled at his chart table. So did the diving officer Petrov. MacKenzie was glad they were paying attention.

'You could look at it like that, Nikolai,' he said. 'But let me ask you this, would it be better to run from the bear knowing he's faster and stronger and if he catches you he'll eat you?'

'I knew it,' Raskin said, pounding a railing happily. 'You *are* up to something.'

'Something,' agreed MacKenzie. 'That far I'll go. The rest you take on faith. Sonar, Conn. Give me a sweep of the area.'

'The *Lenin* is four miles east of us, speed ten knots, depth one hundred meters. The only other ship in the area is a Slava-class cruiser, course two eight zero. Speed fifteen knots.'

'Acknowledged. Conn out. Engineering, this is the captain.'

'Engineering, aye,' came back Chief Engineer Prudenkov's voice.

'Prepare to shut down the main reactor,' ordered MacKenzie. He could hear the other man start over the intercom.

'Did I hear you right, Capteen?'

'Shut her down,' MacKenzie ordered. 'We will be practicing emergency start-up procedures for the next hour.'

'Are you sure you . . . Aye, Capteen. Emergency start-up procedures.' There was some grumbling in Russian. 'Engine Room is ready.'

'More noise, Peter?' said Raskin, choosing not to translate and smiling at Prudenkov's self-censure.

'More noise,' MacKenzie agreed, 'and more practice.'

The ship could not be driven without the reactor on-line. The trick was to hover without propulsion by pumping

189

water in and out of the variable ballast tanks and using *Riga*'s emergency propulsion motor, a tiny motor driven by battery.

'All right, Michman. Let's keep her in trim,' ordered MacKenzie. He began to pump water in and out of the main tanks to stabilize the ship.

It went on like that for hours. After the emergency shutdown, MacKenzie had them running casualty drills, something the Russian seamen seemed totally at a loss over. MacKenzie increased the tempo of the drills. Slowly, the teamwork necessary to transport the 'wounded' had an effect. They were working together better than MacKenzie had ever seen them. In his opinion, the biggest weakness of the Soviet ship was that the men, mostly conscripts, were poorly motivated and woefully undertrained. As their proficiency increased, so did their self-respect and their pride in the ship.

It was close to noon.

'Make your depth three five meters, Mr Petrov,' MacKenzie ordered.

'Three five meters, aye,' echoed Petrov.

'Sonar, Conn. Sweep the area. Active sonar.'

'The *Lenin* is maintaining the same distance, Capteen. The Slava is moving out of the area, heading north. We're now picking up a tanker beginning to cut across the upper quadrant. She is twenty miles west of our position. Very noisy.'

'Should we warn it off?' asked Raskin.

'No. Course and speed on the tanker, Sonar.'

'Course one eight zero, heading due south, speed eight knots.'

MacKenzie said, 'Mr Chernin, I'm going to want some fast data from you when I ask.'

'I am ready, Capteen.'

'Eleven fifty-five hours,' Raskin announced.

'Capteen.' It was Golovskoy, the communications officer. 'This is from the *Lenin*.'

MacKenzie read the message and said lightly. 'It seems the good admiral is questioning our actions and my competence. He asks if we plan to make this a contest or just give up.'

'What is our reply, Capteen?' asked Golovskoy.

'Send this. "Catch us if you can." That's all.'

Golovskoy gave him a curious look. 'As you wish, Capteen.'

MacKenzie's hand flashed out and hit the battle stations alarm. Men ran to their positions who just days before would have walked. The ship had a charged feel. He picked up the intercom and dialed all-ship.

'This is the captain speaking. The time has come for us to be tested, and to test ourselves. This is what all the training has been about, all the tiresome drills. We are going into battle. The *Lenin* will be pursuing *Riga* with intent to harm us as if she were a real adversary. We all know what's riding on this. Remember it. For myself, I do not intend to let an overstuffed, pompous, braggart drink to anything tonight but a bad headache. You are warriors. We can achieve victory. Captain out.'

'One minute to mark,' said Raskin.

'Engine Room, prepare to answer all bells.'

'Engine Room, aye.'

'Helm, prepare to steer course two seven zero. On my order hard right rudder, we want to swing her fast.'

'Helm, aye.'

'Sonar, Conn. Where's the *Lenin*?'

'Still holding her course.'

Raskin said, 'Twelve hundred hours mark. The combat exercise is underway.'

'Start the engagement tapes, Mr Kortzov.'

'Tapes running, Capteen.'

'Engine Room, all ahead flank. Helm, hard right rudder. Steer course two seven zero. Mr Petrov, make your depth six five meters.'

'Six five meters, aye.'

'More noise,' Raskin observed as the Riga shot ahead at her top speed of over thirty knots. 'You're deliberately leaving a trail?'

'One that a baby could follow,' MacKenzie admitted. 'I've done a lot of thinking, Nikolai. It's an interesting situation from a tactical point of view. I'm at a bit of a loss not really knowing the capabilities of my own ship, much less his, so I tried to concentrate my strategy on the thing I do know. The man. Karolov's a bully. That's not hard to see. Sure, I know he must have his own complexities, and his dog probably thinks he's a helluva guy, but deep down he's a bully. And a coward. Someone so insecure that he has to physically dominate his crew to be sure he has the upper hand, someone who didn't get up to hit me till my arms were pinned behind my back, someone so afraid of me that he would attack my officers and crew with this hearing charade to get at me.'

'How do you know he is afraid of you?'

'His hatred. We always hate what we're most afraid of.'

'And what does this tell you?' Raskin asked, nodding.

'That he would welcome an easy victory. That even with all his professed disgust at my lack of professionalism, my making all this noise for so long, he'll secretly be happy thinking he's going to get an easy shot at us. Take home the brass ring in one grab. I wanted him to stay out in the open to show us how brave he is, how simple it's going to be, rather than making our job really hard by having to find him out here in the first place.'

'The admiral frightened . . . I never thought of him that way. What is he most afraid of, do you know?'

'Of me, of my being an American, of anyone showing him up – it's impossible to really know. But it's funny. I could forgive all that. Even the beating. What I can't forgive is that he went after my men to get at me. If I permit that I couldn't maintain anyone's respect, including my own.'

'Yes, I can see that,' said Raskin. 'So that's why all the

training, all the stress on winning. You are fighting him for the crew.'

'Reality is the judge. If we win there has to be merit in what I say. Now let's see if he took the bait. Sonar, Conn. What's the *Lenin* doing?'

'Coming after us at flank speed, Capteen.'

'I am impressed,' said Raskin.

'We have to be careful not to become a prisoner of our beliefs, Nikolai,' MacKenzie reflected, 'trapped by what we want to believe. He wants to believe we're afraid of him so it seems natural that we would run. Okay, now we take that belief away from him. Make him wonder. Mr Petrov, we are going deep. On my order make your depth six five zero meters. Five degrees down bubble. Very slow. No noise.'

'Six five zero meters, aye, Capteen. No noise.'

'That is very deep, Peter. Near crush depth.'

'Better to find out now if she'll hold than with the *Kentucky* on our tail. Engine Room. On my order, we will slow. Reduce speed to five knots and make minimum turns and go to natural flow on the reactor. We need to do it quickly and be careful of the big pressure transient.'

'Aye, Capteen. Dead slow. I'll watch the pipes.'

MacKenzie visualized Karolov in the control room of his faster ship, seemingly swooping down on the slower *Riga* like an avenging angel. They were a tantalizing target, one it seemed the admiral could not resist.

'Mr Raskin, rig for ultraquiet.'

'Ultraquiet, *da*.'

Now it was time to take it away from him, to plant the first seeds of doubt.

'Mr Petrov, take her down. Make your depth six five zero meters. Helm, all ahead dead slow. Engine Room, dead slow.'

'Six five zero meters. Ahead dead slow, aye.'

*   *   *

'Comrade Admiral, the *Riga* is suddenly slowing . . . their sounds are fading. We are losing contact.'

'What? Sweep the area. Active sonar. Maintain contact with them.'

Karolov banged the railing impatiently. For the last eight hours the American had been making enough noise to wake the dead. Then suddenly he goes silent? The change had caught sonar sleeping.

'No signal. We have lost him, Comrade Admiral. The change was completely unexpected.'

Karolov bit back a rebuke. What was the American up to? 'What was *Riga*'s last depth?'

'Sixty meters, Comrade Admiral. Course heading two seven zero.'

He was in the shallow zone. The Black Sea's hypersalinity often caused sonar problems. The American might know that, certainly Raskin would. So he might stay in the shallow zone. Especially if he found a thermal. Karolov flexed his hands and worked his thick forearms. His officers were watching him. They expected a victory. It was up to him to deliver one.

'Standard search pattern. Make our depth sixty meters. All ahead one third. Use passive sonars only. Rig for ultraquiet.'

For now the ocean was quiet, the prey hidden. The *Lenin* slowed to listen, moving forward cautiously.

The hunt was on.

'Mr Dainis, may I have a word with you?' MacKenzie beckoned to the security man. He had stepped into the conn to watch the activities.

'Certainly, Capteen.'

MacKenzie stepped out of the conn into the aft corridor. 'I don't know what your protocol is for discussing these things so I thought I'd step out here with you alone.'

'Very considerate. What is it?'

'I have to know more about the capabilities of the *Lenin*.'

194

MacKenzie put it bluntly. 'Does she have the new sonar?'

Dainis was going against the habits of his professional lifetime to be speaking about such things with an American officer but he responded with only the briefest hesitation. 'No, they do not. There is only one working prototype, the one installed on this ship. When it is time to go north, it will be disassembled and brought along with us to our new sub.'

'Thank you, Mr Dainis.'

'Not at all. I hope we will be victorious.'

MacKenzie reentered the conn.

'We are at ordered depth, Capteen,' Petrov reported. 'Six five zero meters.'

'Acknowledged. Sonar, what have you got?'

'We are still tracking the *Lenin*, Capteen. They are moving forward at ten knots on course two seven zero, slowing, then moving forward again. It sounds like they are searching for us. They are still in the shallow zone. The Slava is almost out of the area of engagement and the tanker is still heading south at eight knots. The area is clear of all other shipping.'

'Very good. Mr Chernin, now I need your good service.'

'Aye, Capteen.'

MacKenzie moved over to the chart table. 'Here's the problem. We are here' – he pointed to the chart – 'heading west. The *Lenin* is behind us, following, also heading west. The tanker is twenty miles northwest of our position, heading south. I want to take *Riga* in a long, slow loop that crosses the tanker's north-south axis and swings in from the far side back onto the tanker's course – one eight zero – matching her position just before the *Lenin* passes. Assuming she continues her present course and speed can you give me that?'

'I can, Capteen,' said Chernin, pushing his glasses higher on the bridge of his nose. 'It's a good problem.'

'I'm glad you like it, Mr Chernin. Sonar, Conn. Report.'

'The Slava has moved out of the area. The *Lenin* is still

on course two seven zero, patrolling in the middle zone now. The tanker remains on a southerly course at eight knots.'

'Mr Kortzov,' MacKenzie directed the dark haired young man whose intensity during both battle maneuvers belied his movie star looks and had increased MacKenzie's confidence in him. 'Prepare a constant fire control solution on *Lenin*. We'll simulate shooting two long-range ASW torpedoes.'

'Yes, Capteen. Constant solution. The tapes are running.'

'Capteen?' It was Chernin. 'Course plotted and ready to be laid in.'

'Very good, Mr Chernin. Let's move her slowly. Sonar, keep me abreast of *Lenin*'s movements.'

'I'm going to walk the boat, Peter,' Raskin advised him. 'Talk to the men.'

'Good idea, Nikolai. Tell them this is the tricky part.'

For the next eight hours, MacKenzie moved the *Riga* according to Chernin's calculations, turning the sub slowly, noiselessly, by small degrees, deep at six hundred and fifty meters. Chernin's course first led them west past the tanker's north-south axis, then they turned north and slid by the tanker at a distance of several miles, finally looping back south to parallel the tanker's course and speed.

There was visible strain in the men after so many hours of intense concentration. Sweat stains sprouted on shirts. The helmsman and planesman kept rubbing their hands on their pants legs to dry them. Michmen checked and rechecked their systems, legs cramped from working under consoles and in tight spaces. The officers knew their careers rested on the day's outcome. They would be forever marked having served on the *Riga*; that could not be changed. But would it be for the brilliant tactics that had defeated the famous Admiral Karolov in mock battle? Or for the recklessness of ideologically impure criminals who were court-martialed and sent to dead-end postings. An officer's life in the armed services was far better than an ordinary average citizen's. They were fighting not only for their careers, in many instances, they were fighting for the quality of the rest of their lives.

By the end of the maneuvers, the *Lenin* was several miles southeast. She had changed course several times, but always returned to two seven zero in the hope of picking up the *Riga*.

'Karolov refuses to budge,' Raskin said.

'What do you expect from an arm wrestler?' MacKenzie said, tired but in good spirits. 'Just let the good admiral come a few miles more and then we'll show him what the *Riga* can do.'

'They are working well for you, the crew,' Raskin said, pleased.

'Better than I hoped,' MacKenzie agreed. 'I'm going to need you soon, Nikolai. I'm as far inside Karolov's head as I can get. Knowledge of tactics, things a Soviet captain would do. You're going to have to help me with that.'

'Need me? That's a surprise.'

'I know we never talked about this,' MacKenzie said quietly. 'It was your ship and I took it. Does that stand between us?'

Raskin shook his head. 'Peter, I am a good captain, but I am not in your league. I'm simply not envious of the unattainable.'

'Then you'll help me?'

'It will cost you dinner,' Raskin said slyly. 'And drinks,' he added. 'I have confidence in you.'

'It's extortion. But it's a deal.'

'In that case I'm happy to help.'

'Thank you. Sonar, Conn. Range to tanker?' MacKenzie asked.

'One mile, Capteen. The noise level is very high. We can barely hear the *Lenin* closing, and only with the new sonar.'

'Then the *Lenin* must be having trouble so close to the tanker,' observed Raskin.

'Let's hope so. It's why we're here. Mr Chernin, my compliments. Very nice work.'

'Aye, Capteen. Thank you.'

'Mr Petrov, make our depth seven zero meters. Still very slow. Five degrees up bubble. We're going to come up directly under the tanker so no sudden moves. Keep us in trim. Mr Chernin, course and speed to put us under the tanker?'

'Twelve knots at one six five degrees, Capteen, and we'll overtake her.'

'Helm, ahead two thirds, Engine Room, make turns for twelve knots.'

'Turns for twelve knots, aye.'

MacKenzie picked up the intercom. 'This is the captain speaking. We have moved into our desired attack position and are about to commence the second phase of our battle plan. In a few moments we will be less than thirty meters under the tanker sailing directly above us. We will wait under cover there until the *Lenin* comes abreast of us and then commence to fall in astern of her. It is a precise set of maneuvers and to some degree dangerous. It's going to get pretty noisy with those big screws turning on top of us. But to comfort yourself, remember, what the *Lenin* can't hear, they can't shoot. Be alert. Captain out.'

The noise level in the control room increased markedly as *Riga* rose toward the surface less than one mile astern of the tanker and made enough speed to overtake it. MacKenzie's desired two hundred foot depth was actually misleading. Depth was measured from the keel at the bottom of the ship. Given the masts on top of *Riga*'s sail and the draft of the loaded tanker, the distance to the tanker was closer to half that.

'Conn, Sonar. We are now directly under the tanker.' The noise in the control room was deafening.

'Sonar, Conn, aye. Helm, steer course one eight zero degrees. Engine Room make turns for eight knots. Sonar, where is the *Lenin*?'

'Four thousand meters off the port bow, Capteen. Closing at ten knots. Still on course two seven zero.'

The noise added to the tension in the compartment. You could feel the heavy revolutions under your shoes, along your spine. Unconsciously, men hunched over from the sense of that great weight overhead.

'Very close quarters,' muttered Raskin.

'Going to get closer,' MacKenzie said. 'All right. Phase three. Nikolai, when the *Lenin* passes us we're going to fall in astern of her. Close follow, we call it.'

'How close?'

'Under a thousand meters.'

'A thousand . . . but why? We have a shot now,' Raskin said. 'Why not fire from under this noisy bucket of bolts sonar kindly calls a ship.'

'Because we have not yet demonstrated one important thing,' MacKenzie said firmly.

'You have him now,' protested Raskin. 'What could be more important that that?'

'Excellence.'

The Russian shook his head mournfully. 'God help us. A fanatic.'

'You might as well get used to it. Like Al Jolson used to say, you ain't seen nothing yet.'

'This Jolson was one of your military heroes, I suppose.'

'Possibly the greatest.' MacKenzie let it lie. But there it was again, he thought to himself. A secret smile inside him that felt damn good after the months of vacuum. If birth was the only thing that stood against death, humor was the one that stood against life. What had he found on board this submarine that made him want to live again?

'Sonar, Conn. Thirty seconds to *Lenin* crossing our track.'

'Distance to her track?'

'Three thousand meters.'

'Helm, stand by to come to course two seven zero.'

'Helm, aye.'

'Mark,' Sonar reported. '*Lenin* dead ahead.'

'Very well. Helm, all ahead full. Sonar, Conn. Continuous bearings to *Lenin*.'

'Conn, Sonar, aye. Two hundred degrees . . . two hundred ten degrees . . . two hundred twenty degrees . . .'

'Right full rudder. Come to new course two seven zero,' ordered MacKenzie. 'Sonar, keep those cards and letters coming.'

'Capteen?'

'Constant reports.'

'Aye, Capteen.'

The *Lenin* passed in front of them and MacKenzie slid the *Riga* out from under the tanker in a fast curve and moved in astern of it. It was as deft a maneuver as any a more modern Los Angeles-class sub could manage. As silent as a sea snake, MacKenzie put his sub behind the *Lenin*. Obscured by the noise of the tanker and its own propellors, the bigger sub was totally unaware the *Riga* was there.

American sub captains called the maneuver 'riding inside his baffles.' There were cone-shaped areas, from thirty to sixty degrees off the sub's main stern line, where sonar could not hear, called baffles. If you snuck your boat into that dead area the enemy sub was deaf to your presence. However, it was a dangerous maneuver. A thousand meters or less was a very short distance to stop a sub almost the size of a football field, so there was a constant danger of collision. MacKenzie held his fears in check. He could not afford another one.

'Distance two thousand meters to *Lenin*,' reported sonar.

'Acknowledged.'

'Steady on course two seven zero, Capteen,' said the helm.

'Very well. Steer two six five degrees.'

'I have never been in this close,' Raskin said. 'It makes my stomach hurt.'

MacKenzie wanted to tell him it made his own stomach hurt. He patted him on the back instead. 'Stop anticipating dinner and pay attention. Next time you may be the one to run this maneuver.'

'God forbid,' said Raskin sincerely.

'Fifteen hundred meters, Capteen. Closing. Now bearing two seven five degrees.'

'Very well. Steer course two eight zero degrees. All ahead two thirds. Engine Room, make one hundred and ten turns,' ordered MacKenzie. He looked over to Raskin. 'Okay, Nikolai,' he said. 'You're a Soviet captain. Think the way Karolov thinks. How often is he going to clear his baffles?'

Raskin considered. 'I would expect a depth change any minute. More than likely he will drop thirty meters. Anticipate something maybe every twenty minutes or so. And watch for a quick high-speed turn. He could come back on you. Or a full stop to hear if you're there.'

'Right.'

MacKenzie picked up the intercom. 'This is the captain. We are now in position directly behind the *Lenin*, right on his tail. Remain alert. We will be in close follow for the next several hours moving back and forth across his baffles. Captain out.'

'Peter?' Raskin was watching the sonar scope. 'I think he's descending.'

'Take us down slowly, Mr Petrov. One zero zero meters.'

'One zero zero meters, aye, Capteen.'

'Watch her, Peter. He's been holding this course too long. I think – ' As if in response to his words, suddenly Kotnikov called out.

'They are turning to port,' he called from the sonar room.

MacKenzie was ready thanks to Raskin's warning. 'Right ten degrees rudder. Steady . . . Keep it coming, Mr Kotnikov.

'New course heading . . . one nine zero. Depth one two zero meters.

'Helm, shift your rudder, steer new course one nine five.

201

Mr Petrov, make your depth one two five meters. All ahead full. Keep it tight. Stay with him.

'Steady on course one nine five. At one two five meters.

'One thousand meters closing . . . nine hundred . . . eight hundred . . .

'All ahead two thirds. Engine Room, make one hundred and ten turns.'

'Engine Room, aye.'

MacKenzie looked around the control room. The men were calm and capable, their performance crisp. So much had been accomplished in a few short days. Close following another sub was a difficult and exacting maneuver. They had just demonstrated their ability. Another few hours of this and they would be as proficient as he could expect.

Then he'd spring the rest on them.

'So, what do you think now?' said Purzov, in the washroom on a break. 'Karolov begins by following us and the captain ends up following him. Right on his tail.'

Kutsky dried his face. 'I have to admit there is something different around here. I feel it myself.'

'This capteen is smart, I admit that,' said Vasilov, the radio tech. 'Karolov must be boiling looking for us by now.'

'Do you think Karolov would hold the hearing anyway?' wondered Purzov aloud.

'It wouldn't be the first time we were lied to,' said Vasilov.

'Let's get home first,' said Kutsky. 'I prefer to worry over my vodka.'

'Over vodka nobody worries,' said Vasilov.

'Precisely,' said Kutsky, tossing his towel into the bin and heading back to the torpedo room.

Karolov was indeed boiling. In fact he was close to apoplexy. It was close to the end time for the engagement and he was no closer to finding the *Riga*. It had disappeared off his screens and never returned.

He was alert for the slightest noise. The tanker had seemed a good bet and he had tried to slip in and make a fast turn to see if the American was lurking there, but sonar hadn't picked up anything in all that noise.

Going active was too big a gamble. It might be just the game the American was playing, outwaiting him, perhaps sitting on the bottom and waiting for *Lenin* to get impatient and expose itself with active sonar, then come in for the kill. Karolov was not going to risk it.

He would do the opposite. 'All stop,' he ordered.

'Capteen, they are shutting down the engines!'

'All stop!' yelled MacKenzie. 'Right full rudder.' Here there was danger. Echoes of the previous day came rushing back to haunt him. Had he stopped and turned the *Riga* in time, or would they crash into the *Lenin* ahead? 'Rudder amidships.'

The systems in *Riga* came to a standstill. The sea was suddenly quiet. *Lenin*'s sonar would be functioning with maximum efficiency. MacKenzie had to wonder if Karolov had heard them in the instant it had taken him to react. A collision was the bigger fear. It could be enough to sink both ships. MacKenzie waited. The crew had reacted as fast as he could have hoped. But was it enough? All over the ship men held their breath and waited. They knew what Karolov was doing. The two submarines moved silently through the sea, drifting slowly and inevitably into one another. It was terrifying.

'Capteen, *Lenin* is underway again bearing one eight five degrees,' said Kotnikov's relieved voice. Men let out their breaths. 'Speed two thirds,' Kotnikov advised.

'All ahead two thirds,' MacKenzie ordered. 'Left full rudder steady course one eight zero degrees. Continue close follow.'

'Capteen?' It was Kotnikov, coming from sonar. 'I would not ordinarily speak, but, well . . . you said . . . you wanted . . .'

'Go ahead, Mr Kotnikov.'

'I have been watching the *Lenin* closely. Admiral Karolov might be trying a slow drift. Perhaps as little as a degree a minute. That way he could clear his baffles and we might not notice.'

Raskin looked at MacKenzie. 'It's one of our tactics. All it takes is five degrees or so.'

'Mr Kotnikov, stay right on him. If there's the slightest course deviation I want to know about it.'

'He has slid right to course one nine two, Capteen. It . . . I mean, I noticed.'

'Acknowledged and well-done,' MacKenzie said to Kotnikov gratefully. 'Helm, come to course one eight five. Stay sharp. It looks like the *Lenin* is executing a slow turn to starboard to clear her baffles. Mr Kotnikov, keep me informed of any changes.'

'Aye, Capteen.'

It was almost twenty-four hundred hours.

'Nikolai? I think we've gotten about as much out of this as we're going to.'

'It has been a harrowing day,' said Raskin, mopping his brow tiredly.

'*Spaseeba*, Nikolai.' Thank you. He meant it sincerely.

'You're welcome. Twenty-three fifty,' Raskin said. 'Time?'

'Yes, it is. Mr Kotnikov, active sonar. Maximum power. Continuous ping. Let them know we're here. Then lay a course for home.'

The shriek of *Riga*'s sonar tore through the *Lenin*'s control room. Karolov and all the others grabbed their ears in pain. His men looked as if they had been betrayed, then turned back to their instruments quickly. But Karolov had seen. It coursed through him like a hot acid.

'Where?' he demanded.

The sonar operator had torn his headset off to avoid ear damage but he had heard enough. 'Directly astern of us, less than three hundred meters.'

Karolov was stunned. So they had been in his baffles all along. How had they managed it? Worse, how long had they waited there, testing themselves against him and continually avoiding his every move to detect them? His rage was a bowel-clenching thing inside him and he felt a flush tinge his skin hotly.

'The *Riga* is turning back to port,' Sonar reported.

The crew was watching him. He had set out to beat the American and the American had beaten him instead, beaten him soundly and everyone knew it. Word of it would spread all over the fleet. He would be a laughing stock.

He felt eyes on his back like driven spikes.

It was not over yet.

MacKenzie walked the ship to speak to the men. It was hard to tell when they had crossed the line together to become captain and crew, but it had happened. There were smiles where there had been blank faces, warmth where there had been distance. Sometimes they talked about home towns. Or families. Distances were bridged. Gulfs narrowed. Some of them asked him questions about himself. He tried to answer as honestly as he could, asked questions in return.

The loudspeaker crackled. 'Capteen, it is Raskin. Could you come to the control room?'

MacKenzie heard concern in Raskin's voice and ran back hurriedly.

'What is it, Nikolai?' he asked as soon as he entered the compartment.

'The *Lenin* is close by. Too close if you ask me. Maybe Karolov is not calling things off so easily.'

'Capteen,' called out Kotnikov's worried voice. 'The *Lenin* is coming straight at us. Collision course.'

MacKenzie felt the icy tendrils of fear again, but this time it was easier to fend them off. Karolov was replaying things from the beginning, wanting to force him off course.

Several maneuvers went through MacKenzie's mind but there was nothing to be gained from engaging the admiral again. The best bet was to get out of there and go home.

'Emergency deep,' he ordered. 'Twenty degrees down bubble. Make our depth three hundred meters. All ahead slow. Call it out, Mr Petrov.'

'Depth one hundred,' called out Petrov. '. . . two hundred fifty . . .'

The throb of the engines died as the *Riga* quieted. Everyone grabbed a railing to hold on to as the deck angle increased.

'Sonar, where is the *Lenin*?' asked MacKenzie.

'Still in the shallow zone, Capteen. We may have lost them.'

'Very good.' Evidently, Karolov hadn't expected him to run. What character flaw caused him not to be able to put it down?

'We are at ordered depth, Capteen.'

'Level off. Zero bubble. Mr Chernin . . .'

The angle of the sub did not decrease. MacKenzie spun around and saw the planesman fighting with his control yoke.

'Capteen,' the man called out in alarm. 'Jam dive. Jam dive!'

'Depth,' MacKenzie demanded.

'Five hundred meters . . . five hundred ten . . .' Petrov called out.

The planes were jammed in a down angle and they couldn't stop the dive. They were already very deep. The planes had to be fixed immediately.

'Engine Room, all emergency back. Keep that plant on line. Nikolai, get men forward to the hydraulics. We'll have to manually shift the planes and pump them back to zero. Move! Mr Petrov, I want to hear our depth. Mr Chernin, you have the conn. Tell the chief he's got to keep that plant on-line no matter what.'

'Aye, Capteen.'

206

'Blowing forward emergency ballast,' MacKenzie said, grabbing the blue lever and yanking hard. He felt the ship slow, but the momentum of their plunge was too great. He needed those planes.

MacKenzie ran as fast as he could down the narrow corridor. For all his bulk, Raskin was out ahead of him, grabbing the men he had already selected in his mind. MacKenzie heard him yell for Kutsky in the torpedo room, a radio tech named Vasilov, Michman Rislov, and a cook named Maryk.

'Five hundred sixty meters,' came Petrov's voice over the all-ship. The engines were screaming. Men stared after MacKenzie as he ran. They knew from the deck angle and the depth something was wrong.

MacKenzie got to the forward cabin first and ripped at the manual control valves for the starboard plane. It could be mechanical or hydraulic or even something physical holding the planes in their down angle. He shifted the valves, but the system was different from an American sub. Where was the handle for the mechanical pump?

'Here, let me.' Taskin shouldered him aside, reached in and extended a red lever. 'Kutsky, you.'

Kutsky grabbed it and began to pump with all his might. Sweat broke out on his face but it gave only the tiniest bit.

'Six hundred meters,' came Petrov's voice.

Raskin was already on the other side of the compartment shifting the valves for the port plane. Again he found the pump lever and extended it. 'Rislov.'

The men struggled to move the planes manually. Raskin had to crawl between their legs to get more leverage. MacKenzie grabbed hold of it along with Vasilov and they both began pumping. Raskin and Maryk took the other.

The noise of the engines was still a loud whine in full reverse as they desperately worked to stop the *Riga*'s mad plunge. It wasn't enough.

'Six hundred thirty meters,' came Petrov's voice.

Every inch of movement of the big planes required

MacKenzie and Vasilov to pump the hydraulic fluid into the holding cylinder. Sweat cascaded from them, getting in their eyes, making their hands slippery. Crewmen wiped towels across their faces so they could see. More worked their way in close to tend to the struggling men.

Kutsky strained like Sampson at the pillars. His shirt was plastered to his body and huge muscles bunched like mountains under his skin. His veins were blue snakes looking ready to burst. The planes moved another inch. MacKenzie stole a glance at Raskin. They were making progress, but it was too slow. He bent back to his task, straining at the pump handle.

'Seven hundred fifty meters,' came Petrov's voice, shaky for the first time. They were deeper than ever before, well below crush depth.

'Push,' MacKenzie grunted, rising to work the plane handles with Kutsky. Together they made it move. This was the man he had made clean the deck with a toothbrush the first day but there was only gratitude in the big man's eyes. He looked near to collapsing but he never stopped pulling. The hull was popping and groaning. The planes moved another inch.

'Eight hundred meters,' came Petrov's strained voice.

'Almost . . . almost . . . Don't let up,' MacKenzie exhorted Kutsky. Side by side they strained at the lever fighting the pressure of the dive on the planes.

'Eight hundred meters,' came Petrov's voice. MacKenzie thought he heard a note of hope in it for the first time but he couldn't be sure.

'Almost at zero,' he heard Raskin grunt from the other side of the compartment.

MacKenzie shook his head to fling the sweat from his eyes. Someone wiped his face again. The muscles in his back were on fire. He pulled on, unable to see through salty tears. Never quit, he heard Justine say. Never quit. There was no winning, just never quitting. He wrenched the lever up with such force that Kutsky grunted in surprise. Kutsky planted his feet to get a better grip. They fought the plane up another inch.

'Capteen . . . we're slowing! Eight hundred ten meters!'

For the first time MacKenzie realized that the angle of the deck was almost back to zero. They were deep, too deep. The hull was popping like mad and the deck felt like the compression was going to snap it any minute, but they were leveling off.

'Zero position,' yelled Raskin.

They kept pumping. 'Up angle,' said MacKenzie finally.

'Six hundred seventy meters,' came Petrov's voice, and now they could hear the excitement in it. 'Six hundred . . . five hundred . . .'

The men cheered. It rang throughout the ship. They pounded each other on the back. MacKenzie would have pounded someone, too, if he'd had the strength, but all he could do was sink down to the deck next to Kutsky who was already lying there gulping air like a stranded fish. Raskin and the others rolled over on their backs, helpless.

It was a good feeling to live, MacKenzie thought lying there. Everything felt sharper, keener. The steel deck under his head, the sounds of the men, the smell of sweat and exhalations, these were the foundations. Crewmen helped him to stand, swaying. Weak-kneed, he was unprepared for the bear hug Raskin threw around him.

'We did it, Peter.' He laughed, continuing on in Russian in his excitement.

'What did you say?' MacKenzie asked, too weak to break the hold.

'I said I would like to get my hands on that bastard's neck.' Raskin laughed. 'But right now I feel too good to care.'

MacKenzie clapped the big man on the back. 'Put me down, you big ape. I think my back's broken.'

Kutsky, Vasilov, Michman Rislov, Maryk were on their feet now. They were bedraggled but recovering. MacKenzie put a hand on the big torpedoman's shoulder. 'Kutsky, if you weren't the ugliest man on board I swear I'd kiss you.'

Kutsky roared with laughter along with the others. 'Capteen,' he said when he could finally speak, 'from you I would accept it.'

MacKenzie smiled and walked over to the intercom. 'Sonar, this is the captain. Any contacts?'

'The area is clear, Capteen. No sign of the *Lenin*.'

'Acknowledged. Nikolai, radio ahead and get a repair crew to meet us. See what fouled the planes.'

'Aye, Peter.'

'And make sure our stores are full. The backup systems, I want a complete reinventory . . .'

Still talking, they helped each other back to the control room.

Only a few days to war, MacKenzie thought as they walked.

They would be ready.

SEVENTEEN

Odessa

MacKenzie sat at a side table in the Storm-at-Sea, drinking with Raskin. A long hot shower in the Odessa Hotel had relieved most of his recurring muscular soreness, and the day's victory put him in a more positive frame of mind than he could remember. A lot of his men were in the bar. The difference between this and the previous night was easily noticeable. Not one, officer or crew, had passed by without a warm hello, *Zdrah'stvooite*, Capteen, or Good evening, *Do'breen ve'cher*, Capteen. There was audible laughter and merriment at their crowded tables as they basked in the aftermath of victory. Word was spreading. His men pointed to him with newfound pride. Other sailors stopped to talk with them, often looking MacKenzie's way. Quite a few bought him and Raskin drinks. As the hours passed, the number of glasses on their table had grown to a precipitous height.

'I've got to stop this,' MacKenzie told Raskin. 'There's a name for it in my country.'

'Good cheer?' Raskin said innocently.

'Alcoholism.'

'Consider it a bond between us,' Raskin said. 'Peter, I wish to say something. Maybe if we were not so drunk I would not. You have accomplished something very remarkable in a very short time. Frankly, I did not think it was possible.'

'Franky, neither did I,' MacKenzie admitted, wondering where he put that *l*.

'Your victory over Karolov was brilliant. Even more important was the way you saved us today. We could have all died at that depth. The men know it. They are yours now.'

'You are a very rare man, Nikolai. Generous when most others are selfish. Broad-minded in a time of increasing pettiness. I have found a great friend in you. No matter what comes, I will treasure that.'

'I, too, Peter. And to cement our friendship, I drink.'

Both downed another vodka, munching on dark bread. 'Ah,' said Raskin delightedly, 'our friend from the other night.'

MacKenzie twisted around. It was the singer from the Odessa Hotel. He strummed a few chords, ones MacKenzie recognized.

'Vysotsky, again,' he said.

'You have a very good ear,' Raskin complimented him.

The place quieted. The singer spoke for a few moments as he softly strummed his guitar. Raskin translated. 'He is quoting Vysotsky. "Poets walk on a knife-edge and cut their soul to ribbons. Truth is a force which pierces the heart." '

The singer began, reaching for Vysotsky's hoarse baritone.

> *Up in the blue sky*
> *pierced by the cupolas*
> *bronze bells, brave bells*
> *now joyous, now enraged.*
> *Cupolas in Russia*
> *are gilded with pure gold*
> *so that God*
> *will see them more often ...*

MacKenzie felt it come over him, the melancholy for which there was no name, the soul numbing sadness he had outdistanced in the last few days but never quite escaped. It was odd to see so many hard men in the bar singing softly, some barely moving their dry, cracked lips from which smoldering cigarettes dangled limply. Tears streamed freely down unshaven faces. Men stroked their beards and looked into their glasses for portents. Vysotsky's song grew deeper, sadder.

> *Along the road*
> *things aren't right*
> *and at the end they're worse.*
> *Not churches. Not bars,*
> *nothing is gained.*
> *No, my friends,*
> *things aren't right.*
> *Not right, friends.*
> *One more time.*
> *Many, many more times.*
> *Nothing's right . . .*

MacKenzie felt his own tears coming but blinked them back. He could not cry here. The feelings grew stronger. An irresistible force pulled him into himself and suddenly he was not in the bar, he was behind the wheel and . . . *He could see them standing on the corner by the traffic light. In front of a grocery store. The woman was holding her little girl with one hand and clutching her coat together with the other. The little girl looked up and saw the car coming at her. Her face creased into a smile. Look, Mommy, she must have said, look at the nice car . . .*

He pressed his face into his hands trying to stop the memories.

'Peter, as a friend, let me speak.'

'Nikolai, please . . . I can't now . . .'

Raskin plunged on. 'We captains are good judges of character. We have to be. Anyone can be taught to know the sea. To know men' – he shrugged – 'that is harder. From the beginning I have seen something bothering you. Something deep inside. A pain. A memory, perhaps. Let it go, Peter. It is consuming you.'

MacKenzie tossed back another drink. It was like raw fire in his belly.

'What is it?' Raskin asked softly.

The guitar strummed louder and more men were singing now, a long slow chant that could have been a funeral dirge but for the sharp demanding beat that got faster and faster. Men stamped on the floor and pounded tables. Most were crying freely now, unashamed of the raw emotion, and finally in this place MacKenzie couldn't fight the ghosts anymore.

'I was driving in a snowstorm,' he began, 'a sudden, freak thing. No one was prepared for it. A car went out of control and came straight at me. I managed to avoid it but I lost control of my own car.' His eyes were haunted, seeing the scene again. 'There was a mother and her little girl on a corner in front of a grocery store. The little girl saw my car coming but she didn't understand it was out of control. I saw her, Nikolai. She was smiling. Then her mother looked up and she knew I was going to hit them. All this took place in a split second. I did everything I could to pull the car away, but I had no traction. It was a solid sheet of ice. A split second. I don't even remember the crash. Just the look on the mother's face when she realized what was happening and she dropped her packages to grab her little girl and then . . . nothing.

'I woke up in the hospital. I was badly broken up. The steering wheel had caved in my chest. My ribs and collarbone were broken and so was my left arm. My spleen had ruptured. It almost killed me but they got me to a table quick and managed to remove it. My face was a mess from the broken glass. I had tubes in my throat and in my arms. I was filled with morphine and who knows what else. It was like floating, but the pain was waiting behind the clouds every time I woke up. I never knew there could be such pain.'

MacKenzie felt tears coursing down his face. For the first time in his life he made no move to stop them. He hadn't cried freely since he was a child. Sobs shook his chest and he had to stop for a moment. His breathing was ragged when he continued.

'I asked about the woman and her daughter, Nikolai. The doctors told me both had survived. I can't tell you how much better that made me feel. I could handle my own pain if they were both okay. They told me the mother had been released with minor injuries. The daughter was in the children's wing, recovering. She would be fine, too. They swore it to me.

'I don't know why, Nikolai, but somehow in all that fog I wanted to see the little girl. Maybe just to say I was sorry. Maybe to tell her to get well soon. I don't know how I managed it but I got out of bed and used the IV stand for a crutch and stumbled down to the ward. It was late at night. No one was around or they would have stopped me ... I wish they had, Nikolai. My God, how I wish they had. The little girl was in her bed asleep. She looked just as cute and pretty as I remembered from that brief moment when I saw her on the corner. I was so relieved. It would all be okay. All my life it had always been okay. I had escaped again. Her sheet was rumpled, she had thrown it partly off during the night. I picked it up to cover her ... She had no legs, Nikolai. Oh, dear God, she had no legs! They hadn't wanted to tell me. The car had crushed her and they had to amputate both of them. Sure she'd be getting out, but not walking. That's what I had done to her.'

'Peter ... '

'I don't remember what happened. It was a long time before I was really conscious again. I must have fallen. They got me back in my bed. All the drugs. All the morphine and anti this and that. Whenever I had the strength I ripped out the tubes. Finally they had to strap me down. Anxiety reaction they said. Posttraumatic stress. Nikolai, I knew. I knew it back then. I wanted to die. I tried to die. That does something to you. It changes you. I ended up losing some central core of happiness that had always sustained me. I never got it back again.'

'But you knew it was not your fault. It was an accident.'

'Sure, I knew. But what did that really change? You see, I had learned something. Something terrible.'

'Peter, I am so sorry.'

MacKenzie drank another vodka and plunged on. 'You know what I realized? That when we are born God places us on the starting line and gives us a gentle push and says go. And we trot off all innocent and unharmed and begin our lives. But what we don't know is that thirty seconds later he places a slavering, grinning horrid monster on that same starting line and points to us and says "Go!" to that monster, too. All our lives that monster is thirty seconds behind us, running after us, hoping to catch up, trying its damnedest to get to us. Some people it catches early. Like my wife. Or crack babies. Or that little girl. Others, we are the fools who go along believing we're somehow in charge, or we're lucky, or God forbid our arrogance, we have some control over our lives. That is the ultimate conceit, that we make things happen. But then the thirty seconds diminishes and we find that monster in our laps and we are never the same again.'

'For the first time you felt despair.'

'Yes.'

'And you think you are less of a man for trying to kill yourself, even though you were out of your mind with pain and remorse and drugs.'

'Yes.'

'Then you are a fool.' Raskin lifted his glass. 'And because of it I will drink to you.'

MacKenzie shook his head. 'I don't understand.'

'Peter, look around you. What do you see? Why do these grown men cry? Do you think Russians drink like there is no tomorrow just because we like the taste?'

'No . . . I . . . don't know.'

'It is because we have *always* known that grinning

216

monsters are right behind us. That is the truth of the Russian soul. That is why Vysotsky touches you. Why he was a national hero, handed from person to person on cassette tapes recorded on tiny players in dark clubs till millions were in existence even though he was never even officially recognized. For most of us that grinning monster is a partner from birth, a twin. Our painful heritage. But this we have learned. That any day the monster does not come to see you is a day to savor. So we drink. Because he is coming and he comes to us all. So drink. Because he has not yet come for you and if God loves you even more than his own son he may never catch up until you are in your grave and the monster stands there with a puzzled look that you were one he could not catch. So drink. Because one day is all you get. And today we did not die.'

Raskin stood and took MacKenzie in his huge arms, holding his friend while the sobs racked his body. 'Let it out, Peter. Strong men can not forget to grieve. Russians know that. Sadness is our national heritage.'

'Capteen Raskin?' It was Chernin, and Kotnikov was with him. They both looked concerned. 'Is the capteen all right?'

Raskin nodded gently. 'The captain is all right. He is very drunk. In the morning he will feel much better than he has in a long time. A fine thing has happened. He came here to make us Americans and in the process we end up making him Russian. Get him some coffee, comrades.'

'Of course. We will tell the others. They were worried.'

'Do that.' Raskin set MacKenzie back down into his seat. He sat there limply, mostly within himself now that the storm was over. Chernin and Kotnikov came back with the coffee and set it down in front of him with some food. MacKenzie looked at it idly.

'Capteen,' Chernin began. 'What you did today. The men . . . Well, we will not forget it.'

'Thank you, Mr Chernin. Is that for me?'

'Yes, Capteen. It will make you feel better.'

'Only a bullet to the head would do that.'

Kotnikov smiled. 'You are joking already. That is good. The vodka is very strong if you are not used to it.'

MacKenzie smiled weakly. 'So Doctor Raskin tells me. What do I say for this one, Nikolai? For the second time today.'

'How do you feel?'

MacKenzie thought it over. 'Lighter,' he said. 'For the first time, lighter.'

'Good. That's your thirty-second head start back. Try not to lose it again.'

'I'll try.' He drank the coffee.

Raskin waved Chernin and Kotnikov back to their seats, but Chernin stopped short.

'Capteen, look.'

For the second time in two nights, Karolov and his officers walked into the bar. This time he had also brought some of his crew, about a dozen men in all. It looked like he had screened them for pituitary cases. Not one was under two hundred pounds. Men carry themselves a certain way when they are looking for a fight. All of Karolov's men were primed. So was Karolov.

Raskin said quickly, 'Let's get out of here before there is more trouble. Help me with the captain.'

Chernin reached for MacKenzie's arm, but it was too late. Karolov didn't even make a pretense of having another agenda. He strode over and stood in front of them.

'You cheated today,' he said loudly.

The singer stopped playing and the bar stilled. Most of the sailors knew of the conflict by now. Tension built like hydraulic pressure.

Karolov said again, 'You cheated and began your run before the appointed time. Therefore the victory was mine.'

Raskin wasn't sure MacKenzie had heard Karolov. He just sat there looking drunk and washed-out with the smallest of smiles on his face and an odd light in his eyes. For all Raskin knew, he could have been unconscious.

'Did you hear me? I say you cheated.'

MacKenzie looked at Raskin. 'Have Mr Kortzov report to me.' Raskin was reassured by the steadiness and clarity of MacKenzie's voice. He nodded and disappeared into the crowd.

'How can you sit there and be insulted? Did you hear what I said?' demanded Karolov.

MacKenzie pushed his chair back. 'Everyone in Odessa probably heard what you said. Be quiet for a moment. You are not helping my headache. Mr Kortzov?'

Kortzov stepped out of the crowd that had formed around the admiral and MacKenzie. 'Yes, Capteen?'

'Did you bring the engagement tapes I asked for?'

'Yes, Capteen.' He handed them over.

'Admiral,' MacKenzie said. 'Do you want to call me a liar again or should we play these tapes for everybody and see who better deserves the title?'

Karolov turned pale. 'You ... you could have faked them,' he stuttered.

'Ah, but your men know I didn't. And they'll soon be talking. And my men know I didn't and they're already talking. You're the worst form of crawling sea life, Karolov. You know you haven't got the guts to be decent so the only way you can live with yourself is by trying to crush the decency in others.'

Raskin murmured to Chernin. 'That was quite a speech. I thought he was drunk.'

'He obviously has Russian blood,' Chernin said proudly. 'What else can explain such a remarkable constitution?'

'Give me those tapes,' Karolov demanded.

'Care to try and take them from me?' MacKenzie said softly. The tension increased. Karolov's men moved in tighter, elbowing people out of their way.

MacKenzie felt something go by his head fast but didn't have the time or the reflexes to duck. It would have caught him if not for Torpedoman Kutsky. Out of the corner of his eye, he saw Kutsky move as fast as quicksilver and block him with his own body. There was the smack of a hard object hitting Kutsky's flesh and a soft grunt, then Kutsky actually lifted the man off his feet and flung him over the heads of Karolov's men. He crashed and lay still. Kutsky winked happily at MacKenzie and pocketed the sap which had been meant for his captain's head.

Karolov's men surged, but it wasn't like the first night. MacKenzie heard chairs move and his men filled the empty space behind him. The presence of his crew was a fine feeling. Kutsky remained on his right, standing lightly on his feet, fists balled.

'Standoff,' MacKenzie said.

'My men will throw yours into the sea,' Karolov threatened.

'Yeah, yeah. And my dad can lick yours. You are one tiring asshole, you know?' He took the revolver that he had drawn from *Riga*'s armory out from under his coat and leveled it at Karolov. The trigger cocked with a sharp click that was very loud in the tightly packed room. Everybody stopped.

'You still won't fight your own battles, will you?' MacKenzie said, shaking his head sadly. 'Karolov, if so much as one more of your men moves I'll drop you right where you stand. I figured with your being such a good sport and all, I should be more prepared than last time.'

'You claim you knew I would be here?' Karolov scoffed.

'Slime behaves in a predictable manner,' MacKenzie said flatly. 'You'd probably like to reinstate the hearing, too, but you can't. After what the tapes show today, you're an embarrassment to your own superiors.'

Karolov reddened. But he made no move to go after him. 'I want those tapes. You are not leaving here with them. Regardless of the gun.'

'Tell you what,' MacKenzie said, coming around the table to stand face-to-face with Karolov. 'I don't want to see anybody hurt. You want these tapes. What say we arm wrestle for them?'

It was probably the moment Karolov had been waiting for all his life. He positively beamed. 'Of course. You want to test me. It will be my pleasure.'

Raskin looked at him like he was crazy. So did Chernin – a very intelligent little man, MacKenzie was learning. It pleased him, however, that most of his officers and men looked like they thought he could actually beat this monster.

'Let me explain the rules to you,' Karolov began.

'No, Admiral, let *me* explain the rules to *you*,' MacKenzie said easily.

Not the hard parts, dear, Justine used to say while she was teaching him. *Hit the hard parts and you only hurt your hands. The soft parts are best*. It bothered him to disregard such sound advice, but MacKenzie knew this punch had to be a bell ringer because it was the only one he was going to get. He put everything into it, bringing it straight off his hip like she had taught him, getting all his weight into it, coming up from the balls of his feet and swinging through his hips and shoulders. As a sucker punch it was a dandy. Karolov never saw it coming. MacKenzie's fist exploded into his jaw propelled by all his dislike of the man and a raging anger at what he had tried to do to the men of the *Riga*, which included nearly sending them to their graves. He had never thrown a punch like it. Karolov's eyes rolled up into his head and he careened backward off his feet, crashing through the bar's big front window and falling out into the street. He lay there unmoving.

No one else budged. MacKenzie turned to an astonished Raskin who was still taking in the events of the previous thirty seconds. 'You didn't really think I was going to arm wrestle him, Nikolai, did you?'

Raskin burst into laughter. It was infectious. Kutsky roared. It convulsed Chernin and then spread to Kotnikov, Kortzov and all the rest until it filled the bar. Karolov's men remained where they were, seething. MacKenzie still had the gun.

He put the engagement tapes on the table. 'Gentlemen, Captain Raskin and I are going back to the hotel. We have plans to make for the morning's sail. Anyone else coming?'

It was little Chernin who spoke up. 'Capteen, we will be along later. There is a, er . . . bill to settle from last night. Is that all right?'

'Of course, Mr Chernin. Have a pleasant time. We sail promptly at ten.'

'Aye, Capteen. Good night. Good night, Mr Raskin.'

MacKenzie walked out of the bar with Raskin. He slid the unloaded gun into his pocket. The cool air hit him about the same time as the noise of the first chair thrown and table breaking. Raskin looked back at the melee inside and winced.

'Er . . . shouldn't we go back in there?'

MacKenzie shook his head. 'They're fighting for their ship. They've found their honor. It's actually better if we leave. That way the stories of their bravery can grow to completely ridiculous proportions by morning. By the way, did you post copies of the engagement tapes to every captain in the Black Sea Fleet like I asked you?'

'As soon as we docked.'

'Good. Make sure everybody is out of jail and on the ship by ten.' He looked down at Karolov still lying in the gutter, and rubbed his hand. 'You know, Nikolai, that punch wasn't as good as the first time I got laid . . .' He grinned. '. . . But it was pretty damn close.'

Raskin laughed, then yawned, stretching his big arms. 'Quite a night, Peter. Want me to drive you back to the hotel?'

MacKenzie took a deep breath. The night air was sweet and the sound of the ocean lapping at the piers below was a balm.

'I feel like walking tonight, Nikolai. Thanks. For everything.'

'Good night, Peter.'

MacKenzie pulled up the collar of his jacket and set off

down the seaside promenade, letting the ocean and the cool night air talk to him of healing.

Karolov felt hands under him, pulling him up. He was groggy. There was noise coming from inside the bar. It sounded like a fight.

'Relax, Comrade Admiral, you will have your chance.'

The voice was right about that. As soon as he was able to stand he was going to find the American and kill him. The entire bar had seen the gun. Who was to say the American had not pulled it out again and in the resulting scuffle was killed by his own bullet? It was the only way to eliminate the humiliation the American had heaped upon him.

But instead of the bar he was taken into the alley, a dank, dark place smelling of garbage and urine. 'Wait, where are we going? The fight is that way,' Karolov protested.

More hands held him firmly. 'We know, Admiral, but first there is someone who wants to speak with you. Someone important.'

Karolov squinted to make out the face in front of him in the dark. He was relieved to see it was the Operations Director of Soviet Naval Intelligence, Viktor Volchek. Volchek was a well-known conservative. He would understand the need for revenge. The director had on a long leather coat, belted at the waist. There were several men around him, all similarly dressed.

'Comrade Volchek . . .' Karolov began, but Volchek cut him off.

'You are not normally a stupid man, Comrade Admiral. What possessed you to interfere in a mission that was approved at a higher level than you will ever achieve?'

Karolov's face got hot at the stinging rebuke. The men around him held him fast. He could see now that not one of them belonged to his crew. For the first time he felt a stab of fear.

'I did not realize, Comrade . . .'

'Yes, you did. Which makes it all the more of a crime. You deliberately went after the American. The collision could have lost the sonar and ended the mission. Today you almost sank the *Riga* with your foolhardy run at the sub after the engagement. It was bad enough to lose, Admiral, worse to be unable to accept it.'

'How could you know . . . ?' Karolov started, but the answer was obvious, his own exec must have talked to the security officer who reported it directly to Volchek.

'Your part in this affair is over,' Volchek pronounced.

'How can I let the American get away with cheating me, Comrade? Please, let me make an example of him. The men must see who is stronger. Surely that is ideologically correct.'

Volchek spoke to someone in the shadows. For the first time Karolov saw there was a man there. Volchek turned back to Karolov, frowning. 'Only a fool would think ideology has anything to do with this.'

Suddenly one of the men holding him dropped a bag over his head, blinding him. Powerful hands stretched his arms straight out in front of him. He struggled but he couldn't break their hold. They bared his wrists.

Igor Dainis stepped out of the shadows and smashed a steel pipe down hard on Karolov's right wrist. It broke with an audible snap. Karolov screamed in pain. They shoved the bag into his mouth to stifle the sound.

'Again,' Volchek commanded.

Dainis brought the pipe down on Karolov's left wrist. He heard the internal crunch that meant broken bones. The admiral passed out in midscream. Volchek's men caught him as he sagged.

Dainis said, 'The last time he will arm wrestle, eh?'

'Take him to the base hospital,' Volchek commanded. 'He will say nothing during his long recuperation, I am sure of that. He'll know we could just as easily have crushed his spine.'

Dainis wiped the sheen of perspiration from his face. It

felt good to hit a man like that. To hear the crunch of bones, to feel the power. It was almost a sexual thing. He took a deep breath of air to slow his racing heart. 'A pity he was so impatient. If he had just waited . . .' Dainis left the sentence unfinished.

'That's true,' agreed Volchek. 'In the end the admiral would have had his revenge. But this is what happens to the man who is not in control of his emotions. We do not suffer from that disease, do we, Comrade?'

'No, Comrade Director, we do not,' Dainis agreed.

EIGHTEEN

Chardzhou, Turkmenistan

The director of the Repetek Sand Desert Station, which stood beside the Amu Darya River not far from Chardzhou, was delighted, if somewhat confused. 'I don't know why I wasn't told anything,' he said again to the big man with a dark, scraggly beard who had given his name as Azrak and was now standing in his office.

'We did have one other delegation of American scientists here. Let me see,' said the director thoughtfully. 'Yes. It was 1934 I believe. Before my time. Well, follow me.'

Azrak followed him out of the office. His feet crunched on the gritty sand that had fallen from his clothing and pooled under his feet. The director was Russian. The assistant director and most of the staff were Turkmeni, with a few Uzbeks thrown in to do the menial jobs. The assistant director was careful not to look at Azrak.

'I am certain the visit was cleared with the ministry. I have the papers here.'

'Yes, well, never mind. I know how things can be.'

The sun outside was a hammer blow after the air-conditioning in the station, but the director seemed to be used to it. 'Over here' – he pointed to one low building, quite pleased to be showing his work with or without the proper documentation – 'we study the desert sands themselves. Did you know we've actually learned to glue the sand down with an oil preparation? Over there are the plant studies we're conducting. We have over ten varieties that actually stabilize the sand. It's the only thing that made planting both sides of the Kara-Kum Canal feasible.'

There were several scuba tanks and regulators hanging

alongside an aging compressor unit. 'What are the tanks for?' Azrak asked.

'Those are very important,' said the director. 'As much goes on under the water as above. We had an algae problem at the canal. It's all this sunshine. It was gumming up the works. We finally found a fish that eats algae. It's called the thickhead, actually a silver carp from the Amur River in Siberia. Now we have another problem. Thickheads and catfish are getting so big we may have to find other fish to eat them.' He chuckled at the thought. 'Never an end to problems.'

'I suppose not,' said Azrak. 'What is that plant?'

'This? Just a common form of heat-resistant – '

The director had never lorded his status as a Great Russian over the Turkmenis who worked at the station, or mistreated any of them. It saved his life. As he reached over, Azrak slid a hypodermic syringe into his left arm and caught him neatly as he fell.

'You have a place for him?' Azrak asked Mamed, the assistant director.

'All prepared. We have been waiting for you.'

Azrak beat sand out of his robes. 'The trip across the desert was very difficult. The Russians had air patrols out. For the most part we were indistinguishable from any water train. Thank the Prophet for ground to air radar.'

'Allah be praised,' agreed Mamed. 'Where are the weapons?'

'On the water-sleds outside, hidden in a false tank. Send your men out. I will supervise the unloading.'

In the summer this place was the hottest spot in the Soviet Union – over one hundred and twenty-five degrees in the shade. If you could find shade. 'We prepared the main lab for you,' said Mamed, following him out. 'I was given to understand the missiles need to be worked on.'

'That is correct. Raza and the American scientist will be arriving later.'

Azrak's men lowered the false side on the water tank.

There were two long boxes containing the cruise missiles, sealed against the desert sand.

'What are those?' Mamed asked, seeing more crates alongside them.

'Automatic rifles and small arms. I want defensive positions dug around the stations.'

'That's fine for your men,' said Mamed, 'but the workers here are laboratory assistants and cooks.'

'We are all soldiers in the service of God. And Raza,' said Azrak. 'Everybody fights if need be.'

'Of course,' agreed Mamed. 'Of course.'

Raza arrived with Lavenhal by helicopter later that night. The scientist set up his equipment in the main research station lab and began working on the modified Tomahawk cruise missiles.

Raza found Lavenhal looking pleased.

'Good news. These weapons are built the same as the others. The electromechanical locks in the arming circuits are open. I can get past them and remove the sensors and then get to the rest of the locks.'

'How long?'

'We're down to forty-eight hours a missile. Four days in all.'

Raza decided he would stay to see only the first part of the job done. Azrak and the transportation people would see to getting Lavenhal back to the main air routes. Raza himself would return to England and rendezvous with the *Kentucky* and its crew. He would be well within the time limits he imposed on Moscow. In this matter he had no delusions. The Soviet president would not grant him his demands. The first missile would fly. He planned to be on board when the *Kentucky* made its attack run on the target he had selected.

Raza had chosen the *Kentucky*'s pilot and officers very carefully. They had all trained on Soviet subs, all were loyal Turkmeni by birth. Finding them was one of the first steps in knowing whether or not his plan would work. When he found a man, he faked a car crash to take him out of officialdom's scrutiny. All his men were listed on their service rosters as dead by vehicular or other accident. Captain Bharkov and his men were now in the Baltic Sea with the *Kentucky* learning its secrets, hidden within a fleet of fishing boats.

Things were falling into place. He didn't know why that surprised him. He had planned everything so carefully. Maybe like any artist approaching the climax of his work, he had a certain amount of doubt that all the carefully laid plots and themes would really come to fruition as expected. There were other doubts, too. He could never be so single-minded as to forget that not every Turkmeni believed in his cause.

Azrak interrupted his thoughts. 'Raza? Can I talk to you?'

'Of course.'

'I know we are going to win because God has willed it. But we must also look hard to see if there are twists and turns inside his grand design, shouldn't we?'

'Speak plainly, my friend.'

Azrak's eyes took in Lavenhal.

'Pay him no attention.' Raza's face was unreadable.

'What if you and the American submarine fail to launch the weapons as planned?' Azrak asked. 'Will the missiles we store here just remain worthless hulks?'

Raza gestured for Azrak to sit alongside him. 'You're asking who will carry on if I can not. The answer is, you will.'

Azrak shook his head. 'I am no leader who inspires others.'

'You will inspire by example.'

'How?'

'Remember, Allah has two hands,' Raza said.

'Open for the righteous, closed for the infidel,' he said. 'I know that. Just as I know your piety is only slightly less a sham than the mask of invincibility you cultivate.'

Raza smiled. 'I thought I had everybody fooled.'

'Most maybe, but not me.' Azrak returned the smile. 'The carpet weavers of Bukhara say spread out your rug and I will read your heart. I know your rug, Raza, and your heart. Even when we were boys in the mosque, you listened but you did not really hear. Always you made your own dreams. But you honor the Prophet so that is acceptable. Perhaps even more than those who quote every verse of the Koran and daily break its commandments.'

'Perhaps. But to your question. Do you know why I chose this station to store the missiles?'

'To shelter us from the desert,' Azrak responded.

'Think, Azrak. You are Turkmeni. I could have put you in the middle of the Kara-Kum and you would have survived for a time.' He looked at his friend closely. 'But what use would it be to us to blow up the desert?'

Azrak's eyes narrowed. 'I see none.'

'Correct. But if you were to draw a circle with a one-hundred-mile radius and this station as its center, you would enscribe a region that produces half the oil for the Uzbek fields and that means twenty percent of all the Soviet oil produced anywhere.'

Azrak made a noise of understanding. 'I begin to see.'

Raza went on. 'There is no way to fire the missiles at a target accurately without a submarine's launch tubes and on-board guidance systems. That leaves them with only one use if the *Kentucky* is destroyed – as a bomb. As you say, I know I am not invincible. So I had the American Lavenhal slave the warheads together and install a triggering device. The warheads will detonate together if the device is activated.'

'How long till the explosion?' Azrak asked, although he felt he already knew the kind of answer he would hear.

'Ten minutes to run through the proper sequence. Long enough to say your prayers. Not much else.'

Azrak looked at him intently. 'But the Turkmeni cause. What will happen to it?'

Raza's eyes were bright. 'Others will lift it. The loss of the oil fields will further cripple the economy and weaken their hold on us. It will make the next battle that much easier. If I fail, or there is no other choice, activate the device.'

'The warrior who dies in battle goes straight to Heaven, blessed by Allah,' Azrak said solemnly.

Raza laughed without humor. 'What does Allah say about the warrior who dies in a nuclear explosion?'

Azrak's eyes had a mischievous twinkle. 'He is thrice blessed.'

'You're making that up.'

'You are no biblical scholar to know.'

Raza laughed. 'I'm scholar enough for that.'

Azrak's face grew serious again. 'Have you chosen *your* target?'

Raza nodded. 'One they will never forget. We are going to blow up the Northern Fleet's main submarine base, the pens at Kola Bay.'

Azrak whistled.

'It is a target made for a small, special craft like the *Kentucky*,' Raza went on. 'The antisub nets are rigged for the big American boats. The underwater arrays won't hear us. And there are plenty of places to hide. The whole geography of the area works in our interest.'

'How many ships will be in port?'

It was one of the few times Azrak got to see the real face underneath, the face of a man totally committed to an ideal, without regard for his own personal safety or that of others.

'Much of the fleet is in for repairs before the summer thaw. The ice cap doesn't refreeze fully for almost five months. A twenty-five thousand-ton Typhoon carrying twenty SS-NX twenties, and two Deltas, along with several attack submarines including a Victor III, two Alfas and a Sierra. Intelligence tells me an Akula may also be in port for repairs. Think of it, Azrak, the cost to them will be in the trillions.'

'It is brilliant, Raza,' admitted Azrak. 'The price is staggering, the loss of life is limited to military personnel, and the West will be delighted to see half the Northern submarine fleet destroyed, especially the missile subs.'

'Once the Western powers see that I have the upper hand, they will return to our cause. An independent Turkmenistan with oil to sell and a strategic position next to Iran would be a welcome member of their alliance. Moscow will have to sue for peace,' Raza said. 'And we will have won.'

'Then Allah guide your hand.'

'Allah and American computers. Now let's get some food. Then we'll see to your defenses.'

NINETEEN

Kara-Kum

Her lips were parched. Her face was as dry as dust. The seemingly endless sands stretched out in front of them, and the feeling that one had to see something different crossing yet another dune was soon replaced by the dulling certainty that only more sand awaited. Which made it all the more astonishing when they topped a high dune and Justine got her first sight of the Kara-Kum Canal.

There, in the middle of the desert, lay a glistening silver ribbon of water over a hundred yards wide stretching from horizon to horizon. The beginning and end of the canal curved into vibrating layers of desert heat, lost in the farthest waves of sand. Equally shocking were the bands of green and brown bordering the canal, which as they drew closer she could see were strips of vegetation from seventy-five to as much as three hundred feet wide.

'It stops everybody like that the first time they see it,' said Kemal, coming up beside her. 'It's almost five hundred miles long. Ten times the length of the Panama Canal. From here it moves west along the Kopet Dagh foothills, all the way to the Caspian.'

'What an incredible feat of engineering to build this here in the deep desert. Why the plantings?' she asked.

'To hold the sand down. Otherwise it would fill the canal in no time. It flows like a fluid. The water comes from the Amu Darya River in the east, fed by high mountain springs.' His voice saddened, carrying anger, too. 'The great pity is that farther north the Amu Darya has been destroyed and half the Aral Sea drained in yet another massive Soviet folly, growing cotton where there should be none. For hard currency, an entire ocean has been destroyed. How could they wonder why the republics want to walk away from seventy years of that kind of devastation and pollution?'

Ezek pulled up beside them. 'The canal, eh? Most of us will never forget the day the water arrived in Ashkhabad. The old men and women never believed water could cross the Kara-Kum, even during the years of its construction. When it flowed in they had to reach down and let it run through their fingers to accept it, touch it to their lips. Many prayed in gratitude. There were feasts for months.'

Justine could understand it. The ribbon of water was a mesmerizing sight. It looked as if someone had taken one perfect shimmering river and put it down whole in the desert, so precisely did its banks cut through the sand.

'Poets wrote about the day and songs were sung about the Canal of Happiness,' said Radi. 'Parents even named their children *Kanal Geldy*, which means "The Canal Has Arrived." '

He gazed down the length of the canal and again Justine was struck by how close the relationship was here between the land and its people. Cut a canal elsewhere and it meant a few more houses, or some pleasure boats had access to the sea. Here, it meant survival, the lifeless brought to life.

'Do we cross it?' she asked.

'No,' said Radi happily. 'We ride it.'

Kemal transacted business with someone Ezek identified for Justine as an official of the canal construction service. Money changed hands and they boarded an eighty-foot launch called the *Oxus*, the ancient name of the River Amu Darya in Alexander's day.

Before they got underway, Kemal let two riders off on the other side of the canal and sent them deeper into the desert.

'Where are they going?' asked Justine.

'They'll check on the first oasis where Raza might have stored the missiles. They will meet us at Merv. If Raza is

234

there we can turn back. If not, we'll go on into the desert.'

'No more desert for tonight, I hope.'

Kemal laughed at her. 'Just a pleasant moonlit cruise.'

'Alla be praised,' she said with real feeling. 'I could kiss you.'

Kemal said nothing and Justine could have kicked herself. Talk about adolescent one-liners . . .

In any event, an hour later she was in heaven, sitting in a deck chair on the upper deck, feeling like Cleopatra on her barge, sipping a cold drink from the galley refrigerator and watching the desert slide by. Karansky had gone to his cabin. Kemal was with his men, tending to the livestock. The sun was setting, painting the horizon with glimmering colors.

She knew to relish tranquil moments like this. Time for reflection. Karansky had noticed it the first time they lunched by the Golden Spring on the way to Firyuza. Here, alone, she found a mental tranquillity that had escaped her in Mac's presence. One of the things she had come to realize was that he could no longer be her sole salvation. She had failed him because she depended totally upon him for all her emotional needs. When he'd had needs of his own she had been blind to them. And impatient.

The saddest part was that she had been where he was. The previous night with Kemal had made her realize a lot of things. She'd felt her own pain again and remembered how bad it was. It helped her to understand Mac emotionally as well as intellectually. They were very different, she and her husband. She was a doer. Her way out was to fight first and understand the emotions later. Mac was the opposite, more cerebral. His way was to come from the inside out. Guilt struck her heavily. Had her leaving made him unable to come out? If she had stayed just a little while longer would he have been able to deal with what had happened to that poor child? How did anyone ever know when it was the right time to leave?

Now Kemal. Did she want to have an affair with him?

A brief respite might bring her closer to Mac, but it could also drive a wedge even deeper between them. She could never tell him, that was for certain. Neither had made a secret of their relationships before marriage. They were both mature people when they met. But marriage vows were sacred. They had promised that.

So could she be just one more person who broke that promise? It happened all the time. Think of it as a business trip. Far away from home. She didn't intend to trade her Washington brownstone for a desert tent. But passion was so scarce in life. How could she let this go? Didn't love cleanse? Or was that just her hormones talking and all love ever did was complicate? Could her love for Mac survive one transgression? Purge your guilt in a fire of passion. It sounded so easy. Blow off some steam and go back whole again to pick up the pieces.

Or perhaps denial was the price she had to pay to atone for leaving. Be selfless for a change. She looked hard at herself. Sure she could fight when the trumpet sounded, but maybe she was just an immature girl who still wanted more than she was entitled to for all that. Grow up, Justine, she chided herself. What are you willing to give to get Mac back?

And what about Mac? She felt herself battered by conflicting emotions. She and Mac had promised each other that their relationship was going to be different from the ones they saw around them. They had shared things about themselves with each other they had never shared with anyone else. Feelings. Honesty. Trust. Those were their foundations. Mac had to matter. Even here. Of course things would be easier if she didn't have to concern herself with his feelings. But that was the point. That was the deal you made. That the other person mattered even if you didn't come home that night, even in another place. She sensed another pitfall here, a more subtle one. She could never tell Mac if she slept with Kemal, but *she* would know – and that would create a place within her she'd have to wall off forever, always closed to him. Too many places and someday, like cancerous cells, they would grow and consume them. She faced a hard truth. Enough secrets and you were strangers.

Something deeper stirred within her, a knowledge of how dangerous the ground was she was treading on. Kemal would get over whatever happened – whether they slept together or not. In many ways he was a better person than she was, his sights on loftier goals. But an admonition echoed deep within her and somehow she knew, without knowing how, that it came from a special private place. It was the age-old place where the wisdom that every woman is born with, and has as her secret source, was located – the reason women would always be braver and older than men.

Kemal was dangerous because in the end you could get over pain. You never got over love.

She awoke in the chair on deck. The sun was rising. Cool, sharp air blew in from the desert. Someone had covered her during the night.

She was ravenously hungry and thoughts from the night had no place here during the day. She rose and went down to eat and wash up. Having a bathroom was like having a suite at the Plaza. It was unlikely they would have such luxury in the conceivable future.

When she came back up on deck the men were wrestling the camels into line. The ship docked with a series of bumps and grinds.

Kemal looked across the restless animals to her. She felt the power of those eyes and knew that his insistent demand had only been postponed, not put aside. Falling asleep had only delayed the inevitable. One of these nights he would come to her and she would have to decide.

TWENTY

Odessa

MacKenzie awoke and knew at once that he had suffered a sea change. He had regained his peace of mind. Like some cathartic medicinal leech, Raskin and his alcoholic elixir, and probably the very deep bones of this medieval place, had bled the poison out of his system and made him pure again. Lightness of spirit might never make the psychiatric profession's top-ten list, but for those who possessed it, it was a blessing every day. MacKenzie knew his monsters had been laid to rest, and it brought tears to his eyes for the second time in twenty-four hours.

How did you celebrate that? he wondered. Throw a paper plane out the window? Drink? His stomach roiled – God forbid. He wished he could call Justine and tell her he was all right again. That he had strength for both of them. But she was out there on her own and he could not reach her. He dressed and sat down at the desk by the window and tried to write her a letter. It didn't do his feelings justice. Some things had to be dealt with in person.

Raskin was waiting for him in the lobby. He noticed MacKenzie's new attitude at once. 'I needed steam for an hour before I could open my eyes,' Raskin groaned. 'You put away enough vodka for a small army and come down with a spring in your step this morning. I don't understand it.'

'It's simple,' MacKenzie said. 'Even my cells wouldn't mess with me today. By the way, I found these outside my door. One of the men must have put them there late last night.'

'They're the engagement tapes you left on the table at

the bar,' Raskin exclaimed. 'It looks like they've been through a war.'

'I expect they have. And the evidence suggests our side won.'

'You know what this means, don't you?' said Raskin.

'It means they did their ship proud,' MacKenzie responded.

'It means they did *you* proud,' said Raskin. 'The officers from the *Lenin* who beat you up were there last night. The crew knew who they were. I expect most of them are back on the *Lenin* this morning looking for their missing teeth.'

Raskin had left their car in front of the hotel. They got in. 'All in all a successful evening, wouldn't you say?' he asked as they drove down Primorsky Boulevard.

'Yes, I would.' MacKenzie was watching Odessa's old buildings and tree-lined streets go by. He said pensively, 'You taught me something last night, Nikolai. All of you did. I guess in a way this city has, too. I'll be sorry to leave it.'

'You don't have to yet. Think of the drinking tonight.' He smacked his lips. 'It will be marvelous.'

'Nikolai,' MacKenzie said warmly, 'you are maybe the most balanced man I have ever met. In a land where almost everybody is afraid, you are brave. Where they are closed-in and run from things, you are open and wise and filled with life, despite your own losses. But my time here is over. The crew is ready, the ship is ready . . . and now I'm ready.'

Raskin studied him for a few seconds before turning back to the road. 'Yes, I can see that. You are very different today. What happened?'

'I'd like to see if I can explain it.'

MacKenzie chose his words carefully, trying to complete his own understanding as well as his friend's. 'I realize now that when I came here I was suffering most of all from a loss of faith. I guess it was the result of what happened to that little girl. The pillars of my life were gone. That's probably what made me try to rip out the IV tubes that were sustaining me. Now I understand. The foundation was gone. I had lost faith in myself, in my optimistic view of the world, and in a kind and merciful God. It froze me up inside. Sure, I could walk around and from the outside I looked fine. My wife and friends kept telling me I was the same man. I could even command a sub, but only because I knew the right words. There was no force behind me. No will. Because I no longer knew what was right in that intuitive way in which I had always functioned. I had become morally lost. What right did I have to be so damn sure of myself? If I was so good how could God use me to tear the legs off that child? And if all that was in doubt, what right did I have to love my wife or find any happiness or command others?

'We all have to have a moral compass, Nikolai. I lost mine. Maybe most people can function without one. But I couldn't. It's a question of standards – and adhering to them even in the absence of knowing what is true with any great certainty. In the end maybe those standards are all we have because we *don't* know what's true with any real certainty.'

MacKenzie watched a bird fly over the harbor and settle on the sea wall. 'Coming here, away from everything I'd ever known, I was a stranger in a strange land. My standards wouldn't have applied even if the accident never happened. One of the shrinks suggested LSD as a possible therapy. It's supposed to be dissociative, he said. Gives you the ability to step outside yourself and see reality from a new perspective. I think that's what happened here. And it was just what I needed.

'These past few nights, last night especially, I became somebody else. For the first time in my life I came from my guts instead of my head. Liberated by your vodka, shown the way inside myself by how accessible your feelings are to you, given the Russian freedom to cry and grieve – I began to be free. My God, Nikolai, the thought

240

of doing back home what I did to Karolov's boat here would be inconceivable. I still don't quite believe I did it.'

'An immortal act,' said Raskin reverently.

'Walking home last night, Nikolai, I realized I hadn't been fighting for the crew, I'd been fighting for myself. If I could beat Karolov by depending on those things that I believed in – that I used to believe in – then maybe I wasn't wrong. Maybe what I had to learn was that faith is always an act of will – that you've got to believe despite all the things that tell you such belief is foolish. And when we did beat him I began to believe again. In my optimistic view of the world, in a kind and merciful God, and in myself.'

'If this is true I am happy for you, my friend.'

'It's true. I have myself back. The shrinks can fill in the technical terms, but that's what it feels like inside. I can put it to rest now. But that means it's over here, too. Time's running out. No more drinking to excess, because that is not my way. The rest cure is over. It's time to leave the Raskin spa. I have responsibilities – to the ship, to the mission and to my family.'

'You are saying you've got to get back.'

'Thank you, Nikolai. Yes, I do.'

MacKenzie gave the order to dive as soon as the *Riga* cleared port and hit the hundred-fathom curve.

'Make your depth five zero meters, Mr Petrov. All ahead flank. Course one nine five.'

'Five zero meters, all ahead flank. Course one nine five, aye.'

'Nikolai, assemble the officers in the wardroom. Chief Engineer Prudenkov, too. Mr Petrov, you have the conn. Avoid contact with any ships, maintain course.'

'Aye, Capteen.'

MacKenzie went back to the wardroom. The steward had been told to bring coffee and tea and they were waiting on the table in big white mugs. His officers filed in one by one. Few could hide at least a brief grin or wry smile at what had transpired the previous night. Chernin had a cut over one eye held together by a small bandage. Kortzov's good looks were sporting a shiner, and Kotnikov limped a little when he walked. All wore their war wounds like medals.

They were waiting for MacKenzie to say something. 'I know,' he said, 'I should see the other guys.'

There was a collective release, chuckles and back slappings. Several let out pent-up breaths. Chernin said proudly, 'It was amazing, Capteen. Single-handedly, Mikhail took on three men and bested them.'

'It was nothing compared to your punch, Capteen,' said Kortzov, his modesty belying the fact that he was about to burst his uniform blouse.

Everyone agreed. 'A thing of beauty, eh, Mr Raskin?' said Communications Officer Golovskoy.

'I have so stated for the record,' Raskin said sincerely.

'Our Mr Chernin, he is a tiger when aroused,' said Golovskoy. 'Many men went down under his fists.'

'I was defending the *Riga*,' said Chernin, a sufficient explanation of his prowess.

'Would you really have shot the admiral, Capteen?' asked Kotnikov.

'Actually,' MacKenzie responded, 'the gun was unloaded. I couldn't take the chance the pigheaded fool would rush me and I might really shoot him.'

They laughed. In the silence that followed, Chernin looked a bit shamefaced. 'We are sorry about the other night, Capteen, when we stood by. We did not yet understand each other, I think.'

'I appreciate that, Mr Chernin, and I want to say something to all of you.' MacKenzie raised his mug. 'I toast your bravery, your courage and your loyalty. You've made me proud to serve on the *Riga*. *Na zdoróvie!*'

'*Na zdoróvie!*' they echoed.

'Now sit down and let me tell you what comes next. I'd like you, Mr Dainis, to pay particular attention because it may put you in the most hot water with your superiors.'

'Very well,' said Dainis.

'The original plan,' MacKenzie began, 'called for us to finish our training on the *Riga* and fly north to pick up another sub out of Kola Bay. This avoided my presence at the top secret facility for an extended period of time. It will mean, however, days, perhaps as much as a week more of shakedown cruising to get all the bugs out of our new ship, a ship we would be totally unfamiliar with. Frankly, we don't have the time. Second, according to Mr Dainis, it also means removing and reinstalling the new sonar, as *Riga* has the only working model. Again, this would necessitate more trials and the real possibility of damage in transport or installation. Last, gentlemen, we are on a roll. We took the *Lenin* twice and your . . . ah . . . private engagement last night has given the crew the kind of morale a captain works his tail off for.'

MacKenzie leaned closer. 'I believe we would be at a distinct disadvantage if we entered combat with anything but the best ship and the crew at peak performance. Who knows what a new ship might need? Worse, who knows how many other Karolovs we might encounter when we get to Kola Bay? This ship and crew are ready and it seems foolish to my way of thinking not to take them both into what may be the toughest battle of our lives. To be honest, I've thought so for a while now. It's part of why I pushed *Riga* so hard.'

'You're saying we should head for the North Sea now?' Raskin asked, reviewing the arguments in his own head.

'I am. We are fully stocked. The cruise will give the men more time to train as a working unit. Mr Dainis?'

'It is hard to say, Capteen. We have been given wide latitude for this mission. Your being here at all breaks iron clad rules. But there is logic in what you say. I will accept the necessity of going it alone, given the security considerations.'

'Thank you, Mr Dainis. Anyone have any other thoughts on the matter? Speak up if you do.'

'Can we afford the time, Capteen?' asked Kotnikov. 'It is a long way to Kola Bay. We have less than a week.'

'Our transit time will be just about the same as the time we'd need to shake down the new ship if we flew up there. This way we arrive as a fighting unit, ready to go. Time is pressing. There's far less than we originally thought. This way we make the best use of it.'

Kortzov was firm. 'If we can find the *Kentucky* and get a shot at him, I want it to be in the *Riga*.'

'As do I, Mikhail,' said Chernin. 'But it can be a dangerous voyage. The way to the Mediterranean is often shallow. The Bosporus narrows severely. We will have to travel much of the distance at periscope depth. We could easily go aground. The Med poses its own problems, including the American navy.'

'It's a little tricky from the navigational standpoint, I agree,' said MacKenzie. 'But there are some alternate routes that may help.'

'What about other subs?' asked Kortzov. 'We'll be crossing the UK Gap. Every inch of those waters is heavily patrolled and rigged with bottom mounted hydrophones. We're bound to be picked up by other subs.'

'We stay clear of any engagement,' said MacKenzie. 'We are a single ship on a special mission. Any company increases our risk of detection by the *Kentucky*. We have an advantage. We know more together about our combined naval practices than any of us knows alone. We ought to be able to slip through the Med and the Gap.'

Discussion yielded to general agreement. It was going to be far more dangerous than fighting taped simulations against the *Lenin*. Every advantage they could bring to bear increased their chances of coming home.

'Very well,' said MacKenzie seeing it in their faces. 'Mr Chernin. Lay in a course for the Bosporus.'

MacKenzie spent the first hours in the sonar room. He had given Raskin the helm, wanting to be as familiar with the new sonar as possible. For long hours he sat huddled over the sonar scopes with Kotnikov and Purzov listening to the sounds of passing ships. The new sonar had better than a ten percent increase in detection sensitivity, MacKenzie estimated, as the day wore on. When the units were put into the Soviet fleet they were going to narrow an already slim American lead in the technology, possibly even surpass it. What Garver had said was true, gaining the new sonar was critically important.

He spent considerable time studying the system engineering manuals. He was at a slight disadvantage because he was stronger in the tactical areas of submarining than in the engineering ones. He wished he had his friend and former exec Tom Lasovic here. Tom's background was as much stronger on the technical side as MacKenzie's was on the tactical. It was the kind of matchup Navy Command tried to make as often as possible. The skilled Annapolis grad would make short work of the technical specs. But MacKenzie had been alerted to look for certain things and as he plowed on, he began to find them.

He took his camera out of his duffel bag and removed the exposed roll of 35mm film as the intelligence people had taught him to do, and shot the pages. A chip in the camera stored the images in digital mode. He ejected a tiny metal disc, the size of a dime with markings to match. It now contained the images. He slipped it in his pocket. The exposed film, the pretty pictures of Odessa Raskin had taken, went into his bag.

He walked down to the trash room. The camera separated into several pieces which he deposited into the barrels about to be ejected. He made sure they were properly weighted, resealed the lids, and returned to his cabin.

He felt a twinge of guilt at the espionage. This was somehow different from the competition to raise the *Red Dawn*. That was out in the open. This was like stealing your host's silver. But the new sonar could tip the balance of power under the seas, and his entire professional life had been devoted to preserving that edge for the United States. The sea change that had restored his peace of mind had reestablished his priorities as well. He was an American naval officer. It was not the first time he'd been called upon to carry out orders that were personally difficult. It probably wouldn't be the last. But this he knew – he had been given a great gift, unique for an officer in the service of his country's military. He would never again be able to look upon a Soviet warship as just a hostile platform filled with faceless enemies. Part of him would always remember the moment men named Chernin and Kutsky and Kortzov and Golovskoy had stood up against a lifetime of training to take his back and embrace things which would always transcend politics and ideologies – honor and friendship.

It was nighttime when Raskin came to wake him in his cabin.

'Peter?'

'Come in, Nikolai.'

'We are nearing the entrance to the Bosporus,' said Raskin, entering. 'You asked to be notified.'

'Right.' MacKenzie went into the head to wash. 'We made good time.'

'Mr Chernin found a strong current,' Raskin said from inside. 'You've been doing your lessons, I see.'

MacKenzie cursed himself for leaving the tech manuals lying around. It was no secret that he had been working with the sonar all that day so he played it as straightforward as he could. 'I wish my engineering background was better. I've absorbed about all I can. Maybe more hours at it will help. You should think about boning up, too.'

'I have trouble hearing the difference between a sub and a whale.' Raskin laughed. 'That is why God created sonar men with their perfect ears.'

'I'm heading for the conn. You coming?'

Raskin said, 'I'll be along shortly.'

Raskin watched MacKenzie depart down the corridor, then turned into his compartment. He waited a minute, then returned to MacKenzie's cabin. It had been his for so long he was familiar with every nook and cranny. He felt guilty not trusting his friend, but it was his duty to do a thorough search. He was relieved to find there was no incriminating evidence of espionage, no supertechnical spy devices, no codebooks, no transmitters. Of course, there was the possibility that spying devices were so sophisticated that he would not recognize one even if he were looking straight at it, but he had done what he could.

He left the technical manuals where they were and debated calling Igor Dainis. He still harbored suspicions about the security officer, but nothing he could really put his finger on. Dainis was too amenable to MacKenzie by half, but realistically, how else could he act? The mission had been approved by Naval Command, he couldn't actively sabotage it. But there was a degree of willingness to his actions that just didn't seem fitting. It struck a jarring note every time Dainis acted like a maitre d' ushering MacKenzie in and out of the sonar. Raskin wondered what Dainis's reaction would be to his concerns? In the end he decided to call the security officer, who agreed to meet him in the wardroom.

'What is the trouble, Comrade Captain?' Dainis asked when Raskin arrived.

'In Russian,' Raskin said, breaking into his native tongue. He described finding the technical manuals in MacKenzie's cabin, and of finding no evidence of any spying.

'Then why are you telling me this?' asked Dainis.

'I am a Soviet officer. You know where my loyalty lies. The new sonar is ours, it should remain ours. But I have a conflict. I consider the captain my friend.'

'So what would you have me do?'

'Protect all parties by removing temptation. His interest may have been just what he said it was, to better command the ship. Fine. Now place the technical manuals under security restriction. I am surprised you haven't done so in the first place.'

Dainis put a firm hand on his shoulder. 'You are to be commended, Comrade. But as much as I find letting Captain MacKenzie have access to everything on the ship professionally and personally disturbing, I am under strict orders. I can not change them.'

'But in this case . . .'

Dainis waved him off. 'You are to be commended. I will record your excellent conduct in my log. It's good you came to me. I wouldn't worry,' he said with a conspiratorial shrug. 'You are to feel blameless whatever happens.'

'What do you mean "whatever happens"?'

Dainis shrugged. 'Nothing. Just a harmless phrase. Is that all?'

'Yes, Comrade Dainis. Thank you for hearing me out.'

Dainis nodded and left the wardroom. Raskin sat thinking about the conversation for some time after.

In the control room, MacKenzie was pleased to see the same crisp performance was still being carried out. 'The captain has the conn,' he announced.

'We have arrived at the Bosporus, Capteen,' said Chernin.

'Very good, Mr Chernin.'

The Bosporus Strait connected the Black Sea and the Sea of Marmara, in effect part of the boundary between Europe and Asia. Turkey maintained control over the eighteen-mile stretch of water which fell within its boundaries. It was a vital route to the Soviets for their southern sea transport.

'You made excellent time. What's our position?'

'We are a mile off the northern entrance to the strait,' Chernin said. 'There is no difficulty entering, it is almost three miles wide. Navigating within the strait is not so easy. The narrows are less than eighteen hundred feet and the depth varies from sixty-six fathoms to less than twenty, even in midstream.'

'The current can be tough, too,' said MacKenzie.

'You've been through here before?' asked Raskin.

'Years ago. We like to check what you guys are up to.'

'We know,' said Raskin baldly.

'Rig control for red,' MacKenzie ordered and the lights in the conn changed to red to permit his eyes to adjust to night vision. He remembered tricky currents, especially in the narrows. A rapid surface current ran from the Black Sea to the Sea of Marmara. A countercurrent below the surface ran along the shores.

The reasons for the complex current were interesting. Geologically, before the connection with the Sea of Marmara, the Black Sea was a deep, brackish lake, similar to the Caspian in its present condition. When the highly saline Mediterranean seawater flowed in, it killed the sea life in the Black Sea's depths, creating a deep, dense layer of lifeless, cold water. Since the rivers that feed the Black Sea carried to it yearly more fresh water than it lost by evaporation, the excess flowed over the deep, cold layer and found its escape route through the Bosporus. The outward rush caused the rapid current. MacKenzie could go under it, depth permitting, but that could be just as tricky because below sixty-five feet, a reverse current flowed back in from the Mediterranean.

MacKenzie picked up the intercom and dialed all-ship. 'This is the captain speaking. To put all rumors to rest, I want you to know we have commenced the battle phase of our mission and are heading for the North Sea to engage the *Kentucky*. We've crossed the Black Sea and are presently at the entrance to the Bosporus, the first leg in our journey across the Mediterranean to the Atlantic Ocean. We will not be leaving the *Riga* behind and picking up a new ship as originally planned. She has shown us she is up to the task ahead. You have also demonstrated you are up to the task ahead. No captain can ask for more. Stay sharp, the way is not without danger. I know the bonds we have formed will see us through. Captain out.

'Periscope depth two zero meters,' he ordered. 'All ahead slow. Mr Raskin, pass the word to keep her quiet. I don't want a Turkish warship on our tail.'

'Aye, Capteen.'

'Up scope.'

The periscope rose up and locked into place. MacKenzie clicked the night scope on and put his face to the rubber eyepiece. The scope magnified the starlight giving him a clear picture of the waters ahead. The entrance to the strait was flanked by naval stations on both sides. Light cruisers were moored at the piers. A freighter flying the Danish flag was heading into the main channel.

'All right, gentlemen. Let's crash the party. Right five degrees rudder. All ahead one third.'

The *Riga* moved into the strait, officially leaving the Black Sea. MacKenzie felt a slight sense of loss. How quickly we adapt, he thought. 'Rudder amidships. I want a constant depth report, Mr Chernin.'

'Aye, Capteen.'

'Sonar, report all contacts.'

'Conn, Sonar. Contact dead ahead, speed five knots.'

'Acknowledged. I've got the freighter.'

'Channel depth one hundred meters,' reported Chernin.

'Acknowledged,' said MacKenzie. 'How does the bottom look?'

Chernin studied his downward looking fathometer which continuously graphed the depth to the bottom. 'It's fairly regular. I'd expect some heavy silt down there.'

'Left five degrees rudder. Hold her steady.'

'Left five degrees rudder, steady, aye.'

They sailed past the freighter. In Florida, MacKenzie had thought it odd how they built little private homes in the shadow of twenty-story apartment buildings. It was like

250

that here as the *Riga* passed the wall of stained steel plates that made up the freighter's hull. He wasn't worried about being seen. The wake from the scope would be hidden by the darkness and the chop from the big ship's passage.

They cleared the freighter. 'Open water ahead. All ahead two thirds. Right twenty degrees rudder.'

'Conn, Sonar. Contact one mile off the starboard bow, speed four knots.'

MacKenzie swiveled the scope. A tanker riding low in the water was heading through the strait. 'Acknowledged,' he said. 'Helm, left ten degrees rudder.'

'Left ten degrees rudder, aye.'

'Channel depth seventy meters.'

'Acknowledged,' said MacKenzie.

Silent as a shadow they slid by the slow-moving tanker giving its big propellors plenty of room.

'Right ten degrees rudder,' he ordered.

Riga sailed into the center of the channel and picked up speed. 'Rudder amidships.'

There was a good-size moon out. MacKenzie had a clear view of the Turkish countryside. Ancient villages lined the densely wooded shores. There were palatial villas on the European side, fantasy towered homes shining silver white in the moonlight. On a balcony, two lovers were kissing. He pumped up the magnification on the scope. They were young. Like all lovers, they were self-absorbed, thinking the moonlight was only for them, never realizing it lit the way for the man-of-war moving silently under the water only a few hundred yards from them.

'Capteen, narrows ahead. Channel depth is fifty meters.'

'Very good. Maintain speed and course.'

'Conn, Sonar. We have a contact dead ahead. It appears to be a warship. One of ours . . . er, Soviet, Capteen.'

'Do you have a signature?'

'It is a minelayer of the Alesha class. Her diesels are very noisy.'

MacKenzie swiveled the scope and turned it to the

highest magnification. The Alesha was surging through the strait with a white plume of wake behind her. She had a single stack and superstructure amidships, with a complex of rails and trolleys behind it for transporting mines and other stores. The stern was built around a ramp with a large gantry above it, making it look like an old whale factory ship.

'The strait is narrowing, Capteen,' Chernin reported. 'Seven hundred meters.'

'Depth?'

'Channel depth fifty meters.'

MacKenzie thought it over. He could wait for the Alesha to run the narrows. Or try and sprint ahead of her. Or go under. He had no time to waste. The fifteenth of the month deadline – talk about an accurate term – pressed in on him like a fist. The fastest way was under.

'Mr Petrov, make our depth three five meters. Five degree down bubble.'

'Three five meters, aye.'

'Down scope.'

'Down scope, aye.'

There was not much room for error. 'Sonar, Conn. Keep me informed.'

'Capteen, we are passing under the Alesha. The noise from her props is deafening.'

The noise was bad in the control room, too. This close the revolving shaft noise echoed in the metal compartment and the steady vibrations rattled bones. MacKenzie took the intercom. 'This is the captain. We are passing under a Soviet warship. Pay the noise no attention.'

'Capteen,' Chernin's voice was alarmed. 'The bottom is coming up suddenly. Sixteen meters.'

'Make your depth two five meters, Mr Petrov. Ten degree up bubble.'

Petrov complied and *Riga* rose sharply. Depth was always measured from the keel. From the keel to the surface or the keel to the bottom. So the *Riga*'s height had to be subtracted from the distance-to-surface figures. The twenty-five meter figure left only five meters from the Alesha's hull and now there was only sixteen from the keel to the bottom.

'Zero bubble,' MacKenzie ordered.

'We are at the strait's narrowest point, Capteen,' Chernin reported. 'Six hundred meters.'

'Acknowledged.' Six hundred meters was a misleading figure, too. The navigable channel was less than a few hundred meters wide. After that it was too shallow. The countercurrent could put them into a sandbar in seconds. MacKenzie felt compressed. The sides of the channel pressed in, the heavy warship overhead. Men hunched over around him.

'I know how a sardine feels,' said Raskin darkly. 'An obstacle or a new bottom?'

'Hard to tell,' said MacKenzie.

'Ten meters,' said a worried Chernin.

'If we take her up any more, we'll tickle that warship's belly,' said Raskin.

'Seven meters,' said a very worried Chernin.

'Let me see that tracing.' MacKenzie crossed over to Chernin's table and picked up the fathometer's extruding paper.

'Capteen, look there. Ten meters,' said Chernin. 'Then it rises again to four. A ridge? Or a ship, maybe.'

'A sunken ship, I think. See that tracing? She looks keel down. The problem could be coming from her stacks. Take us up another two meters, Mr Petrov. Helm, left full rudder. All ahead full.'

Riga shot ahead. There was a screeching sound as the outer hull scraped against something. It combined with the Alesha's propellor noise. Men grabbed their ears. It grew to a piercing shriek.

'No clearance, Capteen!'

'Shift your rudder. Steady as she goes.'

The shriek continued like someone was dragging nails along the *Riga*'s hull. Any minute MacKenzie expected the

outer hull to be breached. The churning propellors overhead never ceased. Someone shouted in pain. Then suddenly the shrieking stopped and Chernin's relieved voice
filled the compartment.

'Ten meters, Capteen ... fifteen meters ... twenty ...
We have depth again.'

The sound of the Alesha's propellors faded as they pulled
ahead.

'Michman, damage report.'

'No leaks in any ballast tanks, Capteen. The pressure hull
is secure.'

'Conn, Sonar. No contacts besides the Alesha.'

'Very well. Rudder amidships. Proceed to periscope
depth, two zero meters. Five degree up bubble. Up scope.'

The Alesha was astern of them, its prow cutting through
the water like a blade. There was nothing on the surface
to indicate the nature of whatever they had run across on
the bottom. He turned the scope forward. The way ahead
was clear, filled with lights from the shining city of Istanbul
ahead, covering both sides of the strait.

'We are reaching the end of the Bosporus, Capteen,'
Chernin reported.

MacKenzie could not take his eyes off the glorious
spectacle. The stars were bright over Istanbul. Medieval
walls encircled the harbor, rising up to its fabled hills. A
bridge lit in rainbow colors crossed the inlet called the
Golden Horn and arced like a comet's tail into the center
of the old city. Traditionally, it marked the boundary
between the Bosporus and the Sea of Marmara.

They passed out of the Bosporus between the twin halves
of the city unnoticed, as silent as any sea creature and
equally as unconnected to the warm, teeming life on land.

Now we are all strangers in strange lands, thought
MacKenzie, watching his Soviet crew move crisply through
their tasks.

All away from home.

* * *

Raskin stopped in the galley for a glass of tea. Several off-duty crewmen were sitting at tables playing chess. Others were eating a meal. The galley was spotless, another consequence of MacKenzie's presence. Raskin was actually in basic disagreement with the American idea that it was good to have kitchens clean enough to double as operating theaters. He had eaten at their fast-food restaurants. They were almost antiseptic, but no one was going to convince him you could tell what you were eating if you were blindfolded. Give him a sloppy street sausage vendor any day for taste. He'd had a pleasant talk on his own with the cook and the food was still good, in spite of the captain's war on germs.

There was an odd smell coming from somewhere. Acrid, burnt. He bent down and sniffed around. The refuse receptacles were empty. The food in the pots on the stove smelled fine. And the men were eating it. He sniffed some more. It seemed to be coming from the ventilator grill.

This was more serious. He decided to check the fan room to see if it was coming from there.

Air on a submarine was constantly being recycled and scrubbed clean of human waste and microscopic organisms that could easily affect everyone in such an enclosed container. In fact, since most of the crew never left the sub at all during their cruise, they all faced severe head colds in the days after returning to home port and breathing an atmosphere that was teeming with normal pathogens.

The corridor was empty outside the fan room. He started to enter, but he heard voices inside. He stopped, hand on the doorknob, because it was Dainis's voice he heard. What was he doing in there? And who was he with?

Dainis was speaking in Russian. Raskin could make out only part of what he was saying over the whirring noise of the fan banks. The other man's voice was tantalizingly familiar but he could not place it. And that smell. It was definitely stronger here. It, too, was familiar. But like the voice it prompted no concrete recognition.

Dainis was saying '. . . after the run, you understand? After . . .' The rest was drowned out. He heard the other man say '. . . shafts coupled . . .' Then the word 'accident.' He heard that clearly. He hesitated, wanting to hear more but fearing Dainis would walk out any second and see him. '. . . electric . . .' the man said. That was all. Then the voices dropped and Raskin hurried off down the corridor, ducking around the bulkhead. He heard the door open. He hoped they would go back the other way and he could sneak a peek, but he heard them approaching. He had to slide down the hatch to the lower deck before he could see whom Dainis was talking to.

When the corridor was clear, he climbed back up and went inside the fan room. He could in fact smell something in there. What was the source? It seemed strongest by the bulkhead and when he looked closer he saw that one of the electrical panels had been pried open. They were big panels, almost as big as the ones in the engine room, filled with wiring and circuit breakers. Two pairs of terminals looked blackened and burnt. Bits of fried wiring lay on the gray metal housing underneath. He sniffed. The same acrid smell. Was this what he had smelled in the galley, someone fooling with the electrical wiring? Why would someone rewire the terminals?

One thing was clear. Something was going on on board the *Riga*. It involved Dainis. His hunch was that it involved MacKenzie, too.

'Depth is one hundred fifty meters, Capteen,' Petrov reported.

MacKenzie looked up from Chernin's charts. He had gotten to sleep after the Bosporus crossing. He felt clear-headed. The ship and crew were functioning fine.

'Acknowledged. Proceed to periscope depth, two zero meters.'

'Two zero meters, aye.'

They had crossed the Sea of Marmara and were halfway

through the Dardanelles, the strait which linked the Sea of Marmara with the Aegean. Once the scope was up he scanned the closer northwest shore of the Dardanelles, the Gallipoli Peninsula. The opposite shore was Turkish Asia Minor, southeast, about three miles away. Longer and wider than the Bosporus, the Dardanelles was some forty-seven miles long and averaged three to four miles wide.

'Conn, Sonar. We have a contact on the new sonar.'

'Can you make it out, Sonar?'

'Capteen, it is an American sub. I believe they have acquired us as well. We heard them come around to our course. They are very quiet.'

Not quiet enough to avoid that sonar. All the more reason to have it, MacKenzie thought to himself. 'Acknowledged. See if you can get a signature.'

As much as he had hoped it wouldn't happen, it was bound to, especially as they came farther into the Med. The American sub was probably waiting to see who came through the strait and picked them up handily. It was ironic. American naval intelligence couldn't alert the *Riga* to where their subs were without alerting the entire Soviet navy. It was too bad. It would have let him avoid this one. Judging by what he himself would do, they had picked up a shadow that would do its best not to be shaken. Even if the sub didn't follow him all the way to the North Atlantic, it would call in others and pass him along as he went.

Having another sub trailing them would be like going into battle wearing a cowbell around their necks. He couldn't communicate with the American captain because Soviet and American systems weren't compatible, for obvious reasons. Tactical cooperation just wasn't possible at this point.

'Conn, Sonar. The American ship is a Los Angeles class attack sub. The *Baton Rouge* according to the computers.'

'Acknowledged, Sonar. And that's Rouge with a soft *g*. It's a French name.'

'Thank you, Capteen.'

It was unnerving to hear an American sub being identified so accurately on board a Soviet warship. He could picture the captain in the control room of the *Baton Rouge* doing the same to the *Riga*. He felt like he was in two places at once.

'He is as fast as we are,' said Raskin. 'Evasion will be difficult.'

'I know how he thinks. What he'll expect. That's going to be our edge, just like when we engaged Karolov. We'll take no action until we're out of the straits,' MacKenzie decided. 'Once we're in the Aegean we have some room to maneuver. Mr Chernin, let's take a look at those charts. We're going to have to be a pretty slippery mouse to get away from this cat.'

TWENTY-ONE

Kara-Kum

Kemal's men returned to say there was no sign of Raza or the weapons at the first oasis. Justine had hoped never to ride her camel again. She cursed the beast and mounted up with the rest. The camel's spindly legs straightened in front and then in back, an ungainly and inelegant ascent, whiplashing the rider.

When Karansky made radio contact with his superiors, they told him Raza intended to attack an unspecified northern target by the fifteenth. Only days remained. She could picture the subs and ASW surface craft at that moment frantically covering the northern seas. Would Mac be among them? Was he coping with his private ghosts? She wondered what she would find if . . . when, damn it, she made it back.

They left the canal and headed north into the desert. Again Kemal dispatched riders ahead of them. They would make better time and return to report if the oasis housed the weapons.

The desert landscape varied from scrub growth to desolation. Endless wind-rippled dunes flowed out to the horizon. The sun was merciless. A few seconds' exposure and her skin burned. Bone-dry, it sucked out the moisture from her body as well. Her lips were cracked within hours. She was grateful when they stopped in the shade of a rocky outcropping. The men gathered in armfuls of a strange looking, black, angular bush they called *saxual* and let the camels feed.

'What is that stuff?' Justine asked, wiping the sweat from her face.

'One of the few plants to thrive in this heat,' Radi explained. 'Watch.' He broke open one of its tubular stalks and squeezed it. A drop of moisture appeared.

Justine licked some off her finger and made a face. 'Sour.'

'It would sustain you in the desert. And the smoke from the wood is sweet, delicious for *shashlik*.' He pointed to where the men were grilling pieces of lamb over a small fire. The *saxual* embers burned like soft coal and the smoke smelled like mesquite.

By the time they finished eating, the sun was lower and the vibrating heat waves had diminished. They remounted and moved off. Karansky had arranged the drop only a few miles farther and soon they saw the plane circling low in the sky. They could be seen easily on the flat desert. The plane made one pass, dipped its wings, then circled back. Twin chutes blossomed in the blue sky and swung down smoothly into the sand.

Justine stood by as Radi and Ezek broke open the first crate. 'AK-47 assault rifles,' she said approvingly. 'The Russian staple. Sidearms, too. What's in the other one?'

'Grenades, night vision gear, a long-range rifle,' said Karansky.

'We should take some time to teach them how to use these,' she said.

'After you, Professor.'

They spent the rest of the day working with Kemal and his men until they were sure no one was going to blow off fifty rounds without meaning to, or jam the firing mechanism. It helped that these men had carried firearms most of their lives. They had no middle-class fear of weapons, no panic at the sight of a gun to unlearn. By dusk, Justine and Karansky were satisfied.

Justine found Kemal looking over his maps.

'The men are as ready as our quick guerrilla course is going to get them in one day. Where to next?'

Kemal looked up. 'As much as I would like to head for

the Desert Station at Chardzhou, I fear we are going to have to stop here for a while.'

She realized he looked worried. 'Why? What's the matter?'

'Look.'

A dark gray swirling cloudlike mass was approaching fast on the rising wind. It towered over the desert, a rolling vortex from sand to sky.

'What is that?' she asked. It was frightening in the same deep down bowel-clenching way as a tornado or a tidal wave.

'A dust storm. I don't think we can make it back to the canal before it reaches us. And we can't let it catch us out in the open without some protection. So we will stay here by the rocks and face it.'

'What about the men you sent out?'

'They will find us,' he said, 'assuming we are still here.'

Radi, Ezek and the others came running. They had seen the dust clouds. They drove the camels in tightly and hobbled their legs to keep them from running. Coverings were erected, little more than sheets over the sand, but the wind would be vicious and anything higher would surely blow away.

The dust storm soon filled the sky and blocked out the sun. The wind had risen considerably and already it was difficult to breathe. Ezek showed her how to wrap the cloth from her head over her mouth so it would keep out the dust. Radi helped her under the covering and sealed it from the outside.

Alone, crouched on the sand, she could feel her own fear. It came rising up like hot bile. This storm was an enemy you couldn't fight with hands and feet or bullets. 'Kindly' Mother Nature picked you up and chewed on you for a while then spat you out like so much gristle any time she wanted to.

Justine remembered being trapped on the polar ice cap. It had taken almost a year to recover. The plastic surgeons had done their work well. Most of the frostbite scars were hidden. She had received excellent preventative first aid on board the Russian icebreaker, minimizing the damage. More skilled in polar survival than anyone, they had cared very well for her and the Navy SEALs, knowing she had been indispensable in saving their ship and their beloved ice officer, Stephan.

She lay there huddled against her camel, afraid. Then she did something she had not done in a very long time. She prayed.

When the storm came it sounded like a million insects buzzing frantically around her, diving into her tent cloth with a rage that could not be denied. The wind drove the grains of sand in and no matter how closely woven the tent cloth was, superfine dust began to filter in clogging her nose and lungs. She dripped the water from her canteen on the cloth around her face as Radi had shown her, increasing the effectiveness of the mask – until it began to cake with mud from the mixture of the dust and water.

The wind screamed and blasted them. She had never felt so alone. She knew intellectually that the others were only feet, perhaps inches away, but she was cut off from them, so completely denied human comfort, that she might as well have been on the moon. She shouted for them but there was no response. No one could hear her over the wind that flayed them like a whip.

She huddled down into the sand seeking a space where the air was clearer. How long could this go on? It seemed like hours already. Breathing was increasingly difficult. How long could they stand this? She listened to the sound of the wind as if it were a song she had to learn. Had it lessened slightly? Was it giving way? Time and time again she thought she heard it fade and hope flared within her. Time and time again it picked up again and howled to a new crescendo.

It happened during one of those times. The wind had died slightly. The weight of the sand on her back was heavy and she wanted to rise to shake it off but she dared not. Suddenly, the camel shuddered and jerked its head up. Sand poured in from the break in the cloth held against its body, choking her. Something must have scared the camel. It bolted up on its spindly legs, tearing the cloth away and exposing her to the full fury of the storm.

She cried out but it was no use. She was blind the moment the wind hit her unprotected face. She stumbled about, thrown by the sandy wind from side to side. She fell, rose again and stumbled over something ending up facedown in the sand. The storm screamed. It drove the sand into her like shotgun pellets. She pulled the cloth over her face and crawled along blindly looking for anything familiar to hold on to, to protect her, to help. Only sand coursed through her fingers. Suddenly there was nothing but emptiness under her. She slid down a dune, rolling over and over again with the sand choking her.

The bottom stopped her. She tried to rise. Still blind she fought the storm but it was no use. Her feet were sinking. The sand was up to her knees. She pulled at the cloth to clear her eyes. Her tears gave her a moment of blurred vision. The sand itself was so fine it was drawing her down into it like quicksand. She tried to calm her panicked mind. It was screaming for her to run. She tried to lift out one foot at a time, but there was no solid purchase. Again and again she slipped back and the sand grew higher around her and the wind screamed and she knew deep within her soul that it was hopeless.

The hand that grabbed her was an iron band around her arm. Heaven might someday open its gates to her but an angel's touch would be nothing compared to the joy that single contact had for her. Somebody was there. Somebody had come for her. Every part of her wanted to embrace that hand and refuse to let it go the way a drowning person claws his way onto the person saving them. But both could drown like that. She forced herself to wait. The sand was up to her waist. She could no longer move her legs. She didn't want to drown in the desert. The thought of sand plugging her nose and mouth terrified her. She wanted to scream but she had no mouth.

Big hands wrapped themselves around her waist. It was Ezek! Powerful Ezek. He unraveled his head cloth and tied it around her. The wind cut his unprotected face until it bled from a thousand places, from the pores themselves. He leaned back and pulled at the rope of cloth trying to drag her legs free. She struggled toward him, getting her hands around his legs. She tried to crawl out. It was no use. The sand was too high. She saw him twist the cloth around his hands for a better grip but try as he might he could not outpull the sand. Suddenly there was another set of hands pulling at her. Kemal had found them, God only knew how. They got a grip on her arms and shirt but the material was too thin. It ripped and she fell back, grabbing at them. They managed to get hold of her belt and pull and finally she was drawn up and out.

The storm, outraged that its victim had broken free, raged to new heights. The wind blinded them. Sand blasted their exposed skin. Justine lost sight of her rescuers although they were only feet away. She threw up her hands to protect her face and ended up sliding backward with nothing to stop her fall. She toppled toward the pit, but Ezek, in a last ditch attempt to save her, threw himself behind her and blocked her fall. She fell into him instead. Pressing her legs against him she climbed away from the sand pool and up the dunes. She rewrapped the cloth around her face and crawled on hands and knees. The wind and the sand cut at her but she climbed. Ezek's body had given her purchase for her legs. She crested the dune and rolled down the other side, coughing and choking. Ezek and Kemal were nowhere to be seen.

She crawled forward searching for the camels. The sand raked her naked back like fire. She was lost until she felt Kemal's hands on her, pushing her on until she came in contact with the sand-crusted fur of a camel. She crawled over it and Kemal pushed her under the tent covering. She was blind and unable to breathe. She fought him in panic, coughing up sand and retching. He held her head until the heaving stopped. Then he pulled her head cloth aside and splashed water into her face. The dust rinsed away and she could breathe again. She gasped air into her lungs, still afraid of drowning in the sand. The water washed the grit from her eyes and her vision cleared. Still panicked, she tried to push his hands away but he restrained her.

Gently, he washed the rest of the sand away, brushing it off her body racked by convulsions.

She was still crying when he took her in his arms and held her, and the storm raged on around them.

Justine stood on the crest of the dune looking down as Radi and the others pulled Ezek's lifeless body out of the sand. They had searched for him when the storm was over, and found him in the pit that had almost killed Justine. He had sacrificed himself to save her, giving her purchase in the sand during the storm. They carried him back to camp, his arms and legs hanging limply. Sand ran out of his clothing in streams.

Kemal came up beside her. 'A snake frightened your camel and made it bolt. We found it under your tenting. In a way, you are fortunate. If the snake had bitten you you'd be dead now. The nearest antivenom is in Repetek.'

'I don't feel very lucky.'

'You blame yourself,' he said. 'But you shouldn't. Right now Ezek is in paradise. To our way of thinking, the warrior who dies in battle goes straight to heaven.'

'This constitutes battle? This crummy dirt?'

'You demean it because it has hurt you. But look around. Remember Shelley's *Ozymandias*? The works of men crumble and the men themselves fade into dust. The desert is greater than all. The sand makes its own determinations. The Russians will go the way of the Turks, as the Turks went the way of the Afghans, who went the way of the

265

Persians, and so on. Perhaps even the Karadeen will be a memory someday. Only the great desert will remain, both friend and enemy.'

'What happens now?'

He shrugged. 'We bury him, we pray, we move on. Ezek was my friend. I will miss him.'

His calmness was maddening. 'One minute you quote Shelley like we're sitting at an English tea and the next you bury your friend in the desert with Moslem indifference.' She was exasperated. 'Who are you, anyway?'

'You know who I am. Just as you know it isn't indifference,' he said and walked away, leaving her to struggle with her guilt and sadness.

She looked down at the linen wrapped body at the bottom of the grave. Did Ezek know he was going to die when he dove into the pit to stop her fall? she wondered. She had risked her life before to save others. This wasn't the first time someone had risked his life to save hers – and lost it. Why did this one bother her so much? Because it was just one more entry on her account, she realized, now even further overdrawn. She had failed Mac. Ezek had died so she could live. Where did it end?

The men gathered around the grave, little more than a hand-hewn hollow in the sand. She joined them, bowing her head silently during the prayers.

The warrior had found his absolution. Where would she find hers?

TWENTY-TWO

Washington, DC

Adm Ben Garver tossed the sighting report filed by the *Baton Rouge*'s commander on his desk and wondered what it meant. He had received it only minutes before an angry Soviet naval attaché came to his Pentagon office in a huff to inform him that the *Riga* had left Odessa unannounced and failed to return. They were screaming that the mission was out of control, searching everywhere for the *Riga*. This close to Raza's date for nuclear attack, they were desperate. Garver looked at the sighting report again. The *Baton Rouge* had picked up the *Riga* in the eastern Med. That was a long way from the North Sea. What the hell was Mac up to?

Garver hemmed and hawed and in the end politely put the attaché off. He didn't have any explanations for Mac's behavior at this point himself. After the attaché left, he sat wondering what the hell Mac was doing and why he didn't communicate his intentions. He looked over Doug Wallace's report again, the psychiatrist who interviewed Mac just before he left for Odessa. The summary passage was most interesting.

> Captain MacKenzie is a prime example of the Lone Wolf type of personality. Very much an individualist, he conforms because he believes, not because his beliefs are compelled by others. This type of 'single warrior' functions very well in the isolated environment of the attack submarine. However, the trauma of being responsible for seriously injuring the unfortunate child with his car has threatened

MacKenzie's essential belief in himself, his world, and the foundations of his personality structure.

One sentence in particular seemed to have special meaning.

A return to Captain MacKenzie's former habits and patterns may well indicate a return to mental health and emotional balance.

A loner, thought Garver, an individual. That was Mac in a lot of ways. Now he was acting like one, taking that Russian sub off on his own. Not communicating his plans to either side. Was this proof that he'd recovered? Or evidence of further decline? Damn shrinks, nothing was ever black-and-white. Maybe. Possibly. If only. He had no time for possibilities. Time was running out. Four days left to Raza's deadline. Raza had had time enough to learn to use the *Kentucky*, time enough to get her into position. He'd even had enough time to arm the nuclear missiles – and heads were going to roll over the suddenly hot issue of using PALS on deployed weapons.

Did he let MacKenzie go or rein him back in? A captain having a nervous breakdown running a nuclear attack submarine was a frightening specter. They were not responsible for Raza, and maybe a surface ship would end up getting him. Right now there were more ships in the North Sea than tics on an old hound. But if MacKenzie went wild, he was the American navy's responsibility. Specifically, Garver's. Garver had seen careers unmade over less drastic mistakes in judgment.

Faith was a funny thing. You were called upon to have it at odd times. He decided he was being called upon to have it now. Mac stayed with the mission. He had faith enough for that.

But Mac would have to prove his skill.

Garver picked up the phone and called in his aide, Cmdr Frank 'Red' Cato.

'Sir?'

'Red, who's the skipper on *Baton Rouge*?'

'Sam Crowitz, Admiral.'

'Cut orders to the *Baton Rouge*. Tell Crowitz to stay on the *Riga* like glue. Close follow if he has to. Who else is in the area?'

Cato thought for a moment. 'The *Phoenix* just put into Holy Loch from under the ice cap.'

'Send her back out. Tell Arlin to patrol the UK Gap. If the *Riga* makes it past *Baton Rouge* and out of the Med, she'll head for the North Sea. I want *Phoenix* to pick her up in the Gap if she does.'

'Yes, sir.'

'Where is *Riga* now?'

Cato checked his watch. 'Assuming they're still running at flank, somewhere off the coast of Italy.'

'Okay, Red. That's all.'

Cato left to issue the orders, but stopped at the door. 'Sir, you think Mac can get past the *Baton Rouge* and the *Phoenix*?'

'It'll prove a lot if he does, Red.'

The two had worked together for a long time. A sly smile spread over Cato's face. 'Care to back up that bet with more than your good nature, sir?'

Garver said in a shocked voice, 'Bet money on the performance of three of our finest submarine commanders?'

'Such a thing never occurred to me, sir.'

Garver arched an eyebrow. 'What have you got in mind?'

'A hundred says he can't lose the *Baton Rouge*. Double or nothing he won't get past the *Phoenix*.'

'Done. My boy, you are going to be responsible for my wife and I having a fine dinner tomorrow night.'

Red laughed. 'Sorry, I already made reservations.' He went to issue the orders.

Garver stared out the window. The trees were in full summer bloom. His first experience with MacKenzie was as a young department officer back on his old sub, the *Skipjack*. Funny how you can spot the really good ones early, like athletes. They possessed the same kind of natural grace, resolve under pressure. Garver had taught him everything he knew and then watched while Mac grew in ways even Garver hadn't expected till the student surpassed the teacher.

Ten days now since they had the ultimatum. So little time to save lives, to stop the deadly game Raza was playing. It might come down to one shot for all the marbles. Well, if that was the case, there wasn't anyone other than Mac he'd want there to take that shot.

I always knew what you had, boy, thought Garver, *and it killed me to see you lose it.* He launched a silent prayer for MacKenzie, thinking of *Baton Rouge* hot on *Riga*'s tail and Phil Arlin in *Phoenix* moving into the Gap to lie in wait.

Now we'll see if you've got it back.

TWENTY-THREE

The Mediterranean Sea

The *Baton Rouge* stayed on the *Riga*'s tail and refused to be shaken loose.

'Sonar, how close are they?' queried MacKenzie.

'Four thousand yards, Capteen.'

'This is the first time in my life I wished the American navy weren't so good,' said MacKenzie darkly. 'We go deep, he goes deep. We turn and come up and there he is.'

'You can pay him your compliments when you return,' suggested Raskin.

'I'd kiss the sonofabitch if I could just get him to leave us alone.'

'Capteen, what do you think he thinks you'll do next?' asked Chernin. 'I mean what would you expect a Soviet commander to do next? Maybe we can catch him off guard.'

MacKenzie thought it over. 'Assuming he thinks we're heading for the western Med, he's probably thinking we'll run the Sicilian Channel staying south of Sardinia.'

'Would you consider an alternate route?'

'I'm all ears, Mr Chernin,' MacKenzie said, moving around to the chart table.

'Sometime when we are being er . . . tailed, as you put it, we sneak northward along the coast of Sardinia and turn here. In between Sardinia and Corsica. The channel is very shallow, but it can be done when the tide is right. He will not expect it, I think.'

'It's a good move,' MacKenzie admitted. 'Should be plenty of noise that close in to foil his sonar. But if he picks us up heading north he's got us in one helluva corset. Could take us days to lose him again.'

'I take it you will not consider a torpedo?' asked Raskin innocently.

'Not even a little one,' MacKenzie said dryly. But a sudden smile came over his features. 'I might, however, consider a depth charge.'

'What are you talking about?' said Raskin. 'We carry no such thing.'

'We are about to,' pronounced MacKenzie.

They met in the trash room. MacKenzie, Raskin, Chernin, Chief Engineer Prudenkov and Weapons Officer Kortzov.

'They'll fit,' agreed Kortzov. 'If the electricians can wire the delay.'

'Ballast?' asked MacKenzie.

'Capteen, we may not need to be very fancy. The straits have sections where the depth is less than fifty meters. Just use normal weights and send them straight to the bottom. The *Baton Rouge* will be very close indeed.'

'Done. Simplicity is always best.'

'I've never seen anything like it,' said Raskin.

'Which makes it perfect for this ship,' said MacKenzie. Get it together. Inform me as soon as you're ready.'

The Sicilian Straits were bounded by Sicily on one side and the Tunisian coast of North Africa on the other.

'The *Baton Rouge* is two miles astern of us, Capteen,' reported Kotnikov from sonar when MacKenzie and Chernin returned to the control room.

'Maintain course and speed,' ordered MacKenzie.

Chernin went to his charts and studied them. 'Shallows to the northeast. Course heading two nine zero.'

'Acknowledged. Helm. Right ten degrees rudder. Come slow to new course two nine zero.'

'Two nine zero, aye.'

For almost an hour they sailed on two nine zero.

272

Suddenly the bottom began to come up fast. 'All right,' said MacKenzie. 'Get ready. Constant sounding, Mr Chernin.'

'One hundred thirty meters . . . One hundred fifteen meters . . . One hundred meters . . .'

The tiny island of Pantelleria in the middle of the channel slid by them.

'Eighty meters . . . steady at eighty meters. The shallows off Cap Serrat extend for several miles outward, Capteen. We should maintain this bottom for about half an hour more.'

'Very well. Return to course two seven zero. Speed ten knots.'

'Two seven zero, aye. Ten knots.'

'Sonar, what is *Baton Rouge*'s depth.'

'They are in the shallow zone with us, Capteen.'

'Acknowledged. Keep me abreast of any change in position.'

'Capteen?' It was Raskin's voice on the speaker.

'MacKenzie here.'

'The devices are all assembled. Mr Kortzov and the electricians tell me you have a twelve-minute delay from release.'

'Acknowledged. Mr Chernin, do we factor in time to bottom?'

Chernin did a quick calculation. 'Six seconds. Negligible. At ten knots we will cover a bit over four thousand meters in twelve minutes.'

'Precisely *Baton Rouge*'s distance,' said MacKenzie.

'Precisely,' said Chernin.

'Some days go that way,' said MacKenzie.

Chernin grinned. 'We are approaching the final edge of the Serrat shallows. Deeper water ahead.'

'Mr Raskin,' ordered MacKenzie. 'Take out the garbage.'

Baton Rouge

Sam Crowitz, the skipper of the *Baton Rouge*, looked over his sonarman's shoulder.

'She's in the shallows, skipper. Not making much of a move to lose us.'

'Not enough water to lose us in,' mused Crowitz.

'Skipper, we've got some sounds. Sounds like an ejection under pressure.'

'Torpedo?' Crowitz asked at once.

'Negative, sir. No motor. Dropping like a rock. Sorry, sir, I guess they're just emptying the trash.'

Crowitz relaxed for the next ten minutes or so. The *Riga* was in no hurry and so neither was he. There was nowhere they could go in these shallows anyway. He considered ordering battle stations once they were out of these waters. He was deliberately provoking the *Riga* on orders from the CNO. Tempers could get frayed under these conditions. Even he had almost jumped at a trash release . . . he stopped. The water here was shallow, less than three hundred feet. You dropped trash down deep so it couldn't be recovered.

'Emergency turn,' he shouted. 'Hard left rudder. Swing her as fast as – '

It was too late. The *Baton Rouge*'s bow, packed with sonar devices, was almost directly over the *Riga*'s trash barrels when they exploded. Packed with nonlethal noisemakers from countermeasures' stores, it sounded like all hell had broken loose. The sonarman tore the headphones off as the shrieking almost deafened him.

'What the hell?' Crowitz exclaimed. The explosions he feared never came to pass. 'What was in those barrels, anyway?' he demanded.

'Apparently, just noisemakers, sir. For cover. They went

off right underneath us,' said the sonar tech. 'We've lost the *Riga* in all the noise. It's going to be a while, sir. There's more stuff going off out there than on the Fourth of July.'

'And we sailed right into it,' said Crowitz bitterly.

'Helluva tactic,' said the XO admiringly.

Crowitz strode into the conn. 'The captain has the conn. All ahead flank. Let's clear this area and try to pick her up on the other side of the shallows.'

He shook his head. Deep water ahead. Once lost it would be dumb luck if they picked up the *Riga* again. Clever Russian bastard. They were making them smarter these days.

'Noisemakers going off, Capteen,' said Kotnikov. 'I feel sorry for their sonarman.'

'A pity,' said Raskin.

MacKenzie said, 'I can see you're broken up about it.'

'You're sure you're not Russian? On your father's side perhaps. Such sneakiness is not worthy of an American.'

'Six hundred fathom curve coming up, Capteen,' said Chernin.

'Acknowledged. Take us deep, Mr Petrov. But slowly. Make our depth six hundred meters. Five degree down bubble. All ahead one third. Engine Room, do not cavitate.'

'Six hundred meters, aye.'

'Mr Raskin, rig for silent running. Engine Room, secure main coolant. Rely on natural flow.'

'*Da*, Capteen.'

'Mr Chernin, lay in a course for Sardinia. We'll go through the islands as you suggested.'

'New course two nine five, Capteen.'

'Helm,' MacKenzie directed. 'Come to new course two nine five. Use minimum rudder. We do not want to cavitate.'

The *Riga* slid down beneath the warm waters of the western Med. Deep, with her engines slowed and her reactor silent, she made less noise than a lamp.

'Sonar, any sign of the *Baton Rouge*?'

'None, Capteen. We picked up a distant active sonar signal a few moments ago. It did not acquire us.'

If the *Baton Rouge* had gone to active sonar they had lost the *Riga*.

'Steady on two nine five, Capteen.'

The *Riga* sailed northwest up the coast of Sardinia.

TWENTY-FOUR

Washington, DC

Red Cato brought in the coded ELF transmission and put it on Garver's desk with five twenties.

'Where?' asked Garver happily.

'The Sicilian Channel. He dropped a bunch of trash barrels loaded with noisemakers and Crowitz ran right into them. By the time he got his sonar cleared MacKenzie was into deep water and long gone.'

'I'm getting a feeling that our good Captain MacKenzie's back in action,' said Garver. 'You?'

'Seems like it. Lousy thing that accident he had. Mac's a good guy. Lot of people pulling for him. Do you want *Baton Rouge* to pursue?'

Garver shook his head. 'It isn't necessary. I'm not even sure he could pick up *Riga* anyway. Alert Arlin they're coming his way.'

'Yes, sir.'

'Any further intelligence on the *Kentucky*?'

'Two possibles,' said Cato, 'one probable, nothing definite. We built her quieter than a hole in the ocean. The Soviets and us are still searching the northern seas, of course. I don't think I've ever seen a combined naval operation of this size. But the range on those Tomahawks gives everybody a lot of water to cover.'

'What about that Turkmeni fishing fleet? You could hide a lot of *Kentucky*s in among them,' said Garver thoughtfully.

'We're covering it. The problem is it isn't a single fleet exactly. Boats keep coming and going. Every so often the entire pack splits up into smaller groups and then recombines in a different location. It's either damn good fishing or damn good camouflage.'

'Keep me informed. I'll hold these,' Garver said, putting the twenties in the drawer.

'Don't spend them yet. Arlin knows Mac better than anybody.'

'I won't.'

Cato left and Garver reread the memo from the Med. Trash barrels full of noisemakers . . . ?

Hot damn. The boy was back in town.

TWENTY-FIVE

Kara-Kum

Justine woke when she should have been asleep. Something penetrated her consciousness. It was a small thing, a movement where none should be, a sense that something was amiss. She didn't move. Her eyes flickered open, scanning the mounds of sleeping bodies in the shadows of the cliff for signs of danger. The sun burned in the afternoon sky like a blowtorch. What had awakened her?

Someone was moving near the camels. She shifted position, got her weight under her and slid off her carpet. She passed Radi's sleeping form, and Kemal's. At the edge of the camp she could see the shape of a man. Sunlight shone off his bald skull. It was Karansky.

He was after the transmitter. Why he wanted it was no secret, either to call in the air strike once they verified where the weapons were, or to call in enough Spetsnatz to steal them for the Soviet take-'em-apart-and-study-them labs. She watched him find it on one of the pack camels and slip it under his shirt. She crawled back to camp and got to her place before Karansky returned.

She lay among the others in the shade, idly soothing her skin where the dust storm had abraded it most harshly, thinking. The storm had raged on for hours after she was pulled out of the pit and Kemal guided her back to camp. They held on to each other in the confines of his tent, her naked chest pressed against his, clinging to him for comfort. If desire was the same thing as action, both were guilty a hundred times over in those hours. Although that was all

279

she had to be guilty about, it brought her even closer to the brink. Closer to him.

In the evening Kemal's scouts returned to tell them the second oasis wasn't Raza's desert refuge. Kemal turned them west at the news, now heading for the desert station at Repetek. Even with the hottest part of the day past them, Justine's eyes hurt from squinting through the glare and her skin was dry and chapped.

They reached the Amu Darya River late in the day and made their way north along its winding length toward Chardzhou on the far western border of Turkmenistan. The Karadeen may be behind the times when it came to armament, but generations of warfare had honed their hunting, tracking and survival skills to the keenest edge. To Justine, every dune looked the same. To Kemal, each was a signpost that pointed him in his desired direction. She felt baked and burnt. He and his men looked as fresh as when they had begun. Finally, Kemal brought them to a stop and dismounted. He pointed, raising his binoculars. Justine raised hers. They were about two miles from the station which she could see clearly.

'Justine?'

She gathered her thoughts. 'First we see if anything's there. Kemal, General Karansky, we three go. The rest of you camp by the river and stay out of sight. We will be back by moonrise.'

They handed their camels over to Radi. Justine checked her weapons. Karansky slung the sniper rifle over his shoulder. A quarter mile away Justine looked back. Men and beasts had somehow melted away, fading into niches in the vegetation on the riverbank.

Kemal led them on foot over the dunes, leaving the river and circling east to approach the station from the desert side. The sun was very low in the sky ahead of them. Once Justine would have enjoyed sliding down the steep dunes. Now it was just physically taxing and mentally depleting.

About a mile from the station Kemal turned them back west. It was already dark.

They made their final approach on their hands and knees over a series of low dunes covered with scraggly undergrowth. Lizards scampered out of their way. Finally, on their bellies, they crested a dune and the desert station lay before them.

Karansky and Justine scanned it with night vision binoculars. After a few moments Karansky grunted in satisfaction.

'Unless this station has need of defensive positions with plenty of armed men, I think we've found Raza's storehouse. Look for yourself, Kemal.'

Kemal took his time examining the emplacements. Finally, he nodded in agreement, handing the glasses back to Karansky. 'Those with guns are not station rangers. They are Raza's men. That big one patrolling the area is Azrak, Raza's number two. Raza would leave him in charge of the weapons. I make out about fifty men. You?'

'Roughly,' agreed Karansky. 'Dug in fairly well.'

'But not along the riverside,' said Justine, still scanning with her binoculars. 'They only have that one outbuilding. There.' She pointed. 'If I had to get inside, and that's going to be the only way to verify if the weapons are here, I'd bring a party up the river commandostyle. They aren't set up to defend that side once we took the outbuilding. Leave some of your men to hold the position while I infiltrate to find the missiles. The rest of your men come in from the desert and we have their front positions in a crossfire.'

Karansky was nodding. 'A sniper set up on that dune over there would make the odds even better.'

'Your job,' Justine said. She wondered what Kemal was thinking now that all his manipulations had led him here with the force he'd bargained for. He was very close to achieving his goals.

'Always nice to be remembered for your work, thank you,' said Karansky happily.

Kemal took a last look at the station and motioned them back down the dunes. 'I say we attack.'

'General?' promoted Justine. 'Do we play it that way?'

Karansky ran a hand over his now dusty pate. 'An air strike would reduce the station to rubble and it might take weeks before we knew if the weapons were in there. Another consideration is that I believe Raza would not be above rigging the missiles to explode. We are in the middle of one of the biggest oil-producing areas in the Soviet Union. I can not take the chance an air strike would detonate them. We have to take the place.'

Which might just be synonymous with taking the missiles, Justine thought to herself. Was Karansky planning a last minute feint at this late date? He could call in Spetsnatz just as easily as he could call in MiGs. The general was nobody's fool and maybe he had been a little too quiet and cooperative till now. What did he really want?

She let out a long breath. 'Okay, then. Much as I'd love to continue in this fashionable hot spot, it's time to earn our pay. Raza's deadline is in forty-eight hours. We'll use the rest of tonight for surveillance to mark out our positions. Tomorrow night we go in.'

TWENTY-SIX

Atlantic Ocean

MacKenzie ran the Straits of Gibraltar in the dead of night, going as deep as the waters permitted. It was threading a very tight needle indeed, but he risked it to lose any other subs close aboard. He slid the *Riga* into the channel with sonar turned to its maximum and Chernin anxiously calling out course corrections every few seconds. At one point MacKenzie took them within a dozen yards of a surface ship, a navy cruiser, using the prop noise to mask their presence from the underwater sound gathering hydrophones that MacKenzie, and now the Soviets, knew were there.

The Atlantic was vast and deep and he wasn't really worried another sub would pick them up as he took the *Riga* north. There was a big thermal layer at four hundred feet and MacKenzie settled the ship tightly under it and got some sleep along with the other senior officers. Eight hours made him feel like a new man and he returned to the control room to go over the charts with Chernin and Raskin. Soon they would have to evade the subs and underwater detection devices in the GIUK (Greenland–Iceland–United Kingdom) Gap, one of the areas in the world most thoroughly saturated with listening devices. There was no doubt someone would be waiting for them.

There was a moment for idle thoughts when the steward brought him coffee and fresh bread. Sailing the strait past Spain had brought back memories. It was familiar territory for MacKenzie, once a very junior officer on one of the attack boats stationed at the now abandoned SSBN base in Rota in the late sixties and early seventies. He was young, on his first cruise. In between trying to qualify for higher rank there were liberties with rowdy buddies in Rota and Majorca. The freewheeling sprees included copious drinking and 'tapa' hopping – eating your way through the street vendors' food stalls filled with fried calamari and squid and chicken – and lying on snow white beaches under the bluest sky imaginable while the lazy blue Med lapped at the sand. There were car trips with dark haired girls to little villages on the coast with white buildings and red roofs where fresh water was unavailable and seawater was pumped in instead. He remembered the bitter taste of seawater soup, and seawater showers that left your hair standing on end. Later, there were white rooms in palatial haciendas with cool stone archways leading up to the highest point on the mountain where the church always stood.

Entire roast chickens were sixty cents apiece. Champagne was a quarter a bottle and instead of drinking it from a flute, you poured it down your parched throat from a spouted glass jug in a steady stream. You could always tell a new man by the wine stains down the front of his shirt. He also remembered dancing with girls in their tiny bikinis at the bars along the beach – the one place their mothers and grandmothers could not keep watch over them. Spain was the vacation spot for most of Europe's young people and the easy morality of the sixties made for some very joyous encounters. One Swiss girl in particular named Katya made the long, long tunnels on the train ride over the Pyrenees interesting . . .

'Peter, you've a funny smile on your face.'

He looked up and saw Raskin watching him curiously. 'Just thinking about old times, Nikolai. I was stationed near here a long time ago. A kid, really. It seems like such a long time ago, and yet, almost like yesterday. Strange.'

'I have a theory on this,' said Kortzov. 'May I share it, Capteen?'

MacKenzie was intrigued. The usually taciturn Kortzov

rarely engaged in idle conversation. It was another mark of how far they'd come together. 'Please do, Mr Kortzov.'

'When we are young, we think in very small times. The time from breakfast to lunch is a long time. The time from afternoon till we meet our girlfriend after school is endless. We get older. We think in terms of school calendars, months at a time. This term I will study such a thing. Next term I will attend that program. Then, even older, we think in terms of years. After university I will go here. Then I will join the ministry for the next few years. Finally, we think in terms of decades. When I am captain, or when my children are grown, or when I retire to the country. And when these things come to pass we are old and we look back and think it is amazing how much time has gone by.'

'So what is the answer?'

Kortzov smiled his movie star smile. He must be hell on wheels with women, thought MacKenzie. 'To live each day fully,' said Kortzov, 'so that at any moment, even if it is your last, you regret nothing.'

'You have previously unsuspected depths, Mikhail,' said Raskin.

'Thank you for your thoughts, Mr Kortzov,' said MacKenzie. 'I find them quite instructive.'

'Thank you, Capteen,' Kortzov beamed.

'Capteen, we are approaching the Gap,' said Chernin. 'Do you wish to hold this course?'

'There's a little group of islands, not much more than shallow spots really. The Faeroes. They could be a good hiding place for the *Kentucky*. Lay in a course. All ahead flank.'

'We will be very noisy, Peter.'

'Quiet or noisy we're still going to be picked up. Let's show them we're not concerned. Maybe draw out our shadows.'

'As you say.'

MacKenzie picked up the intercom and dialed all-ship. 'This is the captain speaking. We are about to enter the

GIUK Gap, an area heavily trafficked by submarines from both our countries. We will most certainly pick up an American submarine. We will attempt to lose her as we did the *Baton Rouge* in the Med. Most importantly, it is here we will face the most critical part of our time together. We believe the *Kentucky* is somewhere in the waters from the Gap to the Barents Sea. The moment we enter the Gap we become a combat ship in hot pursuit of our target. This is not a drill. This is the battle we have trained for. All of you know we have triumphed over considerable odds to get here. Many did not believe we could. For myself, I have every confidence we will triumph over the *Kentucky*. With God's help, this ship and all its crew will emerge from this mission victorious and return home with valor.'

MacKenzie moved the *Riga* into the cold deep waters of the North Atlantic so far from the warm seas of the Mediterranean. They would soon encounter the listening devices mounted along the Gap to pick up Soviet subs leaving their northern ports to attack the vital southern tanker and merchant routes. They worked equally well against subs coming the other way.

MacKenzie drove the *Riga* farther north keeping them as deep as possible, alternately moving slow and fast, hiding in thermals whenever possible and using the natural features of the ocean terrain to cover them. In the end, however, time pressure was his undoing. He couldn't make speed and stay quiet enough to avoid detection. Less than fifty miles from the Faeroes, they picked up company.

'Conn, Sonar. We have a contact. American submarine. Ten thousand yards astern. We are running the signature through the computers now.'

'Acknowledged. Let me know as soon as we have a name.'

Raskin moved to his side. 'It was inevitable.'

MacKenzie nodded. 'We'll see if we can shake him. Mr Petrov, make your depth three three zero meters. Ten

286

degree down bubble. Helm, steer course zero three zero.'

'Three three zero meters. Zero three zero, aye.'

'Engine Room. Stand by for power run.'

'*Da*, Capteen. One hundred percent.'

'You're going to try and outrun her?' asked Raskin.

'I don't know yet. The *Riga's* got plenty of speed. Let's see what we're fighting first.'

'Capteen, Sonar. We have identified the submarine. It is a Los Angeles class attack sub. The *Phoenix*.'

'Well, I'll be,' said MacKenzie wryly.

'You know her, Capteen?' asked Chernin.

'One of my best friends is her captain,' MacKenzie replied. 'We won't have much luck outrunning her unless she has a failure mode. Rig for silent running. All engines ahead slow.' He picked up the intercom. 'Mr Prudenkov, belay that order. We'll shift main propulsion to the EPM for a while. No noise.'

'No noise, Capteen.'

'Helm, come left slowly to two seven zero.'

Cutting her speed, *Riga* began a slow turn to port.

'Conn, Sonar. The *Phoenix* is slowing also. We are losing them, Capteen. Even on the new sonar.'

'It can't be helped. Let's see if they pick us up in half an hour.'

For the next thirty minutes, the *Riga* moved as quietly as a shadow, propelled only by the small battery driven emergency motor. Neither sub had an accurate fix on the other. If luck was with them, *Riga* would drift far enough from *Phoenix* to be out of her sonar sphere. It all depended on Phil Arlin's being able to predict which direction the other sub would move and staying within detection range.

MacKenzie could easily picture Phil Arlin in *Phoenix's* control room. Did he know MacKenzie was on board the *Riga*? The two had staged a good number of mock battles over the years and were familiar with the ways each thought. They'd last worked together before MacKenzie's accident, towing the *Red Dawn* out from under the ice pack.

Phoenix's presence didn't help matters. Arlin would be a tough man to shake and their time problems were never greater. They had less than three days to find the *Kentucky*. The thought of Raza letting the missiles fly was deeply terrifying to one who understood the nature of their destructive power. What was his target? A city? A military installation? Oil fields? Shipping? There were too many possibilities to narrow them down to one.

'Let's move out,' said MacKenzie finally. 'Shift propulsion to main engines. All ahead one third. Return to course zero three zero. Sonar, can we locate the *Phoenix*?'

'We are listening . . . nothing yet . . . Wait, Capteen. Engine noise.'

'*Phoenix*?'

'Yes, Capteen. Range five thousand yards southeast of our position. Coming on fast.'

'They drifted north and west right along with us,' said Raskin. 'The move to the west didn't fool them.'

'Looks like it,' agreed MacKenzie. 'Can't say I'm surprised. Arlin is as good as they get. All ahead full.'

'All ahead full, aye.'

'Capteen,' Chernin called over. 'We are approaching the first of the Faeroes. Depth is decreasing.'

'Periscope depth two zero meters, Mr Petrov. Sonar, surface sweep. Keep your ears out for the *Kentucky*. That new sonar's got to start earning its keep.'

Unable to shake *Phoenix*, MacKenzie brought it along. If there was any sign of the *Kentucky* he'd pull back, but the tiny chain of islands yielded nothing.

'Now we've got a problem, gentlemen,' he said. 'Frankly, I'm hard-pressed to see how to shake the *Phoenix*.'

Raskin looked over to Chernin and a silent communication passed between them.

MacKenzie picked it up. 'Nikolai, what is it?'

Raskin hesitated, then sighed. 'I suppose Mr Chernin and I are considering how fleeting the nature of military secrets is, eh?'

'Well put, Mr Raskin. And since you outrank me . . .'

'. . . it falls on my shoulders,' Raskin finished. 'Get Mr Dainis.'

'What if I promise not to tell?' MacKenzie said straight-faced.

Raskin laughed. 'Of course.'

Dainis met them in the wardroom. Chernin had already spread out the charts. Briefly, Raskin explained the situation with *Phoenix* to the security officer.

Dainis acquiesced almost without argument. Again Raskin was struck by how easily he let him give up their secrets. It was almost as if it didn't matter what MacKenzie learned. What could that mean for the American? But Raskin had no time to ponder things now. He addressed MacKenzie.

'Peter, to put it simply, we have a running route not far from here. In the Norway Gut.'

MacKenzie's astonished expression plainly showed that it wasn't known to American naval intelligence.

'I thought so,' said Dainis.

'We didn't think you had it,' said Raskin, sighing. 'It begins off the Norway coast at Alesund. There's a break in the edge of the continental shelf that extends south-eastward into the Skagerrak almost as far as Oslo.'

'How deep?' asked MacKenzie, tantalized by the hereto-fore unknown highway under the sea.

'Depth increases toward the Skagerrak to more than four hundred fathoms.'

'I'll be damned,' MacKenzie said admiringly.

A running route was one of the most interesting concepts in submarine warfare. Take a deep rift in the ocean like the Cayman Trench or the Norway Gut. If you were lucky enough to stumble on a route through it, and you mapped out every obstacle and pitfall with successive submarine reconnaissance missions, and maybe even placed low-frequency transmitters along its length to guide other subs in the future, imagine the advantage it would be possible to achieve any time an enemy came into the area, or could be drawn into it. Your sub could hit the route at high speed with complete impunity, dive deep, and maneuver into a perfect firing position while the enemy was forced to slow and pick its way amidst the dangerous terrain. Under pursuit, you could use the route to disappear. The depth would mask your sound and your high speed would put you miles away in minutes. You would disappear off your adversary's screens.

'We always wondered how you got in and out of the Swedish shallows,' said MacKenzie.

'I can say no more,' Raskin spoke frankly. 'We have compromised much as it is.'

'But all for a good cause,' said MacKenzie sympathetically. 'Gentlemen, the Norway Gut it is.'

The Skagerrak Sea was bordered by Denmark on the south, Norway on the north, and Sweden to the west. It merged with the Baltic Sea on the bottom of the Scandinavian peninsula. *Phoenix* had not let off the chase all the way south through the North Sea shallows and showed amazing persistence as MacKenzie went through the motions of deep turns and silent runnings. He began to be more and more convinced that Arlin knew he was on board. It seemed as if his adversary could read his mind. But even Arlin didn't know about the running route. If MacKenzie could sucker him into thinking the *Riga* was heading for the Baltic Sea, he could use the Gut to lose him for good.

The entrance, or exit, depending on which way you were heading, to the Gut was in the Skagerrak. Unfamiliar with the route, MacKenzie turned the conn over to Raskin when Chernin announced they were off the coast of Norway.

'Enter code command *zho'ltee*,' Raskin directed Chernin, very aware of MacKenzie's presence. Chernin entered the command into his navigational computer. There was a moment's wait, then the screen flashed a query in Russian.

'Code *krah'snee*,' Raskin said. Chernin input it and the screen flashed a repeating pattern, waiting.

'Command confirmed,' said Chernin, putting a stop-watch on his chart table. Across the room the printer began to chatter, extruding pages. Chernin ripped them out and took one set, handing the other to Raskin.

'These are the precise course changes, timings and navigational information laid down for running the Gut,' Raskin explained to MacKenzie. 'We are ready.'

'You have the conn, Nikolai. Take us in.'

'Forward screens on,' ordered Raskin and the television mounted on the bulkhead came to light. Ahead was the rocky bottom of the continental shelf. Enough daylight filtered down to give them a good picture.

'Sonar, where is the *Phoenix*?' asked Raskin.

'Five thousand yards astern, keeping pace with us.'

'Acknowledged. Helm, come to new course one three zero. All ahead flank.'

'One three zero. All ahead two thirds, aye.'

'Head straight for the Baltic like you're going to give him a run for his money,' said MacKenzie.

'That is the impression I want him to have,' agreed Raskin. 'We'll give him our backside for a few minutes. Make him mad.'

'Conn, Sonar. The *Phoenix* is coming to flank speed.'

'He'll stay close,' said MacKenzie. 'He won't want to put much more distance between us with all these islands around.'

'Good. Just a bit more,' said Raskin. 'When his own speed fouls his sonar . . . Now. Helm, all engines ahead dead slow, speed three knots. Shift propulsion to the EPM. Mr Petrov, make our depth three three zero meters. Twenty degree down angle.'

The *Riga* slid deep into the cold waters off the Norwegian coast.

'Depth three three zero meters, Mr Raskin.'

'Thank you. Mr Chernin?'

'Come right slowly to new course two nine zero.

'Helm, come right with five degrees rudder to course two nine zero.'

It was interesting watching Raskin in command as he doubled back northward toward the Gut. He was neither rushed nor laid back, an adept commander who moved his boat like a chess piece on a board, one steady, contemplated move at a time. On the TV screen, rock formations slid by. Raskin was looking for the entrance to the underground highway among them.

'Activate transponders,' Raskin ordered. These would be the transmitting devices along the route. They would have a short range, emitting brief pulses of electrical energy only when activated by a sub close by.

'Capteen, we are getting a signal. Right ten degrees rudder,' said Chernin.

Raskin corrected their course, searching the screen. He saw it the same time as MacKenzie did, a huge fissure in the shelf.

'Right five degrees rudder. Five degree down angle on planes. Mr Petrov, make your depth one six six meters in . . .' He looked to Chernin who was marking time on his stopwatch.

'. . . ten seconds . . .'

'Ten seconds, Mr Petrov.'

'. . . eight . . . nine . . . Mark!'

'One six six meters now, Mr Petrov. Shift propulsion to the main engines. All ahead one third.'

They were a practiced team and for once MacKenzie had the luxury of watching and not participating. The *Riga* shot forward with a degree of confidence no skipper could have had but for the strict directions already established to run the route. Raskin and Chernin took them deeper and deeper, slowly increasing their speed till the walls of the trench were sliding by fast enough to blur the details.

Both captain and navigator were sweating. Exactly timed course, speed and depth changes shot out from Chernin to

Raskin to the diving officer and Helm, and were translated into movement for the ship. The clearance between the sub and the walls of the Gut was sometimes less than ten yards. With sound bouncing off the chasm walls, sonar was effectively deaf. They were relying completely on the instructions. MacKenzie would have liked to remember them but they were too many and came too fast. The *Riga* rocketed down the Gut at almost twenty knots without a scrape to show for its perilous passage.

'Ten seconds to Alesund,' said Chernin.

Ahead, the walls of the trench narrowed to a tight crevice. It was impossible to pass through. Raskin steadfastly held course, waiting. Seconds would count here.

'. . . nine . . . ten . . . Mark!'

'Emergency blow,' ordered Raskin. His hand hit the emergency ballast blow. Riga blew her ballast all at once and shot up like a cork. On the TV screen the end walls of the Gut shot by like they were on an elevator. They were up and over the edge in a matter of seconds. The water began to brighten.

'Vent all main ballast tanks. All ahead one third,' ordered Raskin. 'Make your depth six six meters. Rudder amidships.' As if presenting MacKenzie with a prize, he turned with a flourish and announced, 'Alesund, Captain. I hope you enjoyed the ride. I return control to you.'

MacKenzie wanted to applaud. 'I have the conn. Sonar, what is the good word?'

'There is no sign of *Phoenix*, Capteen. We hold no contacts within our maximum range.'

'That was quite a performance,' he said. 'Bravo, gentlemen. Mr Chernin, lay in a course for the Barents Sea.'

The seas were clear, nothing stood in the way of their hunting the *Kentucky*.

Having made it past every barrier put in her way from Odessa to Alesund, *Riga* turned north to confront its final destiny.

TWENTY-SEVEN

London

Lavenhal's 747 had been sitting on the runway at Heathrow Airport for over an hour because of engine problems. Lavenhal twisted uncomfortably in his seat. It was wide and spacious but the money belt was cutting into his middle. He wanted to go to the lavatory to adjust it, but the two in first class were occupied by an old woman and a kid respectively – bane to those who rode the skies frequently and knew they could be in there for half an hour or more. Finally, he could stand it no longer and ducked past the curtain separating those who would party and drink champagne all the way to New York in comfort, and those who were treated like cattle in a railroad car. There was a line at the coach lavatories, too, but it was moving. Lavenhal walked back.

As soon as Raza's pipeline had gotten him back to England, he'd wired the director at Sandia that his family responsibilities were over and he would be returning. He did not tell him he would be forty thousand dollars richer, or that he had put nuclear weapons into the hands of a fanatic, but of course that was not really a great concern to him. Lavenhal was actually wondering if buying a Porsche would attract too much attention. Probably not, he decided, not if he set up a cover story about lecture dates for a few months, or maybe fabricated a consulting deal.

The line in the tail moved forward. Lavenhal was happy to be on board. He could finally dismiss the ever-present concern that Raza would betray him. The sub pens at Kola Bay were going to make quite a bonfire for Raza's revolutionary ambitions. Lavenhal would be safely back in New

Mexico. He got into the bathroom finally and lifted his shirt. A buckle had come loose, the pin digging into his skin. He redid it under the nylon flap. He looked at his reflection in the mirror. Who on the plane would venture a guess that the mild-looking scientist was in fact a master spy? He was relaxed and happy, the pleasant buzz the champagne had given him just what he needed. He was so relaxed, in fact, that when the bomb in his carry-on luggage under his seat went off, rocking the airplane and sending a blast of fire and smoke bursting down the center aisle, at first he just looked up in mild surprise. Then the door to the lavatory exploded off its hinges and black smoke filled the tiny room.

He stumbled out into hell. People were screaming and grabbing their children, clambering over each other in their panic to get to the smoke obscured exits. A stewardess tried to stop the stampeding mob but they just trampled her. Someone rammed Lavenhal in the back and he went down hard. People stepped on him. He scrambled to get up and find the exit. Reactions were primordial. The plane was on fire. Thick, acrid smoke made it hard to see. He jammed forward not caring he was kicking people. He climbed over bodies. Scorching flames licked at him. He felt his skin blister. His clothing caught on fire and he beat at it even as he was mashed by the surging mob.

Suddenly there was light and he hit open air, gulping it into his lungs as he fell. He was caught by a wide yellow emergency chute and plummeted to the bottom. Fire engines and emergency vehicles were screaming in the distance. He rolled over and over again to put out the fire. Someone threw blankets on him and smothered the flames.

He managed to get up, weak and dazed. A part of his mind told him he was in shock. People stood around like zombies, glazed and unable to focus. He joined them. Together they watched the plane burn. The front end of the 747 was ablaze. The bomb must have gone off near the cockpit.

Emergency medical technicians raced from the ambulances to tend to the survivors together. Stretchers were laid out. One at a time they were given preliminary treatment, then placed in the white vans and raced to hospitals. Fire engines were dousing the plane. Nobody was coming out anymore. If you didn't make it out in the first few seconds, the windowless tube trapped you like a gas chamber.

'Okay, bloke, just lie down, eh?' said a kind voice.

Lavenhal let himself be put on a stretcher. The man took his pulse, shined a light into his eyes. He felt a needle stab his arm. Another man cut away his clothing to get at the burns.

'Well, well. What 'ave we 'ere?' said Another's voice.

Lavenhal managed to crane his neck and look down. The money belt was burnt partway open and stacks of bills were visible. He tried to grab it, but Another shook his head.

'Don't you worry, Guv. We'll make sure it's safe. See if you can find 'is passport, Bill.'

Lavenhal felt himself lifted, his backpocket explored. He prayed it had burnt away.

'Gaw'd it,' said the first voice. 'A yank Doc. Lavenhal's the name. Priority stamp. Better call security. I'm not gettin' blamed if that bleedin loot's missing.'

'Right.'

Lavenhal tried to speak but he could not.

'Just rest, guv,' said Another's voice warmly. 'We'll take care of everything.'

Lavenhal woke in the hospital. The first thing he realized was that his body was immersed in an ice bath. The second was that there were several hard looking men standing around his bed, all wearing dark suits. Their trench coats were folded neatly over their arms. A man with quiet eyes sat on a chair out of the way behind them, waiting. His suit and haircut said American. Lavenhal had a very high security clearance. He knew those kind of eyes.

One of the men with a trench coat flipped open a wallet. A badge came into view.

'Dr Lavenhal,' he said, 'My name is Peters. British Secret Service. We have some questions for you.'

TWENTY-EIGHT

Washington, DC

'Where do you want the reservation, Admiral?' asked a chagrined Cato, tossing the second hundred on Garver's desk along with the after-action report from *Phoenix*.

'So MacKenzie evaded them both,' Garver said, bemused. 'I guess he's got it back after all.'

'Seems like it, sir. Much as I hate to lose a wager, this one doesn't smart too badly. Phil Arlin's mad as hell though. Chased him all the way to the coast of Norway and lost him in the Skagerrak. Arlin says it's the damndest thing. Dropped right off his screens.'

'I'm sure we'll hear about it.' Garver sat back in his chair. 'Look at this, Red.' He pushed over a folder marked TOP SECRET.

'What is it?'

'Raza had an expert named Lavenhal from Sandia Lab working for him. Seems Lavenhal was a KGB mole and Raza blackmailed him into a little free-lance work for him. The irony is that some terrorist group, possibly Raza himself, put a bomb on Lavenhal's flight from London. Would have blown it to hell and back but the plane was delayed on the ground and Lavenhal was in a lavatory when it went off. The bastards killed over a hundred. The EMTs found Lavenhal wearing a money belt with forty thousand cash in it while they were treating him and reported it to the airport security. Security called in the Secret Service when they saw Lavenhal's government ID. They have him now. As you might expect, he's being very cooperative.'

'What's the damage?'

'The Tomahawks are armed and operational,' said Garver. 'Two are still in the *Kentucky*. Raza's going after the base at Kola Bay.'

'They'll clear the pens, won't they?'

'The subs that can go, will. The ones in for servicing aren't going anywhere, and our intelligence says that means at least one Typhoon-class. No one knows for sure if a nuclear blast will set off the warheads in its missiles.'

'We'd lose a lot of competition if that base went up,' said Cato.

'I wish I could tell you it hadn't crossed my mind, too,' said Garver, 'but it's not to be. Forgetting the Typhoon, even with half the missiles on board, the *Kentucky*'s a nuclear disaster waiting to happen.'

'You said two missiles? Where are the rest?'

'In the desert. Place called Repetek.'

'MacKenzie's wife know about this?' asked Cato.

'The Soviets say she's with the force taking the place now. They're ready to bomb hell out of it as soon as they get the word Lavenhal's information has been verified.'

'Any possibility they might try and grab the missiles?'

'I assume they've covered the possibility.'

'Then it's all in place now. We just stand and wait and hope for the best.'

Garver nodded. 'I wish we could do more, but that's about it. I remember watching a guy line up something like twenty thousand dominoes once, you know, in one of those contests to see who's got the fanciest design. He worked and worked and all of a sudden there was nothing left to do but knock over the first one and let it all happen.' Garver let out a deep sigh. 'Red, I feel like we knocked over that first domino a long time ago. The day I first brought MacKenzie in. Then every day since, more and more dominoes fell. First, that Soviet admiral. Then the *Baton Rouge*. Then the *Phoenix*. You know, I'm beginning to think maybe we can make this one get to that last domino without a hitch.'

He took the two hundred dollars out of his desk and handed it back to Cato. 'Send it to the children's ward at Bethesda.'

'Yes, sir.'

TWENTY-NINE

Repetek

The wet sand along the riverbank compressed darkly under Justine's feet as she led them into the water. The crescent moon gave them a little light to see by but wouldn't expose them unduly. Justine was wearing jeans and a new shirt. A knife was strapped to her leg, commandostyle. The knife felt good when she moved and she was glad that months of desk work hadn't cost her the knack of carrying one gracefully. The time in Ashkhabad and the desert had restored her fighting edge.

The men had shed their robes and wore only their loose fitting trousers and shirts. Their weapons were lashed to a raft made of river reeds floating beside them, rocking from side to side on the current. They slid into the river and kicked away, staying close to the bank and the tall, concealing reeds. Karansky and the others had left almost an hour ago to get into position. Justine checked her watch. They had one hour to take out the rear guard post.

Karansky had spoken to her privately, away from Kemal. He told her he had the radio and had used it to talk with his superiors. They told him their information now was that the missiles were indeed at Repetek. All Karansky and Justine had to do was verify that and stand back. He promised her he had no intention of calling in paratroops to take the missiles. At his signal the jets would come tearing out of the sky and the nuclear threat to this region would be gone. Of course, so would Kemal's dream of freeing his grandfather, the Mahdi. She had no doubt the Russians would renege. Returning the Mahdi to stir up this region again just wasn't in their best interests. They'd hem and haw and try to buy her and Karansky back but Kemal wouldn't cooperate. He'd demand the Mahdi's return. But without the missiles, their leverage value as hostages would just not be sufficient to move the Soviets. They'd abandon the hostages and drive him back to the desert or kill him.

Kemal still expected her to help him. She could tell. He was too principled a man ever to remind her that he had saved her life and all the rest of it. He was simply convinced that his passionate belief in the worth of his cause could not fail to recruit her to it. Sorry, she told herself. She had a mission and it had nothing to do with returning Mahdis. All she had to do was make sure the weapons were in there and back off. Verify and stand back. She and Karansky had worked out a signal. If she sent up the red flare, call in the MiGs.

The river water was cool on her skin. The stars overhead were hard bright points. She put a dark stillness over her mind, one learned long ago. There would be killing done this night. She could see Kemal was keyed up. So was Radi. In fact, all the men looked pumped up. She went the opposite route, inward. She wondered briefly if there might be something in battle that a woman could never fully learn to love, as so many men did. Maybe womanhood was inherently opposed to the destruction of life. She felt a faint stirring in her chest and realized, oddly, that here in the desert, at that moment, she wanted a child more than ever before. Maybe she and Mac would try if . . . Lots of ifs. Too many ifs. Put them aside till later. She found the dark stillness again. Her private song, a melody of shadows sung in the key of death.

The desert station came into view as they swept around a bend. She could just make out the main house and the work buildings surrounding the inner courtyard. She gestured to one of the men. He nodded, took his rifle, and half swam, half waded to the riverbank. He was their first rear cover position. A hundred feet farther she dropped a second man. That left only Kemal and Radi clinging to the raft beside her.

Almost to the compound, they kicked for shore. The rush of the river covered their sounds now, but once over the bank the stillness of the desert would amplify them. They hid the raft in the reeds and tied it fast. Kemal had returned her weapons, taken that day in the mountains. Justine took her Mech 10 automatic pistol and a Beretta handgun. She slipped a small pack on her back containing grenades, night binoculars and flares.

She left Radi and Kemal hidden in the reeds and crept to the crest of the bank. She hid in a clump of tall grass. They had spent the previous day watching the station and she knew its layout perfectly. One of the five smaller buildings was her bet for holding the missiles. She was increasingly sure they were here. Kemal had identified Azrak, Raza's second-in-command. Raza did not have so many senior men that he would waste one guarding this station as a decoy.

She hated being out in the open. By training she was a jungle fighter used to deep cover and thick undergrowth. She hesitated, scanning the grounds again before taking off. It saved her life. She hadn't seen the guard, and because of the sound of the rushing water, hadn't heard him either. He was only five feet from the river with his rifle unlimbered. It would have taken only a second to turn and fire.

She froze. Her slightest movement might catch his eye. Her guns weren't within easy reach. She'd have to twist to get them. Her hand moved slowly down toward her knife, a fraction of an inch at a time. Abruptly, the man came closer. He put his rifle on his shoulder and stood splay-footed at the edge of the river. Kemal and Radi were just below him. If he looked down . . .

He was within a yard of them and she couldn't understand why he hadn't seen them until she heard the familiar sound of tinkling water. She heard him sigh. She slid her knife back in its sheath. His cry might alert others. It had to be done another way. He was close enough and his mind was on other things. She put both hands on the ground and swept her legs out as if she were on a pommel horse. They caught the guard right across his calves and took both his legs out from under him. He fell as if the ground beneath him had dropped away, tumbling head over heels down the riverbank to Kemal and Radi. He didn't have time to cry out. There was a gurgling sound and some splashing, then quiet. Justine did not look back.

She dashed across the compound to the equipment building and slipped inside, hiding along a wall of scuba gear, shovels and the like. The window gave her a perfect view of the guard post. There were four men in all. They were sitting around a small table playing cards by the light of a naked electric bulb on a wire strung over a rafter. Engrossed in the game, they were paying little attention to guard duty. She went to the other side of the building and beckoned to Kemal and Radi. They sprinted across the compound low and fast. She motioned them to stay inside and ducked out again.

Cigarette smoke hit her nostrils and she froze. A guard patrolling the compound walked by and disappeared around another building without seeing her. She wondered if Azrak had pressed the station personnel into service. It would explain the sloppiness. The guard didn't return. The men inside the guard post were talking in Turkmeni and laughing. There was the sound of cards slapped against the table. A long power cord led back to the main building.

She hid herself in the shadows, and gave Kemal and Radi the sign to come. They scampered across to her, barely visible in the wan moonlight. She pointed to the cord and made more hand signs. They nodded.

Justine knelt and plunged her knife into the cord. There was a blue-white electrical spark and the smell of ozone. The light went out inside. The men cursed. She could hear them fiddling with the bulb. Cards were thrown down on the table. She braced herself. The first man came out trailing the power cord through his hands to follow it back to its source. Her knife met him in the chest. She clamped an arm around his throat to stifle his cries.

Kemal and Radi didn't wait. They moved wraithlike into the hut. There were the sounds of a scuffle and the thuds of contact. Then quiet. Suddenly, they were back. There was no need to ask questions. Radi went inside the hut and the snout of his automatic rifle protruded from the window. If Justine sent up a white flare, the rest of their men would attack and Radi would have the defenders in a crossfire. It occurred to her that Karansky, now in a position above the station, would be watching them through the nightsight of his sniper weapon. Did she have to worry that he might take her out? No. Not until he was sure about the weapons.

They had so far been undiscovered. She motioned to Kemal to stay low beside her and they crossed to the next building.

Azrak woke from a sound sleep beside the weapons. Something in the night sounds had changed. He rose silently and went to the window. The courtyard was dark. Quiet. He didn't see anyone moving. Wait, the guard building shouldn't be dark. When he went to sleep the men were playing cards. He checked his watch. Too early for the game to break up. Besides, somebody should have been inside.

He lifted a pair of night vision glasses and scanned the area. There, in the orange light, the muzzle of a gun in the window. Someone had taken the building and now held a fire position on his front line defenses. He had been outmaneuvered before the first shot was fired. Well, he had told Raza he was no military strategist. Who was it? The Russians? Raza had said Moscow was trying to recruit the Karadeen. They knew the desert like the back of their hands. It could well be.

He cursed himself for failing Raza. Then the realization

hit him like a blinding light. In his genius, Raza had foreseen this moment. He had never expected Azrak to hold this position. He expected him to use the trigger Lavenhal installed. Azrak was the southern flank. This far west the explosions would do precious little damage to their home- land. Nuclear clouds would rise over the Soviet Union, first in the south, then in the north.

The beauty of it staggered Azrak as if he had suddenly uncovered the meaning in a beloved but only dimly understood poem. *I will take your wealth and I will take your military might*, Raza was saying, *and I will reduce them to rubble*. Far from a failure, the southern conflagration was an integral part of Raza's brilliant design. He had not failed Raza after all. This was Raza's carpet. It was not Azrak's job to defend the missiles. It was his job to die.

He heard sounds outside. Men were coming all right. The warrior part of him wanted to bolt from the building, rifle blazing, and mount an offensive against the invaders. But he was Raza's man.

So instead, in the darkness, he cradled his rifle on his lap and pressed the trigger activating the timer that would bring down Raza's nuclear holocaust in ten minutes.

Then he waited, meditating on the salvation in Heaven that was his to come.

THIRTY

Barents Sea

They met in the wardroom, all the officers MacKenzie could spare from running the ship in these waters, including Mr Dainis.

'Gentlemen, Mr Dainis has just received word from Soviet Naval Intelligence that one of Raza's men was picked up in Britain. He identified the *Kentucky*'s target. Raza is going after the main sub base at Kola Bay. This is very good news as it narrows the search area down considerably.'

'Kola Bay.' Raskin whistled. 'Can even your *Kentucky* slip in there if they know it's coming?'

'Nothing's changed. They still can't hear her,' MacKenzie said. 'She could bottom out and walk in. Those modified Tomahawks have a long range. She could be sitting on the bottom right now, waiting to take her shot. Remember, this is a radically new type of submarine. She can dive to over five thousand feet. We're the only ones who stand a chance of locating her and we'll be pushing the new sonar to the limit. But I don't think she'll be under the ice.'

'Why not?' asked Raskin.

'I believe I have the answer to that, Capteen, if I may speak my thoughts?' said Kortzov.

'Go ahead.'

'The base is ringed with antimissile systems and we have put a fleet of ASW ships along the coast. The longer the flight track the better chance they have of maybe shooting down the Tomahawks. They are subsonic, after all.'

'Precisely,' MacKenzie agreed. 'So we work on the assumption that they'll bring her in close. How close is still guesswork, but Raza's not a navy man. The idea of sitting below the horizon and lofting a weapon at some out of sight target can't seem very natural to him. And remember, he's only got two. It's got to count. I think he'll want to get in as close to visual range as safety permits. So we'll start our search track as close in as five miles, then extend it out to fifty.'

'Do we let the surface craft know we're here?' asked Chernin.

'Not unless we have to for tactical reasons,' said MacKenzie. 'I don't think Raza can pick up Soviet radio traffic on board the *Kentucky*, but we don't know what modifications he's made.'

'Aye, Capteen.'

'She's out there,' said MacKenzie. 'We've come a long way together. Let's go get her. Any questions?'

There were none.

'Mr Chernin, plot our search pattern. Mr Raskin, sound battle stations.'

Kentucky

Raza was in an aquarium. If he wasn't about to launch a nuclear holocaust, he would have been enjoying himself. Bharkov, his captain, was a likable sort who had grown up in Ashkhabad, the son of a carpet merchant. He was a few years younger than Raza so the two had never met in school. That had come later, when Raza was on a Spetsnatz mission and Bharkov was the submarine captain who ferried them into the African harbor in the dead of night. Raza recognized his accent at once, even though Bharkov tried to hide it under his city Russian.

Months later, Raza had come back to see him. They talked of the country they could build together. Bharkov's parents were dead and he had no wife. Dropping him out of sight had been quite easy. He'd been waiting for this role

308

for a long time. When Raza had turned the *Kentucky* over to him he saw in his face the joy of an actor finally asked to star.

A military man, Bharkov was pleased he had a military target. For him the *Kentucky* was an engineering miracle and he showed Raza how it worked. Except for the minor inconvenience of having to surface every now and then to get a reading from the navigational satellites, much as airplanes did, and replenish their air, the craft dove deeper, moved faster and packed more punch than anything that small ever conceived before. Its systems were so simple anyone could operate them. Laruk, the navigator, put it best – it was like driving a car in the ocean.

Raza had never imagined the sights he'd seen in the inky depths. Fish with bioluminescent lights in their mouths to attract prey. Bubbling volcanoes of sulphur covered with mounds of purple tube coral feeding on the fumes. Whales and sharks and seals and fish of every size and shape, all moving in an endless dance in a swirling multidimensional cauldron of life that one understood the oceans to be once one was privileged to peek below the surface.

Only one other seaman was needed to operate the relatively simple controls. Raza had decided it would be him. His hand would send the missiles on their way. Whether history assigned praise or condemnation, it would belong to him.

They had been in the craft for over a day now but were quite comfortable in the forty-foot black teardrop. Even the head and tiny galley were manageable for surprisingly long periods of time. They slept in their padded, reclining captain's chairs. A man could even curl up in the bathyscaphic sphere amidships. It had a viewport and the controls for the remote manipulator arm.

'How deep are we?' Raza asked.

'Close to four thousand feet,' said Bharkov. 'Deeper than any attack sub or their torpedoes can go.'

'Why so deep?'

'The ocean is full of ships looking for us. Destroyers, small and large ASW craft. It is quite a remarkable display.'

'Then we are in danger.'

'No. They can not hear us,' said Bharkov. 'And what they can not hear they can not destroy. It is that simple. Consider. Unlike in the air, heat is absorbed by the water within a few feet of the craft. Light can not penetrate more than a few hundred yards. Even lasers are short range. The submarine's only enemy is sound, and our sub is near silent. No gear changes, no cooling pumps, no propellor cavitation. We are a hole in the ocean to their sonar.'

'Surely there is some sound,' Raza insisted.

'Some,' admitted Bharkov. 'The rush of the water over the hull, the tiny currents generated by the drive. But no sonar now operating can pick them up.'

'We could be next to the destroyer and it would not know we were there,' said Laruk, the navigator. 'Or we could sail into New York harbor undetected.'

Raza laughed. 'Perhaps we will. After this. How close to shore are we?'

'Fifteen miles,' said Bharkov. 'We will have to come near the surface to shoot. That is a dangerous moment because although we are quiet, the Tomahawks are not. The enemy ships could project their course track back to us and saturate the area with depth charges or subrockets. So we will have to be careful. But we will have many opportunities when the ocean is clear.'

'So we play a waiting game,' said Raza.

'For now. Laruk, do you have a course for me yet?' asked Bharkov.

'Very soon, Captain.'

'We have selected a spot that gives us good advantages, Raza,' said Bharkov. 'We can moor there and not have to worry about an accidental depth charge or the like. And there is plenty of sound to cover a launch.'

'What is it?' Raza asked, watching an ugly reptilian fish with fangs half the size of its length swim into view.

'One of the six major oil drilling platforms in the new Kanin oil and gas fields, about ten miles off the coast,' said Bharkov. 'We can use the hydraulic arm to moor ourselves to it. When the area is clear, we come out and shoot. We may even get the chance to watch the fireball.'

'Very well,' said Raza. 'Go there.'

THIRTY-ONE

Repetek

The first building had nothing but long rows of worktables covered with plant experiments. Justine motioned Kemal back to the courtyard.

It was still quiet outside. Radi gave them the okay sign as they rounded the corner to the second building. The door was locked. She bent down to examine it. It was the merest shadow that alerted her, nothing more than a slightly deeper shade of darkness passing over the wooden door. She reacted before she had time to think, dropping and shoving Kemal aside. The knife blade passed within an inch of her head. The robed assailant grunted in surprise and raised his weapon to slash again. The blade flashed down . . . but suddenly the man's head rocked back and his eyes went white and sightless. The echoing boom of Karansky's shot reached them a second later. He had saved her life a second time. The guard folded in a heap, but the sound had alerted the compound.

Men started yelling and guns erupted. She set off the white flare. Tracer shells coursed through the darkness. She heard Radi's gun going off. The cries of the incoming Karadeen were wild shrieks in the night as they attacked bravely. She drew her gun and blasted the lock away. She searched the building quickly. No missiles. She left as quickly as she came in.

The forward positions had realized shots were coming from behind them and several guards were firing back in their direction, pinning them down. Justine opened up with her Mech 10 and blazed through a full clip.

'Cover me,' she yelled and crossed the courtyard to

the next building like a broken field runner. Radi and Kemal held the guards down firing steadily and accurately. The Karadeen were almost at the forward positions.

She blasted open the door on the next building and went in low and fast. She heard the snick of an automatic weapon being cocked almost subliminally and kept going, throwing her body into a forward roll. Bullets sprayed where she had been seconds before. The door swung shut from its own momentum, shutting off any light. She crouched under a table and stilled her breathing, searching for the unseen gunman.

Outside, the sounds of the firefight raged on, highlighted by the boom of Karansky's big rifle. Justine's eyes were adjusting to the darkness. Lab tables. Electronic equipment. Her gaze came to rest on two long cylinders. Preoccupied with the gunman it took a second for her to realize she had found the missiles.

A successful end to her mission lay ten feet from her but it was the most dangerous ten feet of all. She couldn't shoot freely for fear of blowing herself to kingdom come. The gunman, whoever he was, was no hothead. He was playing a waiting game, silent as a shadow, waiting for her to show herself. She slid her pack off her back and got down on her hands and knees, crawling on her belly under a table into the next aisle.

She rose and tipped over a glass vial. It dropped to the floor and smashed with a loud noise. Justine was already moving as machine-gun bullets stitched across the place where she had just been. She spun and fired behind the muzzle flash. She heard a pained intake of breath and a curse. Then only darkness again.

It was a silent dance they were doing, each jockeying into position against the other. Justine was frighteningly aware of the missiles. A stray shot might send the whole compound up in one big ball of fire. She had to get this guy quickly. But another sound caught her attention. The door. An almost silent opening and closing. There was someone else in the room.

As she was about to move, a voice in the darkness asked in Turkmeni, 'Who are you?'

She froze.

'Who are you?' he asked again.

She understood the words. 'Karadeen,' she answered softly, trying for the accent.

'No, not Karadeen,' said the voice thoughtfully. 'English. Or American. Yes?'

'You've got a good ear,' said Justine, trying to fix the sound. 'American.' She put down the Mech 10 and drew out the Beretta. She couldn't afford to spray bullets. She began to work her way under the tables making for the outer wall.

'The Karadeen brought you here?'

The voice came from another place now. He was moving, too.

'Yes,' she answered. Her fingers found the wires running along the baseboard. She worked her way along them.

'Why?' asked the voice.

'A deal. The weapons for the Mahdi.' Was the other person in the room friend or enemy?

The voice chuckled. 'Then the Karadeen are fools. The Russians will never keep that bargain.'

'You work for Raza?' Justine asked. The wires turned at a corner. She continued to trace them. She bumped into something. A burst of fire spat from the gunman and almost caught her, but she flattened on the floor and it passed over her. There was silence for a few seconds. Justine continued along the wall.

'You work for Raza?' she asked again.

'You are very quick. Yes, I work for Raza. I am Azrak. Together we took your submarine.'

'Some pieces here, I see.' There, a flash of white. Justine snapped off a shot. The boom was deafening. She waited. Disappointingly, the voice spoke again.

314

'We planned for a long time. Raza's carpet is wondrous indeed,' he said.

What the hell did that mean? she wondered. The cord turned abruptly upward. She rose slowly and traced it, felt the light switch in her hand. C'mon, now, she thought. Just give me a fix. Talk your damn head off.

'Raza's a joke,' she said demeaningly. 'So's his midget sub.'

'Raza is a man to die for.'

That scared her. When they started talking about dying gladly, it always scared her. Nobody died gladly but a fanatic. But she thought she had him. Right over there. He was fast. He had shown her that. She'd have maybe a tenth of a second to make the shot.

She flipped on the light . . . and clearly outlined the other person in the room – Kemal.

She had the gunman clearly in her sights. There was only a long table in between them. But it threw her off. 'Kemal, down,' she shouted even as her gun went off. She missed. Azrak spun and fired in almost the same motion. Bullets stitched across her shoulder and jerked the gun from her hand, continuing across the room and hitting Kemal. He went down, red blossoms blooming across his white shirt. Azrak kept his hand on the trigger. The bullets stitched back toward her. She had one chance. She threw herself forward onto the table and went skidding across it scattering equipment before her. The hilt of her knife came into her hand from her leg sheath and she threw it in desperation as Azrak came into view, the deadly muzzle of his gun tracking her as she fell off the table onto the floor. She hit with a crash, expecting his bullets to cut her in half. But they didn't. She looked up.

The handle of the knife protruded from Azrak's chest like a pommel. He had one hand on it, a confused expression on his face. His gun dropped from nerveless fingers. He looked at her as if to say, that was not fair, not in the rules.

He walked stiff legged over to the table where the missiles lay, dying by degrees. Justine tried to get up but pain coursed through her body. Her shoulder was hot and wet. The room was spinning.

'Kemal,' she shouted. She couldn't see him. No answer. A cold hand touched her heart.

She grabbed the lip of the table with her good hand and pulled herself up. Walking was shaky but she made it over to Azrak. He had sunk to the floor, the knife still protruding from his chest. She didn't see how he could still be alive. But any concern she had vanished in a sudden moment of comprehension.

Wires trailed from the warheads to a detonator. The digital numbers told the story. 5:56 . . . 5:55 . . . 5:54 . . . 5:53 . . . Azrak had set off the timer five minutes ago! All this time while they were stalking each other, it was slowly, methodically ticking to nuclear explosion.

'Raza . . .' Azrak tried to speak, but a red froth bubbled out of his lips.

'Shut it off,' Justine demanded. How did you compel a dead man?

'Raza knew,' Azrak managed, and died.

Justine looked at the detonator. 5:44 . . . 5:43 . . . The missiles must be fully armed. No one but an expert could disengage the detonator with any assurance, and she wasn't an expert. Five minutes to a nuclear explosion. No one in the compound, no one within miles could escape. Not even Karansky's jets could get here in time.

Then she heard the sound from the other side of the room.

'. . . Justine.'

Kemal was alive.

THIRTY-TWO

Barents Sea

Raza's deadline.

The *Riga* hung silently a thousand feet below the surface. MacKenzie had shifted propulsion to the EPM and was hovering without propellors, transferring ballast back and forth. They had been on patrol for more than thirty hours without a sign of the *Kentucky*. They were running out of time. Twice he had gone to battle stations when sonar thought it had a contact. Each time they had to stand down. The atmosphere in the control room was tense. The men were getting anxious. MacKenzie was giving sonar all the range he could, shutting down every system in the *Riga* till it was nothing but a noiseless bubble in the sea, listening . . . listening . . .

The intense emotion of the chase had spread to the men.

'So this was what all those drills were about,' said Kutsky in the crew's mess. 'I thought he was crazy always shutting down the reactor and making emergency start-ups. Now we're using them. The captain is one smart fellow.'

'How could he have known?' said Tartakov disparagingly. 'You think he can read the future?'

'Maybe,' said Purzov. 'And maybe that's why he's the captain and you're not.'

'He has you all blinded.' Tartakov spat.

'What's wrong with you?' asked Vasilov, the radio tech. 'We are here in one piece. We beat the *Lenin* and the American subs. He has done us no wrong.'

'No wrong? Do you think we will ever be the same after this mission?' said Tartakov hotly. 'We will be tainted with the stink of the American for as long as we live. What are our politics, what did he tell us while we were on board, what did we tell him? I tell you there is only one way to prove your loyalty.'

'What is that?' asked Vysov.

'Remember what side you're on.'

'Why so cryptic?' said Purzov. 'Explain yourself.'

But Tartakov clammed up. 'I won't say any more.'

Purzov smirked. 'You sound like Comrade Dainis.'

'See how you've changed,' said Tartakov accusingly. 'You used to fear Dainis. All of us did. You may as well admit it. Now you think you are immune. Just like the American. Well, I tell you you're not. No one is.'

'I don't like the sound of that,' said Kutsky. His big arms flexed.

Tartakov pushed his chair away from the table and stood up to go. 'You don't scare me, Ivan. I have other friends now. And all of you, just remember what I said.'

He left Kutsky and the others meditating on that.

MacKenzie was hunched over the charts consulting with Chernin. 'Raza's looking at the same charts. What does he see?'

'A wide stretch of ocean from which to attack. He could be anywhere.'

'The mind doesn't work like that,' said MacKenzie. 'It wants landmarks, identifiable features.'

'Seamarks?' said Raskin, coining a phrase.

'Exactly,' MacKenzie agreed. 'Make a list of possibilities. Then we check them out. One by one. He's around here somewhere.'

'Capteen, the first one is the small island of Ostrov.'

'Lay in a course, Mr Chernin. Engine Room, commence Emergency reactor start-up. All ahead one third. Sonar, keep your ears open.'

'Sonar, aye.'

Kentucky

'Almost time,' said Bharkov.

'We are approaching the oil platforms,' said Laruk. 'Depth is decreasing. Kanin Ledge dead ahead.'

The Ledge was really a flat-topped undersea mountain that sloped up from the much deeper sea around the oil field. The depth of the surrounding waters was more than four thousand feet. The depth on the Ledge was less than six hundred which made undersea drilling feasible in the first place. From the *Kentucky*'s unique undersea vantage point, the drilling platforms looked like giant boxes standing on huge round concrete columns that descended into the depths. Giants standing in water up to their knees would look like this, thick legged in immense shallows.

Bharkov steered for the tallest platform, Kanin *Adee'n*. Kanin One. It towered almost seven hundred feet over the surface, over twelve hundred feet from flame chimney to seabed. All the monstrous four legged concrete-gravity structures were so huge they were held in place on the seabed by their weight alone. As they drew closer, Raza could see the drill core tunnels and was surprised to see as many as twenty separate shafts descending into the sea-floor. He thought he could feel the steady vibration of the huge apparatus, as big around as six city blocks on each side.

Beside it was something Bharkov described as a floating hotel. It looked like a broad flat table the size of a football field, perched on twin submersible catamaran-type pontoons. Laruk monitored the constant flights of helicopters overhead.

The oil fields were relatively new, an important find in these days of Moscow's desperate need for hard currency.

It was going to be even more valuable, Raza thought, if Azrak detonated the missiles in Repetek.

He would be saddened to lose his best friend. People painted a portrait of you, thought they knew you. They didn't. They merely ascribed to you what they needed to see, what they believed they would see in themselves if they were in your position. If the Russians found Repetek, Azrak would detonate the missiles before he let them fall into enemy hands. He hoped his friend understood before he died that Raza had given him the greatest gesture of trust he had ever given anyone – the certainty that he would know that when the time came, alone and unafraid, he was to die for the cause by his own hand.

'There are several surface ships in the area, Raza,' said Bharkov. 'I am going to moor until they pass.'

'Very well. We will launch as soon as they are gone.'

Azrak, Lavenhal and his fellow passengers, the marines at the NATO base in Scotland, his own men at Repetek – the list got longer and longer. He felt the weight of his years and of his struggle. Now the men at Kola Bay.

His hand settled over the covered switch that controlled *Kentucky's* missiles.

THIRTY-THREE

Riga

MacKenzie felt the tension getting to him. He drummed his fingers on the railing, biting back a curse each time they patrolled an area and found nothing. Raza had to be out here somewhere. Had he made a completely wrong assessment of the man's psychology?

'What's our next seamark?' he asked.

'The oil fields on the Kanin Ledge. Six drilling platforms. Very large. Bottom moored. Ten miles off the coast.'

'Manned?'

'Hundreds of workers,' said Chernin. 'A very active field. There is a big mobile accommodation rig next to one of the platforms. It houses all the men and materiel. The platforms themselves have a crew living there, the rest are ferried on and off by helicopter.'

'The *Kentucky* could easily hide among them,' said Raskin. 'It would give them an easy launch to Kola Bay.'

'Good possible,' said MacKenzie. 'The *Kentucky*'s got that hydraulic arm. I've spent some time in Deep Sea Rescue Vehicles. They've got the same type of arm to clear debris off a downed sub's escape hatch. One trick the pilots all used was to use the arm to moor the ship. Then they didn't have to worry about ballast or current. They just held fast.'

'The *Kentucky* could do that here. They are the only man-made structures in the area,' said Chernin.

Kortzov added, 'The drilling sound would cover a launch.'

'We're running out of time. All ahead one third. Let's move in quietly.'

Kentucky

'The surface ships are passing, Raza,' said Bharkov. 'I'm taking us up.'

'Very well. Prepare to launch.'

'It will take a few minutes to lock in the coordinates for Kola Bay,' said Laruk, pressing switches. 'Guidance system on. Satellite relays on.'

Raza wondered if Azrak's time had come, just as his own was coming now. The water around them grew lighter as they rose, a tiny fish among the huge concrete pillars.

He uncovered the switch that fired *Kentucky*'s missiles.

Riga

'Conn, Sonar. Capteen, could you come in here?'

'On my way, Mr Kotnikov. Nikolai, take the conn.'

MacKenzie went into the sonar room. Kotnikov was staring at Purzov's screen over the sonar tech's shoulder. Purzov had his headphones on, looking out into space. His hand was making very fine adjustments on the controls of the new sonar.

'Capteen, we have a new signal,' said Kotnikov, rubbing his thin beard. 'Coming from up on the Ledge by the oil platforms. I don't want to raise hopes . . .'

'Put it on the speaker.'

MacKenzie listened. There, the faintest shush of water – and a scraping sound. Like the kind of sound a hydraulic arm might make grappling a concrete piling or something like it.

'What do the computers say?'

'They have no analog for it. It could be a whale, or a pump, or even a loose piece of equipment.'

'I don't think so,' said MacKenzie.

'You think it's the *Kentucky*?'

'I can't tell yet. Maybe. Keep tracking it.'

MacKenzie suppressed his excitement. He *had* heard something like it once before. For a few moments. When the *Red Dawn*, a diesel boat, had switched off its engines under the ice cap to test its new propulsion sysem. Sonar had tracked them until the system failed, but he remembered that barely audible slushing sound – and *Red Dawn*'s propulsion technology was used to design the *Kentucky*. Of course, the *Kentucky* was far quieter. Only the new sonar would have picked it up.

'There it is again, Capteen,' said Kotnikov.

Shush . . .

MacKenzie felt it in his bones. 'Sonar, that's our target. Don't lose him.'

'Aye, Capteen.'

MacKenzie strode back into the control room. 'The captain has the conn. Battle stations. We have a contact.' He dialed all-ship. 'This is the captain speaking. Sonar has made contact with the *Kentucky*. We are going into battle. Stay alert. This is what it's all been for, gentlemen. Let's show them what the *Riga* can do. Captain out.'

The battle stations alarm rang through the ship galvanizing men into action. Faces tight, men checked and re-checked their systems. What had been a collection of isolated individuals only seconds before suddenly became one corporate entity. They were the body, MacKenzie was the brain. United, they attacked the *Kentucky*.

MacKenzie felt the familiar broadening of his senses, sensing his consciousness expand till the ship became his hands and sinews and blood and bone. *He* drove through the sea to the *Kentucky*. *He* readied his weapons. One will, one desire.

'Sonar, Conn. Your best range to target.'

'Three thousand meters, Capteen.'

'It's near the big platform, Kanin *Adee'n*, Capteen. Kanin One,' said Raskin, consulting his maps.

'Mr Chernin, lay in a course for that platform. All ahead one third.'

'Answers ahead one third, Capteen.'

'Communications. Mr Golovskoy, signal that oil rig to abandon all hands. They have five minutes before we attack. Make sure they understand we mean business.'

'They'll go,' said Raskin. 'They've seen all the ships in the area. They know something's going on.'

'I hope so,' said MacKenzie. 'Fire control. Match sonar bearings and prepare a constant firing solution on the contact.'

'Fire control, aye.'

'Torpedo Room, flood all tubes.'

'Flood all tubes. Torpedo Room, aye.'

'Mr Raskin, rig for ultraquiet. We'll open outer doors on tubes one and four in five minutes.'

'Aye, Capteen.'

'Engine Room. No matter what happens, Mr Prudenkov, keep that plant on line. We can't lose them.'

'We are ready, Capteen.'

'Fire Control,' said MacKenzie, 'keep tracking that contact and make sure you have a firing solution. Mr Petrov, make our depth six six meters.'

'Six six meters, aye.'

'Capteen, we have communication from the platform. They have gone to Code Blue. They are abandoning all hands.'

'Acknowledged. Torpedo Room, set all torpedoes to enable in the mid stratum.'

'Mid stratum, aye.'

The *Riga* raced on under the sea.

Kentucky

'Raza?'

Raza looked up from his reverie.

Bharkov was staring at his screens, concerned. 'I think we are under attack.'

'Impossible,' said Raza flatly. 'The *Kentucky* can not be detected.'

'So I thought, too. But we are picking up the very faint traces of a Soviet submarine behaving suspiciously like it has acquired us.'

Raza thought furiously. One craft. One craft in all this time. Was it possible it alone could hear them? They had sailed past destroyers and ASW ships with impunity. What made this ship different?

'I am picking up sounds above us,' said Laruk. 'Boats in the water. It is possible they are abandoning this platform.'

'If they are,' said Bharkov, 'we must assume they know we are here. They are clearing the field.'

'It is prudent to take defensive action,' said Laruk.

Raza peered into the depths. 'No. Not defensive. Offensive. Attack the sub. We have torpedoes, don't we? And the Americans' best combat system? If this ship can hear us it's the only one. I want it destroyed.'

'Very well,' said Bharkov. He ordered the tech to release the hydraulic arm's grasp on the metal rung of a ladder up the platform's concrete leg and moved the *Kentucky* out into the deeper waters off the Ridge. 'I am locking fire control into sonar. The contact is bearing zero nine zero, range five thousand meters, depth six six meters.' He waited for the computers. The inputs were fed directly into the combat system and the automated rack and feed arrangement fed the first torpedo into the single tube. They felt the jar when it moved in. 'Tube flooded. Pressure is equalized. Outer door is open,' he announced. The automated process continued. 'Torpedo is armed and ready and set in the no limits stratum.' The craft was a wonder. Confirming lights began to flash on his screens, steadying one by one. 'Raza, we have a solution.'

Raza said, 'Shoot.'

Riga

'Conn, Sonar. Torpedo in the water bearing two seven zero. It is coming straight at us. The homing sonar is activated. The computers say it is like the MK-48, but . . .'

'Higher pitch. Around four thousand cycles?'

'Yes, Capteen.'

'It's a modified MK-48, Sonar. Contact acknowledged.' Only one ship on earth had those fish – the *Kentucky*. He had no doubts now. Garver had shown him the specs on the modified torpedo. He wanted to press the attack but the MK-48 would hit them before he could launch his own weapons with any accuracy.

Raskin saw his conflict. 'Peter?'

MacKenzie hit the stanchion bitterly. 'I'm breaking off the attack. That torpedo will follow us to hell and back. Emergency deep. Twenty degree down bubble. Release noisemakers. Hard right rudder. All ahead flank cavitate. Sonar, maintain that contact if at all possible.'

'Sonar, aye.'

'Answering all ahead flank. Diving hard. Three hundred thirty meters . . . three hundred fifty . . .'

'Conn, Sonar. Noisemakers going off. No contact merge. The torpedo's going right past. It has acquired us, Capteen.'

'Sonar, go active, max power.' Sonar poured out acoustical energy at maximum power to confuse the incoming torpedo's homing sonar.

'It's looking, Capteen ... still looking ... no good, Capteen. It picked us up again.'

'Depth, Mr Petrov. Call it out.'

'Four six zero meters ... Four eight zero ... five hundred ...'

'Still coming after us, Capteen,' sonar reported.

'You build them well, Peter,' said Raskin softly.

'Five hundred sixty meters ... Five hundred eighty ... Six hundred ...'

'Helm, left full rudder. Cavitate. Give me a big knuckle for the torpedo to home in on.'

The *Riga* made a sharp turn, propellors churning the water into a huge burst of bubbles. As they collapsed, the sound drew the torpedo's sonar.

'It's turning, Capteen ... tracking ...' He heard the disappointment in Purzov's voice. 'No good, Capteen. Right back on our track.'

The men in the control room looked worried. Their backs hunched against the pursuer. MacKenzie saw sweat appear on their faces. Death was roaring toward them. At this depth and pressure, the slightest tear in the hull would doom them all.

'Easy now,' he said. 'Remember your training.'

'Torpedo range two thousand meters and closing.'

'Depth seven zero zero meters, Capteen. We are at crush depth,' said Petrov. Already the hull was popping and groaning. The flexible deck felt taut like a knife spring. Still the torpedo followed.

They had only one chance left. MacKenzie took it. 'Maintain dive. Going deep.'

A fitting broke. Water sprayed in. Raskin moved quickly working with a wrench to tighten it. Another leak sprang out across the compartment from a small seawater pipe. Chernin took it, and a technician leapt to help him. The men were sopping wet in seconds but they secured the leaks.

'Flooding secured,' Raskin reported, panting.

'Secured here also,' said Chernin, replacing the glasses the spray knocked off his nose.

The hull was a cacophony of frightening groans. Any second it sounded like the skin would split like a ripe fruit and they would be crushed, almost half a mile below the surface.

'Seven three zero meters . . . seven five zero . . . Capteen, seven six zero . . . !'

'How much more can she take, Peter?' It was Raskin, frightened, too.

MacKenzie shook him off. 'It's our only shot, Nikolai. The modified MK-48s were never intended to go after a fast, deep diving target. They're for close in work. They're not enabled below two thousand feet. Too fast and light. This is the only way. Just a few seconds more . . . just a few . . .'

'Torpedo closing, range five hundred meters.'

'Begin to level off,' MacKenzie ordered. *C'mon, just a few seconds more. Don't give in. You're made of better stuff.*

'Capteen, Engine Room, we have a steam leak in the engine room!'

'Isolate it!' shouted MacKenzie into the intercom. 'Keep that plant on-line.'

The hull groanings were ear-piercing shrieks. Men cradled their heads in both hands. One tech bolted from his chair. Chernin grabbed him and forced him down. 'Stay. That is an order.'

'We are going to die,' the man wailed.

'Do you not see the capteen?' Chernin demanded. 'He will not let us die.'

The man quieted. MacKenzie caught Chernin's gaze and wanted fiercely not to let the brave little navigator down.

'Capteen, Torpedo Room. We have a . . .'

Then there was silence.

MacKenzie grabbed the mike. 'Torpedo Room, damage report . . . Report!'

Raskin was holding on to a railing as the *Riga* hurtled

down deeper than she had ever traveled. 'Peter, for God's sake. She can't take any more!'

'She has to.' He held on and waited as the terrible litany continued.

'Torpedo closing, two hundred meters.'

'Depth eight hundred meters . . .'

'Torpedo closing, one hundred meters.'

Pursued by death, MacKenzie let the *Riga* go deeper.

'Depth eight one zero meters . . .'

Someone was praying. MacKenzie hung on.

'Depth eight two zero meters . . .'

Just when he thought the sub could take it no longer, sonar's excited voice burst over the speaker. 'Capteen! The torpedo is suddenly gone off our screens! Crushed, I think. It is gone!'

MacKenzie heard the sob in Purzov's voice. Someone else in the conn cried out in relief even as other men cheered. But they weren't out of danger yet.

'Full rise on both planes. Emergency blow. Move,' MacKenzie shouted. 'Depth!'

'Seven eight zero meters . . .'

'We should have been crushed,' said Raskin in awe.

'Seven seven zero meters . . . seven six zero . . .'

'Nikolai, get back to the torpedo room. Get me a damage report. Quickly.'

'Aye, Peter.'

'Sonar, do you still have the *Kentucky*?'

'Aye, Capteen. Range two thousand meters. Depth one six six meters. Bearing two seven zero.'

'Fire Control, match sonar's bearings and give me a firing solution.'

'Fire Control . . . aye.' Kortzov's voice sounded shaken, but steadying.

'Depth six six zero meters and rising rapidly.'

'Vent main ballast tanks. Make your depth two hundred meters.'

'Capteen, this is Raskin.'

MacKenzie grabbed the mike. 'What's going on down there?'

'A bad leak but it is secured now. We are replacing the shorted circuit boards. Seaman Kutsky came in very handy.'

'He always does. How much time do you need?'

Raskin's voice was positively jovial. 'Give me five minutes and we'll be ready to fire.'

'Excellent, Nikolai. Captain out.'

'Mr Chernin, lay in a course for the *Kentucky*.'

'Aye, Capteen.'

'Depth two hundred meters, Capteen,' reported Petrov.

'Level her off. Zero bubble.'

'Course zero nine zero, Capteen.'

'Peter, Raskin here. Torpedo Room ready.'

'Acknowledged. Torpedo Room, open outer doors.'

'Constant firing solution plotted,' reported Kortzov.

'Prepare to fire tubes one and four,' ordered MacKenzie.

'Ship ready, solution ready. Torpedo Room ready.'

MacKenzie braced himself. It was time to fight back. 'Shoot tubes one and four.'

'Set – Stand by – Fire. Tube one unit away. Set – Stand by – Fire. Tube four unit away.'

Kentucky

'Incoming torpedoes in the water,' said Laruk, shocked. 'Range two thousand meters. The submarine survived our attack.'

Bharkov turned to Raza. 'We have one unit left. Do we attack?'

'No. Not now. Can we outmaneuver their torpedoes?'

Bharkov nodded. 'The ocean floor here is over four thousand feet deep. If we bottom out there is no torpedo in the world that can dive that deep.'

'Dive, then. I want to assess this. Apparently there is a sub that can hear us. It changes things.'

'I don't know how he eluded our torpedo. He went well below his crush depth. He is either a very brave or a very foolhardy captain.'

'Perhaps he is both. But he is just another obstacle.'

Riga

'Conn, Sonar. They're diving deep. Our units are following. He's below two thousand ... they're losing him, Capteen.'

It was frustrating. The *Kentucky* had used MacKenzie's tactic, diving deeper than the torpedoes could follow. Complicating the picture, it was no strain for the *Kentucky* to bottom out even here, with the ocean floor almost a mile deep. But he had only one torpedo left. That was going to make him cautious. And now he knew that there was at least one ship in the sea that could track him. It was going to make him damn careful.

'Our units have trailed away, Capteen. No contact.'

'Acknowledged.'

He was down there all right, MacKenzie could almost feel him. Time pressure could work both ways. If he'd filled his tanks before he went under he had at least twelve hours' bottom time. But only a few hours remained in the fifteenth. Raza had been bold enough to include a specific date, he would want to make good on the threat.

For the first time since this affair had begun, time was working against Raza. He was down there, and for the first time he'd be worried.

Raskin returned to the control room. 'The damage is worse than we thought, Peter. We can't make full power on the reactor. The best will be a one third bell till we can replace the isolated steam fittings. *Riga* was never built to take all that pressure, Peter. By all rights we should have lost her.'

'I need more speed. Tell Mr Prudenkov to pull out all the stops.'

'I already did, but it's still going to take hours. Where is the *Kentucky*?'

'On the bottom, I think.'

'We can't touch him there.'

'I don't know. Maybe we can. For now I'm going to resume patrol in this area. We'll maintain ultraquiet and keep sonar at maximum. Now that he knows there's someone around who can hear him, let's let him sit for a while and think.'

THIRTY-FOUR

Repetek

Justine raced over and cradled Kemal in her arms. The wounds were bad, but not fatal. She fished the medikit out of her pack and stuffed bandages over the wounds. A shot of stimulant and his eyes began to clear.

She was suddenly aware that Radi was standing over her, dozens of the Karadeen behind him. 'The station is ours,' he announced. 'Kemal . . . ?'

'He'll be okay. But all of you have less than five minutes to get out of here. The bombs are rigged to explode. Evacuate everybody. I'll do what I can.'

'You . . . can't stay,' Kemal managed.

'Radi, take him. Tell Karansky. Go.'

They picked up Kemal and bore him off. Radi hesitated only a moment, then ran off.

The detonator ticked on steadily. 4:23 . . . 4:22 . . . 4:21. How the hell was she going to disarm the missiles? These kinds of devices were usually booby-trapped. Cut the wrong wire and they went off. It was mesmerizing. 4:11 . . . 4:10 . . . 4:09. She couldn't risk cutting the wires. It was that simple.

It came to her that she was going to die in Repetek.

Suddenly, she saw the rightness of it. This was the balance. This was what it had all come to. This was the payment for Ezek and Kemal and even for Mac. This was where she reconciled her books and closed her account.

Her mind was working overtime. Nuclear missiles had been set on fire, even dropped from airplanes, like those that landed in the Med off the coast of Spain. There hadn't been any nuclear explosion. Blowing the core in any way but a precise implosion would just make for a very dirty mess scattering radioactive particles all over. It was logical. If the MiGs could come down and blow them up, why couldn't she do it on the ground? She reached into her pack. There was no way out for her. The grenades would only give her about ten seconds.

4:01 . . . 4:00 . . . 3:59 . . .

Not enough time to escape. Not even enough time to write Mac. By now the Karadeen were riding like mad to put distance between themselves and the station. Who knew how far the explosion would carry? She felt bad for the river behind the station. It wasn't going to be worth much for a few years, just like the Aral Sea farther north. She took a grenade out of the pack and found some tape on a workbench.

'Just what is it you're doing?' Karansky asked behind her.

'C'mon, Goren,' she said blithely, 'didn't you ever want to go out in a blaze of glory?'

'You're going to blow them?'

'Yep.'

'You'll die.'

'If there was any other way I'd take it. Look.'

3:31 . . . 3:30 . . . 3:29 . . .

He was silent. It is not often we are given to know the exact moment of the holocaust.

'What about Kemal?' he asked.

'Radi's got him. The wounds aren't serious. He'll live.'

'You're doing it for him, aren't you?'

She gave him no immediate answer. 'For him. For Mac. For me. I don't know. It's been coming for a long time, Goren,' she said finally. 'I owe too much. This cleans the slate.'

'I see.'

'Go now,' she urged him. 'I have things to do.'

But he was thinking. 'Look, if you have any shot at all

it's in the river.' He moved off with increasing energy. 'You understand me? The river. Head for it.'

'Sure, Goren. Good working with you.'

He stopped. There was admiration in his tired eyes. 'And you.' He said, 'The river,' once again. Then he was gone.

She looked at the timer. 3:13 . . . 3:12 . . . 3:11 . . .

The tape peeled off the roll with a pasty sound and she wrapped it around the four grenades she had. Pop the pins and put a piece of wire around the handles and it was set to go. Not the state of the art in explosives, but it would do the job. She noticed several gas cans and added them to the pyre. Maybe the heat would sterilize some of the debris.

2:31 . . . 2:30 . . . 2:29 . . .

She wanted to give them as much time to get away as she could. She'd blow it with one minute left, just to make sure there was nothing tricky in the detonator. It was remarkable how peaceful she felt. Maybe this had been coming all her life, ever since she sat on the back of her father's truck and played for the troops so her brothers could kill them. Maybe there just came a point when the balance sheet demanded you turn yourself in for all the accumulated weight of your life.

Mac had helped for a time. He had made her alive. But deep down this had always been lurking, like a motif heard once and then not again till the climax of the piece. It was all the more startling because it had been there all along, beautiful in its own right, demanding to be heard.

In spite of that, she'd give it a shot. She owed life that much. The river, Karansky had said. Well, it was as good a place as any and she didn't fancy just standing here and being blown to pieces. She got a head of steam up, tried to work herself into a good solid rage. Mac would like that. Don't take it lying down, he would have told her. Give it one more shot. Tenacity. It was always her best thing.

Well, once more for Mac. Optimism.

1:02 . . . 1:01 . . . 1:00 . . .

She pulled the handles.

They came into her hand so easily that it surprised her. Ten seconds.

She ran.

Nine.

The building didn't seem so long the first time.

Eight.

She hit the corridor and made for the back door.

Seven . . . six . . .

She hit the sand before she knew it was there and fell, sprawling forward into it.

Five . . . four . . .

She pushed up and sprinted across the compound. The dark vegetation by the river beckoned.

Three.

She left the compound and hit the long stretch to the beach. Her legs pumped like a track star.

Two.

The riverbank loomed before her. She ran for the edge. The water was several feet below. She dove into the air.

One.

The blast caught her in midair and slammed her into the water like a giant fist. It forced her down deep and drove the air from her lungs. It came to her frightened mind that she was going to drown. Then it came to her that it didn't matter. Above her the sky was exploding and pieces of the station were raining down on the surface. Burn to death in a radioactive fire, or drown. There was nowhere to go but to die.

Her lungs were on fire. In a second she'd have to take in air. She fought the panic that rose within her. Her mind screamed. She had to open her mouth. Just when she thought she could stand it no longer she felt hands on her body, turning her, grabbing her face, jamming something against her lips, telling her, urging her, forcing her . . .

She opened her mouth and Karansky shoved the regulator in and pressed the purge button. Air spilled into

336

her tortured lungs. She was almost unable to comprehend she was alive and breathing twenty feet below the surface of the river. He slipped a mask over her face. She clamped the sides and cleared it. She could see now. He also had on a mask, fins and a tank. Where the hell had he gotten them? Then she remembered – there was scuba gear in the storage building! He must have seen it there the day they spent studying the station!

Karansky helped her get her tank over her back and secured it. She breathed steadily in and out, bubbles rising comfortingly around her ears. She kicked off her boots and he slid fins on her feet.

He gave her the thumbs-up query.

She nodded, wanting to kiss his bald-headed, goggled face. Sweet air flowed into her lungs. She was alive when she had no right to be. She was happy.

She threw her arms around him, anyway. He looked funny smiling around the regulator. He pointed upstream and swam off. There was at least an hour of air in the tanks. They could go a far way.

She cleared her tears out of the mask along with the river water and swam after him.

THIRTY-FIVE

Riga

The hours passed. It was a waiting game now, a battle more of wits than weapons. The *Kentucky* had taken refuge on the bottom, but Raza had to come up to the stratum limit that would allow him to shoot. However, he knew *Riga* was on patrol with the ability to hear him. What he did not know was that the best *Riga* could muster now was one-third speed. Stalemate, of sorts. The problem for MacKenzie was how to make the best use of his damaged craft to get *Kentucky* to move.

Uncharacteristically, MacKenzie had called in help.

'Conn, Sonar. The surface ships are moving into position as you requested. Depth charges are in the water.'

MacKenzie had moved *Riga* well out of the way of the attack pattern, but even so the force of the explosions carried to them through the water, rocking the sub. Anyone who'd ever been depth charged never forgot the experience of being in a metal cylinder and shaken beyond endurance. Fear knotted your guts. Your ears and sinuses burned. It would be even worse in a craft the size of the *Kentucky*.

It seemed to MacKenzie, standing in the conn listening to the far-off booming of the depth charges, that somehow this mirrored his own experience. He'd learned you couldn't do everything yourself. Somewhere along the line you had to have help. Raskin and his vodka had loosened him up, and in that loosening he found the means to express, and finally expel, his pain. What did you learn? he always asked himself at the end of any experience. Here he had learned that sometimes you couldn't do it alone.

He had been wrong to shut out Justine. His arrogance, and that's what it was, had demanded he find his own solution, his own absolution. He thought no one truly strong needed help. Now he knew. Sometimes you couldn't do it alone.

If anyone had told him that this particular understanding would result in his calling in the Soviet navy to assist him, he would have told them they were crazy. But there they were. His leaving Odessa without permission had been rendered a moot point now that *Riga* was engaging the *Kentucky*. Soviet naval command cleared his use of the surface ships. Their deep-set charges were going to make a mess of the bottom. If by accident one got the *Kentucky*, so much the better. If not, they were going to make her pretty damned uncomfortable. Hopefully, uncomfortable enough to run.

You can't do it all alone.

He checked his watch. 'Sonar, Conn. The first pattern is coming to an end. The *Kentucky* might make a move.'

'We will be listening, Capteen.'

Kentucky

The pounding was indeed having an effect in the *Kentucky*.

'We can not remain here, Raza,' said Bharkov as the ocean floor turned into another muddy geyser and rattled the ship violently again. 'A system failure will send us back to the fishing fleet. We might not be able to make repairs.'

'How long can they keep this up?' Raza demanded. His face was drawn and pale.

'Indefinitely,' said Bharkov flatly. 'Half the Soviet navy is up there, and the other half is probably steaming here.'

'But they've been there for days. What makes this different now?'

'It only takes one set of ears to guide them, Raza. I can only guess they have some kind of experimental sonar unknown to the designers of this sub, or to me. Apparently they have that in the sub that is shadowing us.'

'Then we have to move.'

Another explosion, this one closer, shook the fillings in their teeth. Bharkov looked around the cabin worriedly. 'A near miss would be as good as a hit at this depth.'

'Can we make it back to the oil rigs?' asked Raza. 'We would be safe there.' As if to underscore his words, yet another explosion rocked the ship. 'I can't take much more of this,' he said grimly.

'No one can,' agreed Bharkov. 'The devastation is as much psychological as physical. The pounding raises ancient fears. There's over two thousand pounds of pressure on every inch of us. Your subconscious knows that and is scared to death at every creak. We must move. Soon. I would like your permission to try something.'

'What is it?'

'Sooner or later they will stop depth charging to analyze the results, perhaps change the settings on the charges and so on. They know we know that, and I think it is when they will expect us to move. It would be better if we took the risk and moved off sooner. We may be able to pick up the sub that way and fire on her. It would be worth our last torpedo to eliminate their sonar advantage.'

Another explosion. This one, closer, tossed them around in their seats. The hull groaned. Water dripped from some of the pipe joints. It was just a matter of time until a system failed, or the hull burst.

'Take us out of here,' Raza ordered, his hands white knuckled on the arms of his chair. 'Prepare to shoot if that sub comes out of hiding.'

Riga

MacKenzie forced himself to stay cool. The *Kentucky* couldn't take the pounding too much longer. They were going to move. He felt sure about that. But where would they head? They might feel safe under the oil rigs. They'd be right in thinking that, too. No one would risk hitting one of the platforms. Twenty wells spewing oil into the Barents Sea would be a disaster of unparalleled magnitude. The resulting spill would make the Alaskan accident look like a minor mud puddle. He decided to guard against that eventuality and move there before Raza did. Engineering was still effecting repairs. He couldn't afford to get caught out in the open. Once again, he decided to get some help.

'Sonar, Conn. Surface sweep.'

'Several ships, Capteen. The *Vice-Admiral Sulakov*, a Udaloy-class antisubmarine warship, heading west on course two seven zero at ten knots. There is also the *Vasil Chapeav* and the *Marshal Timoshenko*, both Kresta II-class ASW ships. The *Chapeav* is heading east on course zero nine zero, speed eight knots. The *Timoshenko* is heading south-east on course one three zero, speed eight knots. All three ships have ASW helicopters in the air. Smaller ships are as follows . . .'

'That's all, Sonar. Keep listening for the *Kentucky*.'

'Sonar, aye.'

Raskin had an ear cocked to the far-off explosions. He moved closer. 'I think they've got to move soon, Peter. Probably back to the oil fields.'

'I've been thinking that, too. I'm going to double back under cover of the *Chapeav*.'

'Underneath it?'

'It's the safest way to traverse the attack zone. I can't let the *Kentucky* pick us up again without having full speed.

Last time they almost sunk us. We couldn't outrun those modified MK-48s again. Can we manage eight knots?'

'Yes, I think so.'

'Very well. Mr Chernin?'

'Capteen.'

'What course will take the *Chapeav* past the oil field?'

Chernin bent to his chart and ran rapid calculations. A few moments later he looked up. 'New course zero five zero. It will take twenty minutes at their present speed.'

'Acknowledged. Communications. Mr Golovskoy, radio the *Chapeav*. Message: *Riga* requests cover under you. Come to new course zero five zero. Rendezvous in . . .'

'Seven minutes,' supplied Chernin.

'. . . seven minutes,' MacKenzie finished. 'Ask acknowledgment. Send it as soon as our masts are up. Mr Petrov, periscope depth, two zero meters.'

'Periscope depth, two zero meters, aye.'

'Torpedo Room, status of tubes one and four.'

'Tubes one and four loaded with ASW torpedoes.'

'Set all torpedoes with below limits stratum. Flood all tubes and open outer doors.'

'Torpedo Room, aye.'

'At two zero meters, Capteen,' reported Petrov.

'Acknowledged.'

MacKenzie felt they were close. One more engagement. The *Kentucky* would be cautious with only one torpedo remaining. They'd want to survive to shoot their missiles. It was time to take the *Riga* on the offensive again, push them hard. As hard as he could with two thirds of his engine power gone, he mused. *One good shot. That's all. Just give me one good shot.*

'Capteen.' It was Golovskoy, the communications officer. 'Message from *Chapeav*. Mikonev, Captain. Cover and course change acknowledged. Welcome to the Soviet navy. There is an added, Congratulations, *Lenin*, Capteen.'

Raskin grinned. 'You've made some fans.'

'Or Karolov was an even more disliked bastard than we

342

thought. All right. Let's make use of their good nature. Make our depth three three meters. Right ten degrees rudder. Helm, match *Chapeav*'s course and speed and keep us steady directly underneath her.'

Kentucky

'Sonar scan,' ordered Bharkov, preparing to move the *Kentucky* toward the surface. The sounds of the last explosion had barely faded.

'No submarines, Captain,' said Laruk. 'The surface craft are still all engaged in the attack pattern.'

'I can hear that. My ears are about to split open. I'm sure the American submarine must be well clear of the area in which the surface ships are laying down the depth charges. I'm moving us back to the oil platforms.'

Bharkov powered up the craft and moved silently off the ocean floor. A thick cloud of silt enclosed them and extended upward for hundreds of feet. It reflected the *Kentucky*'s lights and gave the cabin an eerie gray-blue glow. He was guessing they would not expect him up in the shallow zone. From the settings on the depth charges they thought he was on the bottom. Well, the *Kentucky* was just as noiseless in the shallows. He took them up slowly, satisfied when he heard continued explosions coming from the depths.

Raza wiped the sweat from his forehead, glad to be off the hellish bottom. They would be in the oil field within minutes and soon after moored to one of the concrete legs, unmoving and undetectable. Then let the surface ships exhaust themselves blowing the ocean floor to bits. When it was all over, the *Kentucky* would rise like a phoenix and blow Kola Bay to bits.

'Depth five hundred meters,' called out Laruk. 'Four hundred fifty.'

The explosions were distant now. Bharkov fed power to the drive and ran for the oil rigs.

Riga

'Capteen, we have contact on the new sonar. It's the *Kentucky*! Course one three zero. Speed twenty knots. Range three thousand meters. Just below the above limits stratum, Capteen.'

'Acknowledged. Fire Control, match sonar bearings and prepare a constant firing solution.'

'Fire Control, aye.'

This was it. MacKenzie slapped the stanchion. 'We've got him, Nikolai. He's running.'

'Heading right for the oil platforms.'

'He won't get there this time,' affirmed MacKenzie. 'We'll get our one good shot. Time to leave papa. Make our depth six six meters, Mr Petrov.'

'Six six meters, aye.'

'We will fire a salvo of torpedoes from tubes one and four.'

'Fire Control, aye.'

'Depth six six meters, Capteen,' reported Petrov.

'Level her off. Zero bubble.'

'Conn, constant firing solution,' reported Kortzov.

'Stand by to fire tubes one and four,' said MacKenzie. He could feel the tension in the control room. Let nothing stop them now. Let those fish ride the track right to the *Kentucky*. Five minutes more and she would be hidden in the oil fields again. She was out in the open now.

'For all the marbles,' he whispered and saw Raskin nodding, his eyes fixed on the screens.

'Capteen, ship ready, solution ready. Torpedo Room ready.'

MacKenzie braced himself. It was time to take it to the max. 'Shoot units in tubes one and four.'

'Set – Stand by – Fire. Tube one unit away. Set – Stand by – Fire. Tube four unit away.'

Kentucky

'Captain, more incoming torpedoes in the water,' said Laruk, shocked. 'Range two thousand meters. The submarine has appeared out of nowhere.'

Bharkov scanned the screens in fear. 'He must have been hiding . . . yes, under the surface ship. He must have. They are too close, Raza.'

'Torpedo one thousand yards and closing.' Laruk saw the fear on Bharkov's face. He watched the screen wide-eyed.

'Do something,' shouted Raza. 'Fire the missiles.'

Bharkov shoved his sleeve across his face to wipe away the sweat. He tried to concentrate. 'They are too close. We can't make the platforms. We have to dive. Maybe we can outrun them again.'

'Torpedo five hundred yards and closing.' Laruk couldn't tear his eyes from the screen.

'Take no chances,' Raza demanded. 'We are expendable. Fire the missiles!'

'I am captain of this ship and I say we dive!' Bharkov's hand shot out and the *Kentucky* dropped like a stone.

'Depth,' he demanded. 'Laruk!'

'Captain, I will shoot you.'

Bharkov looked at the pistol suddenly in Raza's hand and laughed. 'Do you think you can threaten me with that with a torpedo on our tail? Shoot me and run this ship yourself, Raza.'

'Depth one hundred sixty . . . one hundred eighty . . . two hundred . . . the torpedoes are still following us.'

'Let them come,' said Bharkov hotly. 'Raza?'

'Resume command,' said Raza tightly.

'Two hundred sixty . . . two hundred eighty . . . three hundred . . . still following. Torpedo range is six hundred meters. We are outdistancing them, Captain!'

'We will beat them. Laruk, match sonar bearings and shoot our remaining torpedo back on their course track.'

'Acknowledged,' said Laruk. 'Unit armed and ready.'

'Fire.'

They felt the jolt as the torpedo left the *Kentucky*.

'Depth.'

'Three hundred meters . . . three hundred twenty . . . three hundred thirty . . .'

'We are going to outrun them,' exclaimed Raza. There was hope in his voice now.

Bharkov nodded, so intent on dodging the pursuing torpedoes that he never saw the danger coming.

Laruk saw it first. 'Captain! In the water. Dead ahead on my screen!'

'Dear God, I see it! Emergency turn . . . ! Emergency . . .'

Whumpf.

The second pattern of depth charges laid down by the *Chapeav* and her sister ships had all but gone unnoticed in *Kentucky*'s run from *Riga*'s hotly pursuing torpedoes. Had the charges not been reset for the middle zone on MacKenzie's orders, the *Kentucky* might have made it deep enough below crush depth to evade them and destroy the torpedoes. But the *Kentucky* was too close and the sensors in the depth charges felt her presence for the split second that she dove past. They detonated, catching *Kentucky* in a pressure wave that sent her spinning out of control. Systems badly stressed during the initial depth charging finally failed. She slowed, taking on water, drifting out of control.

Raza yanked his head up from the controls. Bharkov was slumped over. Something hot and wet was pouring from his scalp. Raza searched for the fire button on the console but the lighting kept shorting out. When he wiped his eyes

346

his sleeve came away bloody. He made the mistake of looking out the front view port to clear his head.

What he saw transfixed him like a bug pinned to a specimen board. The first of *Riga*'s torpedoes came hurtling in riding the tiny wake from its propellor, growing larger and larger as it came homing in straight for him. He screamed at the unavoidable head-on collision. The torpedo smashed right through the window spearing into him with a torrent of glass and seawater, cutting him in two only a microsecond before the electronics in its warhead told it contact had been made and enough explosive to kill a ship ten times larger erupted and destroyed the *Kentucky*.

Moments later the second torpedo passed through the quieting turbulence and the flakes of debris settling softly to the bottom.

Riga

'Capteen. Contacts have merged. Explosion on bearing of *Kentucky*. Unit one has hit the *Kentucky*. It is off our screens!'

'Acknowledged, Sonar. Well done. Communications, inform the fleet. Send this: Clean sweep. *Kentucky* destroyed by *Riga* this day and time. All hands performed with valor. Sign it, MacKenzie, Captain, *Riga*, United States Navy.'

Wild cheering started in the conn and spread throughout the ship as word spread. MacKenzie accepted the claps on the back, but inwardly there was a moment of silence. The souls lost on board the *Kentucky* had threatened countless others and he had completed his mission, but he would not cheer death in any form.

'Capteen, Sonar.' MacKenzie heard the concern in Kotnikov's voice and called for quiet. Heads turned to listen.

'This is the captain. What's wrong, Sonar?'

'Torpedo in the water. *Kentucky* may have launched, Capteen. Heading right for the *Chapeav*.'

'Warn them,' MacKenzie directed. 'Hard left rudder.'

They waited. Overhead, combat systems were activated. The helicopters would be dropping decoys.

'We are hearing some strange sounds. Another high-pitched motor. Can it be an echo of our torpedo?'

'On the same course?' asked MacKenzie.

'No, Capteen. Heading straight for us.'

It was Raskin who understood first and shouted to MacKenzie. 'Peter, the second torpedo may be running afoul. If it doubled back it could have easily acquired us.'

'Sonar, did you track unit two?'

'We thought it was lost in the depths, Capteen.' He hesitated. 'Capteen, a stronger signal. It is definitely our second unit. Homing sonar is on. It has acquired us.'

'Damn,' MacKenzie cursed. It must have gone right past the target after it was destroyed and made a long sweeping turn. Why the hell wasn't it crushed? 'Bearing?'

'Three five zero. Range three thousand meters.'

'What's our depth?'

'Two hundred sixty meters,' reported Petrov.

'Acknowledged. Countermeasures, release noise-makers.'

'Noisemakers away.'

'It's not falling for them, Capteen. It is still locked onto us.'

Suddenly the sea was alive with danger again.

'Inform the surface ships of our situation,' MacKenzie ordered. 'Warn them to stand clear. Helm, right-hard rudder. All ahead flank, cavitate.'

He had little confidence in the knuckle but it might buy them some time. He couldn't outdive the torpedo. *Riga* had been stressed badly the last time. She'd never handle that depth again.

'Torpedo slowing . . . searching,' advised sonar.

'Mr Chernin, Kanin Field. Describe it again.'

'Kanin Field sits on a flat-topped undersea mountain sloping up from the bottom. The bottom is more than one thousand meters deep. The distance from the top of the mountain, what we call the Ledge, to the surface, is less than two hundred meters.'

'How far?'

'Two thousand meters to the Ledge. Due east of us.'

'Conn, Sonar. The torpedo has passed through the knuckle and is coming straight for us. Distance two thousand meters. Speed thirty knots.'

'Helm, steer course zero nine zero. All ahead flank, Engine Room.'

'Conn, Engine Room. We can not answer the flank bell!'

'Maximum turns, Mr Prudenkov. Give me everything you can. I need speed.'

'We can't do much more than one third, Capteen.'

'If we don't do much more we won't have very long,' snapped MacKenzie.

'Engine Room, aye.'

'Make your depth two five zero meters, Mr Petrov.'

'Two five zero meters, aye.'

'Capteen, Communications. We are informed the *Chapeav* has been hit. Damage amidships. But she is still afloat.'

So the *Kentucky* had left a legacy of destruction after all. 'Acknowledged,' he said.

The whine of the engines picked up a pitch. They were running as fast as possible – right for the Kanin Ledge. There was no way to outrun the torpedo that was breathing down their necks. This was a move of desperation. It had to be timed just right or he was going to bring down the kind of environmental holocaust he had been sent here to avoid. But he had to save his ship.

'At ordered depth, Capteen.'

'Acknowledged. Distance to the Ledge, Mr Chernin.'

'Eight hundred meters.'

'Call it out. Every hundred. Closed circuit screens on.'

'Aye, Capteen.'

The TV screens came on. Still too dark to see anything but murky water at this depth. 'Nikolai, I need your help.'

'Anything. What have you got in mind?'

'You gave me the idea. You and Mr Chernin. In the Norway Gut. I thought you were going to hit the wall. But you didn't. You took her up faster than I've ever seen. You're going to have to do it again.'

'Seven hundred meters to Ledge,' said Chernin.

'Torpedo closing, six hundred meters,' reported Sonar.

The torpedo was gaining on them. MacKenzie looked at Raskin intently. 'At this depth we're running straight into that undersea mountain. It goes up to two hundred meters below the surface. I'm going to make as sharp an ascent as possible right before the wall and try to run that torpedo right into it. If we don't, if we take the torpedo over the top with us, we'll end up destroying one of the platforms and doing what the *Kentucky* could not do. So we can't. It would be better that we fail and both go into the wall. I'll wait for the last second and even then some. It'll be up to you and Mr Chernin to take us over with that practiced maneuver you used.'

Raskin looked pale. 'We had markers there, Peter.'

'I'll tell you when. I can't turn that decision over. I have to wait until I'm sure the torpedo can't climb over the Ledge. If we can, so be it. If not . . .'

'Four hundred meters to Ledge,' said Chernin.

'Torpedo closing, three hundred meters,' reported sonar.

'Mr Chernin, you heard my orders?'

'Yes, Capteen. I will do my best. Three hundred meters to Ledge,' said Chernin.

'Torpedo closing, two hundred meters,' reported sonar.

Both Raskin and Chernin were sweating. The picture on the TV screen came into focus. Dead ahead was a stone wall – the outer limit of the Ledge. They would be crushed into an unrecognizable hulk of metal if they hit it. It raced toward them with frightening clarity as the *Riga* rocketed on, death speeding only slightly behind.

'One hundred meters to Ledge,' said Chernin.

'Torpedo closing, one hundred meters,' reported sonar.

'Stand by for emergency blow,' said Raskin, worriedly. The strain of the maneuver alone might break *Riga's* back.

'Nikolai, you have the conn on my order to execute.'

'Understood, Peter.'

'Ten seconds to the Ledge,' said Chernin.

MacKenzie could see the wall. He steadfastly held course. Seconds counted. The torpedo roared after them, only seconds behind. The men in the conn held their breaths.

'. . . seven . . . six . . . five . . . four . . . !'

'Capteen . . . Capteen!'

'Now, Nikolai. Execute!'

'Emergency blow,' ordered Raskin and his hand hit the emergency ballast blow. *Riga* blew her ballast all at once and shot up like a cork. 'Full rise on all planes. All back emergency. Watch that pressure transient.'

On the TV screen the walls shot by closer than anyone could have imagined. There was a sharp, scraping sound. It rose to a gut-wrenching pitch. They were too close. Adding to it, the ship was suddenly rocked with explosive force. Men who couldn't grab railings were thrown about.

'Capteen, the torpedo hit the wall and detonated.'

'Acknowledged,' said MacKenzie gratefully, holding on as the *Riga* shot upward. At least they had that.

'Keep pumping,' ordered Raskin. The scraping sound grew worse – but they were rising. Still rising. The water was brighter. The wall began to curve away . . .

They almost made it.

The outcropping that caught them must have projected fifty feet beyond the top of the Ledge. It tore into the bottom of the keel like a knife and breached both outer and inner hulls. The ship was torn open. Men were tossed around the conn like rag dolls. Water poured in.

MacKenzie picked himself up off the deck. At first he

didn't understand the light on the TV screen. Then he saw it for what it was. Daylight! They had surfaced the ship. At least the main tank was holding for now, too.

'Damage reports,' he demanded on the all-ship.

'Conn, Engine Room. We are flooding.'

'Torpedo Room, we are taking on water, Capteen.'

They wouldn't hold for long at the rate they were taking in water. MacKenzie hit the alarm. 'All hands abandon ship. This is the captain speaking. All hands abandon ship. Stay calm. There are surface ships in the area. Make for the platforms if you can. Communications, send out the SOS.'

'Sending, Capteen.'

The intercom crackled. 'Capteen, this is the engine room. Please come quickly. It is Mr Prudenkov . . .'

'On my way,' MacKenzie shot back. 'See to the men,' he ordered Raskin and ran out of the conn.

'Wait, Peter . . . !'

He ran back. Water was spilling into the main passageways and men were scrambling to get to the escape trunks. He calmed where he could, directed where he had to and provided the welcome presence of authority. Sweet salt air was flooding the ship from the open hatches. 'We got them, Capteen,' said one man proudly.

'We sure did,' MacKenzie acknowledged.

He made his way back to the engine room. The compartment hatch was open. He ducked inside. Chief Engineer Prudenkov was lying on the deck, his head held above the rising water by Seaman Tartakov.

'What are you doing here?' MacKenzie asked. 'What happened to Mr Prudenkov?'

'Arisha is my best friend. I came back to help him out. It is a good thing I got here.'

'I suppose it is. Let me help you.'

Water was pouring in. The reactor was still on-line but the main shaft was disengaged. When the water hit the reactor control equipment it would shut down the plant, but fires had started and the oxygen flasks could rupture and blow them sky-high. They had minutes at best. MacKenzie stepped into the water and got an arm under Prudenkov's inert form.

'I'll hold him. We'll need more help. Call Mr Raskin.' It was only then that he noticed Tartakov's rubber gloves and boots.

'Why are you . . . ?'

Security Officer Dainis's voice from behind stopped him. 'He is wearing them because unlike many on this boat, Capteen, he did not succumb to your tainted politics or your false heroics.' Dainis came out from behind an instrument console. 'Heroics, I might add, which have finally cost us the *Riga*.'

MacKenzie said nothing. Dainis was wearing boots and gloves, too. Suddenly Tartakov was holding a gun.

'It was originally planned that you would die in an accident,' Dainis said. 'Comrade Tartakov wired the bilge pocket that takes the overflow from the after trim tank and propellor shaft leak off. You would have taken one step into it to observe some problem and have gone up in a blue spark.'

'What happened to Mr Prudenkov?'

'Comrade Prudenkov saw the cable and tried to stop us. A pity you contaminated him, too.'

'I see.'

'It doesn't matter. Losing the *Riga* makes it all unnecessary. It will be your grave, and his, the brave captain who went down trying to save his men. Fitting, eh?'

It was a ghastly surprise. Dainis wore a face MacKenzie had never seen before. The man was a consummate actor. It suddenly made sense, all the help. No secrets. Security be damned. He should have seen it coming. Dainis, with or without his superiors, had planned to kill him from the start rather than let him leave the ship having learned so much. Why protect the Gut or the codes or the technical manuals for the sonar – the good captain was never going home to share them.

Tartakov moved to cover him with the gun, leaning on the propellor shaft which went through the hull out into the water, in effect, a hole in the hull. It couldn't be tightly sealed or the shaft couldn't turn, so some water came in, was collected in the bilge pocket at the bottom of the compartment and pumped out again. Seawater made a pretty good conductor. Wiring it for high voltage was a neat and effective trap.

'They'll want to recover the sub for the sonar. Do I get sent home with a bullet in my head?'

'Even that is unnecessary now,' said Dainis. 'Simply locking you in here will assure a clean autopsy should anyone care to perform one on you after several weeks underwater.'

'He's learning.' Tartakov laughed. 'Just like you said the admiral did.'

MacKenzie was surprised. 'Karolov? Was he your idea?'

'No, actually. He acted on his own. As submarine commander of the fleet he knew your operating area and went out looking for you. To prove your victories over Soviet subs were flukes. His exec informed on him. It was a foolish move. What Seaman Tartakov is referring to is the night of your final argument in the bar. My superiors thought it best to have a talk with the admiral afterward. To get him to stand down. He was going to go to your hotel to kill you, you know. We broke his wrists,' said Dainis, obviously relishing the memory.

'Why?' said MacKenzie.

'We couldn't let him interfere anymore. You might actually be able to destroy the *Kentucky*. It had to be afterward, to protect security.'

The water was rising. The ship couldn't have more than a few minutes. The discussion was so unimportant it amazed him. But he went along with it, stalling for time now because he thought he felt something that they could not see.

In his arms, a faint stirring from Prudenkov.

'Where's the Capteen?' Raskin demanded at the escape trunk.

'He went aft,' said Kortzov, sending more men up the ladder. 'He hasn't come back.'

'And Dainis?'

'I haven't seen him,' Kortzov looked around at the dying ship sadly. 'No need for security now, though.'

Raskin was worried. Something about that call from the engine room bothered him. Where was Dainis if he was still on the ship? Could MacKenzie be in danger? Electrical wiring in the fan room. The big electrical panels like in the engine room . . . Suddenly, what Kortzov said caused a flash of realization and it all added up. Dainis hadn't worried about security because he didn't need to. MacKenzie was doomed from the beginning. And with the *Kentucky* destroyed and the ship sinking, what better time?

He saw Kutsky ahead, wading through the knee-high water.

'Ivan, come with me. Quickly!'

MacKenzie felt it again. More than a faint stirring. Prudenkov was trying to tell him something.

Tartakov was still leaning on the shaft indolently. Dainis was acting as if he had all the time in the world. MacKenzie realized he was savoring the moment. MacKenzie had beaten Karolov and the *Baton Rouge* and the *Phoenix* and finally the *Kentucky*. He'd even beaten the *Riga*'s own torpedo. Now Dainis was going to beat him. He wanted to make it last. That was why Tartakov was here, to witness it. To report how clever Dainis was, later.

Prudenkov kept shifting slightly to his right. MacKenzie suddenly saw why.

'If I'm going to die I'll be damned if I'm going to keep some Russian pig from drowning,' he said irritably and thrust Prudenkov from him. To the right. He hit the ledge

355

of the deck and slumped there. His head barely stayed above water.

'You see,' said Dainis approvingly to Tartakov. 'The truth comes out. We are not men to him as he would have us believe. We are pigs, animals. Things to be used and thrown away. Like this sub.'

'And you lose, boys,' said MacKenzie easily. 'Because I've already sent the specs for the new sonar to my navy. Go and report that to your superiors. Somebody will, someday. I completed my mission, You blew yours.'

Prudenkov was inching toward the console.

'You're lying,' said Dainis, but MacKenzie could see he had cracked his calm.

'How could you?' Dainis demanded.

'In one of the trash barrels,' MacKenzie said. 'Remember when we dropped them filled with noisemakers for the *Baton Rouge*? In there. It was all planned from the start and you never even saw it coming.'

Almost . . . Prudenkov was reaching and no one noticed. Dainis looked at Tartakov, who took his eyes off MacKenzie . . .

MacKenzie dove to the left and shouted, 'Spin her!'

Prudenkov's hand shot out and hit the control button that engaged the main engines. The main shaft Tartakov was leaning on was suddenly engaged and spun around. Used to bearing the weight of the giant propellor, it lifted Tartakov effortlessly into the air as if he weighed no more than a few ounces and flung him down on the other side. If Tartakov had not struggled he might have survived, but he tried to shoot as he fell. The shot went wild, ricocheting around the compartment, and his arm was sucked under the shaft. It dragged him under and he was crushed in an instant. A scream died on his lips.

Dainis was on MacKenzie in a flash pushing him toward the still open electrical panel. He was a man insane. The panel was only five feet away, the contacts exposed. There was more than enough power to electrocute him. Dainis planted his rubber clad boots and pushed him closer, his arms wrapped around MacKenzie. MacKenzie fought as hard as he could but couldn't break his hold. Dainis was enraged, a man possessed. He came closer . . .

Suddenly, only inches from the panel, MacKenzie felt Dainis's weight come off him. Kutsky was holding the security chief over his head like a toy. MacKenzie stumbled out of the way aided by Raskin's strong grip.

'Peter, are you all right?' demanded Raskin.

'I'm okay now. Glad to see you, Nikolai. Nice work, Mr Prudenkov.'

Prudenkov was holding his head. 'I thought you'd never get the message, Capteen,' he said wryly through his pain. Raskin pressed a compress against the open wound and helped him up.

'I'm slow sometimes,' said MacKenzie. 'Like with him,' he indicated Dainis with a thrust of his chin.

'An old breed,' said Raskin. 'One we will all do better without. I heard him talking the other day to someone. Planning. Now I see it was Tartakov. When you were called from the conn, well, it took a while, but I realized what it all meant.'

'What do I do with him?' asked Kutsky. He was still holding Dainis over his head with one hand on Dainis's collar and the other hooked in his belt. If Dainis moved, Kutsky could break his back.

'It is a serious matter, what to do with him. If he reports we helped you, Peter, we will all go to prison. It would be considered treason. Have no doubt.' Hard looks passed from man to man. The water was rising. They had to go. Finally, Raskin stood up. He had a deep, sad stillness on his face. MacKenzie said nothing. This was not his place.

'Perhaps we should discuss this in the passageway,' said Raskin slowly. 'Come, Peter. Senior officers. Ivan . . . ?'

'Yes, I will guard him,' said the big man. 'Go now.'

They waited in the passageway. A moment later Kutsky came out and closed the hatch behind him.

'He died trying to save Seaman Tartakov,' said Raskin solemnly. 'It will be in my report.'

'A brave man,' agreed Prudenkov. 'I will bear witness.'

'We haven't much time,' said Raskin. 'Come.'

They reached the main deck through the aft hatch. Helicopters from the oil platforms, long used for pulling men out of the ocean, were already circling above. MacKenzie was relieved to see that most of the crew had been picked up. They dove off the doomed *Riga* and swam out to clear water. Ropes came down to pull them into the sky. One by one MacKenzie, Prudenkov, Raskin and Kutsky were brought into the helicopter.

It was a bright, clear day and the air tasted like candy. The *Riga* was listing badly in the sea below now, filling past the point where her remaining tanks could support her. Slowly, she turned bow up and sank below the waves.

'A fine ship,' said MacKenzie, moved more than he could say.

Raskin nodded. 'She took us a far ways.'

The helicopter hovered, looking for more men. Silently, they watched the water rush in over *Riga*'s grave. Soon, even the bubbles were gone.

'Poets walk on the knife-edge and cut their souls to ribbons,' Raskin quoted softly. 'Vysotsky. You remember?'

'I remember,' said MacKenzie. 'It turns out old friends and sea captains walk there, too.'

Raskin put a hand on his shoulder and the helicopter whisked them over the copper sea into the sky.

THIRTY-SIX

Kara-Kum

The fires from the blazing station still lit up the night sky as Justine and Karansky dragged themselves from the river. They dropped the scuba gear on the bank and sprawled on the grass.

'What can I say, Goren?' Justine lay back and savored the star filled night sky. She felt whole again. A new person. She had cleared her accounts. Her mission was complete and Luck or God or maybe just Gen Goren Karansky had decreed that she would not die this night. Nuclear fires had been prevented. She had paid back all the people who had died to get her here.

Karansky took a waterproof flare from his pack and shot it into the sky. It trailed across the darkness in a yellow arc, dying in a spiraling plume of smoke at the last. They didn't move.

Soon, the Karadeen came.

Kemal was riding his own camel, his shoulder trussed up in bandages. She was very glad he had survived. Radi was there, too. In fact she saw only two riderless camels. The Karadeen had given a good accounting this night. Kemal dismounted and came over to her, his eyes sparkling with pleasure.

'How . . . ?' He indicated the station.

'Grenades. Goren met me in the river with scuba tanks. We swam out of it.'

Kemal looked at Karansky in a new light. He saw the unspoken understanding that passed between him and Justine. Kemal knew that to them he would always be just a passionate player. They were professionals – and now their job was done.

'What happens now?' he asked.

'You get your Mahdi,' Justine said.

'Without the weapons? What is to ensure it? Surely not you and he as hostages.'

'Nobody knows the weapons are destroyed but us,' said Justine. She had regained her strength and rose off the desert. A warm clear wind was coming off the sands and it dried her clothing. It smelled of bittersweet saxual.

'He knows,' said Kemal. 'And he must have the transmitter. I can not find it.'

'I'm sorry, Kemal,' said Goren. He looked genuinely saddened. 'It has to be this way. The money is still yours if you want it. We appreciate what you did.'

'Keep your money,' said Kemal bitterly.

'Will you kill me as you promised?' asked Karansky. It was almost an abstract question. At this moment, neither death nor life were very real for him and Justine. After what they had been through they were suspended somewhere in between.

Kemal shook his head sadly. 'I can not. I owe you too much. A debt of honor exists between us.'

'As you wish,' Karansky said simply.

'Funny thing, honor,' said Justine idly. 'I kept trying to figure out who I owed. Kemal saved my life in the dust storm. You saved it at the prison and just saved it again in the river. Now that my mission is over, I suppose I'm free to choose.'

'Choose what?' asked Kemal. 'What can be changed now?'

'Lots, actually. Look.' She showed Kemal Karansky's transmitter. 'Sorry, Goren. But it's time your people gave them back their Mahdi.'

Karansky grabbed his pocket and found nothing. 'But you made a deal with me . . .' he began. A rueful smile spread over his features. 'I suppose I didn't lose it in the river, eh? Well, it serves me right for forgetting what a good pickpocket you are.'

'I made a deal with you, Goren, to ensure the weapons would be destroyed. That had to be the primary goal. Even more important than your grandfather, Kemal. We couldn't let those weapons loose on the world. Not for any one man no matter how important he was to you. Or you are to me.'

Kemal's face was alight with understanding. And something deeper. 'I understand,' he said gratefully.

'I'm glad. I took Goren's transmitter not only to cover you but to prevent him from calling in paratroops to take the weapons once I saw we could take the station ourselves. Now they're gone. As long as he stays with you, nobody's the wiser. Say you took them before burning the station. Send them a piece as proof. I promise my agency will keep it quiet until the Mahdi is returned. Treat Goren well. He saved my life, too.'

'Like a brother.'

Justine stood up and brushed the sand off herself. As wet and bedraggled as she was, she still felt exhilarated. It was over now. She looked to the Karadeen. One by one the men reached out their open hands to her. Warriors, they saluted one of their own. She returned each clasp firmly.

'Thank you. Now if you will all excuse me . . .'

The men parted respectfully and let her wander off into the night.

She knew he would come. Just as she had always known that she could never betray him.

'The Karadeen will sing your praises long after you are gone,' he said quietly behind her, sometime later.

'You have a habit of sneaking up behind me,' she said. She was sitting on the sand, letting it sift through her fingers, savoring this last night.

'I haven't really thanked you.'

'Yes, you did.' She felt more clearheaded than she had in a year or more. 'I saw it on your face.'

He knelt beside her and took her hand. 'Stay here. We are soul mates, brought up to be the same thing. I've seen the cities. Don't go back to supermarkets. Build a country with me.'

She turned to him and touched his face gently. 'I've already helped build one country. I *want* supermarkets. And maybe babies. And I want my husband. Before you say anything more, I've thought this through. There's only one reason I'm going back. I love him. He is still the reason I get up in the morning. When I thought I was going to die right before Karansky shoved that regulator in my mouth, I knew. It's Mac. If he's not whole by now, I'm going to help him get whole. Somehow, I don't think it will be so hard now. That is your gift to me, Kemal.'

'And me?'

'If not for him. You. That's the truth.'

'I see.' He was silent for a while. 'We will head for the canal then. We can have you back in Ashkhabad in a few days.'

She smiled. 'Actually, I came out here to use Karansky's transmitter. My people know the missiles have been destroyed. They've agreed to keep it quiet. They'll be sending transport in the morning. See? I'm a modern person again. I'd like to get home before Mac does.'

'It is only a few hours to dawn. I don't think I can sleep.'

'Me neither.' She sighed. 'I'm too keyed up. So let's spend the last few hours talking about anything we like. In the morning I'll get on that helicopter and someday you will invite me back to meet the Mahdi as a distinguished guest of your government. Okay?'

He kissed her and she returned it. For a single moment a realm of possibilities opened, and closed.

'Done,' he said gently.

'Done,' she said.

EPILOGUE

Washington, DC

Justine held the letter Mac had written before he left. Ben Garver brought it over and they had a long talk about his mission on the *Riga*. She had his assurance that Mac was okay and very much his former self. This she could not take on faith. She waited, knowing that she would know the instant he walked in whether it was true or not.

Lifetimes pass in minutes. So much had transpired since they'd last seen each other. Once things happen we are never the same. She knew that. Just as she knew she had been irrevocably changed the minute she gave her life away to destroy the missiles, and in doing so, surrendered herself to a larger sense of God and Fate than any she had known before. Maybe it was what Mac called peace of mind.

Sitting in the comfortable living room of their renovated Capital District brownstone with its stuffed chairs, oriental rugs and polished hardwood floors, it was hard to reconcile the events of the past weeks. Part of her was still disconnected from her real life, but another part felt oddly fresh and new. Adding to things was the shock of returning to the US and home so quickly. CIA helicopters airlifted her out of Turkmenistan. A NATO jet whisked her back to Washington. Now, here, showered and clean and dressed in a fresh skirt and blouse and, God love them, stockings, Kemal and the desert were as far away emotionally as they were geographically.

She could still see him standing with Karansky, his black robes blowing in the prop wash, his dark visage glinting, so much hidden, as much a part of the desert as the sand. He had not waved. She smiled at his stubborn pride.

Emotion would have been unseemly. In many ways he was as sparse as the desert.

The desert. It was out there in the black sands of the Kara-Kum that she had come to understand herself and her life in a new way. In one consummate moment she had reconciled a cosmic balance sheet that had been growing increasingly lopsided for a long time. In one column were all the lives she had taken. In the other, her own life. It had begun to prey on her how long she could live with the imbalance, finding it increasingly hard to accept. Now the sheet was clear. The balance tallied. The columns equal. She had freely given up her life when conditions demanded it, without any thought of escape. In that moment she had taken her place among the dead and settled the score, repaid the debt. It was remarkable how calm she felt.

She still needed Mac, needed his optimism and his strength, needed him because she *loved* him. In the place where her despair had always been, all the more startling because it had been there for so long, there was stillness and quiet, a peacefulness she had looked for all her life. Mac would understand. They'd give it another try. Tenacity could apply to their relationship as well as to their careers, couldn't it? Mac said sometimes love is an act of faith. They would start with that.

The late afternoon sun fell golden through the high windows onto the furniture highlighting dust motes dancing in the slowly cooling summer air. The shadows on the old buildings grew longer. Outside, the capitol traffic moved slowly, sometimes backing up on the narrow street. Every now and then someone honked impatiently. It was so very quiet in between that she could hear her own heart.

It came to her how little she had known up until now, how much was left to discover. But this much she knew . . .

She was the hunter home from the hill.

Justine smoothed out the yellow-checked pattern of her

364

skirt on the couch, and waited for her sailor to come home from the sea.

MacKenzie stood for a long time on the street in front of the brownstone watching the lacy white curtains fluttering in and out of the library and the living room windows on the first floor. It meant Justine was home. It was her habit to open the windows to coax even the slightest breeze into the house rather than use the central air-conditioning. He always wondered if she flung them open for fresh air, or economy, or an escape route.

He understood a lot more about her now. How pain could be debilitating. How if the monster caught you early you would always see life differently. Maybe she should have stayed longer. Maybe he could have let her in sooner. They would never know. What mattered was that he was back, and whole again, and they could start over.

He had seen Garver and the rest of the brass first, at the Pentagon. The intelligence boys were overjoyed when he handed them the 'coin' he had carried from the *Riga* containing the information on their sonar. And there was something about Garver winning a two hundred dollar bet that he didn't understand but that made Red Cato wince. Alone later, Garver told him he had seen Justine, told him what he knew of her time in the desert. He said he noticed changes. Mac hoped so. He wanted very much to tell her what he found on the *Riga*. She could explain what happened to her in the desert. Changes. We never stay in the same place for long. It was a good place to start.

Raskin . . . He smiled at the memory. Raskin who said he had his thirty-second head start back again. Comrade Nikolai Vladimirovich Raskin, captain in the Russian navy, chaplain-without-frock, therapist extraordinaire, champion drinker, his friend. He had to have such a big frame. No smaller vessel could contain such a man. He last saw Raskin on the flight deck of the Russian 'floatel' – floating hotel – moored next to the main Soviet drilling platform. The rescue copter had flown them all there. They were fed and clothed while congratulations poured in from the ships of both fleets and their respective Navy Commands. It was the first time since the fight in Odessa so many days before that they were around other people. *Riga's* officers and men gathered protectively around their American captain and bristled at the stares from the hard-faced Russian workers in the mess. They moved to one side like a pack in some other animal's territory, guarded, closed in. No one approached. Together, over hot food and drinks and a sense of things coming to an end, they talked of the mission, of the *Lenin* and the *Kentucky* and the *Riga*, of those first days and times.

Someday when there are no more boundaries, someone said . . .

When word came that an American helicopter was coming, every man from the *Riga* gathered on the flight deck. In silent formation, one by one they shook his hand. Crewmen, officer – rank made no difference. There was Chernin and Purzov and Kortzov and Kutsky and Prudenkov and Kotnikov and Golovskoy and Petrov, till each and every man had come forward. The only record of Dainis and Tartakov was a brief hard glint in Kutsky's eyes, and even that melted like northern ice in the warmth of his smile.

'*Dasvidanya*, Peter,' said Raskin. Good-bye. For a second the embrace of his huge arms blocked out the sun. Then MacKenzie felt something pressed into his hands. He knew without looking what it was.

He smiled. 'From hand to hand. I'll listen to it often. Thank you, Nikolai. All of you. No captain has ever served with finer men. *Dasvidanya.*'

A car horn interrupted his reverie, pulling him back. From there to here. The Soviet drilling platform in the North Atlantic was replaced by the brownstone on his home street. A thought nagged at him. Would a drink help his homecoming, loosen him up? He shrugged it off. It was the wrong route. A thirty-second head start had to be enough. The monster would always be there. Laugh at him. It gave you a better than even chance to beat the bastard.

So what was he waiting for?

Impressions. The shallow depressions in the concrete steps from countless feet. The gritty sound the soles of his shoes made. The key that needed to be coerced into the bottom lock. The number sequence on the alarm – his birthday, then hers. He hung his cap on the rack in the foyer and put down the presents he'd bought at the transit base in Europe.

'Just?'

'Mac?' Her voice from the living room. 'Is that you?'

'I'm home.'

It came to him as she rushed into the hallway and into his arms that he had never seen anything as beautiful. The yellow dress was a splash of color as grand as spring's first daffodils. Her black hair hung down free and straight and he knew she had left it that way because he liked it. Small thing. Important. The smell of her blasted along his nerves and suffused his head and awakened in him a longing that was incredibly vast and pure.

'Oh, Mac . . . I want to talk about so many things.'

'I know. Me, too.'

'I'm so sorry . . .' she began.

He shushed her by planting his mouth over hers and saw merriment sparkle in her eyes. Then he picked her up as he winked his best and most outlandish wink. Her laughter bubbled under his lips.

In that instant they knew.

There was plenty of time to talk.

Later.